CW00358184

Saffron Skies and New Beginnings

Rita Bradshaw was born in Northamptonshire, where she still lives today. At the age of sixteen she met her husband – whom she considers her soulmate – and they have two daughters, a son and six grandchildren. Much to her delight, Rita's first novel was accepted for publication and she has gone on to write many more successful novels since then, including the number one bestseller *Dancing in the Moonlight*.

As a committed Christian and passionate animal-lover her life is busy, and she enjoys reading, eating out, visiting the cinema and theatre, and walking her beautiful little rescue dog, Angel, who's love on four paws, as well as being involved in her church and animal welfare.

BY RITA BRADSHAW

Alone Beneath the Heaven
Reach for Tomorrow
Ragamuffin Angel
The Stony Path
The Urchin's Song
Candles in the Storm
The Most Precious Thing
Always I'll Remember
The Rainbow Years
Skylarks at Sunset
Above the Harvest Moon
Eve and Her Sisters
Gilding the Lily
Born to Trouble
Forever Yours
Break of Dawn
Dancing in the Moonlight
Beyond the Veil of Tears
The Colours of Love
Snowflakes in the Wind
A Winter Love Song
Beneath a Frosty Moon
One Snowy Night
The Storm Child
The Winter Rose
Believing in Tomorrow
A Woman of Courage
Saffron Skies and New Beginnings

RITA BRADSHAW

Saffron Skies and New Beginnings

PAN BOOKS

First published 2024 by Macmillan

This paperback edition first published 2024 by Pan Books
an imprint of Pan Macmillan
The Smithson, 6 Briset Street, London EC1M 5NR
EU representative: Macmillan Publishers Ireland Ltd, 1st Floor,
The Liffey Trust Centre, 117–126 Sheriff Street Upper,
Dublin 1, D01 YC43
Associated companies throughout the world
www.panmacmillan.com

ISBN 978-1-0350-0036-4

1 3 5 7 9 8 6 4 2

A CIP catalogue record for this book is available from the British Library.

Typeset by Palimpsest Book Production Ltd, Falkirk, Stirlingshire
Printed and bound by CPI Group (UK) Ltd, Croydon, CR0 4YY

MIX
Paper | Supporting
responsible forestry
FSC® C116313

For our six precious grandchildren who are all growing into the most amazing, funny and wonderful people: Sam and Connor, Georgia and Emily, and Reece and Chloe. I hope you know that you're all the light of my and Pappy's lives, and that we love you all the world and bags of sugar!

And my lovely granddogs: Lily, Topsy and Yoschi, and the much-missed Bailey. All very different but with the most quirky personalities and loving ways – each a real little blessing with four paws! As is our new arrival, Angel, who's simply perfect.

Acknowledgements

Several avenues of research proved useful when I was writing this book – museums, films, TV programmes, news clips from 1939–45 etc., but books that deserve a special mention are as follows:

Millions Like Us: Women's Lives in War and Peace 1939–1949 by Virginia Nicholson

Our Wartime Days: The WAAF in World War II by Squadron Leader Beryl E. Escott

The Second World War by Antony Beevor

History of the RAF by Chaz Bowyer

Children of Allah: Between the Sea and Sahara by Agnes Newton Keith

Contents

Prologue

Belinda stood in front of the full-length mirror looking at her reflection. Her fine lawn nightdress hinted at the curves beneath and she had brushed her hair for some time so that it fell in a shining silky curtain down her back, rather than plaiting it as she usually did at bedtime.

She was trembling, and she bit down hard on her bottom lip, her pale and somewhat babyish face staring anxiously back at her and her deep-blue eyes wide. She had to do this, she told herself, and tonight. Every day, every hour was crucial.

Her fingers were joined so tightly at her waist that her knuckles gleamed white, and she slowly relaxed them, taking several long, deep breaths.

Everything – her marriage, her life, her future – rested on her succeeding and she had waited too long already. If she had been thinking straight she would have done this weeks ago. She had to seduce her husband into sleeping with her and in a way that made it seem it was his idea . . .

PART ONE

The Secret

1918

Chapter One

Seven weeks earlier

Belinda stood gazing at the glittering, noisy throng in the ballroom. Her eyes lifted for a moment to the glass chandeliers, which seemed like a host of twinkling stars, before returning to the dancers. The orchestra on a raised balcony at the end of the vast room were in full play, and many of the couches and velvet seats arranged against the walls were empty. There was a feverish gaiety pervading the atmosphere tonight, she thought, as she watched a group of ladies she vaguely knew pass her, laughing and talking loudly in what she considered a most unseemly manner and taking great gulps from their wine glasses.

Of course everyone would be excited with it being Armistice Day and the end of the war; when the guns had boomed out all over the country at eleven o'clock and the church bells had rung, crowds had poured out of the offices and shops and factories to sing and dance in the streets. Archibald had been in Newcastle and he'd returned saying strangers were kissing in doorways and he'd been grabbed and hugged by several folk on his way to the railway station. He didn't hold with such behaviour and had appeared distinctly ruffled when he'd come home.

She glanced at her husband standing stiffly at the side of her. Archibald didn't care for dancing either or a host of other what he called 'frivolities'. She rather suspected that was one of the reasons her parents had pressed her to marry him, her father being a minister of the cloth. She had been brought up strictly, she supposed, but had enjoyed her childhood in the big rambling vicarage with her brother and sisters, and as her father had been wealthy in his own right they had wanted for nothing and had had some influential friends in County Durham, Archibald being one of them.

It was five years after his first wife had died that he had asked for her hand in marriage, and her parents had immediately given their consent. She'd had very little to do with it. The fact that Archibald was thirty years older than her hadn't concerned them. It was an important step up the social ladder, her father had informed her coldly when she'd tentatively mentioned Archibald's age, and she ought to be grateful that a fine man like Mr McFadyen had noticed her.

The gratefulness on her part had lasted for a while after the wedding and honeymoon in Paris, but gradually Belinda had realized she'd made a terrible mistake. Archibald cared for her in his way, she was sure; he was kind enough but in the manner of an absent-minded father, and he was so dull and staid and *old*. Furthermore, the intimate side of their relationship wasn't at all what she had expected. She had read enough stories to know that when a man fell in love with a girl the physical side of things was important to him. Not so her husband. Weeks, months, could slip by without him making any demands on her. In fact, there were times when she wondered why he'd wanted another wife. Mrs Banks, the housekeeper, ran the house like clockwork and she and the butler oversaw the rest of the staff. Archibald dealt with the household expenses and any financial matters, and of course he had his businesses too.

Belinda sighed. The unrestrained merriment in front of her emphasized her unhappiness. She was bored, she admitted. She wanted to have some fun for once; was that so wrong? She'd had to persuade Archibald to leave his study and books and he'd said he didn't want to stay long. She did. She wanted to dance and dance, she thought mutinously, and if Archibald wouldn't ask her she would accept anyone who did.

Loud laughter brought her head turning, and she saw Colonel Wynford in a group of ladies a few feet away. Everyone always maintained that the Wynford dinner parties and dances were the best in the county and she didn't doubt it. She always felt as though she'd been swept into a different world when she came here, a place of colour and light, laughter and extravagance. Although the Wynford estate bordered Archibald's, it could have been a thousand miles away. Her husband's grand house and surrounding land which included a large farm paled into insignificance beside the splendour that was Evendale, the Wynford family's country seat.

The house itself was an enormous and beguiling classical-style residence with over sixty rooms, and Archibald had told her that didn't include the attics where a number of the servants slept, and the laundry tucked away at the back of the building where there was more servants' accommodation. A wing had been added to the original house two decades ago for gentlemen with bachelors' bedrooms, a gun room and an enormous sitting room where the men could sprawl and drink to their heart's content after a day of hunting, shooting or fishing. The colonel's wife, a beautiful, cold woman distantly related to royalty, was adept at entertaining the ladies on sunlit lawns or in front of roaring fires in the colder weather while the men indulged in their pursuits, but invariably the women would abandon their pleasant conversations and card games to join their menfolk for luncheon, elaborate picnics in the grounds where the servants would provide first-class fare with various wines and spirits. Belinda hated these occasions with the bloodied bodies of pheasants and partridges and other birds hanging on display but she kept her revulsion to herself. It wasn't done to voice such sentiments.

In the spring any entertaining at Evendale had come to an abrupt halt. Philip Wynford had been home on leave from the front and a riding accident had put him in a wheelchair for several months. The party tonight was the first big occasion since then, and it was clear he was back on fine form. A tall handsome man of thirty or thereabouts, Philip cut a dashing figure with his military bearing and rakish good looks and the ladies flocked round him like bees to a honeypot.

Belinda had always got the impression that Archibald didn't altogether approve of their charismatic neighbour, perhaps because the two men were so very different. One, quiet and sober and intensely private, and the other the life and soul of any gathering with a quick and somewhat irreverent wit. She wondered how Philip was feeling now the war was over; he was an army man through and through as had been his father and grandfather before him. Again, in stark contrast to Archibald. Her husband had a heart murmur which had prevented him joining up and although he'd said he would have done his duty for King and country, Belinda knew he was relieved he hadn't felt pressured to fight.

She hadn't been aware that she was still staring at Philip Wynford until a pair of piercing blue eyes honed in on her. For a moment she was transfixed, his gaze drawing her in, and then she turned away, hot colour staining her cheeks. She always felt gauche and nervous on these occasions, and her natural shyness hadn't been helped in the early days of her marriage when she had overheard some ladies in the Wynford crowd refer to her as 'that little mouse from the vicarage'.

Philip noticed her confusion and smiled to himself. Archibald's wife was a sweet girl but why she had tied herself to a stuffy individual like his neighbour he didn't know. He'd said the same to his wife and Felicity had raised her perfectly manicured eyebrows and told him not to be naive. 'Where else would she have the opportunity to marry so well? No doubt he wanted young flesh to warm his bed and she had no objection with all the benefits that would ensue. She's pretty enough but no raving beauty after all.'

He hadn't argued with Felicity – he rarely did these days even though he found her acidic cynicism unattractive – but he thought Belinda McFadyen had a certain something that was more appealing than mere beauty. An innocence, a gentleness, that was missing in most women of his acquaintance. Some of their set took lovers as casually as selecting a new item of clothing, and the ladies were as bad as the men.

This thought was at the forefront of his mind now as he turned his attention back to the group he was standing with. Two of them had been his mistresses for a time in the past and the other three wouldn't rebuff his advances if he made it clear he wanted an affair with them. If Felicity weren't such a frigid creature sexually he didn't doubt she would have taken a lover; it wasn't any sense of morality or faithfulness that had prevented her, just the fact that she found the whole process of intimacy distasteful. How he had managed to produce four sons from her unyielding body he didn't know, but for the last few years they'd had separate bedrooms and no physical contact except the odd chaste kiss on the cheek. But he'd got his boys, and she was quite happy for him to seek his pleasure elsewhere as long as he was discreet. All in all he was happy with his lot. He was back on his feet again after that terrible time when the physicians had warned him he might never walk again, and although his back gave him constant pain he could put up with that. Yes, he was happy. No one could claim to have everything they wanted in life.

In spite of himself he turned and searched the crowd for Belinda. There was a dance in progress, a waltz, but he couldn't see her among the weaving figures, and then he spotted her sitting on a couch against the far wall, her amber-coloured gown spread primly to each side of her. Archibald was standing at her side, for all the world like a sentry on duty, Philip thought wryly, as he watched the other man stare straight ahead, unsmiling and stiff.

He might have left it at that, he might have never asked her to dance, but for the fact that one small slippered foot caught his attention, tapping in time to the music.

Taking his leave of the ladies, he walked across to the couple, engaging Archibald in conversation for a few moments as the orchestra finished playing. Then, as they struck up again, he bent towards Belinda, saying, 'May I have the pleasure?' before glancing at Archibald and adding, 'With your permission?'

For a split second he thought the man was going to refuse and then Archibald smiled coolly, his eyes cold, as he said, 'Of course.'

Belinda knew she was blushing again as she rose.

Archibald wasn't a small man at nearly six foot, but the colonel was several inches taller and seemed to tower over her as she extended her arms, placing her right hand tentatively on his shoulder and the tips of the fingers of her left hand in his palm. She felt his arm go round her waist and for some reason she shivered inside, and then she was swung into the dancers. She had danced a few times with Archibald, mostly on their honeymoon, and on occasion with other partners, but this was different. She felt as though she was floating with the music and her feet hardly seemed to touch the floor. He was looking down at her and smiling and she smiled back at him, slightly breathless as she said, 'You – you dance very well.'

'I've had a lot of practice.' His face came closer as he murmured, 'You dance beautifully too.'

She found she was hardly aware of the other couples on the dance floor after some moments, just the sensation of being held in his arms and being twirled around as though she was as light as thistledown. It was intoxicating, heady, and she didn't ever want it to end. When the music stopped, instead of leading her back to her seat he said softly, 'You need some refreshment. There's some very fine punch, my butler has a gift for making it, or perhaps a glass of wine?'

He had guided her to a long table where several liveried footmen were serving drinks and before she knew it she had a glass of punch in her hand. She wasn't used to alcohol; her father had never imbibed beyond the occasional glass of sherry at Christmas and Easter, and although wine was served each night at home she rarely finished a glass, despite Archibald often having three or four with his evening meal. She found wine somewhat sour, it made the insides of her cheeks tingle, but as she took a small tentative sip of the punch it was delicious and like nothing she had tasted before.

He smiled at her. 'Good choice?'

'It's lovely, different to wine.' And then she bit on her lip, realizing how unsophisticated she'd sounded. Her voice low, she murmured, 'This tastes fruity, like apples with honey.'

'Skelton guards his recipe like the crown jewels but beware, it has a hidden kick.'

She took another sip, feeling the punch warm her stomach and melt her nervousness. 'It's lovely,' she said again, her voice more confident as she found herself relaxing.

She smiled at him, and Philip was taken aback by the way it changed her face. She had smiled before, of course, but there had always been a restraint there. He could see why Archibald, dull and staid as he was, had wanted her for his wife, but it only strengthened his opinion that Belinda was wasted on him. His gaze flicked to where Archibald was standing on the other side of the ballroom, now deep in conversation with a couple of older men, one of whom was a Member of Parliament. No doubt the talk would be earnest and political and as boring as hell, he thought derisively, as he turned his attention back to the young woman in front of him. He was amused to see her glass was empty and he took it from her, saying, 'Would you care to dance again?'

'Yes, please.'

Her eyes were bright and her cheeks faintly pink and as he led her to the dancers he thought that Felicity's summing-up of Belinda was quite wrong; she was more than pretty but her beauty was of the fragile kind and not immediately obvious like some of the full-blown, painted faces around him. Why had he never really realized this before? he asked himself as he whirled her towards the middle of the floor, but she seemed different tonight.

Belinda felt different. She danced several more times with the colonel before another guest cut in on them with a smile and a bow, and then after that she was never short of a partner. But no one danced as well as Philip Wynford.

When a servant informed everyone that dinner was ready Archibald appeared at her side, taking her arm as they walked into the enormous dining room where the guests were seated according to the ornate name cards at the individual places. His tone was indulgent rather than annoyed when he murmured, 'You seem to be having a good time, m'dear.'

'I am.'

'I'm glad. Gone are the days when I could dance all night, it's the prerogative of youth, I'm afraid.'

She glanced at him as they took their seats. She couldn't

imagine that Archibald had ever had the inclination to dance all night but she didn't say this, being relieved that he didn't seem to mind that she was enjoying herself. She felt a sudden rush of affection for him and rested her hand on his for a moment. He couldn't help being the way he was and she was lucky to be married to a good man; some of the men were clearly drunk, their voices over-loud and their faces red as they ogled women other than their wives. Archibald would never behave like that.

As usual at the Wynford get-togethers there were four wine glasses in front of her to accompany the huge variety of food that was served, but when the first glasses were being filled by the liveried footmen as the meal commenced, she saw that it was the punch and not white wine that was being poured for her. She opened her mouth to comment but as she did so she caught the eye of Philip, who was seated at the middle place of the upper table. He winked at her and grinned, mouthing, *Enjoy*, and she smiled back, feeling inordinately pleased. Archibald didn't appear to notice and by the time they came to the puddings the footman had refilled her glass twice. She didn't think she had ever enjoyed herself so much; the conversation seemed more witty than normal, the different courses more delicious, the ladies more sparkling and the men more charming.

The meal lasted for two hours and as was customary the dancing wasn't resumed immediately; the ladies adjourning to the drawing room and leaving the menfolk to their port and brandy and cigars.

It was as Belinda rose from the table that she felt her head begin to swim. She felt hot too, her cheeks burning, and rather than following the majority of the ladies into the drawing room she made for the powder room with the intention of dabbing her face with cold water.

She had hoped to find the room empty but there were a number of women already seated on the small velvet-backed chairs, each of which faced an ornate little dressing table. They were busily powdering their faces and fiddling with their hair, chattering away like a group of magpies, and all seemed to know each other very well. She always felt like an outsider in situations like this and so she walked further down the room and, opening the door of the cubicle at the end of the row she went inside, closing it behind her.

The Wynfords had had all the indoor closets replaced with modern ceramic lavatories and plumbing – there were no remaining wooden boxes with holes in the middle and leather seats at Evendale – and she waited, standing quietly until silence reigned, and then emerged to find she had the powder room to herself. Walking across to the row of small washbasins on the far wall, she ran a little water into one of them and took a small hand towel from the pile next to the bowls. Wetting it, she dabbed at her hot cheeks for some moments, examining her appearance in the mirror.

Her mother would have described her as bright-eyed and bushy-tailed and it wouldn't have been meant as a compliment, she thought ruefully, as she took in her flushed face. Strangely though, considering she had always lived in fear of displeasing her parents, she didn't give a fig tonight. She couldn't remember ever having enjoyed herself so much and the evening wasn't over yet. She intended to dance some more, hopefully with Philip, because in his arms she felt as though the rest of the world didn't exist and she was no longer the little mouse from the vicarage, the newcomer who didn't really fit in.

She smoothed a few tendrils of hair which had escaped the chignon at the back of her neck into place and dabbed at her face some more until she was satisfied her complexion had returned to its normal peaches and cream before leaving the powder room. The band had been tuning up and as she entered the ballroom it began to play a polka. She spotted Archibald conversing with the two men he'd been deep in conversation with before the meal and a number of people were standing talking or sitting on the couches at the edge of the room, and for a moment she hesitated, unsure of what to do. The next moment a hand took her elbow and a voice in her ear murmured, 'I wondered where'd you'd got to,' and she turned her head to find Philip smiling down at her. 'I thought I'd lost my dance partner.'

And then she was whirled onto the floor again and as other couples began to join them she let herself relax and be led by him. When he drew her over, breathless and laughing, to the refreshments as the dance finished and the footman poured more punch she didn't object. She was thirsty and the drink was so delicious.

They danced some more and when, after a short interval, another guest claimed her before Philip could she felt quite cross with the poor man, nice though he was. Whether it was the fact that he held her too tightly and whisked her round too quickly she didn't know, but when he paid his respects as the music finished and she sat down on one of the couches her head was spinning and she felt hot again. She had the desire to leave the noise and laughter and heat of the ballroom for a while and get some fresh air. She felt increasingly dizzy and not at all like herself.

Where was Archibald? She glanced around but the room itself seemed to be moving and she couldn't focus very well. And then to her relief Philip was standing in front of her, his voice soft when he said, 'You look a little perturbed, is anything wrong? No one has upset you, have they?'

'No, no, I'm just too hot. I think I need some fresh air, that's all.' She was finding it difficult to pronounce her words and with a little shock of horror she wondered if she was tipsy. But she had only drunk the punch and it had tasted more like the fruit juice her father's cook had made when she was growing up than anything else.

'Shall I fetch Archibald? Do you want to leave?'

'No,' she said quickly. This evening had become a moment out of time and she didn't want to return to normality just yet. 'No, perhaps just to step outside for a minute or two.'

'It's too chilly and there's a keen wind blowing – you'll

freeze to death – but there's plenty of rooms where the fires won't have been lit.' He helped her to her feet as he spoke and kept hold of her arm as they left the ballroom, guiding her through the anteroom and then into a corridor which led into Evendale's baronial hall. There was a roaring fire burning in the massive fireplace and it was a little cooler than the ballroom but not much.

He led her towards the end of the hall past the magnificent curving staircase and a number of doors, opening one and standing aside for her to precede him as he said, 'This is my study and I rarely have the fire lit. I don't feel the cold myself but Felicity could live in a hothouse and still not be warm enough.'

It was a large room with bookshelves taking up two walls, and several items of furniture dotted about. The enormous walnut desk and big leather chair were facing them and behind them two huge thick curtains had been drawn against the winter night. He gestured towards a big sofa which was richly upholstered in thick tapestry. 'Do sit down. Can I get you a drink?'

She shook her head. It was lovely to get away from the noise and heat for a few minutes but she'd become aware that their being alone like this wasn't quite proper. Sinking down on the sofa, she kept her back straight and folded her hands in her lap, although what she would really have liked to do was to lay her head back and shut her eyes.

She watched Philip as he poured himself a good measure of brandy from a decanter on a table next to the desk.

He was so handsome, she thought as he turned towards her, and nice. Not at all stuffy. And he wasn't patronizing like some of the assembled company.

He didn't sit down beside her but pulled one of the two armchairs in the room close to the sofa so he was facing her. Seating himself with a soft sigh, he said, 'A little peace and quiet away from the madness, eh?'

She didn't want him to think that she was finding fault with the evening and this was reflected in her voice when she said, 'Oh, but it's wonderful to dance too. I've never danced so much in my life. Archibald – well, he doesn't care for it.'

Philip nodded. He could imagine, he thought drily. The amount of alcohol he'd consumed loosened his tongue and he found himself saying, 'You don't seem to have much in common, from what I've observed.' And then, as her eyes widened, he hastily added, 'Forgive me, it's none of my business. I have no wish to offend you.'

'You haven't offended me.' In fact, it was a relief to speak the truth for once. 'And you're right, we don't have much in common.'

'Why did you marry him?' he asked quietly, leaning forward.

'My parents thought Archibald was a good match.'

'And you? What did you think?'

'He – he was kind and he said he loved me.' She paused. 'He *does* love me, but—'

'But?'

His mouth was fascinating her and he had dark stubble on his chin. She'd noticed when she'd danced with him that he smelled good too, a mixture of cigars and fresh scented linen and something else too, something indefinable but which had caused shivers in her stomach. She'd forgotten what she was saying and swallowed hard, trying to remember through the fog in her mind. Archibald, that was it. Her voice a whisper, she murmured, 'I feel lonely,' as her bottom lip quivered. 'All the time I feel lonely and there's no one to talk to.'

He put his glass down and took one of her hands. 'You can talk to me.'

She blinked. He was so close now she could see the tiny laughter lines radiating from the corners of his eyes and the feeling that had engulfed her when they'd danced was stronger now. 'Talking won't do any good really, will it? It won't solve anything.'

The man must be mad, Philip thought. He had hold of both her hands now and could sense the trembling within her through them. To have this enchanting creature as his wife and neglect her as he was clearly doing. She was fresh, young and so innocent. Oh, he didn't doubt that Archibald had taken her, but in essence she was still unawakened sexually, and that after three years of marriage. It was nothing short of a crime.

He found it impossible to stop his next reaction, moving to sit beside her, whereupon he took her into his arms and kissed her. He hadn't known what to expect, but when she didn't push him away or protest but was pliant in his embrace he kissed her more deeply, bringing all his considerable expertise to bear.

Her mouth opened beneath his like a flower and he felt the thrill of conquest down to his toes, his body hardening as the blood surged through his veins. After some moments he pulled the bodice of her dress down to reveal her small full breasts, caressing them and feeling the tips respond under his fingers. By the time he lifted the skirt of her dress and peeled away the lace panties she was moaning softly at the things he'd done to her and when he entered her they moved together as one. It was like the first time he had ever made love, he thought with a touch of wonder. He'd forgotten it could be like this.

When it was over he held her tightly in his arms, kissing her flushed face and murmuring endearments, but when she began to quietly cry, he whispered, 'What is it? Did I hurt you?'

Belinda shook her head, overwhelmed with what had happened to her. She'd never imagined in her wildest dreams that making love could be like this but she had betrayed Archibald, her marriage vows, even who she was, swept along on a tide of passion she hadn't thought herself capable of.

'Belinda, it's all right.' Philip held her gently, tenderly. 'Don't cry.'

'We . . . I . . . I shouldn't have.' She pulled away from him, the stickiness between her legs bringing a surge of consuming guilt. Even a kiss would have been wrong, a form of unfaithfulness, but *this*. And to think she had looked askance at some of the ladies in their social set who flirted and perhaps drank a little too much on occasion, even joined in Archibald's censure of such women. *Archibald. Oh, Archibald.* She would never be able to look him in the eye again but she couldn't tell him what had occurred. He would be appalled and disgusted, it would be the end of their marriage and what would her parents say when they knew the facts? They would disown her. And if Archibald insisted on a divorce the scandal that would ensue would destroy them all. She must have been mad to forget herself so far.

'It's not your fault, it's mine.' For once in his life Philip was feeling some remorse as pangs of conscience made themselves felt. He'd had many women besides his wife but they had been a certain type – mostly married and all worldly wise. He had known Belinda wasn't like that, so why had he taken advantage of her? he asked himself, knowing the answer and despising himself for it. Because he had wanted her. His desire had grown all evening and when the opportunity had arisen to assuage it he hadn't had the moral strength to resist. But what was done was done, and it wasn't as if anyone had stumbled in on them. Now that really would have put the cat among the pigeons.

Gentling his voice further, he murmured, 'I'm sorry, truly sorry, but I repeat it's my fault, not yours. You have nothing to reproach yourself for. I – we – were swept away by our emotions but the responsibility is mine alone.

The thing is, no one knows what's happened. No real harm is done.'

She stared at him as though he had lost his mind.

He was about to say that such incidents were commonplace among their friends and acquaintances but thought better of it. Instead he said quietly, 'When you are ready we will rejoin the party. No one will have missed us.'

She had dried her eyes and smoothed down her clothes and now, rising to her feet, she said stiffly, 'You go. I – I need a few moments.'

'Belinda—'

'*Please.*'

His eyes narrowed at her tone. 'As you wish.' When he reached the door and before opening it he turned, and now his voice was soft and tender. 'Please try and look at this as one of those things that just happens sometimes. You are beautiful and enchanting and I took advantage of your innocence, I know that, but I shall remember these few minutes with great fondness.'

She made no reply, she couldn't have. *One of those things*? It might be a casual encounter for him but for her it had been anything but, on many levels.

When she was alone she sank down onto the sofa again, trembling and bereft. After a few minutes the panic and desperation subsided and a strange kind of numbness took over. It enabled her to stand up and walk over to a large mahogany and gilt mirror on the wall and check her reflection. To her amazement she appeared no different in spite of the fact that she felt the word 'adulteress' was seared across her brow.

Taking a few deep breaths, she tidied some loose strands of hair and squared her shoulders. She had to go back in there and pretend that nothing had happened, in spite of the fact that her whole world had just crashed about her. It was the only way.

Chapter Two

The band were taking some refreshments when Belinda entered the ballroom and people were standing in small groups or sitting on the couches lining the walls. There was a great deal of laughter and loud conversation, interspersed with the footmen filling empty glasses and offering trays of canapes and sweetmeats, and quite a number of the assembled throng were clearly the worse for wear. In contrast Belinda found she was now painfully sober and wanted nothing more than to go home.

She stood hesitating and then saw Archibald making his way towards her. Just the sight of him brought her fighting back tears. He smiled as he reached her, his tone indulgent as he murmured, 'There you are, m'dear. I've been looking for you.'

'I – I've been powdering my nose.'

He nodded. 'One or two folk are beginning to take their leave but we don't have to go if you would prefer to dance a little more? I might even take to the floor myself if you ask me nicely.'

It wasn't like Archibald to joke or tease her and it made the lump in her throat worse. He was such a good man, she thought wretchedly. So kind and solid and reliable. He wouldn't dream of looking at another woman. Swallowing hard, she said quietly, 'I'm a little tired and ready to go home.'

He drew her hand through his arm. 'Come along then and we'll make our goodbyes.'

Their hosts were standing with another couple as they approached, and while Archibald spoke to Philip, Belinda kept her gaze concentrated on Felicity as she said, 'Thank you so much for a lovely evening.'

'It's been fun, hasn't it,' Felicity drawled languidly in her highfalutin voice as she cooled her face with an ornate fan. 'It's wonderful the war's over at last. Those beastly Germans needed to be taught a lesson, ghastly creatures. Bringing them to heel makes it all worthwhile though.'

Belinda gazed at her. Philip's wife always reminded her of a cat her mother had had: sleek and beautiful but ready to show its claws at the slightest provocation and totally devoid of affection. Millions of men, women and children had died over the last few years because the power-mad Kaiser had invaded Belgium and plunged the world into conflict, and she didn't think anything was worth that. But Felicity probably hadn't meant it the way it had sounded.

She didn't know how to respond, but the woman of the couple who Philip and Felicity were standing with cut into the conversation before she could speak anyway.

Her voice gushing, she said, 'Absolutely, Fliss, but that's foreigners for you, always forgetting their place.' She didn't even glance at Belinda. 'And have you heard there's been high jinks in all the towns and cities? Desmond said it's like a giant school being let out. Cakewalks in the squares, fireworks, shop and factory girls accosting men in uniform and throwing their arms round them and that's the least of it. Such goings-on and so exciting.'

Felicity wrinkled her aristocratic nose. 'It sounds a little vulgar, darling.'

The other woman's face fell. 'Oh yes, yes, of course, but then what can you expect of the common masses?' she said hastily. 'Desmond always says they're like children.'

Belinda decided that she didn't like Desmond or his wife.

Archibald had finished talking to Philip and had caught the tail end of the conversation. Noticing her expression, he smiled and nodded at Felicity, drawing Belinda away. She went gladly without meeting Philip's gaze although she was aware he was looking at her. How she would ever face him again she didn't know, she thought desperately. The Wynfords were holding a Christmas Eve dinner party the following month and they had already accepted their invitation. It had included her parents, who were going to stay with them over the Christmas period.

Her father had recently retired from the ministry, and he had bought a substantial property in its own grounds on the outskirts of Brandon, not far from Archibald's estate. Belinda didn't know if this was a good thing or not. She'd made the most advantageous marriage among her siblings and had consequently become the favoured daughter, a role she'd found to be a mixed blessing when it involved seeing more of her parents than the others did.

Once they were in the hall, a footman was sent to tell Archibald's coachman to bring the vehicle to the foot of the steps at the front of the house, while the maids helped them on with their coats and hats. It was bitterly cold outside – the day had been one of granite skies and intermittent icy rain – but as they stepped into the fresh air the clouds had dispersed and a heavy frost was already beginning to turn the grounds white.

Fairley, their coachman, was waiting with the coach and horses and came forward to assist them into the vehicle, and Belinda was glad of her thick furs as a biting wind almost blew Fairley's peaked cap off. Once in the coach she sat quietly at Archibald's side. He made no effort to take her hand or put his arm round her – he rarely made gestures of affection – but began to recount the conversation he'd had with the Member of Parliament regarding the likelihood of a General Election now the war was over.

Since her marriage, Belinda had become adept at listening to Archibald with one ear while her mind was occupied elsewhere. Now she made the occasional appropriate response while continuing to silently berate herself as the coach trundled homewards. When it passed between huge gates set in a high stone wall and on to the winding drive leading to Fellburn House, she felt an uncharacteristic warmth for the house as it came into view. She was home.

It was the first time that she'd really thought of Fellburn in that way, beautiful though the honey-stoned building was. Since they had arrived back from honeymoon and she had formally taken up the position of mistress of the house at just seventeen years old, it had seemed more like a prison than anything else. Magnificent, certainly, compared to what she had been used to, and luxurious too, but a prison nonetheless.

It wasn't so bad in the warmer months when she could walk in the ornamental gardens and read in the bowers covered in sweet-smelling roses and clematis, or wander in the woodland and wildflower meadows bordering the farm. She'd only visited Archibald's farm once when she had first taken up residence in the house. He had introduced her to Mr Irvin, his farm manager, and Cissy, his wife, but had made it clear that the farm was no place for a lady and of course Belinda had adhered to his wishes on the matter.

The oval forecourt was lit by lanterns and once the coach had stopped, Archibald descended and helped her down. He kept hold of her arm as they climbed the broad steps leading to a large stone terrace. The front door was open and Wright, the butler, was waiting with one of their two housemaids at his side.

'I trust you have had an enjoyable evening, sir,' Wright

said in his cold ponderous way as the little maid took their coats and hats just as Mrs Banks, the formidable housekeeper, appeared from the direction of the green baize door which led to the kitchen and servants' quarters. She came swiftly towards them in her black alpaca dress, the belt of which supported a chatelaine of keys. 'There's a good fire in the drawing room, sir,' she said primly, 'and Cook's preparing coffee and sweetmeats.'

Belinda stifled a groan. She couldn't, she just *couldn't* go through the usual routine that occurred each time they returned from an evening out. Refreshments in the drawing room while Archibald dissected the evening in minute detail. No matter the hour, it was something he liked to do and she always obliged him, but not tonight. Her nerves were screaming with guilt and shame. Touching his arm, she said quietly, 'Would you mind if I went straight up? I feel rather tired.'

'Of course, m'dear. All that dancing has taken it out of you. Go ahead and I'll make sure I don't wake you.'

He patted her arm and as she turned towards the staircase, Mrs Banks said, 'I'll send Johnson straight up, ma'am.'

'There is no need tonight, Mrs Banks. I would prefer to see to myself. Tell Johnson she can go to bed.'

'As you see fit, ma'am.' Mrs Banks's plump chin drew into her neck. The housekeeper had many ways of expressing disapproval and this was one of them. Belinda had always been aware that Archibald's senior staff thought he had married beneath him.

His first wife had been well connected and great friends with Felicity Wynford by all accounts. Johnson, her personal maid, was a thin individual with a beak of a nose and hard eyes and she never missed an opportunity to make Belinda feel gauche, but only when Archibald wasn't within earshot. When he was present, Johnson put on the mantle of the attentive older servant helping the young mistress to adapt to her new role with kind solicitude.

A few months after she had been married she had tentatively asked Archibald if she could choose a personal maid for herself but he had been askance. 'You'd go a long way before you found someone as experienced as Johnson,' he had said with a frown. 'Verity thought the world of her and the woman's discreet and efficient. I confess after Verity died I didn't quite know what to do with her, but she'd been with us so long I kept her on to assist Mrs Banks where she could and help with any problems with the female staff. Why do you want to replace her? Is there a problem?'

It was then she should have stood her ground, she had realized some time later, and explained that Johnson was not what she seemed. Instead she had fudged it and dismissed the matter.

She was weak, she told herself now as she climbed the stairs to her room. All her life she had been timid and easily intimidated, first by her parents and siblings and then by Archibald. She had always allowed the people in her life to dictate to her in one way or another, anxious not to displease them or cause friction, compliant to the last. The model daughter, the model wife. But she had well and truly blotted her copybook tonight, hadn't she.

She stood on the wide landing for a moment, biting down hard on her bottom lip to prevent herself crying. Time enough for that when she was in bed and Archibald was asleep. Sometimes she felt the very walls of this house had eyes and ears, and there was always one of the servants popping up when you least expected it.

As though on cue, the door to the master bedroom opened and the first housemaid emerged, dipping her knee when she saw Belinda and saying, 'I've just brought up the hot water, ma'am, and your bottle's already in the bed.'

'Thank you, Vickers.' She always had a stone hot water bottle to warm her feet in the winter, although Archibald didn't avail himself of one.

Once in her boudoir she undressed and let down her hair, but before pulling on the cream satin and lace nightdress that Johnson had laid out for her she washed between her legs with soap and water, scrubbing away for an unnecessarily long time. It was cold in the small room, there was a fire in the bedroom but not in her boudoir or Archibald's dressing room, and she was shivering by the time she climbed into bed, her feet seeking the warmth of the bottle.

When Archibald came up an hour or so later she pretended to be asleep, and long after he lay beside her snoring she remained stiff and still but with tears flooding down her cheeks.

It was as dawn began to lighten the sky outside the window that Belinda finally drifted into a troubled slumber, her dreams as disturbing as her thoughts had been while she was awake and populated by dark figures and strange longings. And deep in her body, had she but known it, a change was beginning to take place . . .

Chapter Three

Christmas had been a strained affair, at least as far as Belinda was concerned. Everyone else had appeared to enjoy it. Her parents had arrived a few days before Christmas Eve and she knew Archibald had liked their company, particularly that of her father. The two men had spent hours discussing the cost of the war economically and socially, along with the possible outcome of the proposed General Election in which women were allowed to vote for the first time, something her father vehemently disagreed with. It had meant she had had to entertain her mother, something she found difficult at the best of times. It hadn't helped that she had been feeling particularly tired and somewhat unwell in the lead-up to Christmas, as well as dreading the dinner party at the Wynfords on Christmas Eve.

Somehow she had got through the evening, forcing herself to eat a little of what was put before her and joining in the cross-talk and chatter where she could. She'd been careful to keep her gaze on the lady and gentleman seated opposite her on the whole and hadn't let it stray. She'd had to speak to Philip and Felicity when they had first arrived at Evendale, but as they'd had her parents with them and her father had engaged Philip in conversation immediately, she'd barely met Philip's eyes.

In the coach driving home her father had waxed lyrical about the grandeur of the house and grounds and what excellent hosts the Wynfords were in a way that was embarrassing, but as it had meant she hadn't had to make conversation it had suited her. Christmas Day had been a quiet affair. She had awoken with a feeling of nausea first thing which had passed sufficiently for her to enjoy a small lunch, but when the same thing had occurred the following morning, flutters of panic made themselves felt. When she had missed her monthly two weeks after the Armistice Day ball she had put it down to the stress and overwhelming remorse she was feeling, but now another due date had come and gone. She was feeling subtly different in her body too. She knew women were often sick in the mornings when they were expecting a child because her eldest sister had suffered in that way.

Her parents left the next day after lunch and it was a relief. Her mother had a way of noticing things and had already made one or two comments about her looking a little peaky, hinting that she might have something to tell her.

Now it was the fifth morning in a row that she had felt nauseous and she couldn't pretend to herself any more. She was expecting a baby and Archibald couldn't be the father. They hadn't been intimate for months.

She was dressed to go down for breakfast and Johnson had just left the room. Belinda sank down on the edge of the bed, desperation tearing at her. What was she going to do? Archibald might be gentle and reticent but he was a proud man. He would demand to know the name of the individual responsible and confront him. Even if he agreed to keep the matter private to avoid a scandal it would destroy their marriage, and what would become of her baby? From a little girl she had always wanted children, but not in these circumstances. Her baby, her poor baby. She rested her hand on her stomach, although as yet there was nothing to show for the new life inside her; nevertheless, she felt a flood of protective love.

After a few moments she made herself stand up and go downstairs, and as she entered the breakfast room she saw Archibald immersed in his morning paper. Their housemaids were hovering in front of the long sideboard with its covered dishes, the table was beautifully set with silver cutlery and fine crockery and a roaring fire was burning in the black-leaded grate. The room was cosier than the more formal dining room where they ate their evening meal and usually she liked the start to the day but today she felt lost and terribly afraid, feeling she was teetering on the edge of a precipice.

'There you are, m'dear.' Archibald looked up and smiled, folding his newspaper and putting it to one side. It was the signal for the maids to begin serving them. He always enjoyed a hearty cooked breakfast but Belinda rarely ate more than a rasher of bacon and a little scrambled egg with a slice of toast. The last few mornings she had struggled to even force that down.

Somehow she got through her small meal. Archibald always left the house every morning at eight o'clock and she knew he would be gone for most of the day. Along with the house and farm and grounds, he had inherited a thriving rope-making works and a pottery near Easington some miles east of the estate, and he liked to visit both businesses daily when he could. He often called in to see his bank manager in the afternoons to discuss his investments and have a glass of whisky or two with the man, who was also a friend, arriving home early evening. It was a routine he'd had since he was a young man and he had seen no reason to change it when he married again.

Once Archibald had gone Belinda decided to go for a walk in the grounds to clear her head and get some fresh air. She needed to be on her own and think.

They'd had flurries of snow over Christmas followed by a thaw the day after Boxing Day, only for the weather to turn bitterly cold once more. There had been a hard frost during the night and the morning sky was high and blue with wisps of silver. Lacy spiderwebs glinted and sparkled on the bushes and shrubs, and the frozen white ground looked as though diamond dust had been sprinkled over it in the cold sunlight. In spite of her abject misery, Belinda stood for some moments just breathing in the clean, icy air, which carried the elusive smell of woodsmoke at the heart of it, before she began walking.

She was warmly dressed in the sable coat and matching hat Archibald had given her for Christmas, and her boots were fur-lined too. He had given her a very generous clothing allowance when they had got married and was far from being a mean man; she knew she only had to ask for something and it would be hers. She had once tried to explain to him that the only thing she really wanted was more of his time and affection, but it hadn't gone well. He had been somewhat annoyed and had cut the conversation short, and she had been left feeling rebuffed and highly embarrassed, as though she had said something indelicate.

She was thinking of that humiliating episode now as she made her way along a path which led to the pleasure gardens, passing under a high, ivy-covered arch set in stone walls and into an area of sculptured trees, flower beds, fountains and arbours, all frozen and still in the late December morning. She had walked for some minutes before she reached one of the little grottos, a small ornamental cave-like structure which had a bench seat at the back of it where one could sit in the shade at the height of summer and listen to the fountains tinkling. Today the frozen water was silent and not even the twittering of birds disturbed her solitude.

She sat down, her gloved hands in her lap, seemingly calm and composed but her brain was racing. Somehow she had to find a way out of this nightmare that wouldn't affect her child, but how? If she told Archibald the truth the repercussions would be unthinkable; even if he agreed to continue with the marriage he wouldn't tolerate bringing up another man's child, and she couldn't blame him. And the same would apply if she sought refuge with her parents. They would insist the baby was put away somewhere, that's if they didn't disown her and refuse to help in any way, which was highly likely. If she went to Philip the consequences would be scandalous – even if he agreed to take responsibility, and there was no guarantee of that – and again the child would carry the stigma of illegitimacy.

In spite of herself a little whimper escaped her lips and she put her hand tightly across her mouth although she was quite alone. The feeling of nausea had lessened considerably but she felt no relief, the turmoil in her mind consuming.

How long she sat there before Palmer, the head gardener, disturbed her privacy she didn't know. It could have been minutes or hours, such was the state of her mind. As it was she made the old man nearly jump out of his skin when he caught sight of her as he shuffled along, his pipe hanging out of his mouth and his cloth jacket unbuttoned despite the cold.

'I beg your pardon, ma'am,' he said, doffing his tattered cap as he spoke. 'Didn't mean to intrude.'

She smiled at him. Palmer always reminded her of one of the ancient sculptured trees he tended so lovingly, gnarled and bent but strong nonetheless. 'It's me who's intruding, Palmer,' she said softly. 'This is more your domain than mine.'

The old man smiled back. He liked the little mistress, as he always thought of her. She had no side to her, unlike most of the gentry. He was well aware what that lot up in the house said – that she didn't carry herself the way the master's previous wife did and had no presence about her – but like he'd said to Cook only last week when he'd called in to the kitchen for his morning cup of cocoa, presence be damned. The little mistress spoke to you as if you were a real human being rather than muck under her feet, and to his mind that was a good thing. Some of them up there were more hoity-toity than the gentry themselves and he couldn't be doing with 'em.

'I'm just on me way to the forcing house, ma'am. I've got a nice lot of raspberries that should be ready today.' The little building near the greenhouses was his pride and joy. It was tucked away out of sight and hidden from the house and pleasure gardens by high stone walls. He spent most of his time in there these days; it was as warm as toast with the two stoves burning night and day and the pipes heating every inch of the place, and it suited his old bones. The forcing house meant the master and mistress could have peaches and other fruit in the midst of winter, and fresh flowers for the table displays.

Belinda inclined her head. 'That's lovely, Palmer. Thank you.'

Palmer doffed his cap again before walking on. He knew she had a particular fancy for raspberries because she had told him so in the summer when she'd met him in the grounds one day. He never used to see hide nor hair of the first Mrs McFadyen and she wouldn't have deigned to speak to him if he had, he thought, but this one spent more time outside and always spoke pleasantly if she saw him. His missus said she thought the little mistress was unhappy and she might well be right. He hoped not though. It'd be a crying shame and her so young and bonny.

Belinda watched the bent old figure shuffle off. Palmer had taken a great delight in showing her round his beloved forcing house one summer's afternoon, proudly explaining this and that and the mechanics of what he did in the colder months to produce his bounty. He'd been as pleased as punch to have an audience. It *was* quite miraculous what he did in there though, she told herself, changing time and nature.

She stiffened. *Changing time*. Her heart began to race. That was what she had to do. No one was aware of her condition as of yet. If she and Archibald made love shortly, tonight even, and in a few weeks' time she announced she thought she was pregnant, who would be any the wiser? The baby would have to be 'early', of course, but that happened. Her own sister's first child had been nearly six weeks early if she remembered rightly.

She pressed one gloved hand against her chest; her heart was pounding so hard it felt as though it was going to escape her body.

It was the answer, the only answer, she told herself as

she rose to her feet, her agitation such that she needed to walk. But how was she going to accomplish the first part and make Archibald want to be intimate with her tonight? Although they shared the same bed, the most he did each night before they went to sleep was to give her a perfunctory kiss on the cheek. Walking slowly, she wound her way out of the pleasure gardens and a large area of lawn beyond them and entered the woodland that led to the wildflower meadows, her favourite spot in the spring and summer. Today, though, she didn't leave the woodland, stopping and standing with her back leaning against a tree trunk as she looked up through the bare branches to the blue sky.

She could count on two hands the number of times Archibald had taken her since they'd been wed, she thought apprehensively, and she had no idea how to tempt him in such a way that he would take the initiative. Their wedding night had been a gentle, tender affair for which she had been grateful at the time; he had been considerate of her inexperience and anxious not to hurt her, and although it had been slightly painful she hadn't found it unpleasant. He had taken her once more during their honeymoon and then on returning home to Fellburn it had been a good three months before he had made love to her again.

Making love. Could you call Archibald's brief, almost passionless performances in bed *making love*? She hadn't known what pleasure meant until that night in Philip's study when his hands and tongue had brought forth responses she wouldn't have dreamed herself capable of, and more than once since she had had such erotic dreams that she'd awoken hot and flushed and damp between her legs.

Mortified at the way her thinking had gone, she shook her head in despair and began to walk again. During the day she could usually keep control of her mind and the strange desires Philip Wynford had called forth, but the night was a different matter when her subconscious had free rein. Every time it happened she awoke feeling drenched in shame and guilt, as though she was betraying Archibald all over again.

It was nearly three hours before she returned to the house and at some point during the morning she had made up her mind that she would do whatever was needed to bring Archibald up to scratch. She would have to be careful, she warned herself, once she was sitting in front of the fire in the drawing room with a tray of coffee and little pastries. The walk had done her good and she had an appetite. She couldn't appear immodest or bold, just the opposite in fact, but somehow she had to manipulate things so that the protective, almost fatherly affection he had for her was stirred into something more for a few brief minutes. That was all she wanted, just a few minutes, and then he needn't touch her again for the rest of his life if he didn't want to.

All that day she alternated between determination and despair and then that evening, just before Archibald was due home, salvation arrived in the unlikely form of her parents. She had changed into an evening dress – even when it was just the two of them dining Archibald liked the proprieties to be upheld – and was sitting in the drawing room waiting for him when one of the maids announced her parents. Her mother swept into the room in her usual high-handed manner, but then shed a tear or two as she announced that their eldest grandchild was at death's door. Apparently they'd spent the afternoon sitting at his bedside with his distraught parents.

It transpired that little Cuthbert had caught a chill playing in the garden in the snow with some friends. It had gone to his chest and according to the doctor, had turned into a severe form of bronchitis. The situation was dire, her father said grimly, and the next twenty-four hours were crucial. They had come to ask that Archibald and herself would join them in praying all would be well.

When Archibald walked into the house he found his mother-in-law wiping her eyes and his father-in-law declaring the Lord's will be done. They prayed together for the little boy and the in-laws stayed for dinner before they left. It was a sombre affair; no one had an appetite.

Later that evening as they stood on the steps waving her parents off, Belinda was surprised when in an unusual show of affection Archibald put his arm round her. 'The poor little chap might well pull through, m'dear,' he said softly. 'Don't lose hope.'

She looked up at him, her eyes liquid with sudden tears. 'It would be too cruel if he was taken so early. He's only seven years old, Archibald. He has the rest of his life in front of him.'

'I know, dear, I know.' Cuthbert was the son of the oldest of Belinda's siblings, Robert, and Archibald knew the child had been instrumental in giving his father the will to live when Robert had returned home from the war unscathed in body but deeply troubled in his mind. Archibald found children an irritation on the whole and certainly Belinda's nieces – two girls aged five and three from one sister and a girl of two from the other – bore this out with what he considered their incessant whining and demands, but from the first he had warmed to Cuthbert. The stocky little boy was charmingly comical but always well-mannered and Archibald considered him a grand little fellow. He said this now, adding, 'I'm sure he will be all right. He's strong and sturdy and a fighter and that's important. Take heart.'

She nodded, allowing him to lead her back into the warmth of the house where he ordered coffee and brandy to be served in the drawing room. He didn't sit in the armchair he normally favoured but drew her down beside him on the sofa, keeping his arm around her until Mrs Banks bustled in with the tray.

His kindness and affection when added to the heightened emotions she was feeling about the baby and now Cuthbert brought the tears to her eyes again as she sipped her coffee, but at the same time it cemented her resolve that she must follow through on what she had decided earlier. He wanted to comfort her and she could use that to her advantage; she might not get another chance like this.

She finished her coffee and then said, 'I think I'll go up if you don't mind.'

'Of course.' He patted her hand, knowing how distressed she was. She felt things deeply, that was the thing, he told himself. His first wife hadn't been like that. Verity had, he supposed, been a female version of himself in some respects – reserved and undemonstrative – but she had had a grandeur about her he knew he didn't have. She hadn't liked the physical side of marriage and had made that clear on their wedding night which had been something of an ordeal, and had left him feeling brutish and shamed and coarse. Their marriage had never really recovered from it but had limped on for another twenty years; years in which they had lived very separate lives while putting on a show for the outside world. When she had died, he hadn't touched her intimately in nineteen years. He knew the course he should have adopted years ago; several of his friends had mistresses or paid for their pleasure elsewhere, but a certain fastidiousness in his nature had prevented that. He had got used to subjugating his body and desires until it had become second nature.

'Archibald, you won't be long, will you?' Belinda's voice was soft, hesitant. 'I – I don't want to be on my own tonight with my thoughts.'

He often spent an hour or two reading after she had gone to bed and more times than not she was asleep when he eventually entered their bedroom, but now, his voice gentle, he said, 'I'll finish my brandy and come straight up, dear.'

When he had fallen in love with Belinda he'd told himself things would be different. *She* was different. Young and warm and vulnerable in a way that Verity had never been. He had been as nervous as a schoolboy still wet behind the ears on their wedding night, he remembered now. Terrified of disgusting his new wife as Verity had said he'd disgusted her, the words she'd hissed at him making him feel like a wild beast and stripping his virility. Belinda hadn't been like Verity, but he knew he had hurt her when he'd taken her because there'd been spots of blood on the sheet in the morning.

He watched her leave the room and swallowed the remainder of the brandy in his glass before pouring himself another.

Perhaps, in the early days of their marriage, he should have plucked up the courage to ask her how she felt about intimacy, but he'd been too afraid of the answer. Instead, he'd reverted to suppressing his feelings, and on the rare occasions when desire overcame him he made sure he got it over and done with as quickly as possible for Belinda's sake. She always lay docile and still and made no objection, but he had no idea what she was thinking.

He knocked the brandy back in one and stood up, knowing she needed him for once, which was a good feeling although he didn't want her to be so distressed. He would hold her in his arms and soothe her, reassuring her that all would be well so she could sleep peacefully, he thought as he climbed the stairs. Just that, nothing more, although it had been a long time . . .

Belinda stood in front of the full-length mirror looking at her reflection. Her fine lawn nightdress hinted at the curves beneath and she had brushed her hair for some time so that it fell in a shining silky curtain down her back, rather than plaiting it as she usually did at bedtime.

She was trembling, and she bit down hard on her bottom lip, her pale and somewhat babyish face staring anxiously back at her and her deep-blue eyes wide. She had to do this, she told herself, and tonight. Every day, every hour was crucial.

Her fingers were joined so tightly at her waist that her knuckles gleamed white, and she slowly relaxed them, taking several long, deep breaths.

Everything – her marriage, her life, her future – rested on her succeeding and she had waited too long already. If she had been thinking straight she would have done this weeks ago. She had to seduce her husband into sleeping with her and in a way that made it seem it was his idea. She'd heard Archibald come into the bedroom and walk through to his dressing room a few minutes earlier, and now she left her boudoir, her heart pounding. Johnson had lit the oil lamps and put extra coal on the fire in the small grate before she'd left and the bedroom was warm and welcoming, the thick velvet curtains closed against the winter night.

As she stepped into the room Archibald emerged from his dressing room. He was wearing a deep red velvet dressing gown and his hair was brushed behind his ears; in the dim light he appeared younger and this impression was heightened when he moved towards her almost hesitantly, saying, 'Come and get into bed, you must be cold,' as his eyes moved over her, lingering on her hair.

She remained where she was, and when he reached her she said softly, 'Thank you for your understanding about Cuthbert.'

'Of course I understand. I care about the little chap too.'

She looked unbearably sweet standing there, he thought as he put his arms round her, and when she nestled into him his heart began to pound faster. She tilted her head after a moment, inviting his mouth to take hers, and he was filled with what was almost wonder. *She wanted him to kiss her.*

He cupped her face in his large hands and at first his lips were gentle. Then, as he felt her response, the kiss deepened and for the first time in their marriage he threw off the restraint that normally bound him. Whisking her off her feet he carried her over to the bed, quickly divesting himself of his dressing gown before he lay down beside her, and when her arms reached out to him he wouldn't have been able to put a name to the emotions that filled him, so complex were they.

Chapter Four

The next weeks were ones of severe snowstorms and gales, and the north in particular suffered the brunt of the freezing conditions. The wind howled night and day and in some places the snowdrifts were over eight feet high, deep enough to bury a horse and cart. Belinda had never minded the snow – in fact, she had always found the winter months had a charm of their own when the landscape was clothed in white and after a walk outside one could sit in front of a roaring fire and have tea and toasted muffins dripping with butter. This year, though, everything was different. She felt weighed down – though not in her body for as yet, apart from the nausea first thing, she appeared no different and her stomach was still flat. It was her heart that was heavy.

She had thought that once Archibald had been intimate with her she'd feel better mentally and emotionally, but if anything she felt worse. That night when they had learned how poorly Cuthbert was had been different to any other. *Archibald* had been different, not just in his lovemaking but the way he had lain next to her afterwards and talked softly in the darkness about his first marriage and the way Verity's rejection of him had moulded his thinking. She'd had no idea how damaged he was as a man and something had changed in her that night. She hadn't realized for some days that she'd fallen in love with him.

She was sitting in the drawing room listening to the wind howling down the chimney and she stood up, walking over to the windows that looked over the ornamental gardens. If only she hadn't betrayed Archibald everything would be wonderful. Cuthbert had recovered and was back to his usual self; she and Archibald had a new understanding which boded well for the future and already he was home more, and although he would never be a particularly adventurous lover he was passionate and loving. The nausea which had dogged her in the mornings had improved and fortunately it had never been bad enough that she'd been unable to hide it. She was feeling less tired too.

She sighed, biting down on her bottom lip as remorse overcame her. Now had come the time when she had to lie to him and pretend that the little life in her womb was his; she wished so much that it was. Allowing Philip Wynford to make love to her had been wicked but she was going to further compound that by doing something worse. But what choice did she have?

It was snowing again, feathery flakes that were being whipped into a frenzy by the wind, and although the room was warm she shivered. Her father had always had a ready answer when his parishioners had asked why a loving God had let evil enter His world. He'd maintained it was necessary as a means of sorting the saints from the sinners. If that was so, then she knew which category she fell into now.

She was still standing gazing out of the window when Archibald arrived home. He had taken to having lunch with her over the last weeks and some afternoons he didn't go out again but would sit with her in the drawing room reading. Belinda would either read or work on her embroidery and she enjoyed his company even though they didn't talk much. He'd proposed that once the weather improved they must go for outings together in the small landau rather than the larger coach and horses. He would drive – it was more intimate than being driven in the coach, and on fine days when the weather was clement there was nothing nicer than bowling along in the fresh air.

Belinda knew he was trying to make an effort and she appreciated it, even though it added to the crushing guilt and shame. She would have given anything to be able to go back to the night of the ball and change what had happened but of course that was impossible. This morning, for the first time, she had thought she detected the slightest mound in her belly; she was now eleven or twelve weeks pregnant or thereabouts by her reckoning so it could be the baby, and the knowledge had caused such a flood of love for the tiny creature inside her it had taken her breath away. She would do anything, *anything*, to protect it.

As Archibald came into the drawing room she turned to him, and something in her face made his cheerful expression falter. 'What is it? Don't tell me Cuthbert is poorly again?'

'No, no.' The feeling inside her was like a pain, an ache, and suddenly she knew she couldn't wait and agonize further. She had to follow through on what she had planned; she was between the Devil and the deep blue sea and there was only one way out. 'I – I've been feeling a little unwell the last few mornings.'

'Unwell?' Concern wrinkled his brow.

'Nauseous and – and a little tired.'

'I'll call the doctor right away. Fairley can take the coach and bring him—'

'I don't need to see a doctor. At least not yet.' He clearly didn't have the faintest idea what she was trying to say, she thought with a mixture of affection and desperation.

Archibald had gone a little pale. Verity's illness had begun in much the same way; nausea and exhaustion closely followed by severe bloating and pain in her abdomen. Cancer, the specialist from London had gravely told him, and well advanced. It was one of these silent diseases and even if the local doctor had picked up on it when the first symptoms had become apparent it still would have been too late. Thinking of this, he said, 'Nonsense, I don't want you to wait, m'dear.'

'Archibald, I'm expecting a baby.'

He had come and taken her hands when she had said

she was feeling unwell, and now he remained perfectly still, staring at her for some seconds before he whispered, 'What did you say?'

'I'm with child.'

She watched as her words sank in and when his face changed the expression that lit it up from within brought tears to her eyes.

'You're sure?' he said softly.

'Quite sure.' She forced a smile. 'Are you pleased?'

'Oh, my darling.' He gathered her in to him, holding her tight. 'Mere words couldn't express how I feel. I never thought—' He broke off and his voice was thick when he murmured, 'I wondered if I would ever be a father. My own father and his grandfather before him were only children; it seems the McFadyen line has always been sparse.'

She raised her head from his shoulder and her eyes blinking away tears, whispered, 'I love you.'

It was the first time she had ever said the words and they were both aware of it. He didn't speak, he didn't hold her tighter, but again the look on his face smote her heart and when he took her mouth in a long, deep kiss their mingled tears flavoured it with salt.

Over the next months, life settled into a harmonious pattern. After a harsh winter the arrival of spring was gradual but in March flowers of wood anemone poked their heads up to lie like spots of snow in sheltered spots of the grounds and primroses tentatively made their appearance. April was a month of warmth and cold, sunshine and showers, with bees stirring once again and the call of the cuckoo echoing from the woodland and announcing that winter was really over.

Archibald had insisted that she pay a visit to their local doctor to make sure all was well when he'd first learned of her condition. Belinda had made sure that he remained in the waiting room, and once with Dr Hogarth had explained that she was pregnant, giving him the supposed date of her last monthly and saying she felt quite well and did not want to be examined. Assuming it was on the grounds of modesty and not wishing to upset her, the doctor had concurred and told her to contact him if she had any problems. Otherwise his midwife would call to see her in a few weeks, he'd said, and from what she had told him she could expect the confinement to be towards the end of September.

She had rejoined Archibald and once they were in the carriage had reported the doctor was satisfied she was in good health and everything was as it should be at this early stage. She knew if he'd had his way he would have liked to wrap her up in cotton wool, but from that point on she'd insisted on taking her normal walks in the gardens every day when the weather permitted. Now though, Archibald mostly accompanied her, having reduced his visits into town to once a week.

Nature had conspired with her and she was carrying the baby snugly, still able to wear her normal dresses into May, although towards the end of the month the mound in her stomach was obvious. She'd always loved the spring when the scent of flowers filled the air and pink and white blossom loaded the boughs of apple and cherry trees, but with new life growing inside her the season was even more special. The baby had been moving for weeks but she had kept this to herself – she was only supposed to be five months pregnant, after all – but in the last week of May she felt she could at last share the experience with Archibald.

It was a beautiful afternoon and they'd taken a walk to the little dell in the woodland that was one of Belinda's favourite places on the estate. The area was awash with bluebells that reflected the sky high above, and Archibald spread out the thick tartan blanket he'd brought with him and helped her to sit down. The essence of summer was in the air and the day was almost hot, orange-tip butterflies and honey bees making the most of the blooms all around them. Skylarks were swooping and soaring in the thermals, singing their songs of pure liquid notes and joyful trills, and Belinda felt a sense of peace steal over her.

The baby would have Archibald's name, growing up in his house and calling him Father, and it *would* be his son or daughter, she told herself. In everything that mattered. What was the brief moment of conception compared to bringing up a child? Fatherhood was compounded of so many things and she knew Archibald would be the best he could be. He was so thrilled with the prospect and maybe they would have been unable to conceive a child of their own? He'd said himself that the

McFadyen men weren't the best in that regard. Perhaps this was meant to be?

She had to forget about that night with Philip Wynford, those minutes that had had such repercussions, and concentrate on making Archibald happy and contented within their family unit. She would never be able to atone for what she had done but if good came out of it maybe God would forgive her, even if she couldn't forgive herself?

The baby kicked, as though in agreement with her thoughts, and she reached out and took Archibald's hand, placing it on her stomach. 'Can you feel your child?' she murmured softly.

He was very still for a moment, and then, as the movements came again more strongly, he looked into her eyes, his own full of love as he whispered, 'He's strong.'

'Or she's strong?'

'Yes, or she. Boy or girl, if it's healthy and strong we'll be content, won't we, my love.'

She smiled, and as she'd done several times in the last weeks she reached up and kissed him. As he gathered her into his arms so that she was nestled in his lap, she told herself again that it would be all right. She would carry her secret to the grave and never breathe a word to anyone. Her child would grow up with two loving parents and that, after all, was the most important thing.

June proved to be a disappointingly wet and cloudy month after the fickle promises of May, but in July the weather turned exceedingly hot. The sun burned down from a cloudless sky day after day, and Belinda found the heat trying.

By her reckoning the baby was due some time in August, although of course as far as everyone else was concerned it would be a good few weeks later. Thankfully Archibald was anxious to acquire their nursery maid in plenty of time – his pedantic nature meant he believed in leaving nothing to the last minute – so Belinda found herself interviewing several applicants towards the end of the month from an agency in Newcastle, and others from an advertisement Archibald had placed in the *Newcastle Journal*. Most were of middle age or over and Belinda didn't take to any of them particularly until a small round woman with rosy-red cheeks and a bright smile was ushered in by Mrs Banks.

Belinda returned the smile as she said, 'Good afternoon. And your name is?'

'Dodds, ma'am. Nancy Dodds.'

Belinda found the relevant letter from the small pile on the table at her side. Nancy Dodds was forty-six years of age and had been dealing with children from the age of fourteen. First at a vicarage close to where she'd lived in Newcastle, and then some years later by becoming nursemaid at the residence of a Captain and Mrs Lyndon. She had been in charge of six youngsters there but when the last child had been dispatched to boarding school, had decided to move on. Her references were glowing.

Belinda remarked on this as she said, 'Mrs Lyndon was clearly sorry to lose you.'

'Aye, ma'am. She wanted me to stay on and see to the grandchildren when they visited but that wouldn't have been all that often. The thing is, I wouldn't have known what to do with meself most of the time if I'd stayed. I was happy there and Mrs Lyndon was lovely but I like being with bairns. That's the long and short of it.'

Belinda nodded. 'I understand.'

'And Mrs Lyndon did too, bless her.'

'I'm afraid there would only be one child here, certainly for the present.' Belinda smiled. 'My baby is expected towards the end of September.'

'Oh, there's nothing nicer than a new baby in the house, ma'am. Mind, they might be small but they keep you busy, sure enough.'

'I'm sure they do. I have a nephew and three nieces and when they visit it can be demanding but not as much as when they were tiny.' Belinda wanted to know a little more about Nancy but she knew in her heart that she had already made her decision. This little woman was nice, warm, and that's what she wanted for someone who would have a hand in looking after her child.

By the time Nancy left the house an hour later it was all arranged. She would return in two days' time and take up residence in the nursery maid's bedroom and sitting room. Belinda had shown her these quarters which were next to the day and night nurseries and washroom and closet. Everything had been newly decorated in the colours Belinda had chosen – lemon and cream – and no expense had been spared. There was still the perambulator and crib to buy, along with the rest of the paraphernalia the infant would need, and Belinda had suggested that Nancy accompany her into Newcastle and advise what would be required once she had taken up residence at the house.

It had been a pleasant hour. Belinda had felt more at home with the little woman than she'd felt with any staff since leaving the vicarage to be married. There was something innately natural and wholesome about Nancy, and Belinda felt she could be trusted not to take advantage if she was less formal with her. This thought caused her to say as Nancy was leaving, 'The staff here are addressed by their surnames – it's something my husband's family have always done – but in your case I would prefer to call you Nancy.'

Nancy beamed. 'Oh, I'd like that, ma'am. Mrs Lyndon was the same. Of course, their establishment was nothing compared to this. I mean it was nice, grand even, but this, well . . .' She appeared to run out of words.

Belinda nodded. She knew what Nancy meant. She had been over-awed when she'd first seen Fellburn House after living at the vicarage.

Once the little woman had left for North Shields, where she was presently staying at her sister's, Belinda went to find Archibald, who was going through some papers in his study. She had grown considerably larger in the last two months, but mercifully the baby was lying in such a way that she still didn't look enormous. Her mother had unknowingly contributed to the deception, saying on a number of occasions that Belinda was carrying the child in the same way she'd carried her first baby. 'A little in the front and a little in the back. Now with you and your sisters it was all at the front and much more uncomfortable, so be grateful.'

Belinda *was* grateful and she knew that her shape and the fact that the baby showed no signs of coming early was all to the good, but with the heatwave she was still finding it difficult to sleep at night and had lost her appetite.

Archibald looked up as she entered and immediately stood up, coming over to her and seating her in the big leather armchair opposite his desk. 'So, how did this batch of applicants go?'

'You make them sound like chickens or something.' She smiled. 'Actually, very successfully. I've found the perfect nursemaid.' She filled him in on Nancy Dodds, including the fact that she was going to call Nancy by her Christian name.

'Do you think that's wise?' he asked mildly. 'It sets her apart from the rest of the staff.'

She did really hope so. Johnson was a constant thorn in her side, and Mrs Banks and Wright weren't much better, often adopting a faintly superior attitude if Archibald wasn't around. The pair were only in their forties but they both seemed so much older, always so stiff and correct and unbending. The other staff weren't too bad, she supposed, but if she could have an ally in the house she'd feel so much better, and she had a feeling that Nancy would be able to hold her own with the lot of them. She shrugged in answer to Archibald. 'It's what I've decided. I shall be happier calling her Nancy rather than Dodds.'

'Then that is fine, m'dear,' he said at once.

She almost smiled; she suspected that if she asked for the moon he would do his best to get it for her, and at the moment he wasn't about to overrule her on anything.

He had perched on the edge of his desk and now as she stood to her feet he rose with her. 'I'll leave you to it,' she said softly, 'but later, after dinner when it's cooler, I thought we could go for a stroll in the gardens before bed.'

'Of course, but see how you feel.'

Belinda nodded. On her last visit to the house Mrs Howard, Dr Hogarth's midwife, had noticed her patient's ankles were a little swollen. She'd suggested Belinda sit with her feet up as much as possible in the coming weeks and unfortunately Archibald had been within earshot of the conversation. Since then he had fussed even more.

But she was fortunate to have such a caring husband, Belinda told herself as she left the study; in every respect she was more fortunate than she deserved. If the baby could remain tucked away where it was for a few more weeks – perhaps even past the date when she knew it should arrive – then she would be for ever thankful. She had refused any invitations from the Wynfords over the last months, saying to Archibald she would prefer to remain quietly at home due to her condition, and he had been more than happy to agree. The only folk they had visited or who had come to them were family, and they had completely dropped out of the local social scene. And she had no wish to resume it once the baby was born. She would be content with her husband and child, she promised herself, and if sometimes those heady minutes with Philip Wynford came to mind she dismissed them instantly.

Once Nancy was installed in her rooms in the nursery suite, Belinda experienced a lightness of spirit that had been absent for a while. Nancy worked on her like a tonic. Over the next days they shopped for everything the baby would need. Besides practical items such as nappies and clothes and small soft blankets, they had great fun purchasing toys and books, Belinda's favourite being a huge teddy bear who sat in a corner of the day nursery on his own small chair. Archibald had some of his old toys brought down from the attics where they'd been stored for decades, along with his childhood desk and chair.

His attitude towards Nancy was as formal as to the rest of his staff. Belinda understood this – it was the way that Archibald had been raised. Naturally intuitive, Nancy would make herself scarce in his presence and even when he wasn't around she was always careful not to take advantage of the special way her mistress treated her. She was a natural-born comedian, however, and this made every day entertaining and enjoyable for Belinda, who had been starved of fun and laughter for so long. Nevertheless,

Nancy possessed a streak of iron in her nature and this served her well with the other staff in the house. From the first day she had nailed her colours to the mast and she and Edith Johnson had loathed each other on sight.

The heatwave continued into the first week of August and just when Belinda felt she couldn't endure it any more, violent thunderstorms and torrential cloudbursts brought the temperature down to a bearable level.

Belinda's stomach seemed to double in size each week in the last month and when, at the end of the third week in August, she awoke one morning with cramping pains in her stomach she knew the baby was coming. She'd had a disturbed night with severe backache and niggling pains in her belly, but these pains were something else.

Mrs Howard was duly sent for, and as the labour progressed satisfactorily Nancy sat by the bedside holding her mistress's hand and chatting with the midwife, bringing an air of normality to what was a painful and somewhat scary procedure for Belinda. Dr Hogarth was summoned just before midnight when Mrs Howard felt the birth was imminent. In view of the fact that the baby was some weeks early she'd felt the doctor needed to be present in case there were complications, but she hadn't mentioned this to the patient, of course.

When the doctor arrived at the house he found Archibald pacing the drawing room in a terrible state, and spent a minute or two trying to reassure him that the baby arriving early was neither here nor there considering Belinda was in good health and everything had appeared normal when Mrs Howard had seen her just a few days ago.

An hour later, Belinda gave birth to a daughter who weighed six and a half pounds. A good weight, the doctor said, considering the early arrival. With Belinda being slight and narrow in the pelvis, Mother Nature had known best after all. Another few weeks and the baby could have been ten pounds or more, which could possibly have meant a difficult and complicated birth. As it was, the child was breathing well and appeared robust.

Archibald was ecstatic after the long hours of crippling anxiety when he'd been tormented by thoughts of losing both of them. When he came into the bedroom Belinda was lying in a fresh nightgown with her hair loosely tied with a ribbon and a big smile on her face, and he kissed her first before cradling the baby in his arms. The look on his face brought tears to the eyes of the three women, and even Dr Hogarth's voice was gruff when he said, 'There you are, Mr McFadyen. Didn't I tell you that all would be well? You have a fine healthy daughter.'

Archibald gazed down at the tiny scrap of humanity in his arms. His voice thick, he murmured, 'She's beautiful,' before his eyes met Belinda's. 'Thank you, my darling. Thank you for the priceless gift of our daughter.'

PART TWO

Tangled Webs

1938

Chapter Five

'Don't look at me like that, Bella. I'm only saying that you can understand why some Germans, like Werner and Karl last night, resent the Jews so much. Werner said where he was born in the Mitte district of Berlin many factories, workhouses and businesses in the streets were under Jewish ownership and his family were exploited by rich Jewish bosses. He can remember his father coming home from the factory where he was employed and coughing and wheezing to the point where he vomited, and his face and hands were stained black from smoke and oil. That would have an effect on any child. Anyway, I don't see why we couldn't have arranged to see them again; even when you disagreed with them they were so charming,' she added somewhat wistfully.

Mirabelle McFadyen, or Bella as she preferred to be addressed, glared at her best friend. The two young women were sitting in a smart café in Halle-an-der-Saale near Leipzig in Germany having coffee and cake, and discussing the dance they'd attended the night before. A number of dashing Luftwaffe officers who were training at the nearby Air Wireless School had been present, and two in particular had displayed their interest in the girls. Initially Bella had been as flattered as her friend by the young men's interest, but as the evening had progressed she'd become more and more disturbed by their views and attitudes. She had challenged them on various things, not least the political regime they espoused.

Now her voice was fierce as she said, 'Well, I'm sorry but I don't understand at all how Werner and others like him blame everything that's been wrong in the past on a certain segment of society, and all the rallies with their drums and marches and beautiful young people in uniforms waving flags won't convince me that there's not something evil abroad here. Jewish families are being turned out of their homes and hounded and synagogues and businesses set on fire – how can that be right, Cecilia? I've only been here a few months but this Nazi "masters of the world" thing is making my skin crawl.'

The Honourable Cecilia Chiswell-Fitzgerald glanced about her. On the next table were two elegant ladies with stylish hats and silk stockings, accompanied by a couple of gentlemen with walking sticks and golden watch chains. It was that sort of place. Genteel and refined. And Bella's voice had been loud. She adored Bella of course, she told herself, but sometimes her friend could be overly single-minded when she had a bee in her bonnet about something or other. But then Bella had been the same since they'd first met at the elite day school for girls they'd both attended in the north of England. They'd become inseparable, both being only children, and had gone to Paris together to be 'finished' for six months once their school days were over, but after that their paths had diverged. Instead of following the expected route and embarking on the London season, Bella had rebelled and pursued her love of languages here in Germany where a branch of her mother's family were living.

Cecilia reached out and patted Bella's hand. She'd had a lot of practice in placating her friend in the past and now her voice was conciliatory when she said, 'I'm not saying it's right, Bella, but really it's none of our business, is it? This isn't our country after all, and the people who live here know better than we do.' Werner and Karl had insisted that Adolf Hitler was the architect of a wonderful new Germany and the future would be glorious once the country was cleansed of all its dissidents. It had sounded plausible to her but Bella had been furious and said so in no uncertain terms. They'd ended up leaving the dance early.

Bella shook her head. 'The Nazis are bullies and thugs on the whole, can't you see that? And those officers last night were just repeating what they'd been told since they were small. It's indoctrination of the worst kind, Cecilia, and there's something terrible happening here. My aunt and uncle have heard of Jews being beaten up, even murdered, and families being sent to camps and all sorts.'

'Have you seen someone murdered?'

'Well, no, of course not, but others have.'

Cecilia settled back in her chair, taking a sip of coffee before she said, 'Well, everyone I've met since I've been here has been charming.'

'Yes, but that's my aunt and uncle's social set, isn't it,' Bella said wearily, wishing Cecilia would *listen*. She supposed her friend was an innocent – certainly she always accepted everyone at face value – and she knew Cecilia's hope for the future was to rise to the pinnacle of social success through an excellent marriage which would include vast wealth and possessions on an unimaginable scale. She was like a child, seeing the world as pleasurable and fun and ignoring anything that might cause a shadow to fall on her perfect life. When she'd tried to talk to Cecilia about the rumours of war that had been gathering pace, her friend had flatly refused to countenance the credibility of it. She knew she ought to be patient with Cecilia – her friend couldn't help the way she was, she supposed – but it was annoying.

Cecilia leaned forward. 'Darling, I'm due to fly home tomorrow, so let's not talk about this any more. Oh, I do wish I could stay longer but there's Amelia's wedding, so I have to go.' Amelia was one of Cecilia's cousins and she was having eight bridesmaids, of whom Cecilia was one.

Bella nodded; she wished she could say that she would like her friend to stay longer but in truth she couldn't. She'd been excited about her coming to stay for a few days but in actual fact it felt as though Cecilia's presence had been like someone holding up a mirror in front of her, forcing her to stare at the reflection, and she didn't like what she saw. If she had stayed in England and done the London season and all the country balls that led on from it, she'd probably be just like Cecilia now, she thought ruefully. Not that she had ever planned to do that; she'd known in Paris that she wanted to develop her language skills and the best way to do that was to live in a country and absorb the different styles and use of words and so on. Her French and Italian had already been good, and she knew the four months she'd spent here had improved her German enormously. Languages had always come naturally to her, and if she'd had her way she would have loved to travel to Italy too, but her parents had only allowed her to come to Germany because one of her mother's sisters had settled here. She'd been chaperoned every minute – her uncle had even taken and collected them from the dance last night – but in spite of her aunt's efforts her senses had become sharpened as to what was happening in Germany.

Dutifully, she said, 'I'll miss you,' to Cecilia, but as her friend began to prattle on about the wedding and her bridesmaid's dress and the best man who was an earl's son and still fancy-free, Bella's mind was elsewhere. She'd heard her aunt's two maids whispering about gangs of Nazi thugs who owned the streets, driving around in trucks, flashing their guns and their swastika armbands and hooting at pretty girls. If they wanted to pick someone up or beat them they did so apparently with impunity, and any resistance meant being taken away to one of the camps which were prisons where opponents of the Nazi regime were detained. The maids were sisters and looked Aryan, with fair hair and milky white skin, but from what she'd overheard that morning there was a Jewish grandmother. The old lady had gone shopping a couple of days ago and had not returned.

Horrified, she had made herself known and tried to talk to them but when they'd realized she'd been listening they'd scuttled away without saying any more. Coming on top of the anti-Semitic tirade from Werner and Karl the evening before, it had made her realize the severity of some of the things she had heard her aunt and uncle discussing and why they were making plans to leave their home and return to England. They weren't Jewish but they were frightened, and for the first time she fully understood why.

Her aunt's chauffeur arrived to pick them up from the café, and once home in the beautiful apartment on the outskirts of the city the two girls got ready for the dinner party her aunt was hosting that evening, but all the time Bella found she was mulling over the events of the last twenty-four hours. Nevertheless, she tried to respond to Cecilia's chatter; her friend was leaving early the next day and she didn't want to put a damper on her last evening in Germany.

It wouldn't be long before she returned home to England herself. She'd had to persuade her parents to let her come, and the agreement had been that she'd spend the summer with her aunt and uncle – he was some kind of diplomat for the English government but she'd never quite understood exactly what he did – and then leave some time in October. It was now the end of September and tomorrow was the first day of October, so time was limited.

Would she be sorry to leave Germany? she asked herself as she stood with Cecilia sipping pre-dinner cocktails with her aunt and uncle before the arrival of the dinner guests. She had been so excited when she'd first arrived but had soon discovered that she would actually have had more freedom at home than with her aunt and uncle. The political situation coloured everything; non-conformity was a very dangerous path to choose and as bad stories had begun to filter back into Germany as to what was happening to Jews in some of the camps, her aunt in particular had become paranoid that Bella didn't speak to anyone outside the house and express views against the Nazis. Her aunt and uncle's group of friends spoke freely in the confines of the house on social occasions, but even then they often stopped what they were saying if she approached. Bella didn't know if this was because they didn't trust her, or whether her aunt had asked them to do this. Intrinsically curious, she'd become adept at eavesdropping and as she was blessed with acute hearing had heard several conversations which had disturbed her.

As the first guests arrived, she thought of one evening in particular a week ago which had given her a sleepless night as she'd tried to make sense of what she'd overheard. One of her uncle's colleagues had been talking to an elderly

German couple about the Bund Deutscher Mädel, a female Hitler Youth organization. The couple were distressed about their two granddaughters, who had previously been in the Jung Mädel for ten- to fourteen-year-old girls and had recently moved up to its senior equivalent, the BDM. The girls had become increasingly hostile to their parents as they'd become entrenched in the organization and obsessed with racial purity and hard physical exercise; their bible was Hitler's *Mein Kampf*, apparently, and they studied a whole range of anti-Semitic writings and Nazi literature. When their parents had expressed some concern, the sisters had threatened to denounce them to the authorities and had treated them with utter contempt.

'I don't understand it,' the grandmother had said despairingly. 'They used to be such a happy family and the girls were so sweet when they were little. My Ursula is heartbroken.'

Her uncle's colleague had shaken his head. 'I'm afraid Ursula and her husband said too little too late. All children are little vessels ready to be filled with good things or bad by their parents and educators. In fearing the wrath of the Reich and social ostracization years ago they chose to conform and to allow the girls to absorb the views of their Nazi teachers. You know that – we have discussed it before, my friends. We are "old Germany" – at least, that is how your granddaughters have been taught to see us and their parents.'

The three of them had become aware of her presence at this point and changed the subject, and when she had tried to discuss what she'd heard with her aunt the next day she wouldn't be drawn. 'The less you know about such things the better,' her aunt had said firmly. 'You will be going back to England soon.'

Quite what that had to do with anything Bella didn't know, but she hadn't pressed her aunt. And last night the two Luftwaffe officers had earnestly extolled the virtues of the Hitler Youth, insisting that through religious debate their teachers had shown them that the destruction of the Jew within German society was an intended course of history and God's will, with a logical conclusion as to the amputation of a diseased portion of the evolutionary mechanism of the human race. God had appointed Hitler to save Germany, and the Germanic Aryan race would one day inherit the earth. It was at that point she had insisted on telephoning her uncle and asking him to pick them up early.

Within a few minutes of all the guests gathering, Bella sensed something particular was afoot. Cecilia, who didn't speak a word of German, was blissfully oblivious to the tense atmosphere and by encouraging her friend to natter on about this and that, Bella was able to tune in to other conversations.

It didn't take long before she grasped that the undercurrents in the room were because of an announcement in Munich that afternoon stating that there would be no war over Czechoslovakia. It had followed a conference lasting nearly twelve hours between Chamberlain, Mussolini, Hitler and others.

Bella didn't quite understand at first; she would have thought that no war was a positive thing, but the more she listened the more she understood that the solution was not to everyone's liking – certainly not the Czechs who hadn't been present – for it granted almost all of Hitler's demands.

'Unfortunately Chamberlain showed Hitler that he's spineless days ago,' her uncle said quietly to one of his colleagues. 'You don't react to the sabre-rattling of a tyrant by letting him know that armed conflict between nations is something you'd go to any lengths to avoid. We've abandoned the Czechs to their fate and that's unforgivable but worse, Hitler now knows he's unstoppable.'

The man her uncle was speaking to said something Bella couldn't catch and at the same time she realized Cecilia was waiting for her to respond to their supposed conversation. Hoping she was saying the right thing she smiled and said, 'Right,' and it must have been appropriate because Cecilia launched off again with more details about Amelia's wedding.

At this point, much to Bella's annoyance, her aunt chose to join them, and Bella just knew from the look on her aunt's face that she'd realized what she was doing. Suddenly angry at the way she had been treated like a child ever since she had arrived in Germany, Bella said flatly, 'So Uncle thinks a war will still happen despite the agreement today?'

Prudence Myers sighed. She loved her niece. Bella was beautiful and vivacious with her golden-brown hair and large dark-blue eyes, but she was too intelligent by half. And Germany was no place for intelligent young women who spoke their mind. She'd had misgivings when her sister had written at the beginning of the year asking if Bella might come to stay with them for a few months, but hadn't liked to refuse. But she should have done, she knew that now. She had been horrified when Bella had told her about the Luftwaffe officers last night – or to be exact, horrified at what Bella had said to them, she corrected herself. People had been arrested for far less and in spite of Geoffrey's diplomatic status they might have been unable to protect her. She had written to Belinda this morning asking if she and Archibald could come and take Bella home immediately, rather than waiting another three weeks as had been agreed.

Taking a deep breath and keeping her voice light, Prudence said, 'Darling, don't worry your head about such things,' before turning to Cecilia and adding, 'Only a few days until Amelia's wedding now. You must be very excited. I hear it's going to be a grand occasion.'

'Uncle Geoffrey is right, isn't he.' Bella's voice verged on truculent. 'And I agree with him. The only way to deal with a bully is to stand up to them, even if it means a fight, and Chamberlain has backed down.'

Cecilia was looking from one to the other, her eyes wide and her face faintly alarmed.

Her voice stiff now, Prudence said, 'Please, Bella, that's enough. This is Cecilia's last evening with us so let's make it a pleasant one.'

Bella stared at her aunt. Her uncle and all the people here, English and German alike, believed a war was coming and Aunt Prudence was talking about a pleasant evening? If half of what she had picked up on since she had been here was true, then Germany was a hateful country run by a brutal and wicked regime. How had it been allowed to happen? Why hadn't her aunt and uncle and others challenged the authorities long ago? 'Don't you care?' she said tightly. 'About what's happening now, about what's been happening for years here? All the families, women and children—'

'*Bella.*' Prudence's voice wasn't loud but it stopped Bella in her tracks. 'You have no idea of what your uncle and others like him have been doing and I have no intention of explaining. It's too dangerous. For you and for us. I suggest you say nothing more.'

Geoffrey had joined them and now he took Bella's arm, saying to his wife and Cecilia, 'Would you excuse us a moment?' before he led her out of the room and along the hall to his study. Once inside he shut the door and turned to face her. 'Sit down,' he said quietly, and when she still remained standing, he added, 'Please?' Once she was seated, still in the same calm, quiet voice, he said, 'Your safety has been your aunt's main concern and I understand this, but I feel the time has come to explain just a little of where your aunt and I stand in all of this. My job is important, Bella, and I have done my duty to the best of my ability, but at the same time I and some of my friends – German friends, I might add – have been instrumental in providing –' he hesitated – 'help to certain members of the community who through no fault of their own have been targeted by the Nazis. I can say no more and I only say this because in a day or two your parents will arrive to take you back to England where you will be safe.'

Bella's hand went to her throat; she wanted to say she was sorry but instead she whispered, 'I don't want to be safe. I want to stay here and help.'

'That's commendable and I know you are sincere but forgive me for being blunt. You would be more of a liability than an asset, m'dear. Things are going to get swiftly worse here and your aunt and I are prepared for what might happen. Chamberlain spoke about "peace for our time". I don't know if he is incredibly naive or ill-advised or what, but it is absurd to imagine that the fortifications in the Rhineland which Hitler's boasted about are not for the purpose of war. Czechoslovakia has already been sacrificed, Mussolini is cosying up to Hitler, and Poland is in the Führer's sights. War will come.'

Bella nodded. In England, where everything had been normal and peaceful, she'd have found it difficult to believe war was inevitable, but the last months in Germany had convinced her otherwise. 'I'm sorry, Uncle Geoffrey,' she said shakily. 'I shouldn't have said what I did to Aunt Prudence.'

'The fault is ours, m'dear. In our determination to protect you from any unpleasantness we went too far. We should have sat you down weeks ago and had this little chat. You're a fine young woman and it's been a pleasure to have you here. I shall be sorry to see you go in one way but in another I shall be relieved. Do you understand?'

'Yes, I understand.' She stood up and kissed her uncle on the cheek. War was coming. Thousands of people would die, millions, and who knew what the outcome would be? Suddenly she wanted her mother.

Chapter Six

Belinda arrived in Germany within days. Archibald didn't accompany her, on doctor's orders. He'd had a couple of mild heart attacks during the summer – which they had kept from Bella, knowing she would worry – and as Dr Hogarth had said in his blunt way, Archibald had recently had his seventieth birthday and was no spring chicken to go gallivanting.

Bella and her mother spent another day with Prudence and Geoffrey before returning home, and it was only when they drew up outside Fellburn House that Belinda told her daughter about Archibald's heart condition. Bella scrambled out of the car and entered the house at a run, finding Archibald in his study and flinging herself into his arms. 'Why didn't you tell me you'd been ill?' she accused once they'd finished kissing and hugging. 'I can't believe you didn't say anything. I'd have come home at once.'

'Which is exactly why we didn't let you know, my darling. You couldn't have done anything and we wanted you to have the time as planned with your aunt and uncle.' Archibald smiled at the beloved daughter who was his sun, moon and stars. He'd often thought that he hadn't known what true happiness was until she'd been born. He had said that once to Belinda and she'd smiled and said she hoped he had a little love to spare for her too. They had been the words of a wife who knew she was adored and he had taken them as such.

There had been no more children. He knew Belinda would have liked another baby but he was content with Bella, and in truth she had always kept them on their toes. Even as a toddler Bella had been headstrong and full of spirit, but these characteristics that were somewhat alien to him, and to Belinda too as she was as placid as he knew himself to be, were offset by an innate compassion and kindness. As a child, Bella had always been bringing home any injured birds or fledglings that always seemed to manage to come across her path, along with rescuing a large litter of kittens one of the local villagers had been about to drown in a bucket, and a couple of stray dogs.

His daughter had caused them a good deal of embarrassment among their friends too when she had spoken out against hunting and shooting more than once; the country set they moved in here were obsessed with such activities, which Bella found abhorrent. But that was his Bella and he loved her for it. They had named her Mirabelle after his mother but she'd become Bella almost from day one. It suited her.

'How are you feeling now?' Bella said anxiously as she searched her father's face, only half-reassured by his firm reply that he was perfectly well. Admittedly she'd been gone a number of months but he seemed to have aged as many years.

'Now, I want to hear all about your time abroad and what you've been up to.' Archibald put his arm round her as they left the study. 'You said in your letters that it's helped your German enormously, but you were fluent before you left. Did you have fun too in the midst of improving yourself?'

They had reached the drawing room where Belinda was waiting, and as Bella's face changed, he said, 'What? What is it?'

Once they were all sitting down with the coffee the maid had brought, Archibald said again, 'What's wrong, darling?'

Bella raised her head, looking at her father and then her mother and then back to her father before she said, 'Aunt Prudence and Uncle Geoffrey were lovely and their friends were nice but . . .'

'But what?'

'It's the things that are going on in Germany. Aunt Prudence did her best to shield me from it but terrible injustices are happening to lots of people, especially the Jews.' She related some of what she'd become aware of, finishing with the story of her aunt's maids and their missing grandmother. 'Aunt and Uncle are trying to help but they wouldn't tell me how because it could have put me in danger – which speaks for itself, doesn't it. They're taking the most terrible risks, I'm sure of it.'

Archibald sighed, his face grim. 'I'm not going to insult your intelligence by saying that the times aren't grave, Bella. Like Mr Chamberlain I'm a man of peace, but that doesn't mean closing one's eyes to the strategies of a tyrant. Hitler won't stop in his quest for domination until he's made to stop.'

'But surely Hitler doesn't want war?' Belinda's face had gone pale. The political problems at home and abroad didn't interest her and she had always preferred not to think about anything unpleasant, besides which she was still mourning Nancy, who had died the year before. When Bella had outgrown her nursery maid, Nancy had stayed on as Belinda's companion because the two women had become so close.

'We can only hope and pray, m'dear.' Archibald's voice was gentle. 'Now don't worry your head about it.'

Bella stared at them both. How many times had she heard her father speak to her mother in that soothing tone? Hundreds. He babied her, he'd always babied her. She supposed it was because he was so much older, but through his example she'd grown up believing her mother had to be shielded from life and that she was fragile, unable to cope with stress. She was delicate and mustn't be upset in any way, and any problems she'd naturally taken to her father. Oh, she did so love her father.

Knowing instinctively that he wanted her to change the conversation for her mother's sake, she said in a brighter voice, 'Cecilia was full of the details about Amelia's wedding when she came to Germany. I think she's got her eye on the best man.' She forced a smile at her mother. 'I wouldn't be surprised if we hear another wedding's in the offing soon.'

'Really?' Belinda was immediately intrigued. She was fond of Cecilia and always got on well with her when Bella's friend came to stay. She would never have admitted it to a living soul, but much as she loved her daughter she often didn't understand her, whereas Cecilia was more of an open book. 'What's his name? Do we know him?'

The diversion had worked, and as Bella and her father exchanged a knowing look, Bella began to divulge all the gossip. Nevertheless, she'd made up her mind she would seek her father out and have a quiet chat without her mother present. She wanted to fully understand what was what, the background to everything that had been happening in the last months and years and what it meant for the future. And she needed to tell her father something else, too. She had no intention of returning to what she termed as the somewhat meaningless existence that many of her peers like Cecilia enjoyed – lunches in town, dinner at the best places along with all the balls and parties and social functions that were mainly for one purpose as far as she could see – that of marrying well. She'd been blessed with a privileged lifestyle – she had come to realize that over the last little while – and while she thanked God for what she'd had, she didn't want to drift into a future that was aimless. She wanted to *do* something,

something worthwhile. The only trouble was that she didn't know what. But it didn't necessarily include marriage.

The next morning she emerged from the talk with her father better informed about current events and more determined than ever that from this point on she would dictate her own destiny. If she was honest with herself she was frightened at the changes that would occur if the country was forced into a war with Germany, but was coming to terms with the inevitableness of it. And she liked to *know*; it was uncertainty or beating about the bush she'd never been able to tolerate, even as a child. Sidestepping an issue wasn't in her nature. Her father was as sure as he could be that war with Hitler was on the cards and that was enough for her.

The next few days she adjusted to being at home again but it wasn't difficult; for one thing, she had far more freedom than she'd experienced over the last months under her aunt's care. For another, the close relationship she'd always enjoyed with her father had deepened if anything, and she spent hours with him in his study discussing this and that.

The Germans marching into Czechoslovakia and occupying the once-Czech Sudetenland; Duff Cooper resigning as First Lord of the Admiralty over Chamberlain's appeasement of Hitler; President Beneš resigning in Prague, and in Berlin the Jews being ordered to hand in their passports amid brutal persecution which involved many being expelled to Poland – they covered it all, and slowly, as her understanding grew, so did her appreciation of all the complexities involved. She knew her father enjoyed their conversations as much as she did and he was never condescending, unlike some of the men in their social set who made no secret of the fact that they considered women intellectually inferior.

Over the next weeks, Bella gave a great deal of thought to her future. She wanted to work. She had made up her mind about that. It would horrify her mother and perhaps even her father too, especially as she intended to do something worthwhile and gritty – nursing maybe, something where she could make a difference, albeit in a small way. Whatever she did, she knew she'd need training. At the moment she wasn't good for much other than speaking a few languages, she told herself ruefully. She had been enclosed in a kind of elite bubble up to this point in her life, but going to Germany had opened her eyes to many things. She had never really given much thought to the way some folk were forced to live. Poverty, and all the oppression and injustice that went with it, just hadn't registered on her in a real way – she'd simply accepted it. Although the terrible things happening in Germany weren't happening here, there was a huge divide between rich and poor and she felt guilty and ashamed that she'd lived nineteen years without *seeing* it.

It was a couple of weeks into November when Bella attended a dinner party at Evendale House, the Wynfords' country estate. She knew the Wynfords well – they were close neighbours, after all – and when she was younger she'd played with the youngest son of the colonel and his wife, James Wynford. He was some years older than her but unlike his three elder brothers had always been patient and kind, letting her traipse around after him even though she realized now she must have got on his nerves. The last she'd heard he was away at medical school and she hadn't seen him in years.

She hadn't felt like accompanying her parents. They'd received a letter from Prudence that morning and reading between the lines of what her aunt had written, she and her father had gathered that her aunt and uncle had been greatly affected by what was being called Kristallnacht or Crystal Night, a night of anti-Jewish attacks that had occurred some days before. They'd read in the newspapers that the whole of Germany's Jewish community had been subjected to a night of terror without precedent in modern times in a civilized country. An orgy of violence and arson had swept the nation with more than seven thousand Jewish shops being looted, hundreds of synagogues burned down and Jews being beaten senseless and murdered by youths with lead piping, while fashionably dressed women clapped and cheered and held up their young children to watch. It had been sickening, and in her letter Prudence had described the amount of broken glass lining the streets which amounted to millions of pounds' worth of damage, and the fact that Geoffrey had been warned by German officials to stay well away from the town that night.

It was clear the attacks had borne all the hallmarks of

an officially organized event; they'd begun simultaneously throughout the country and had followed a clear pattern.

Prudence had written that Goering had expressed his annoyance when he'd heard that most of the replacement glass would have to be imported and paid for in scarce foreign currency, remarking that 'They should have killed more Jews and broken less glass.' Her aunt had made no comment about Goering's statement but the fact that she'd written it at all revealed a lot. She'd added that she hoped to see them soon; Geoffrey was experiencing a few 'problems' at work and a break away would do him good.

Bella and Archibald had stared at each other when Belinda had finished reading the letter aloud at the breakfast table. It didn't sound good. Belinda, on the other hand, had blithely ignored most of what her sister had written, remarking that it would be lovely to see Prudence and Geoffrey and if they paid a visit she hoped it was at Christmas. Christmas was such a festive time for families to get together.

All in all, Bella wasn't in the best frame of mind when they drew up in the huge forecourt of Evendale, the thought of making polite conversation with the Wynfords' guests as frustrating as it was tiresome. She didn't mind Colonel Wynford – she'd always liked him and she knew he had a soft spot for her too – but his wife was a different matter. She found Felicity Wynford a cold fish. Still, as her parents had said, they'd been invited and it would be rude to decline the invitation without a good excuse, especially as the colonel had remarked to Archibald only the week before when he'd seen him in town that it would be nice to see Bella again after her months abroad.

It had just begun to snow when Fairley stopped the car. Archibald had sold his beloved carriage years before, but not the two horses. They were of a good age and were enjoying their retirement in a large field in the grounds of Fellburn estate with a cosy stable block for the winter which they shared with Bella's childhood pony, a little piebald mare called Meg. Small as she was, she kept the two bigger horses in check and wasn't above giving them a nip if they stepped out of line. Archibald had once commented that in his opinion the pony and Bella had a lot in common.

Once inside the brightly lit house a maid took their coats and then Bella followed her parents through to the drawing room, where a number of people were assembled. Some she recognized and some she didn't, but the women were all dressed up to the nines and the men were in dinner jackets. The buzz of conversation and occasional laughter was the same as at any other dinner party Bella had attended but tonight it grated on her. Cecilia would have loved it, she thought, but her friend had managed to bag the earl's son at her cousin's wedding and was devoting every minute to trying to persuade him to put a ring on her finger, so she hadn't seen anything of her. Which actually suited her, she thought guiltily, sipping the cocktail that she'd been given.

'Bella, m'dear.' The voice of Colonel Wynford brought

her turning. He kissed her on the cheek, saying, 'It's wonderful to see you again, and looking exquisite, if I may say so.'

'Thank you, Colonel.' She dimpled at him. There had been real pleasure in his voice.

'I was only telling James this morning how you'd scorned the London season and all those debutante dances and forced poor Archibald and Belinda to let you venture forth into the big bad world.'

'Hardly, Colonel,' she said, laughing. 'Firstly, I wouldn't dream of forcing my parents to do anything, even if I could, and secondly I was hardly out in the big bad world. I was staying with my aunt and uncle, as you know full well.' Her glance took in the tall blonde man standing at the colonel's side.

Noticing the look, Philip said, 'You remember James, of course. My youngest. You two used to play together, but that was more years ago than I like to remember.'

Before Bella could reply, James held out his hand. 'It's been quite a while, certainly, and the little tomboy that I recall is no more. In her place is a beautiful young woman. How do you do, Miss Mirabelle McFadyen?' He used to tease her as a child by giving her her full Christian name, knowing she preferred Bella.

'Very well, thank you, Mr Wynford,' she replied in like, thinking how good-looking he'd become. The boy of years ago had been thin and lanky with an unruly mop of hair he was forever pushing out of his eyes. The man he'd become had filled out with broad shoulders and a wide chest, his hair thick but neat and his eyes a vivid blue.

Her hand was taken by his large one. His flesh was firm and warm and she felt the contact right down to her toes. Her skin tingling, she retrieved her fingers, her voice more composed than she was feeling inside when she said, 'How is medical school?'

'Done with.' His grin widened. 'You're looking at a fully fledged doctor now, I'd have you know.'

'That's wonderful.'

'It would be if he wasn't set on practising in the worse part of town somewhere here in the north-east, rather than in a suitable establishment in London, Harley Street maybe.' Philip shook his head. He loved James, perhaps more than the rest of his offspring, but he could be as stubborn as hell, he thought sourly. 'All that money on his education and the years at medical school, and he wants to throw it away.'

Bella stared at James's father. The colonel was old school, she'd always known that, and staunch to his class – he certainly had no revolutionary social ideas – but even so . . . Her hackles rising, she said quietly, 'How is working where the need is greatest throwing anything away?'

'I couldn't have put it better myself.' James beamed at her and again she felt his attraction envelop her. 'I keep telling him that there are more than enough physicians dancing attendance on those who can afford to pay them well, and I never had any intention of becoming one of them.'

Philip glared at his son. 'Stiff-necked and stubborn,' he grumbled. 'I'd got it all arranged, a London surgery and a foot in one of the larger hospitals. Illness is illness, after all, and a doctor is supposed to alleviate suffering, isn't he?'

'Which, God willing, I shall do,' James said with remarkable good humour considering his father's attitude, 'but in a place of *my* choosing.' He put an arm round his father's shoulders for a moment before he added, 'Now stop showing Bella your grumpy side or she won't come here again. Will you?' He smiled at her.

'Definitely not.' She softened her words by putting her hand on the colonel's arm for a moment as she said, 'You should be proud James is prepared to stand firm for what he believes in. I think he's a lot like you, actually.'

'Now, I might be getting old but I know when I'm being soft-soaped, m'girl.' The words could have been in the form of a rebuke but for the gratification he couldn't hide. He had always thought that if he and Felicity had been blessed with a daughter he'd have liked her to be in the mould of Bella McFadyen. She'd always had a bit about her, had Bella.

Just then the gong was sounded to summon the guests into the dining room and as Philip hurried off to attend to his hosting duties, James offered Bella his arm. 'Shall we?' he said softly.

Once in the dining room Bella found herself seated next to her father on one side and Sir Miles Rathbone on the other. Sir Miles was an ancient little gnome of a man who she knew from past experience was stone deaf, which made any conversation extremely stressful. She looked down the table. Felicity had placed James next to her and on his other side was a young woman with beautifully coiffured hair and a dress that showed rather a lot of cleavage. The girl was glittering with diamonds and appeared animated as she engaged James in conversation. Bella's eyes narrowed. A spot of matchmaking on his mother's part, perhaps?

Then she caught at the thought, annoyed to find it had rankled. What on earth was the matter with her? she asked herself. She was being ridiculous. The girl might already have an understanding with James for all she knew, and it was absolutely nothing to do with her anyway. She hadn't seen him in years.

As the meal progressed the number of courses seemed endless. When she wasn't virtually having to bellow at Sir Miles, Bella picked at what was on her plate. She was careful to keep her gaze from wandering down the table, but nevertheless was conscious of the girl's shrill laugh every so often. She hoped James found it as jarring as she did.

When a suitable opportunity arose, she plucked at her father's sleeve, murmuring, 'Who's the young lady seated next to James Wynford? I don't think I've seen her before.'

In an equally low voice, Archibald whispered, 'I've no idea. There's a couple of families from London staying with the Wynfords for a few days and I understand one of them owns half of Kensington. Or is it Chelsea?

Something like that. The young lady might be part of that group – one of the daughters?'

Bella nodded. So perhaps she hadn't been too far off the mark in her initial assumption? Felicity Wynford could well be parading suitable young fillies in front of her youngest son? The other three sons were all married and settled, so she could imagine Felicity had decided it was time for James to find himself a wife from the upper echelons of society. Only the best would be acceptable for Felicity.

And then Bella reprimanded herself. She was being spiteful about James's mother, she knew that, but the woman was so *obvious*. Everyone here tonight would be fully aware of what was intended with the seating arrangements but it was Felicity's house after all.

In spite of herself she glanced towards James and saw he was laughing at something the girl had said, his head bent towards her. Suddenly she wished she were anywhere else but here. She wanted to go home but they hadn't even begun the puddings yet. She sipped at her glass of wine, willing the time to fly by. Of course it didn't.

Eventually the meal was over and the ladies adjourned to the drawing room while the men enjoyed their port and cigars. Bella had always considered this a somewhat archaic custom although tonight it meant she could observe the young lady who had monopolized James. It didn't take her long to discover that the girl in question was a Miss Rowena Silverstone and from the way that Felicity Wynford was gushing over her it was clear she was much in favour. Bella was sitting with her mother and a couple of younger women, one of whom was Felicity's cousin. This didn't stop the lady in question murmuring, 'Felicity has set her sights on this one, that's for sure. Of course with Daddy being positively *filthy* rich and Rowena being an only child, other considerations can be put aside.'

'Other considerations?' Bella said softly.

'Darling, it's well known that dear Rowena has been a little too free with her favours in the past. The girl's man mad actually, anything in trousers – or without them.'

'*Grace*.' Belinda was shocked and it showed.

'Oh darling, you know it's true.' Grace gave a little tinkling laugh. 'And James is the fourth son after all, not even the spare, so a rich wife will be needed to keep him in the manner to which he's become accustomed. I mean, a doctor, for goodness' sake.' She wrinkled her nose. 'A general practitioner, not even a consultant or specialist. Poor Felicity was quite *devastated* when James told them his plans.' She leaned forward, saying in an undertone, 'There was the most awful scene but James won't be moved – Felicity says he's like his father in that respect. He's like Philip in looks too, don't you think? Handsome devils, the pair of them,' she added somewhat wistfully.

Bella noticed her mother had gone quite pink and assuming she was embarrassed at the other woman's frankness made an effort to change the conversation although she had found it riveting. As soon as she could she excused herself, saying she needed to powder her nose, but instead of making her way to the cloakroom she walked to the orangery at the back of the house. When she had visited Evendale as a child the structure, with its orange trees and tropical plants, had always fascinated her and it was kept warm even on the coldest winter days. She had often curled up in one of the big cushioned basket chairs while the adults were occupied, sniffing the air which had its own perfume unlike anything else, although if James had been around they'd play hide-and-seek or some other game until she had to go home.

She walked to the far end of the orangery. One side was made up of glass panels that overlooked the grounds, some of which opened on a tilt and some of which didn't, and she stood looking out at the falling snow. It was wonderful to get away from everyone and the incessant chatter. And then she jumped violently as a voice behind her said, 'I see we had the same idea.'

She turned to see James sprawled in one of the basket chairs partly hidden by a huge fern. 'You startled me.'

'Sorry.' He stood up and joined her. 'Beautiful, isn't it, the snow, when it first falls. Pure and clean and untainted. It's a shame it can't remain like that. It's the same with human beings, I suppose. As babies we're innocent and unsullied by life but then –' he shrugged as he gazed out across the manicured gardens – 'we change.'

She turned to look out again as she said quietly, 'That sounds very jaundiced.'

'Does it?' He didn't glance at her. 'I prefer to think

realistically. I've found that on the whole people are selfish and self-serving and intent on having their own way.'

'Perhaps you've been mixing with the wrong people.'

He laughed out loud, looking into her face as he said, 'I wouldn't argue with that.'

She smiled back. There were no lights burning in the orangery but the illumination from the snow outside made it possible to see every feature of his face. Grace had been right, he was handsome.

'Do you remember when we were children and we used to escape the adults and play in here?' he said softly.

Bella nodded, her smile widening. 'I remember that you were very patient with a little girl who followed you everywhere when you were home from school. I must have got on your nerves.'

'No, you never did.' She was quite lovely, he thought as his gaze wandered over the creamy skin and amazing hair that seemed to be made up of so many shades of gold. 'Actually, I liked you,' he said quietly. 'I still do.'

There was a note in the last words that sent a frisson of something warm through her and suddenly the orangery seemed very intimate. 'You've said yourself that people change,' she said lightly. 'Perhaps if you got to know me now you wouldn't like me at all.' She arched her eyebrows, tilting her head and openly laughing at him.

'There's only one way to find out,' he said, a quirk to his mouth at her teasing. 'Would you do me the honour of having dinner with me tomorrow evening, Miss Mirabelle McFadyen? There's a little pub not far from here that does the most glorious steak pies. If you like steak pies, that is.'

A little pub. Not a fancy restaurant. She was finding she liked the adult James more and more. 'I adore steak pies,' she said solemnly, 'but what about Rowena? Should we ask her too?'

He grimaced. 'That laugh. No, I think we'll keep it to just the two of us if that is all right with you?'

She looked deep into the blue eyes. 'Quite all right.'

And that was the beginning.

Chapter Seven

Belinda stared at her reflection. She was sitting in front of her dressing-table mirror and had sent Johnson away some moments before, saying she'd finish the last of her toilette herself. She adjusted one of the combs in her upswept hair and sighed heavily. She'd have to go down for dinner in a minute, she told herself, but she didn't feel like eating. The fear that was with her day and night curbed her appetite and gave her a constant headache.

Bella and James. Who would have imagined such a thing? There were so many people in the world and they'd had to fall in love with each other. But then they were brother and sister, so maybe that hidden bond had had something to do with it? The last few months Bella had been so happy, her eyes sparkling and always laughing. Bella, oh, Bella. And Archibald. He adored his daughter. What was she going to do?

It wasn't a new thought. From the first day that Bella had announced she was going to dinner with James in November the previous year, she had prayed incessantly that this attraction that was obvious between the two would fizzle out. And it still might. She shook her head. She was clutching at straws. And of course everyone else had been delighted at the match, except James's mother, of course. She'd had to abandon her matchmaking with Rowena Silverstone.

If only she could have escaped the north-east after Bella was born and put some distance between their family and the Wynfords, but of course that had been impossible. The two adjoining estates had been in each respective family for generations. Archibald would never move away; Fellburn was in his blood. And she wouldn't have been able to give a good reason for wanting to leave.

She stood up, taking a long deep breath as she told herself for the umpteenth time that this thing between Philip's son and their daughter might come to nothing. Young people were always falling in and out of love after all, and with the shadow of impending war hanging over everything who knew what the future held? The thought of war filled her with dread, but she had to admit that if it was the means of separating James and Bella she'd actually welcome it, which was terrible.

On leaving the bedroom suite she made her way downstairs to the drawing room. Bella and Archibald were already enjoying a pre-dinner glass of sherry and as she entered the room they were laughing at something or other one of them had said. Two smiling faces turned towards her, their love for her apparent in their eyes, and again the fear rose up in a great flood. Somehow she forced herself to smile and take the glass of sherry that Archibald passed her, but as she sipped at it she barely tasted what she was drinking. Everything seemed like ashes in her mouth these days.

The following morning Bella awoke early, just as dawn was breaking. It was a beautifully soft, warm June day and slipping on her silk negligee over her nightgown she opened the doors leading on to her small balcony and stepped outside. The sky was rose-tinted and the air was fresh; it seemed impossible on such a lovely morning that the country was preparing for the very real possibility of war, but already in April the government had announced that conscription would take place along with plans for the provision of air-raid shelters and the evacuation of children should hostilities begin, and farmers were ploughing up grazing pastures to increase the proportion of food produced on home soil. The grounds of the estate stretched away in front of her, peaceful and tranquil in the early morning light, and in the far distance she could hear cows mooing and the occasional barking of a dog. Downstairs, Mrs Banks would be chivvying the house-maids and Wright would be about his duties. The old retainers were as much a part of Fellburn as its bricks and mortar, even though the years had taken something of a toll. Everything was the same as it had always been but it was going to change, she had prepared herself for that. Even Cecilia had recognized the urgency of the times; she'd persuaded her earl's son to tie the knot some weeks before, but even as Bella had danced at their wedding she'd sensed the fear in her friend's frenzied gaiety.

She sat down at the little table and chair on the balcony and, as they so often did, her thoughts turned to James. He'd gone to inspect a doctor's practice that was for sale in the town of Gateshead the day before and his father had accompanied him. The elderly doctor was retiring and moving away and the adjoining four-bedroomed house was part of the sale. James had told her that the property was in the poorest area of the town, but that suited his plans to live and work among the people he wanted to serve. It also meant that the purchase of the practice and house was within James's reach, unlike one a couple of months ago that had been in an affluent area of Newcastle. James's maternal grandparents had left him an inheritance and although the purchase would take every penny of it, that didn't faze him at all.

Bella smiled to herself. He was so excited, and although nothing had actually been said between them she knew that if the practice and house were suitable, he'd ask her to marry him. He was old school; he'd want to be able to provide a home for them and she understood that. Not that she wouldn't have married him if they'd had to live in a hut; they were soulmates and they both knew it. She couldn't imagine life without him now and she shared his vision to work among the poor. Although it would be a bit of a struggle at first and life would be very different from the lifestyle they'd both been used to, they were united in purpose.

They wouldn't be able to afford even a maid until James was established, but she could learn to cook, and as a doctor's wife in a working-class community she'd be at his side helping him. She could be his receptionist in the practice and his wife and partner in the home. They would share everything, they were determined about that.

She hadn't mentioned their plans to her parents; much as they liked James she knew they would be concerned at what she would be giving up to become his wife, but she knew she could talk them round. She and James loved each other, the sort of love that came once in a lifetime, and what was more important than that? They'd want her to be happy and she couldn't be without him.

Suddenly she wanted to get out of the house and be nearer to him. They had planned to meet later that morning but there was a spot in the grounds where she could see the Wynford house in the distance. Just seeing it would bring him closer.

Dressing quickly, she went downstairs. Mrs Banks was in the hall and she told the housekeeper that she was going for a walk to work up an appetite for breakfast.

Once outside, she made her way towards the pleasure gardens, which were beautiful at this time of the year and saturated with the perfume of roses. She would miss them when she got married. She walked towards the woodland, passing through and into the wildflower meadows. When she reached the border of their property there was a drystone wall where she could see Evendale's imposing facade. Of late, she and James had sometimes sat in this spot between their two homes and made plans for their future. Now she sat there again.

The sun had risen high into the clear blue sky while she had been walking and already the day promised to be a hot one. She took off the cardigan she'd slipped on over a sleeveless dress and shut her eyes, lifting her face to the warm rays as they caressed her skin. She could hardly believe that this time a year ago James hadn't featured in her life; now he *was* her life, he made it whole.

Bees were buzzing in the meadows behind her and birdsong filled the air. For a moment the sense of sheer joy that welled up was overpowering and she put a hand to her chest as though to restrain it.

When she heard James's voice calling her name she almost thought she'd imagined it, but then she opened her eyes and there he was hurrying towards her, waving. Jumping down from the wall into the Wynford grounds she flew to him, and as his arms went around her he lifted her right off her feet and swung her against him. Then he was kissing her and she was kissing him back, their bodies pressed into each other. When at last he released her they were breathing heavily, their faces alight.

'I was coming to see you,' he murmured, his eyes drinking her in. 'I couldn't wait till later.' He kissed her again, long and hard. 'I missed you yesterday, so much.'

'I missed you too.'

'I made an offer on the surgery and house and he accepted it.' He took her hands in his. 'You know what this means, don't you.'

It was rhetorical and she didn't speak, but every part of her was aware that this was the most precious moment of her life.

'Will you marry me?' he said softly, going down on one knee. 'You know I love you, I feel I have loved you all my life without realizing it and though I can't offer you much in the way of worldly wealth I can promise you that I'll make it my life's work to make you happy. No woman will be adored as you are adored—'

His words were cut off as she flung herself at him and then they were rolling in the thick grass, their arms around each other as she said, 'Yes, yes, yes, a thousand times yes,' as their lips met. Some moments later and in the circle of his arms, her head strained back from him as she gazed into his face. 'I love you so much,' she said softly, 'so very much.'

'And I you, my love.' He sat up, pulling her onto his lap. 'I'll speak to your father this morning. I don't want to wait too long, do you?'

She shook her head. She just wanted to be his wife as soon as it could be arranged. The times were uncertain and there was no need to delay; a simple wedding would suffice even if it caused a few raised eyebrows. Their families would expect a high society affair, of course, but they would stand their ground together. Nuptials at the local parish church and a small wedding reception at Fellburn would be perfect. She voiced this and James smiled. 'We could go and see the vicar tomorrow and ask for the banns to be read.' He stood up, drawing her with him. 'And I'll take you to see the practice and the house in the next few days. The house has been rather neglected since Dr Robson's wife died five years ago and needs decorating throughout—'

She stopped him by reaching up and kissing his mouth before she murmured, 'I'll love it whatever it's like because it will be our home, somewhere we can live and work together, bring up a family the way we want to.' As in so many things, they were in perfect agreement that children should have equal opportunities regardless of their sex.

'I can hardly believe you love me,' James whispered softly against her lips. 'You could have any man you wanted, marry well—'

'I am marrying well,' she said, taking his face between her hands and looking deeply into the blue eyes. 'I'm marrying you and men don't come any better.'

Now he grinned at her, shaking his head as he said, 'You wait till you're fielding off a difficult patient who wants my guts for garters. It happens, you know.'

'Oh, I can be very firm when I want to be and I shall start as I mean to carry on. The doctor's wife won't be a pushover.'

'I didn't think for one moment you would be.' His grin widened. 'Do you think it would be impolite if I walked back with you now and spoke to your father?'

'I think it would be wonderful. He's very fond of you, you know.' As she spoke the words, her mother came into Bella's mind. She couldn't explain it but of late she'd got the impression that her mother didn't approve of James the way her father did. She could be imagining it, of course – her mother wasn't one to wear her heart on her sleeve – but her face took on a kind of closed look sometimes when James was mentioned. Bella shrugged the thought away. Whatever her mother felt, they were going to marry and they would be happy.

They walked back to the house hand in hand and Bella felt she was floating on air. She had imagined this day so often, the moment when James would ask her to become his wife, and it had been more wonderful than any of her daydreams.

They entered the house by the way Bella had left – through the French doors of the breakfast room – and found her father already seated at the table. He was reading his newspaper while he waited for her and her mother to join him and looked up in surprise at their appearance. With no preamble, James said, 'I wondered if I could have a word with you in private, sir?'

Archibald's eyes moved to his daughter's face and what he read there caused him to smile as he stood up, saying, 'Of course, dear boy. Come into the study.'

Left alone, Bella sank down onto one of the upholstered chairs, her thoughts tumbling over themselves as she stared vacantly at the flower arrangement in the middle of the table, and she was still sitting like that when Belinda walked into the room.

Belinda glanced at the covered dishes standing on the long sideboard and then at her husband's chair and his discarded newspaper, a cup of coffee gently steaming beside it. 'Where's your father?'

'In his study. With – with James.'

'James?'

'I went for an early morning walk and met him. He – he had some news, he's going to buy that doctor's practice in Gateshead.' Bella found she couldn't continue. There was something about the way her mother had said James's name that told her she hadn't been mistaken when she'd imagined her mother didn't like him.

Belinda stared at her daughter. She didn't need to be told why the two men were ensconced in Archibald's study. The thing she had feared had come to pass and it couldn't happen. It would be a crime against God and man, she thought sickly, and what about any children? They could be impaired, crippled in mind or body or both and the fault would be hers. She had to speak out.

'*Mother?*'

It was Bella's cry of alarm that brought her back from the verge of fainting and as she groped for a chair, her daughter's arms came round her.

Once she was seated, Bella knelt in front of her saying, 'What is it? Are you ill?'

She grasped at the lifeline, and the weakness in her voice wasn't feigned when she murmured, 'Yes, I think it was something I ate last night, I've been feeling unwell.'

'You should have stayed in bed this morning.'

Belinda nodded. 'I think I'll go back upstairs.'

'I'll help you.'

'No, stay, and tell – tell James I'm sorry I missed him.' In spite of her protests Bella insisted on ringing the bell for Mrs Banks and then between them the housekeeper and her daughter escorted her up the stairs and into the bedroom, where she insisted she would be fine. One small mercy was that she had given Johnson leave to go and see her ailing mother in Newcastle; she really couldn't have coped with the maid's sharp eyes and insincere concern.

Once she was alone, she walked over to the window and sat in one of the velvet upholstered armchairs, gazing blankly ahead as her mind raced and her stomach churned. It was only a matter of moments before Archibald came hurrying into the room, clearly perturbed. 'What is it, m'dear?' he said, taking her hands in his after drawing the other chair closer and sitting down at her side. 'Shall I send for Hogarth?'

'No, no, I don't need a doctor. Something I've eaten has disagreed with me and upset my stomach, that's all. I felt a little faint but it is passing.' She looked into his dear face. Whatever happened now, he was going to be hurt terribly; knowing the truth about Bella would break his heart. Was there any way out of this where he could be spared? She shut her eyes. It was actually painful to see the love and worry on his face. 'An hour or so and I'll be quite recovered, I'm sure.'

'Shall I help you into bed?'

'I'd rather sit here now I'm dressed and as I say, it is passing.'

'Would it help to hear some news I think we have both been expecting?' Even as he said the words, Archibald admitted to himself that he wasn't sure how Belinda was going to react now that James had officially asked for Bella's hand. The subject hadn't exactly been a bone of contention between them for the simple reason that Belinda had refused to discuss it, saying that the relationship between their daughter and Wynford's youngest son wouldn't last whenever he had mentioned it. He didn't understand her attitude about James. He liked the man, respected him too, and although he would have preferred his daughter's future husband to be able to keep her in the manner to which she'd been accustomed, he could see that the pair of them would make a go of things. Bella had never been a social butterfly, and dinners and dances hadn't interested her in the least. He would make sure that he gave them a very handsome wedding gift straight into the bank as well as paying all the wedding expenses and so forth, and he didn't doubt the Wynfords would be generous in that regard too.

Belinda's voice was quiet and flat when she said, 'I presume James has asked for her hand in marriage and you have agreed?'

'Just so.' He was about to say more but stopped himself. They could discuss any reservations she had when she was feeling more herself. 'He's gone off home to tell Philip and Felicity. Apparently he and Bella don't want a big wedding, they'd prefer a small reception here after the service and no fuss. I don't suppose that will suit Felicity.'

He waited a moment, and when Belinda said nothing, added, 'Can I get you anything, m'dear? A hot drink perhaps?'

'No. No, thank you.' She shut her eyes, leaning back in the chair. 'Go and have your breakfast with Bella.'

She was aware of him standing looking at her for a few moments more and then the sound of him leaving the room, but she still didn't open her eyes. Something had clarified in the last minute or so. She needed to go and talk to Philip. She should have done so when she had first realized their children were seeing each other rather than letting the affair gather steam. She didn't harbour any hope that he would have some kind of miraculous answer on how to proceed, but nevertheless, he needed to know. That was as far as she could think at the moment.

After some minutes she rang for Mrs Banks and told her to inform Fairley to bring the car round to the front of the house, after which she went downstairs. Archibald was eating breakfast with Bella and he immediately rose to his feet, saying, 'Oh, there you are, dear. Feeling better?' as he pulled out a chair for her. 'Come and have something to eat.'

Ignoring the invitation, she said quietly, 'I am going to go for a drive. I could do with some fresh air.'

'Of course, dear, of course. I'll come with you.'

'I'd prefer to go alone.' She softened the words with a forced smile. 'I won't be long but I have a headache.'

Archibald looked at her, nonplussed, but when she

glanced at her daughter she saw Bella's face was expressing something more than just bewilderment. She was angry, Belinda thought, angry that her mother had spoiled what was after all a special day for her.

And this was borne out in the next moment when Bella said tightly, 'I can't believe that you are acting this way. I thought you were really ill but you just don't want me to marry James, do you? Is that why you're in a blue fit?'

'Bella.' Archibald shook his head. 'Don't speak to your mother in that tone.'

'What have you got against him? Is it because he's not wealthy or influential? Is that it? Because let me tell you he's worth a hundred of men like Augustus Hammond or Timothy Osbourne, for all their riches. James is prepared to work at what he believes in and so am I. We love each other. Doesn't that count for anything with you?'

'*Bella, enough*.' Archibald silenced his daughter. 'Your mother is not well.'

Belinda's gaze swept across them one last time. There was lots she wanted to say; that she loved them, that they made up her entire life in different ways; that she was going to cause them such heartbreak they'd hate her for ever and if she could die right at this moment and spare them the grief she would gladly do so. Instead she turned and walked out of the room into the hall, ignoring Archibald's call for her to stay.

Fairley had the car waiting and he opened the door

for her just as Archibald came hurrying out of the house. He reached the car as Fairley started the engine and she lowered the window. 'I won't be long,' she said again, her eyes moving over each feature of his face, 'but I need to be alone right now.'

He reached out with his hand and touched her cheek for a moment, and as she began to wind up the window he said softly, 'We'll talk when you return, dearest, and whatever is the matter we'll sort it out, all right? I love you.'

Belinda couldn't speak. When she came back she was going to destroy him and there was nothing she could do to prevent it. The die had been cast all those years ago on Armistice Day and the time in between had just been a lead-up to this day.

Chapter Eight

Philip Wynford was highly delighted with the day thus far. He had risen early and gone for a ride round the estate before breakfast. This used to be a regular occurrence before the riding accident in his younger days which had put him in a wheelchair for some months, and he still suffered with back pain all these years later. It meant that there were occasions when he felt unable to ride or even walk very far. But the last few days he'd felt better than he had for a long while. Added to his physical improvement, James had returned to the house a few minutes before and informed him that he'd asked Bella McFadyen to marry him. Felicity didn't know yet – she often stayed in bed till noon these days – but he could just picture the look on her face when she was told and he was relishing the moment. But it wasn't just because he knew it would annoy Felicity that he was pleased by James's choice of wife; he was genuinely fond of Bella.

He smiled to himself as he sat drinking a cup of coffee in his study, the sunshine streaming through the open window and bringing with it the sweet scent of the roses that clung to the wall of the house. Bella had been a proper little tomboy when she was small but she'd grown into a beautiful woman who knew her own mind, not like some of the simpering young ladies Felicity had had in her sights for James. And Belinda had been a different person since she'd had a child, that had become obvious pretty quickly. Bella seemed to have provided the focus in her parents' marriage and he was glad about that; he hadn't liked to think that Belinda was unhappy.

He stopped his thoughts from going down the path they were apt to do when he thought about Bella's mother. He couldn't in all truthfulness say he regretted their brief encounter but he knew he'd taken advantage of Belinda when she was tipsy and her guard was down, and it wasn't something he was proud of. But life had gone on. They'd never spoken of it again and she and Archibald had clearly come to an understanding in their marriage that suited them both. And now their two families would be connected through the marriage of their children.

When a knock came at the study door and the maid put her head round to say that Mrs McFadyen wanted a word with him in private, he stared at her in surprise for a moment. Belinda here? And apparently without Archibald. He was about to say he would see her in the drawing room and then changed his mind. Felicity might be down shortly and if Belinda had asked to see him in private his study was more suitable. 'Show Mrs McFadyen in here, please, Davidson,' he said shortly, sitting up straighter. He moved the papers he'd been looking at to one side and when the door opened again and Belinda came into the room he rose to his feet, saying, 'Belinda, m'dear. This is a nice surprise and on a day of such good news too.' He stopped abruptly. She was staring at him in such a way that he realized something was terribly wrong. Recovering himself, he said, 'Sit down, m'dear, please, and tell me what I can do for you.'

Her hands were gripped together at her waist and she didn't take the seat in front of his desk that he'd indicated but remained standing as she said, 'Bella and James can't be married.'

His eyes narrowed. 'I don't understand.'

He watched her take a deep breath and the words trembled as she said, 'They can't be married because they are half-brother and -sister.'

He began to say again, 'I don't—' and then it dawned on him what she was intimating.

'Bella was conceived on Armistice Day.'

'But it was months after that when you and Archibald announced a baby was on the way, Belinda.'

She said nothing to this, merely staring at him with desperate eyes, her face as pale as bleached linen. Afraid that she was going to faint away on the spot, Philip came to her side, and taking her arm gently pushed her down into the big leather armchair opposite his desk. Softly, he said, 'Are you sure of the date?'

She nodded.

'And there is no way at all that Bella could be Archibald's?'

'None.' She swallowed hard. 'After I realized I was pregnant I made sure that we – we slept together and then weeks later I told Archibald I was expecting a baby. As far as anyone else knows, Bella was born a few weeks early. And in every way that matters she *is* Archibald's daughter.'

He ran a hand tightly across his mouth before he said, 'In every way but one.' *Hell, what a mess.* 'Why didn't you tell me before?'

'I didn't think I would ever have to. What happened between us didn't mean anything, you said so yourself.'

Had he? He couldn't remember. He might have said something similar but surely he hadn't been so callous?

Her voice came small and broken when she whispered, 'What are we going to do? They – they can't marry.'

No, they couldn't marry. He slid off the side of the desk and walked over to the window, standing with his back to her. 'They'll have to be told the truth. I know my son. Nothing but that would prevent him marrying Bella.'

Belinda gave a little choked sob and he turned quickly. 'I'll take full responsibility and make it clear that no blame is attached to you. I took unfair advantage of you that night, we both know that. You were in essence an innocent and I seduced you.'

'I was a married woman, Philip,' she said painfully, 'and I could have stopped you at any time. You didn't force yourself on me.'

'No.' His tone was emphatic. 'You weren't used to

alcohol and the effect it can have and you were sad and lonely. I knew that. The fault is mine and mine alone.'

Bella, his daughter? That delightful, impish little girl who had grown into an enchantingly lovely woman was his? It was incredible, but he knew if Belinda said it was so then it was. And this was going to tear both their families apart and wreck two young people's lives. Nevertheless, he couldn't let the engagement continue, now that he knew. Why hadn't Belinda come to him before when she had seen the way things were going between James and Bella? He could have sent the boy to Europe on some pretext or other – further experience in the medical field, anything. And then reason kicked in. James wouldn't have gone; from the night he and Bella had been reacquainted last year, he had loved her. It was as simple as that. And none of this was Belinda's fault; when he'd said that he had meant it.

'We'll have to tell them now, today, before the engagement becomes public,' Belinda said weakly.

She watched him draw in a deep breath: his waistcoat expanded and then slowly sank back into place and, on a sigh, he said, 'The sooner the better, but first it's only right that you tell Archibald the truth and I put the matter before Felicity.'

She nodded, tears wetting her cheeks. 'Bella is his world, she always has been. I don't know what this will do to him.'

'Do you want me to come with you?'

'*No, no.*' It was vehement, the first time she had spoken

with any force. 'I need to tell him when we're alone, to make him understand . . .' Her voice trailed away. To make him understand what? she asked herself. That she'd betrayed him, that their beloved daughter wasn't his, that she was going to break Bella's heart? That she'd ruined all their lives?

'All right. Perhaps it's better we tell the children individually,' he said, trying to think straight through the turmoil in his mind. 'They'll no doubt want to meet afterwards but initially, with the shock and all, it might be kinder to let them absorb the facts when the other isn't present.'

Kinder? This was a death blow they were talking about. She didn't say this, however, merely nodding and standing to her feet. It flashed through her mind that this was the very place where the tragedy that was now being enacted had begun all those years ago. She had been young then, young and silly and – yes, and shallow. She hadn't appreciated what she'd had in Archibald or even considered that beneath his distant manner was an insecure and troubled man who had been terrified of repulsing his young wife.

Philip walked her to the door and out to the car, where Fairley was sitting impassively in the driver's seat. The chauffeur jumped out at their approach but Philip gestured him away, opening the back door himself and helping her inside. Whereupon he said very quietly, 'I'm more sorry than I can say, Belinda,' before he closed the door.

Sorry. She felt a surge of hysteria well up and fought

it down, knowing that if she gave in to it she would start screaming and screaming and where would that end? As the car gathered speed, she shut her eyes and leaned back in the seat. Philip's relationship with Felicity was nothing like the one she and Archibald shared. Since the night when he had talked to her about his first marriage and revealed so much, the feeling she'd had for him had deepened from day to day. He had become a tender and loving husband, his devotion and care encasing her and making it easy for her to love him back with an intensity that surprised her. When Bella had been born things had got even better, the three of them wrapped up in a peaceful happiness that she'd imagined would last for ever.

She stifled a moan, conscious of Fairley, opening her eyes and pretending to look out of the window on the short journey home. Archibald must have been looking out for her because he was standing on the front steps as the car pulled up, and came to meet her as Fairley stopped the engine and walked round the car to open the door. 'How's the headache?' he said gently.

She didn't speak until Fairley was back in the car and they were at the top of the steps and walking into the house, whereupon she said, 'I need to talk to you about Bella and James.'

'I know you're troubled about their relationship but James is a good man and—'

'Please, Archibald, I have something to tell you and it's – it's not pleasant.'

Wright was waiting in the hall and after glancing at

her white face, Archibald said to the butler, 'We'll have coffee on the terrace, Wright.'

'Very good, sir.'

Archibald took her arm and led her through the open French doors of the breakfast room and out onto the long stone terrace that ran the length of the back of the house. Once she was seated on one of the cushioned chairs at the wrought-iron table he sat down beside her, taking her hand in his. Her flesh was cold despite the warmth of the June morning; she felt chilled to the very core of her. 'What on earth is it, darling?' he asked softly, the worry he had felt when she had left the house deepening.

As she sat, her gaze fixed on their joined hands, Belinda told herself that she had to speak, she had to tell him, yet she couldn't begin. It was a full minute before she whispered, 'I did a terrible thing, an unforgivable thing.'

'What? Come, come.' There was an indulgent note in his voice now. 'Whatever it is, you can tell me. We have no secrets between us, my sweet, and nothing you've done is worth this.'

'It was on Armistice Day.'

'Armistice Day?' His voice was high with surprise. 'But that's over twenty years ago.'

'We were at the Wynfords', they had a ball—'

'Yes, I recall it now you've said,' he interrupted her, 'but surely nothing that happened then has caused you to be so distraught? And what's it to do with Bella and James?'

She swallowed deeply, moistened her lips, then said, 'I

drank too much and I was alone with Philip in his study. He – we –' She put her hands over her eyes, bowing her head.

There was silence for a moment and then Archibald said, 'He kissed you? Is that what this is all about?'

'It was more than that.'

The silence was longer this time. 'How much more?'

She removed her hands from her eyes and looked at him, and what he read in her face caused him to draw back in his seat. 'No.' He shook his head. 'No, it can't be. You wouldn't.'

There was a hard burning place in her chest that had spread into her eyes and prevented her from crying. 'No words can tell you how sorry I am—'

'Was it just the once?'

'What?'

'Did – did you go with him more than that one time?'

'No, no.' She shook her head. 'I hated myself for what I'd done and if I could have undone it, I would. I love you, I've always loved you and I don't know how it happened but I was tipsy and he—' She gulped. 'And then it was too late.'

'He took advantage of you,' Archibald said slowly, using the very words Philip had expressed earlier that morning. 'The man's always been a womanizer and a rake but I would have thought better of him than to use *you* in that way.' He suddenly banged his fist on the table, making her jump. 'I could kill him,' he said tightly, dark red colour searing his cheekbones. 'To think I've sat at his table eating his food when—' He stood up, pacing the length of the verandah and swearing under his breath.

Belinda watched him; she'd never seen him like this or imagined she could feel frightened of her mild-mannered husband but this was a man grievously wronged. She stood up, and as he approached her she whispered, 'I know you will never be able to forgive me and I wouldn't ask you to, but believe me when I say I've always loved only you.'

He closed his eyes for a moment and then looked at her. 'So this . . . mistake is the reason why you are against James marrying our daughter? You think the son might be like the father, is that it? Because I see little of Philip in James.'

She stared at him, the words that would destroy their marriage sticking in her throat. Her heart was pounding so hard it hurt but when the words came they were flat, lead-weighted. 'They can't marry because James and Bella are half-brother and -sister.'

Archibald's eyes narrowed in bewilderment.

'Bella was conceived on Armistice Day. Philip Wynford is her natural father.'

As she finished speaking she became aware of Bella standing in the doorway of the breakfast room holding a tray of coffee she'd clearly intercepted from one of the maids. For a split second they made up a frozen tableau. Then Archibald clutched at his chest, his face contorting as he fell, and Bella screamed, dropping the tray with a mighty crash.

The next minutes for ever remained a jumble in

Belinda's mind. The servants had come running and Wright reached his master first, kneeling at his side with Bella, who was making terrible moaning sounds like an animal in pain.

Mrs Banks and one of the housemaids took their mistress's arms as Belinda's knees gave way and held her up as another maid pushed a chair beneath her bottom, and then as Bella rose to her feet screaming and came at her mother, one of the gardeners who'd been working close by held her back as best he could.

Overall though, it was the still figure of Archibald which was imprinted on Belinda's brain. She knew he was dead even before she saw Wright shake his head as he glanced at her. She'd stopped her husband's heart from beating when she had told him that his beloved daughter wasn't his.

Dr Hogarth had come and gone. The body had been removed and the terrace returned to order. Quiet reigned in the shocked household. The doctor had insisted that Bella be sedated but Belinda had refused any medication. She sat in numbed silence in the drawing room staring into space, refusing the refreshments a concerned Mrs Banks tried to press on her. When Bella's screams had subsided as the sedative had taken hold, Dr Hogarth had told her that Bella would sleep until the next morning and wake more herself. She hadn't contradicted him, although she had known her daughter would never be the same again.

Not knowing what else to do, Wright had taken it upon himself to send a message to their nearest neighbours, the Wynfords, when evening came and Belinda still hadn't moved or spoken. Twilight was falling as he showed Philip and Felicity into the drawing room. Felicity had insisted on accompanying her husband even though he had told her what had occurred between himself and Belinda and that Bella was the result; she was determined to prevent a scandal at any cost, and this was made clear in her first words once Wright had left the room. Her voice as cold and clear as glass, she said, 'I trust the servants are unaware of what caused Archibald's collapse?' ignoring her husband's outraged, '*Felicity!*'

Belinda had risen to greet them and now she stared into the haughty face. 'I don't know,' she said vaguely. 'Perhaps.' What did it matter? What did anything matter?

'I won't have James's good name tainted or brought into disrepute,' Felicity said icily, 'and I suggest you make this plain to your daughter. James is fully aware of the situation and understands that any association between himself and Bella is over.'

For the first time since Archibald's cardiac arrest Belinda drew herself up straighter, and her voice was as autocratic as Felicity's when she said thinly, 'Have you said all that you came to say? Because I would like you to leave now.'

'Don't you dare take that tack with me, not after what you've done—'

'*Felicity.*' Again Philip's voice was like the crack of a

whip and this time Felicity heeded it, glaring at Belinda as she muttered something under her breath.

'I'm sorry, Belinda,' Philip said softly. 'We came here tonight to offer our condolences and see how you and Bella are and if there's anything we can do.' He waved his hand helplessly. 'I know this is one hell of a tangle but we're still friends and—'

'No, we are not friends.' She looked at them both, her voice stiff. 'We never were.'

'Well, really!' Felicity flounced round, saying, 'Come along, Philip. I came here in good faith but the woman has no breeding or class, that is evident enough.' She marched to the door, opening it and saying again, 'Come along.'

He ignored her. 'I mean it,' he said quietly. 'If I can help at all, talk to Bella and explain that it was my fault, I'll gladly do so.'

She shook her head. 'Just go.'

For a moment she thought he was going to say more but then he turned, following his wife out of the room and shutting the door behind them. She sank down onto the sofa but the numbness that had blanketed her before their arrival had dispersed and now grief and sorrow and guilt and shame swept over her in bitter waves. *God, God, help me.* She thought it as a prayer, joining her hands and swaying back and forth. *Help me through the next days because I can't go on.*

Chapter Nine

It was gone noon before Bella emerged from her drugged sleep the next day, and then only because the maid had come into the room and opened the curtains. As the bright sunlight streamed in Vickers came to the bedside, her voice soothing when she murmured, 'I've brought you a cup of tea, Miss Bella. Shall I adjust the pillows while you sit up?'

Why was Vickers talking as though she was an invalid? Bella thought, struggling to open her eyes. Her limbs were leaden and her eyelids heavy, but then something pierced the fog in her mind. *Her father*. Coming fully awake, she saw the maid staring at her with sympathy, her round face solemn.

Her father had died out there on the terrace. The terrible dreams – nightmares – were true. She heard a scream start somewhere in her head, the same screams that had spiralled out of control the day before, and from deep inside she found the strength to tell herself, *No, don't start that again, none of that.* Forcing herself to speak, she said shakily, 'What time is it?'

'Nearly half-past twelve, miss.' Vickers busied herself arranging the pillows behind her young mistress's back as Bella sat up. The poor lass, Vickers thought sadly. They all felt terribly sorry for Miss Bella – she'd been so close to her da after all and for him to go sudden like that. It must have been such a shock. Mr Wright had said that the master had been as right as rain a few minutes earlier when he'd ordered coffee for him and the mistress, and then to drop down dead with no warning. Mind, as Mrs Banks had pointed out, the master's heart had been dicky for a while and when your time was up, it was up. But for Miss Bella to be there and see it . . .

She must have been asleep for twenty-four hours, Bella thought hazily. She vaguely remembered Dr Hogarth's voice, he must have given her something. She took the cup of tea Vickers passed her, nodding her thanks, and then as the maid asked if she wanted anything to eat she shook her head. 'My father?' she asked quietly. 'Is – is he here?'

'No, miss. The master's been taken away. Dr Hogarth saw to all that. We're all very sorry, miss. He was such a lovely gentleman if you don't mind me saying so.'

'Yes, he was.' She felt strange, as though nothing was real. Was that the effect of whatever Dr Hogarth had given her?

'I'll come back in a little while when you've finished your tea, miss.'

The maid bustled out of the room and Bella stared about her. Everything looked the same but it wasn't. Her father was dead. She breathed deeply, fighting the panic, because she couldn't deny what her mind was telling her. He was dead because her mother had told him something that was unbelievable but, nevertheless, true. Her mother had slept with Philip Wynford. James's father was *her* father. Which meant she had lost James too.

She moaned softly, like an animal in distress, and the cup tilted, spilling tea on the bedcover.

She had to see James. Did he know? And then she answered herself immediately. Of course he would know by now. Had he tried to see her while she was asleep? Had he come to the house? Flinging the covers aside, she slid out of bed just as there was a knock at the door but instead of it being Vickers who entered after her 'Come in', it was her mother. They stared at each other and now the last remnants of the strong sedative she'd been given melted away as an emotion, terrifying in its intensity, emanated from the core of her. She had disliked people before, strongly at times, but she had never hated. Glaring at her, she said bitterly, 'I don't want anything to do with you.'

'I have to talk to you, to explain.'

'There is no possible explanation for what you did. He worshipped you, do you know that? How could you? How could you be so cruel? And with Philip Wynford, James's father.'

'I was young and had too much to drink at a ball—'

'*I don't care.*' Her voice had verged on a scream and she moderated it as she repeated, 'I don't care. There is nothing you can say that could excuse what you did so save your breath. You killed him, you know that, don't you? And for him to die like that knowing—' Her voice caught on a sob but she choked it back. 'And me and James. You let us fall in love, believing we could be together. I'll hate you for ever. You've ruined everything.'

'I know, I know. I'd give my life if I could change things.'

Tears were streaming down her mother's face but if anything they made Bella more angry. All her life her father had treated her mother like a fragile piece of Dresden china – she must never be upset, never troubled, never bothered by the harsher things of life – and all the time she'd been hiding this terrible secret, this wicked, horrible thing that she'd done. Her mother wasn't delicate and vulnerable, she was as hard as iron, and Bella wasn't about to be fooled by crocodile tears as her father had been.

'But you didn't give your life, did you,' she said grimly. 'You took his, and you have wrecked mine and James's and everyone's. I wish it had been you who had died yesterday—' She stopped abruptly; she hadn't meant to say it and even in her rage and grief the look on her mother's face smote her. But she wasn't about to take it back. She squared her shoulders under her thin nightgown, her face defiant.

For a few more moments they continued to stare at each other, and then her mother reached into the pocket of her day dress and brought out an envelope. 'The

Wynford chauffeur brought this earlier and I promised I'd give it to you once you were awake.'

Belinda turned, stumbling as she left the room, blinded by her tears.

Bella had read the letter and every word was burned into her mind. '*Dearest Bella*,' it had begun. She had teased James about his handwriting in the past, saying it was very much a doctor's scrawl and barely legible, but he had written carefully this time.

'*I am so very sorry to hear about the sudden death of your father. Archibald was a fine man and I liked him very much. He will be greatly missed. I thought it only fair to let you know that I am going to France tonight* –' she had glanced quickly at the top of the page and had seen it was dated the day before – '*and will be away a few weeks. In view of the circumstances I thought it best for both of us and I'm sure you will agree. No good could come from us torturing ourselves on what might have been and a meeting just now would be too painful. I will be, for ever, your James.*'

She was sitting in a chair by the window, her hand pressed tightly across her mouth, her eyes staring wide but without seeing the vista in front of her. Her whole being was yelling, *No, no, he wouldn't leave me without saying goodbye in person. James wouldn't do that, not after all the things he's said and what we mean to each other. We were going to be married.*

Vickers came in with a luncheon tray at one point,

pointing out that Cook had made her a light omelette and she should try to eat a little, and whether it was that simple act of kindness that released the tears that thrust up from the depths of her and flooded her face she didn't know, but once the maid had gone she cried for some time. She was overwhelmed with a pain so great she thought she'd die from it, because surely no one could survive such agony of mind? At some point she must have slipped from the chair to sit on the carpet, curled into a little ball, but when she eventually stood up she was no longer crying, nor was there present in her the frightening feeling that she was going mad. Instead, the anger she felt towards her mother had fanned out to include James too, his father, his mother, all of them. Humiliation made up part of the white-hot rage, mortification that he could leave her when she knew she couldn't have chosen to leave him, and shame was in there too. Stupid though she told herself it was, she felt debased and dirty, as though some of this was her fault and James was blaming her. And perhaps he was, deep inside?

Eventually she walked across to the tray and forced herself to eat every morsel. Then she got dressed. Her mind had cleared and it was telling her what to do as though it was separate from her being, presenting her with a plan. She didn't question it: on the contrary she welcomed the feeling of detachment.

She packed a suitcase with clothes and shoes, and then the small portmanteau she'd used when she went to Germany, which she filled with personal items along with her bank book and other documentation including her passport.

Leaving these in her room, she made her way downstairs. She met Vickers in the hall, who said, 'I was just on my way up for the tray, miss, and Cook wondered if you'd like a cup of coffee?'

'No, thank you, but there's a suitcase and portmanteau in my room that needs bringing down, and could you tell Fairley to bring the car round, please.'

'Yes, miss.' Vickers stared at the young mistress. As she said afterwards in the kitchen, Miss Bella didn't seem like the person they all knew.

Bella walked through to the drawing room. As she had expected, her mother was there; she was sitting in an armchair in one of the two large bay windows looking out into the garden. Maintaining an air of decorum in front of the servants, Bella thought bitterly. As if that mattered.

With no preamble, she said, 'I'm going to London to stay at the house for a while. I trust you have no objection?' Their London residence was a fairly small Kensington Mews house with a resident cook and maid.

Belinda stared at her daughter's white face. 'I have no objection but would you let me explain—'

'Don't.' Bella shook her head. 'Don't waste your breath. There's nothing you could say that would make this any better. Don't you realize that?'

There was silence between them for a moment, and then Belinda said, 'Are you going to see James before you leave?'

'No, I am not going to see James,' Bella ground out tightly. 'Apparently he's run off to France, no doubt at the behest of his dear mother, who I'm sure is secretly delighted that her son's on the marriage market again. He left last night so he obviously couldn't wait to get away.'

'Oh, Bella, I'm sorry—'

'Don't.' She made a movement with her hand as though throwing something off. Turning, she said over her shoulder, 'Goodbye, Mother.'

'Bella, don't leave like this.'

Ignoring the plea, she retraced her steps into the hall where Wright was standing with her summer coat and hat, his lined face troubled. As he helped her on with her things, he said quietly, 'I'm sorry, miss, to speak out of turn but the mistress needs you at a time like this. Perhaps you could delay your departure for a while?'

When she was a little girl she had always been slightly afraid of the butler; he was so stiff and correct, stern even, not like the other servants, although Mrs Banks had expressed silent disapproval on a number of occasions when she'd returned to the house muddy or with torn clothes after playing in the grounds. But Wright had been devoted to her father and there was real grief in his face as he looked at her. It tempered her reply. She put a hand on the old man's arm, her voice soft as she said, 'I'm sorry, I would if I could but there are things I can't explain that mean I have to go straight away. I know I can leave everything in your capable hands, Wright – between you,

you and Mrs Banks have always run the house, haven't you, and I know my father relied on you. But more than that, he thought a great deal of you.'

Wright's bottom lip quivered but he recovered almost immediately. 'Thank you, miss. You'll – you'll be back for the funeral?'

'I don't know.' It would cause tongues to wag if she was absent but she didn't care about that. And her father was gone – whether she attended his funeral or not would be of no concern to him where he was now, but she wanted him to be buried with the dignity and respect he deserved and she just didn't trust herself to hold her tongue if she saw her mother standing piously in church. No one would understand, of course. They'd think it deplorable, but other people's opinions had ceased to be of importance, except, perhaps, that of Wright.

Even more softly, she said, 'I can only tell you that I know my father would understand my reasons if I don't come and that I loved him more than I love anyone. Can we leave it at that?'

The rheumy old eyes moved over her strained face and his eyelids blinked. 'And he loved you, Miss Bella. He was a different man after you were born and that's a fact.'

She nodded but couldn't speak, fighting back the tears. Father, oh, Father. The look on his face as he'd died . . .

Wright cleared his throat, his voice gruff as he said, 'Your things are in the car, miss, and Fairley is waiting.'

Pulling herself together, she said quietly, 'I shall be at

the London address for a while so any correspondence that might come for me can be forwarded there. Would you see to that, please?' She needed time to be alone and think about what she was going to do. In the last months she had imagined her future was all mapped out. She was going to be a doctor's wife and work in the community at James's side. Now that dream was gone and she had to think again, but without the loving support of the man she would always think of as her father. Philip Wynford might have impregnated her mother but it didn't make him her father, she told herself fiercely. She wished she'd been able to tell Archibald that.

She and Wright walked to the front door and he opened it. She pressed the old man's arm in goodbye and then stepped outside, knowing that if she had her way it would be the last time she saw her family home. She walked swiftly to the car, where Fairley was standing impassively by the open back passenger door, and just as she reached it thunder growled overhead and a flash of lightning rent the sky. The hot spell had broken and the sky looked dark and stormy. It was fitting somehow.

'Where to, miss?' Fairley asked as he helped her into the back seat.

'The railway station.' She settled back in the leather surrounds, and as the engine started and they set off down the drive she didn't look back.

PART THREE

Bedbugs and Naked Airmen

1939

Chapter Ten

Bella was always to look back on the next few weeks as the worst of her life.

It was dark and windy and raining hard when she arrived in the capital. The few folk on the wet shiny pavements were scurrying along under umbrellas with their heads down and it could have been a March day rather than June.

She took a taxicab from the station and when it pulled up outside their London residence she found the cook and maid had been forewarned of her imminent arrival. Once she'd had a light supper she retired to her room, exhausted and heartsore, and there she remained for the next two weeks. She escaped her misery by sleeping much of the time; a strange lethargy had overtaken her and the fatigue affected both her body and her mind. Later, when she thought about it, she realized it had probably saved her sanity, but at the time she simply slept between crying bouts that consumed her.

It couldn't last, of course. One morning she awoke

knowing she had to face the outside world and come back into the land of the living. She had cried an ocean but no more, she told herself painfully. She'd lost everything and everyone she had ever known in one fell swoop and she wished she could have died with her father, but she hadn't. She was here and he would expect her to carry on. The hate that burned inside her for her mother and the colonel hadn't lessened, but her feelings regarding James changed from moment to moment. One minute she felt she hated him as much as his father for leaving her the way he had without seeing her one last time; then she found herself making excuses for the way he'd behaved – he'd thought it less painful for both of them; he had been considering her as well as himself; he still loved her – but she'd always rein in her thoughts at that point. Their love was tainted in the worst possible way. It was unclean, incestuous, and she couldn't rid herself of the feeling that James blamed her in some way. Or perhaps it was her own shame that was causing her to think that way? Shame that she knew had no basis in logic but which, nevertheless, was very real.

Throughout July and August events on the world stage began to crystallize her thoughts regarding the future. She sat in the small courtyard garden of the Kensington property in the bright sunshine, with the heady perfume of the climbing roses covering the stone walls sweetening the London air as she pored over the newspapers. The dire happenings took her mind off her own situation.

The persecution of the Jews in Germany was growing

more extreme as the weeks progressed, and in Vienna the Archbishop, Cardinal Innitzer, was beaten up by Nazi thugs, causing widespread shock and condemnation. Hitler closed the border with Poland in Upper Silesia amid mounting tension, and Britain and France reaffirmed their pledge to assist Poland in the event of invasion by Germany and Russia. These two nations, in a complete turnabout after years of mutual vilification, had made a pact to join forces.

At home, the army and RAF reserves were called up as Europe's mobilization for war intensified, and it was announced that everyone would have an identity card and number in the event of war. All movable treasures were taken to safety from the major museums and galleries and even from Westminster Abbey.

If Bella hadn't been so heartsore and utterly miserable she would have been frightened, but as it was she just wished she could have discussed the news reports and wireless announcements with her father. Her mother had written to her shortly after she had arrived in Kensington, pleading for her forgiveness and explaining how the episode with Philip Wynford had come about. It hadn't helped.

She had read the letter and then destroyed it, sickened to the depths of her. A few days later the colonel had written. He had insisted that he was entirely to blame for what had happened and that he took full responsibility. She had burned his letter too and she hadn't replied to either of them: if anything they'd made her hate her mother and the colonel more. There had been nothing from James, and although at the bottom of her she hadn't expected him to write again, it still hurt.

As the Polish crisis deepened at the end of August, children began to be evacuated from Britain's towns and cities and London became strangely quiet. Seventy-two underground stations were partly closed to the public to speed up the long-planned operation, and when Bella took her morning walk the streets seemed almost dead.

Everyone expected that the country would be at war within days. It had become horribly inevitable, but if nothing else it had made her come to a decision about her future. The King had approved the formation of the Women's Auxiliary Air Force at the beginning of July and she intended to join up.

Hitler was determined to promote a world war and nations would be forced to take sides; it had become apparent that Germany had been planning for this for years under his leadership. He was a madman, but a clever, devious one. Her Aunt Prudence had written to her at the London address to let her know that she and Geoffrey were back in England, and Bella was deeply relieved that they were safely home. She wondered what her mother had revealed about everything; her aunt hadn't mentioned anything beyond the fact that they were grieved at Archibald's demise and hoped London was proving something of a diversion.

Bella doubted her mother would have confided in Prudence; she would want everything brushed under the carpet, she told herself bitterly.

August had proved a baking hot month; the summer had been the hottest one Bella could remember for years. Thunder was in the air day after day, giving everyone headaches, and even in the little shaded courtyard the air was stifling. Everyone prayed for rain to cool things down as the roads sizzled and flies buzzed. Her twentieth birthday had come and gone and she'd spent the day alone, throwing away any cards without opening them and giving the cashmere jacket her mother had sent to her to the cook, Mrs Graham, saying the colour didn't suit her. Mrs Graham had been over the moon. She had amused Bella by ordering an entire case of Bromo lavatory paper and a large supply of sugar and tea, 'In case that little Charlie Chaplin –' as she referred to Hitler – 'does his worst.' So now the broom cupboard was jam packed with lavatory paper and the wardrobe in one of the spare bedrooms with foodstuffs. Clearly, as long as Mrs Graham could wipe her bottom and drink tea, she'd be happy. She'd told Bella to buy up hairpins for herself, along with Kirby grips and elastic for knickers and extra soap, 'Because no one wants to smell, do they, miss.'

Bella had said that no, they didn't, but preparing for rationing seemed singularly unimportant the way she was feeling, although she wouldn't have offended the cook by saying so. The number of tins of corned beef and salmon Mrs Graham had salted away would have fed a small army, but if it kept the cook happy so be it. She, herself, would hopefully be in the WAAFs anyway.

Throughout the year the women's auxiliary services

had started to muster, though as yet there was no formal recruiting drive. Nevertheless, the publicity made the services like the Women's Royal Naval Service, the Women's Land Army, the Auxiliary Territorial Service and her own favourite, the WAAFs, sound benign and appealing, like a glorified Girl Guide camp:

> *Some are learning to be cooks, others are doing orderly and clerical work . . . The Woman's Army is a very human institution – the use of powder is allowed, and even a touch of natural lipstick . . . Not an easy life, perhaps, but a healthy, friendly one. And a grand Army . . .*

Bella was sceptical. Reading between the lines, there was little to distinguish these female soldiers from militarized maidservants or secretaries, but in a less than comfortable environment, added to which the public as a whole was by no means ready for female soldiers. It was barely ten years since women under thirty had had the vote, and there were plenty of people who made their feelings clear about the possibility of belted and booted women square-bashing it like the men. Far from discouraging her, however, any opposition made her more determined. The anger inside her needed an outlet and she wanted to take the world, especially the world of men, by the throat.

She had watched a trial run for an air raid when the traffic had been stopped for the duration of fifteen minutes and air-raid wardens had told people what to do. Perhaps because of their ridiculous appearance, dressed in regulation overalls so ill-fitting that the trouser seats were between their knees, she couldn't take it seriously. When the siren had wailed and the exercise had got under way, everyone around her had been grumbling that it was silly play-acting and it was unthinkable that there would be air raids on England. It had been a beautiful summer's day; down by the Embankment the river had glittered in the sunshine and in the nearby Physic Garden the trees had been full of chirping birds. Suddenly vivid pictures had stormed her mind – guns firing, buildings exploding, droning bomber planes overhead dropping their deadly merchandise with no thought for the civilians below. Mayhem, destruction on an unbelievable scale.

She'd walked back to the house later that afternoon feeling sick; not that the idea of death frightened her, just the manner of dying. She didn't want to lie trapped and suffering beneath rubble or bleeding in the streets, but it could happen, and the people around her who had refused to accept such a possibility were living in cloud cuckoo land. Or perhaps it was that they were happy and had more to live for, people they loved and who loved them? she asked herself.

On the first day of September Bella awoke early, before it was light. She tiptoed down to the kitchen and made herself a cup of coffee, taking it out into the courtyard, where she sat and watched the sky lighten. The mass exodus of children from London that week meant the world beyond the walls of the courtyard was quieter than normal and that in itself felt odd.

Some time later she heard Mrs Graham come down and begin talking to Shirley, the maid. Bella had told Shirley that she would call her by her Christian name the day after she'd arrived in London – she was done with convention. When Mrs Graham came into the courtyard half an hour later she thought it was to ask what she'd like for breakfast. Instead, the woman said, her voice trembling, 'They've just said on the radio that German troops have invaded Poland, miss.'

Bella stared at her. The die was cast. Britain and France would have to declare war on Germany now. Suddenly she was aware of everything around her with the clarity of a photograph: the sun glinting on a pane of glass in the kitchen window behind Mrs Graham; a honey bee busy collecting pollen from one of the full-blown climbing roses and the shrill melody of a blackbird singing its little heart out in the sunshine. Suddenly the longing for James swept over her with such ferocity that she actually winced.

The next day was a Saturday. The BBC Home Service incessantly interrupted its schedule of gramophone records with gloomy announcements. It was a day of deep foreboding and that night storms hit Britain, rain coming down in sheets and thunder crashing overhead. Bella couldn't sleep. She sat by her bedroom window watching the lightning flashes and thinking that Mother Nature was providing the finishing touch to what had been weeks and months of waiting. Her mother had phoned twice but she'd refused to talk to her, telling Shirley to say that she was busy. She didn't know what the young girl and Mrs Graham thought but she didn't care.

Sunday morning dawned crystal clear with bright sunshine, a perfect September day with the world washed clean. Shortly before eleven-fifteen, Bella joined Mrs Graham and Shirley in the drawing room as she'd arranged the night before so they could all listen together to the expected broadcast from Downing Street. Mrs Graham was grim and white-faced and Shirley had clearly been crying, but Bella was more impatient than anything else. She could almost hear her father saying, 'Enough of the shilly-shallying, let's get on with it now.' She had felt him near that morning, the first time she'd sensed his presence since he had died. It was as welcome as it was unexpected and whether she was imagining it or not didn't matter, she told herself.

Even in London, Sunday was a day when all the bustle of the week came to a stop. Shops closed, factories were silent and workplaces empty. There was church, a nice roast lunch if you could afford it and an afternoon dozing in the parlour or taking the children for a walk in the park. Today, though, the atmosphere was different; the country was holding its breath.

The delicious smell of roast beef faintly flavoured the air as the Prime Minister began to speak the fateful words they'd all been waiting for:

'This morning the British Ambassador in Berlin handed the German Government a final note stating that, unless we heard from them by eleven o'clock that they were prepared at once to withdraw their troops from Poland, a state of war would exist between us. I have to tell you now that no such undertaking has been received, and that consequently this country is at war with Germany.'

Shirley immediately burst into tears, earning a sharp rebuke from Mrs Graham, who ushered her out of the room saying that she needed to start peeling vegetables and enough of her shenanigans. Left alone, Bella turned off the wireless and followed them, walking through the kitchen and out into the small courtyard. Nothing had changed and yet everything had changed. The September sun still shone down, warming the good and the bad, bees continued to bumble amongst the roses and fragile, beautifully coloured butterflies fluttered on the buddleias. There were no brass bands playing, no stirring call to arms, just a hushed quiet. But they were at war.

And then suddenly the Sabbath silence was broken by the eerie wailing of sirens, causing Mrs Graham and Shirley to come hurrying outdoors rather than down to the cellar, which they'd kitted out as an air-raid shelter. The three of them stood looking up into the clear blue sky, Shirley clutching hold of Mrs Graham and still with the vegetable knife in her hand, but it was empty of aircraft as far as they could tell. They could hear people in other gardens shouting to each other above the din, but within minutes the all-clear was sounding.

'Must have been a false alarm,' said a shaken Mrs Graham. 'I'll make a pot of tea, miss.'

Bella smiled as the cook and maid disappeared back inside the kitchen. War might have been declared and they'd just had a taste of what could happen for real in the next weeks and months, but a cup of tea always put things to rights. What chance did Hitler and his Nazis have against the likes of Mrs Graham?

Chapter Eleven

Bella stood in line clutching her bottled specimen which she had been told to give in at the medical centre while she listened to a sergeant shouting instructions at the top of her voice. She had reported to the Royal Air Force training centre just outside London that morning, along with a coachload of other girls, and had been trying to find the medical centre when they were ordered on parade. No one seemed to know what was happening, not even the corporals or sergeants who were striding about looking officious.

'I think we've caught the RAF on the hop,' the girl next to Bella whispered. 'I heard they didn't expect any WAAFs yet and no one's prepared for us. RAF stations have little enough accommodation for their men, let alone women. My brother's a pilot and he said everyone's in a state of panic. There's no proper uniforms in some camps and goodness knows where we'll be sleeping tonight. The powers that be have messed up, that's what he said.'

Bella stared at her in alarm.

'Some of the stations are opening up old married

quarters and others are putting girls with local landladies or in hostels. Jim, my brother, said they'll be getting in Nissen huts as soon as they can but it's a real flap. I'm Lucy, by the way. Lucy Pickford.'

'Bella McFadyen,' Bella whispered back, just as the sergeant told them to follow her to the air-raid shelters. Thirty or so girls trotted after the straight-backed sergeant and she brought them all to a halt before she said, 'You can't use these at the moment because they're full of water. If you need to take shelter – which I doubt you will – take cover under the sandbagged petrol pumps.'

'Did she just say petrol pumps?' Lucy squeaked nervously. 'I thought it was the Germans who's trying to kill us, not the RAF.'

Bella grinned. She thought she was going to like Lucy Pickford.

Once they had been dispatched to the gas centre for masks, they were told to give their bottles in at the medical centre and return there the next day for a full medical inspection. Having already endured one by a doctor attached to the recruiting station, Bella wasn't looking forward to a second. From the medical centre they were taken to the clothes store and here pandemonium reigned, mainly because the odd bits of uniform that were available were ancient, including the underwear. Corsets with bone, vests tied with tape, huge winter knickers – Bella had never seen such monstrosities.

'You know what the powers that be are doing, don't you?' said the irrepressible Lucy. 'We're on a station where we're outnumbered by men six to one at least and they're hoping these passion killers will prevent any hanky-panky. It's no coincidence that these old uniforms are all several sizes too big as well – we'll look like we're wearing sacks.'

'Actually, I could make something of a sack, but this . . .' Bella eyed the jacket and skirt she'd been given with distaste. It was old and smelled of mothballs.

She was absolutely starving too; she'd only had a couple of slices of toast before she had left the house in Kensington that morning and it was now four o'clock in the afternoon. It was strange to feel hungry again. Over the last weeks her appetite had gone completely but now she could eat a horse, she thought wearily, as someone else pushed a faded rain cape on her.

'You'll all get new uniforms in a few weeks,' the sergeant bawled across the din, 'but make sure you look after what you've been given today. You're lucky, some stations have nothing and you'd have to wear your own clothes for a while.'

'She thinks this is lucky?' Lucy rolled her eyes. 'What have we let ourselves in for?'

What indeed? Bella thought longingly of hats adorned with flowers and feathers, high-heeled shoes, silk stockings and kid gloves – items she'd taken for granted in the past.

By the time they were marched in a line to the cook-house armed with their irons – knife, fork and spoon – which, they were informed, must not be lost or bent or otherwise damaged, Bella wasn't the only one feeling dazed and confused. She was sure everything she'd been told had gone in one ear and out the other, and she still had no idea where she would be sleeping that night. All their suitcases and bags were still piled up in the reception area and girls were tripping over themselves in their disorientated state. One poor girl who looked a couple of years younger than the official entry age of eighteen actually walked into a door and nearly knocked herself out, earning a furious reprimand from a passing corporal. The whole place was buzzing with sergeants and corporals and they all seemed to have eyes in the backs of their heads, showing no mercy to the new recruits.

When they filed into the cookhouse the smell of food was overpowering, making Bella's mouth water. Once the queue reached the long tables where the food was being dished out by several cooks dressed in white with mob caps, Lucy, who was in front of her, turned to say, 'Well, I can see it but I have no idea what it is.'

They were given one plate each and on this some kind of stew made of unidentifiable meat swam to join jam roly-poly pudding with no central divide. Having found two seats at a table with some other raw recruits who had been in their group earlier, everyone exchanged smiles but then tucked into the food as quickly as possible to avoid the dishes meeting in the middle of the plate. It was a vain attempt but Bella found that jam roly-poly soggy with gravy was quite edible if you were hungry enough. What the lumps of meat were in the stew she had no idea even after she'd eaten them.

Once she'd cleared her plate, she became aware of a

large plump girl with frizzy fair hair eyeing her. 'Didn't think your sort'd eat that,' the girl said in a ripe cockney accent.

'My sort?'

'Top-drawer.' In spite of her words the girl's manner was friendly. 'I knew there'd be a lot of posh birds in the WAAFs,' she continued, 'but I still fancied it more than the army or the navy. There's somethin' about pilots, isn't there, and I love their uniform. It makes the ugliest bloke worth looking at. Mind, any officer'd do for me, I ain't fussy.' She laughed uproariously and Bella found herself smiling. There was something likeable about the girl even though Bella wasn't sure if she was being got at.

'So, do you classy birds think you'll stand it then? Bet it's different to what you've been used to.'

Knowing she needed to start as she meant to carry on, Bella said pleasantly but coolly, 'Oh, don't underestimate classy birds – we're as tough as old boots when the chips are down.'

'Is that so? Well, the proof of the pudding is in the eating, that's what I always say, so I'll reserve me judgement.'

'That's very generous of you.'

'I'm Kitty by the way, and this is Maud and Delia. We used to work in a fish canning factory and joined up together. If nothing else we won't stink all the time now – it didn't half used to put some blokes off.' She roared with laughter again and the two girls she'd indicated, who were clearly twins and small and mouse-like, smiled nervously. They hadn't said a word.

'I'm Bella and this is Lucy.'

It was the cue for the other girls to introduce themselves and as they finished the tea in the tin mugs they'd been given – which tasted as though it had been stewed for days – they learned a bit more about each other. Lucy, it appeared, could dance and ride a horse to hounds and had lived what was mainly an ornamental life thus far, although she could drive a car. Anne, a ginger-headed, lanky girl, had worked as a library assistant, and had joined up with her cousin, Sybil, who had worked as a housemaid in a big hotel in Slough. The eighth girl on the table was Arlette from the East End, who had a French mother and an English father and who, she said, had worked as a model before the war.

'What sort of a model?' Kitty asked in her forthright manner.

Arlette shrugged her slim shoulders and smiled with a languid wave of her hand.

'Oh, right, that sort,' Kitty said with a knowing nod.

Bella and Lucy looked at each other, shocked in spite of themselves. Kitty caught the look and grinned, clearly delighted, but whatever comment she might have made was lost when their sergeant appeared at the table barking orders.

They all jumped up and she led them back to the reception area where their things were, telling them to collect everything and meet her outside. Once they were assembled they saw a lorry with an RAF driver leaning against it, smoking a cigarette as he surveyed them through narrowed eyes.

'Those girls with surnames that begin from A to L step forward, please.' A number of the recruits followed the sergeant's command. 'You'll be staying here on camp, some of you in married quarters that have been opened up and some in the huts behind the women's washroom.' Bella had visited this and it hadn't been a pleasant experience. It had clearly been hastily adapted with one side holding wooden cubicles containing lavatories, and the other a row of baths and basins with no dividers. Under each bath ran a water gulley and the washroom was nothing more than a corrugated-iron shack with a gap between the walls and roof. It might not be too bad in the summer but in the winter it would be freezing, and it certainly wasn't for the shy and retiring.

'Now, you others will be billeted with local landladies for the time being,' the sergeant said briskly. 'Your driver has the name and address of each lodging house and will arrange a common rendezvous where he will pick you up at six o'clock sharp in the morning. You will not be late.' She glared at them to emphasize her words. 'And you will not fraternize with the locals. Is that clear?'

A few mumbled affirmations sounded.

'*Is that clear?*'

This time the 'Yes, Sergeant' was louder.

'I'm sure I do not need to remind you that you carry the pride of the Royal Air Force name with you wherever you go.' Eyes as sharp as those of any bird of prey swept their faces. Bella found herself feeling guilty even though she hadn't done anything.

The next few minutes were chaotic. Bella noticed that the twins were among those who were staying put and were clearly upset that Kitty wouldn't be with them, although Anne, Sybil and Arlette were also remaining in the camp. She, Lucy and Kitty climbed into the back of the lorry, which had long benches down each side, and once all the girls were aboard their driver slung their suitcases and bags into the middle of the space. To say it was a squeeze on the wooden seats was an understatement: they were packed in as tightly as sardines in a can. Once the lorry revved up and got going a cacophony of screams ensued as girls clutched hold of each other and others were catapulted amongst the luggage. In any pauses in the lorry's journey they could hear the driver whistling to himself in the cab at the front, and Bella wondered how often he'd enjoyed himself in this way. She got the distinct feeling that he was loving every minute.

Once they arrived in the town the lorry stopped and the driver opened the back flaps. 'Four for Mrs McGinty's.'

The girls all looked at each other, thoroughly traumatized.

'Are there four of you who want to stay together?'

Four girls scrambled out, dragging their suitcases from among the pile, and the driver pointed to a particular house in a street of terraced properties. 'That one.'

He then turned his attention to the rest of them. 'There's room for another three in this street at Mrs Darling's,' he said flatly, before calling after the first four, 'Hey, you lot, I haven't told you where I'm picking you up in the morning yet.'

As the girls retraced their steps, Kitty said, 'Come on,' nudging Bella and Lucy as she grabbed her suitcase. 'I like the sound of Mrs Darling.'

Once they'd joined the other four, the driver said, 'I'll see you all at six o'clock near that drinking fountain, all right?' pointing to somewhere in the darkness.

It was a moonlit night, but with the residents of the town paying heed to the blackout warnings hardly a chink of light showed anywhere and they could barely see a thing, let alone some fountain or other. Nevertheless, Kitty said, 'Yeah, all right. So which one is Mrs Darling's?'

'Next to McGinty's. I'm dropping some more of you at the top of the street on the corner, and the rest'll be housed in the next street but you'll all meet at the fountain. If anyone's not there when I come they'll have to make their own way to camp but I tell you now I wouldn't want to be in their shoes if that happens.'

'Well, aren't you a little ray of sunshine,' Kitty said sarcastically.

'I'm just saying, that's all.' He turned and climbed back into the cab, revving the engine once more. As the lorry trundled off along the long terraced street of identical houses, the seven girls looked at each other.

'Come on then, let's see what the RAF have reserved for us,' Bella said, lugging her suitcase across the dark street as the rest followed suit. The two houses the driver had indicated each had a basement with steps leading down to it behind a row of railings and the front doors had big brass knockers. Mrs Darling's was in the shape of a particularly hideous grinning gnome and Kitty lifted it and rapped hard enough to wake the dead, making Bella and Lucy wince.

The door opened in the next moment and a large woman stood in the aperture, clearly enraged as she bawled, 'What do you think you're playing at, banging like that? Think we're deaf in these parts or summat?'

Completely undeterred, Kitty squared up to her. 'You shouldn't have such a big knocker if you don't want people to use it.'

'I'll give you big knocker, m'girl.'

Feeling that things were getting out of hand, Bella said quickly, 'I'm sorry, we didn't realize how loud it would be. We've been sent by the RAF camp. Mrs Darling, is it?' She could feel Lucy shaking with laughter that she was trying to conceal and she felt like laughing herself but kept her face straight with some effort. 'It's very good of you to put us up.'

Slightly mollified, Mrs Darling said shortly, 'You'd better come in,' standing to one side so they could pass her and glaring at Kitty, who glared back.

The hall was narrow but Mrs Darling squeezed past them after she'd shut the front door. 'Leave your things there a minute,' she said, pointing to the foot of the steep stairs, 'and come into the lounge.' She opened the first door on the left and led them into a small parlour that was cold and smelled fusty. It contained a three-piece suite in a horrible shade of sickly green, a huge aspidistra and little else. 'I don't normally allow my guests to come in here, it's my private space.'

'Oh, right.' Bella nodded, somewhat bemused.

'I just want to go through the house rules. You'll be leaving every morning just before six o'clock, I understand, and I don't expect to hear anything of you – there's my other guests to consider. They said you'd be getting your meals at the camp so don't expect anything here. I don't allow gentlemen callers, I don't do no washing and I lock the front door at eleven sharp every night. If you're going to be later than that you'll have to stay at the camp.'

'We couldn't have a key for those occasions?' Bella asked politely, earning herself another glare.

'No, you're right, you couldn't.' Mrs Darling hitched up her ample bosom with her forearms in indignation. 'You keep the curtains in your room closed day and night – I haven't got time to go in and close them once it's dark and I'm not having the warden banging on my door shouting the odds. And you don't fraternize with the other guests – I'm not having any hanky-panky in this house.'

From this they assumed, rightly, that there were men staying under Mrs Darling's roof too.

'I change the sheets once a month and your day for a bath will be on a Friday. There'll be enough hot water for one bath so you'll have to take turns and use each other's water. I don't have no bad language, no drinking –' here she singled out Kitty for another glare, who stared back innocently – 'and no food brought on the premises. Now, I'll take you up to your room and be quiet, please. One of my gentlemen is of a nervous disposition and doesn't like any noise.'

A kind of hysterical squeak came from Lucy that she turned into a cough. Kitty grinned at them both, clearly unconcerned what Mrs Darling thought.

They heaved their things up one flight of stairs and then another to the second floor. Mrs Darling pointed out that the bathroom was on the first floor and if they needed to use it at night, again silence must be observed. Once on the landing they passed one door and then the landlady opened the second, standing aside for them to enter before shutting it again without another word.

'Darling by name and darling by nature,' Kitty said, deadpan.

Chapter Twelve

Later that night, as Bella lay in the three-quarter-size bed next to a sleeping Lucy listening to Kitty's snores emanating from the single bed under the window, she reflected that the day could have been worse. She had made two friends for a start, and she hadn't had time to think about James at all till now. The grief about her father was always with her but she was learning to live with it bit by bit. She had no other option. Certainly everything was different to what she'd been used to, not least her present accommodation.

The room was devoid of any creature comforts. It held one three-quarter-size bed which they'd agreed was more suitable for herself and Lucy, as their build was smaller than Kitty's, and the single. The mattresses on both were lumpy and uncomfortable, and the thin brown blankets were just about adequate for now but in winter they'd freeze. Not that they'd be here in the worst of the weather, she told herself. Once they'd completed their training they could be stationed anywhere.

The floorboards were bare without even the luxury of the thinnest rug and they creaked loudly with every footstep. Besides the two beds, there was a rickety old wardrobe crammed into the small space and a speckled mirror on one wall. That was it. And mouse droppings. Lots of mouse droppings.

Kitty had pointed these out quite matter-of-factly, laughing at Bella and Lucy's grimace of disgust. 'Just thank the Almighty it's only mice, my fine ladies,' she'd said, giggling. 'It's the rats you have to be wary of.'

Kitty had apparently been born in London's East End, the sixth of twelve children. They'd lived near the docks and the family had shared their two-up, two-down rented house with numerous rodents of all sizes and plenty of lodgers of the insect variety before her father had been killed in an accident unloading crates from a cargo boat. All the family except the four youngest children had been farmed out to various relatives and her mother had taken the little ones and gone to live with one of her sisters in Kent eight years ago, the last Kitty had heard of her.

Bella and Lucy had stared at her with wide eyes as Kitty had related her background; it was like something out of a Dickens novel. 'Who took you in?' Bella had asked as they'd sat on their beds with blankets draped round their shoulders to combat the damp chill in the room.

'Me dad's cousin's son and his wife but he was a nasty bit of work, the son. He'd belt you as soon as look at you but it was when he tried to interfere with me that I pegged it. I was only thirteen, the dirty beggar.'

'Oh, Kitty.'

'It's all right.' Kitty smiled at the note in Bella's voice. 'He did me a good turn really because when I scarpered Maud and Delia's mum took me in – we'd been at school together and when some of the kids used to pick on 'em cause they were timid and a bit slow I'd stick up for 'em and their mum liked me. I knocked on their door and asked if I could stay till I found somewhere and that was it. The son come round theirs throwing his weight about and saying I'd got to go back with him and the twins' dad and brothers set on him. He didn't come back after that.'

'Gosh.' Lucy had leaned back against the wooden bedhead, causing the bed to creak and groan. 'The most I've gone through is when my pet pony had to be put down. What about you, Bella?'

'My father died a few weeks ago.' She told them a little of what had occurred but was careful not to mention James. 'My mother and I don't get on so I doubt I'll go home again.'

'Really? That's a shame.' Lucy had touched her arm in a gesture of sympathy and Bella had changed the subject, but in the next few minutes before they settled down for sleep, she had been aware that Kitty was looking at her searchingly. She had the feeling that the loud, outgoing Londoner was more perceptive than she let on. Lucy, on the other hand, didn't seem to have an intuitive bone in her body and would happily breeze through life accepting everyone and everything at face value.

But she liked them both, she thought in the moments before she fell into an exhausted sleep, and perhaps because they were all so different she felt they'd get on well. She was glad she had joined up – it had been the right thing to do – and although she wouldn't have wished for the country to be at war, if it had to happen it had probably come at the right time for her, all things considered.

The next days passed in a blur of lectures in the classroom, running here, there and everywhere half the time in a state of utter confusion, and marching. Marching, marching, marching.

Kitty swore that the constant drilling by their flight sergeant, often with blistering results, was because the RAF had no idea what to do with their intake of female recruits. Most of them were as green as grass and the parades in a large hangar where they marched round and round out of step, swinging their arms haphazardly, made the poor man apoplectic – the more so when his swearing and cursing made some girls cry. If nothing else, the girls' vocabulary increased by the day.

Bella and Lucy and even the twins got the hang of what they were required to do fairly quickly, and Anne and Sybil weren't far behind. Arlette had tended to sashay rather than march at first, causing the instructor's face to go bright red as he had screamed at her, but it was Kitty who really drove the poor sergeant to his wits' end on more than one occasion. Try as she might, she simply couldn't coordinate her arms and legs into anything resembling a march. The more he shouted, the more confused she got.

After one particularly stressful drill for all concerned he strode up to her, quivering with rage so that the veins on his forehead looked as though they were going to burst, and growled, 'I'll say it just one more time. Step off with your left foot and swing your right arm forward. Dammit, woman, a monkey could do it. And swing your arm higher when you salute.'

Visibly affronted, Kitty glared back at him. 'It's all very well for you, sergeant, and probably the monkey, but these get in the way.' She tapped her enormous breasts, which were straining against the ill-fitting jacket she'd been given. 'And I can't see my feet, which doesn't help.'

For once he was speechless.

Nothing proved as traumatic as the first thorough medical inspection, however. Modesty went out of the window as airwomen in various states of undress waited to see doctors and nursing orderlies – herded together like cows for milking, as one disgruntled WAAF wailed. Knowing that this was something that they'd have to go through not once but many times didn't help, and the checks for such things as pregnancies, venereal diseases and head lice were rigorous.

Bella sat, practically naked, between Lucy and Kitty on a hard wooden bench, trying hard not to stare at anyone in particular. Then Arlette's name was called. Their friend strolled by totally unconcerned in her birthday suit, flicking back her long dark hair as she smiled at them, as casually as though this was an everyday occurrence. Which, as Kitty pointed out in an aside in the next moment, probably hadn't been too far from the truth in Arlette's previous life before she'd joined up.

Bella giggled. 'I suppose once you've sat bottom to bottom in the altogether it levels everyone out if nothing else.'

Kitty nodded solemnly. 'I shall never be in awe of you posh birds ever again.'

'Not that you ever were.'

'That's true.'

It was the day after the medical inspection and three days after they'd been lodging with Mrs Darling that Kitty started itching. The following morning she woke up covered in spots and told Bella and Lucy she was sure they were bedbug bites. Knowing their landlady wouldn't accept it unless it was proven, they set the alarm for two o'clock the next night and managed to catch a couple of the disgusting little creatures in a matchbox which Kitty showed a disgruntled Mrs Darling before taking them to the sergeant at the camp and explaining the issue.

The result of that conversation was special Dettol baths for all of them, although Bella and Lucy insisted they were fine, and the same day the three girls were told that they were leaving Mrs Darling's and moving onto the station forthwith, much to their delight. Camp beds were squeezed into the central walkway of the hut that the twins and the others were in, and although it meant walking over beds to get from one end of the hut to the other, no one complained.

To cheer the three up after their toxic delousing baths, Arlette got hold of a couple of bottles of gin. She'd bestowed her favours on one of the airmen who apparently frequently visited the village pub. Once it was lights-out and they knew the corporal wouldn't bother them everyone got tiddly by the glow of the hut's pot-bellied stove; exchanging stories, laughing hysterically and declaring they were all friends for life.

At three in the morning, Bella became aware of Kitty shaking her by the arm. 'I need the lavatory and it's pitch black out there, come with me,' she pleaded, hiccuping violently and nearly falling over as she attempted to put her shoes on.

Giggling helplessly, the two of them stumbled out into the darkness, completely disorientated. The September night was warm but clouds obscured the moon and stars, and after they had tottered about for some minutes it was with great relief that they saw the bulk of the wash-room loom up in front of them. Kitty completely missed her footing as they stepped over the threshold, going headlong and then sitting on the floor laughing, which stopped abruptly as an airman, as naked as the day he was born, suddenly stood up in a bath in which he'd been sleeping.

It transpired that they were in the men's washroom and the airman was even more drunk than they were.

Having left his bed some time before on a similar mission to Kitty's, he'd decided that the walk back to his hut a few yards away was too much and had settled down to take a nap in one of the bathtubs. In spite of being in the altogether, he insisted on helping them find the way back to their hut, having draped a towel round his nether regions, which Bella thought was very chivalrous of him in the circumstances.

It was only once they were safely back in their beds that Kitty whispered, 'Bella? I still need to go.'

'I tell you now that we're not leaving this hut till morning when we can see outside,' Bella said in a fierce whisper. 'You'll have to cross your legs.' So saying, she turned over and was asleep in moments.

Thanks to some extra coaching by Bella and the others, Kitty had just about mastered marching in time and saluting by the day of the passing-out parade.

Quite a few girls had been homesick and so miserable that they decided to go home, including Anne and Sybil and a long-faced girl called Patricia who'd cried herself to sleep every night. Bella, Lucy and Kitty had promptly claimed the three vacant beds, so at least there was more room in the hut and everyone wasn't in danger of breaking their necks attempting to get from one end to the other.

Bella found she'd got used to a lot of things in the short time she'd been at the camp – liver, which had a green tinge, and onions for breakfast; being shouted at by every corporal and sergeant all the time for anything and everything; bathing in front of umpteen other girls in the ladies' washroom, where privacy was non-existent; washing one's knife, fork and spoon in a murky trough from which they emerged more greasy than when they'd gone in – the list was endless. On the other hand she knew she had toughened up considerably, made friends for life, laughed on even the worst days and developed a healthy appreciation of food after hours of incessant marching that she wouldn't have believed herself capable of.

Trade training courses followed basic training once the passing-out parade was over, and on the day it dawned there were mixed feelings in the hut. Everyone knew that even if they were lucky enough to be going to a new camp with a friend or two, there were others they were being forced to say goodbye to and with the times so uncertain, who knew if they'd meet up again?

Bella had heard she was being posted to the RAF casualties office at Ruislip. In the last year of school she and Cecilia had thought it fun to take advantage of a typing course that had been offered as an extra to the curriculum. Neither of them had done particularly well but she'd thought she might as well put it down on her RAF application form, but now she wished she hadn't. Some of the others were being dispatched on wireless operators' courses or meteorologist programmes and even radiographers. It was of slight comfort that the twins were being sent to the RAF camp in Cranwell, where kitchen orderlies were needed; Arlette to somewhere in Scotland as an equipment assistant; and Kitty, to her disgust, was going to be trained as a spark plug tester. Everyone knew that was one of the filthiest jobs there was, the proverbial short straw. Lucy, on the other hand, because she could drive, had landed the coveted job as an MT driver. As Kitty had said, 'There'll be you swanning about driving an officer around with your posh accent, all neat and clean and hail well met, and me grubbing away cleaning hundreds of spark plugs in petrol.'

'Not necessarily,' Lucy had protested, laughing in spite of herself. 'I might be driving a refuse lorry for all you know.'

'No.' Kitty had sighed, her voice resigned. 'It's bound to be a group captain at the very least and ten to one he'll be dishy into the bargain.'

'I'll invite you to the wedding, I promise.'

'Many a true word is spoken in jest.'

Bella had smiled along with everyone else as the two had ribbed each other, but secretly she had to admit that she was desperately envious of Lucy. It was a plum job and very different to being stuck in an office all day, although she'd been told hers was an important post in that it released airmen for first-line duties.

None of them were thinking about anything, however, other than getting through the marching without disgracing themselves on the morning of the passing-out parade. It was now the beginning of October and the weather had turned markedly colder after the Indian summer they'd been enjoying for most of September. The heavy sky was dull and overcast and a keen wind was blowing. Compared to the biting north-easter Bella had grown up with she didn't think it was too bad, but a number of the girls were shivering uncontrollably as they gathered together. Once the air force band struck up it acted as a shot in the arm, though, and everyone strode out in perfect formation, even Kitty.

The camp had had a shipment of uniforms delivered the day before, much to the delight of the girls, and for the first time everyone had clothes that actually fitted. They looked like WAAFs, so maybe that helped.

When they were finally dismissed their training officers were full of smiles, which was a good sign – it didn't happen very often. The burly sergeant who'd made Kitty's life a nightmare came over to her, grinning. 'I knew you could do it, lass. Well done.'

Kitty stared at him in shock, and then surprised everyone including herself by bursting into tears. All in all, it was an emotional day.

The next morning there was much hugging and exchanging of addresses, promises not to lose touch and quite a few tears. From the first day of training they'd all supported each other to the hilt, class had been forgotten and strong friendships forged. Now they were being torn from the arms of their new-found chums and sent off to a *real* RAF camp and it was terrifying. Even the twins, who at least had been kept together, were distressed.

Once they'd had their last breakfast together they returned to the hut and packed the brand-new kitbags which had been delivered with the uniforms. Shoes at the bottom, underclothes next, followed by other belongings and then shirts and jacket, with tin hats sitting on the top of everything. Simple. Except Bella found that the long white tube of a thing weighed a ton. Kitty knocked one of the twins clean off her feet as she swung her kitbag onto her shoulder, and the rest of them staggered about bent almost double, helpless with laughter. Eventually they managed to get to the waiting lorry that was going to transport them to the railway station where the RAF driver took pity on them and threw the kitbags in the back as though they were as light as feathers. Once they were all aboard and the tailboard was in place, off they set, singing now, as much to keep their spirits up as anything else.

Bella looked round at everyone, her gaze resting on Lucy and Kitty. In just the short time they'd known each other she realized she was closer to them than she had ever been to Cecilia. Without either of them being aware of it they had helped her through the worst period of her life. She would always grieve for her father and especially the manner in which he had died, and she never wanted to see her mother again, she told herself fiercely, but somehow in the last weeks, in the companionship of Lucy and Kitty and the others, she had been able to let go of James. Even forgive him for not having the courage to come and say goodbye in person, although she still felt he had owed her that after what they'd meant to each other.

Perhaps she had never really known him after all, she thought pensively, because she would never have dreamed he would leave the way he had. Maybe no one ever really knew someone else at heart? Her father had imagined her mother was different to what she was but she'd betrayed him and lied for twenty years, ultimately causing his death.

It was a stark lesson for the future and one she would never forget. She was done with love – it was a fool's game and she was no fool. The only person you could trust was yourself and she would never let herself become vulnerable again.

The girls had gone into a spirited rendition of 'Pack Up Your Troubles in Your Old Kit Bag', and she winced as Kitty dug her hard in the ribs. 'You're not singing.'

'I'm just thinking about Ruislip,' Bella lied. 'I don't think I'll be any good at office work.'

'Aw, don't worry.' Kitty slipped her arm through Bella's. 'If anyone can cope with whatever's thrown at them it's you, gal. You're as bright as a button up top and with your looks you can always charm your way out of any difficulties. Men'll be putty in your hands. Even Sergeant Travis fancied you, you know, and he was a right beggar.'

'I don't think so,' said Bella, laughing. 'And anyway I'll probably be working with a load of women.'

'Ah, that might be a problem then.'

'You're a proper Job's comforter, aren't you?'

They grinned at each other but as the lorry trundled on and the girls started on 'Good-bye-ee' with a lot more enthusiasm than melody, Bella faced the fact that her future was going to be very different to the one she had dreamed about, not just because of the war but because even if she survived it she would never marry and have a family. She couldn't risk going through the pain she'd felt when James had left again.

But she wasn't going to waste another minute crying for what might have been; there was a war to fight and she would do her bit, and that was enough for now. What would be, would be. It was out of her hands, and strangely that brought a sense of peace.

Chapter Thirteen

Over the next months, Bella found her equilibrium was challenged every single day. Her main function at Ruislip was sending letters of condolence to the families of killed or missing airmen. She often worked late into the night, eyes streaming with tears, typing out the fateful messages destined to break the hearts of the mothers and wives and sweethearts who read them. Try as she might, and she did try – every single day – she couldn't separate herself from the horror of what she was typing:

> *It is my painful duty to inform you that your son [or husband], airman X, has been reported Missing [or Missing, believed killed] as a result of operations etc. etc. etc.*

She'd been told that no typing errors were admissible; these were precious letters that the families would keep for ever.

She worked with some other girls in the casualties

section and they all found their menial but important work distressing. She had been billeted with one of them, an amiable brunette called Rachel, and it was comforting to live with someone who understood how harrowing the job was. Home was one of a number of old requisitioned houses that had been taken over by the services in which the bedrooms had been made into dormitory-style accommodation to maximize the space. Poor maintenance in the past meant the whole building was damp and draughty, and as regulations decreed that all personnel must sleep in a room with an open window, that didn't help matters. As the weather worsened in December everyone dressed for bed as though going on an Arctic expedition; the only warm place in the whole house was the kitchen, with its ancient and temperamental range.

The fuel shortages meant utilizing any wood they could find and when one of the girls' RAF boyfriends offered to cut down an old dead tree in the garden he was treated as a hero. This was a precarious undertaking – it was a big tree – but along with considerable swearing and cursing from the boyfriend and squeals and screams from the watching girls, the tree was eventually cut down without the man in question being rushed to the nearest hospital. The end result meant they had enough wood to see them through the winter, which was just as well. In January the Thames froze over as a cold spell swept across Europe, bringing snow and the worst storms of the century. Rationing was brought in at the beginning of the month for the first time since 1918 and the country was told to economize wherever possible.

All this, along with the streets being blacked out, which made the winter nights seem even longer and darker, created a feeling of gloom everywhere. Suddenly the world had changed out of all recognition and carefree summer days full of light and warmth were just a distant memory. Even soaking in a hot tub was a thing of the past. In the house, the girls had agreed on a rota whereby they'd each take a bath just once a week because it took so long to fill the tin bath with hot water from the range.

There were fourteen of them squeezed into the three bedrooms upstairs and the front room which had been converted into a fourth bedroom. This meant that the two girls whose turn it was on any particular day would bathe – one at a time – in the tin bath in front of the range. It was the only warm place in the house. Everyone else would be sitting talking at the table or on the long settle bench which stood along one wall. Shyness and modesty had, of necessity, gone out of the window. Bella had been mortified the first couple of times she'd stripped off but had found you could adapt to anything if you had to.

The lavatory for the property was at the end of the garden in a brick-built structure that didn't seem overly safe to Bella; some of the bricks were beginning to crumble and the old wooden door was nearly falling off its hinges and wouldn't shut properly. Sitting there in the dead of the night in pitch blackness was in Bella's opinion scarier than anything Hitler could throw at them, especially as some of the girls had noticed big rats running about once twilight fell. It was emptied fairly regularly by council workmen via the back lane, but that in itself was a mixed blessing. Sitting in situ with one's ears straining for the sound of the truck wasn't exactly relaxing.

Nevertheless, everyone adapted to the present circumstances, whatever their background. As Rachel pointed out when one of their company was moaning about the lack of an indoor bathroom, they were still fortunate enough to be living in a country where right ruled over might.

Life that winter was a constant struggle against the cold once Bella left the confines of the office, but one night in February as she trudged up the garden to the lavatory over crisp white virgin snow under a brilliant full moon, clad only in pyjamas, boots and her RAF greatcoat, she stood for a moment taking in the silence that surrounded her and the fragile beauty of the night. Sooner or later the air raids would come, it was inevitable, and then the war would blast its way into people's homes and lives in a new way, she told herself. The letters she had to type each day were the tip of the iceberg.

She stared up into the heavens, serene and tranquil for the moment like the calm before the storm, and for once she couldn't prevent thoughts about her mother from flooding in.

She breathed out a deep, bitter sigh, her breath a white cloud in the frosty night. How could her mother have done what she did; not just sleeping with another man but then compounding the betrayal by all the lies afterwards? She had thought they were such a happy family, the three of them.

A sob caught in her throat as she pictured the look on her father's face that day as he had died. He would still be alive if she hadn't fallen in love with James.

Guilt and shame rose up in an overwhelming flood, catching her unawares, and all the sadness in the world crushed down on her – the letters she had to type; the terrible things that were happening beyond Britain's shores; the grief and sorrow and heartache people were going through, but most of all, *most of all* the fact that she had, albeit unwittingly, had a hand in killing her father. She had been fighting acknowledging it for months, pushing the shadows aside when they'd tried to intrude on her consciousness, but tonight her strength was gone. The guilt, however erroneous, was crucifying. Rage, worthlessness, sorrow, regret rose and fell in great surges of emotion that took her breath away.

Within the layers of sorrow she cried for her father, for James, for the past, for the future which would be so different now, for the children she would never have, and for innocence lost – the innocence of believing that your mother is the most precious and perfect of women.

How long she cried in the silent night she didn't know, but eventually the sobs lessened and she began to breathe deeply, slowly, regaining a measure of calm. The knowledge that she had been trying to banish for so long about her hand in the death of her father had been faced and now she had to live for the rest of her life – however short or long that was – with all the emotions wrapped up in it.

If only she had known the truth she'd have behaved differently, she told herself. She would have treated James as the friend he had been throughout her childhood, nothing more. But she hadn't known. And now, however much she regretted the outcome of their love affair, it was too late.

She became aware that she was frozen to the marrow and shivering uncontrollably, but still she didn't move. It was a full ten minutes later before she could rouse herself, and in that moment she knew that if one of Hitler's bombs had fallen and blown her to pieces she would have welcomed it.

It was in the spring, as the German army across the Channel moved nearer, that the course of Bella's life and career changed dramatically. She was summoned into the presence of the commanding officer at Ruislip, an elderly man who sported the most enormous handlebar moustache.

Wondering what she had done wrong that necessitated being reprimanded by such an august personage, she stood in front of his desk trying to keep calm. He eyed her without blinking and then, to her surprise, told her to be seated. 'What do you know about Y Service?' he barked without any preamble.

Bella blinked. 'I'm sorry, sir?'

'Y Service, Y Service! Heard of 'em?'

'No, sir.'

He nodded. 'You might or might not be aware that by the time this war broke out the governments of most European countries had been pouring resources into intelligence for some years. It'd become clear that electronic eavesdropping on the enemy was going to play a vital part in complementing military might. And key to these operations here in Britain is the section known as Y Service, which is responsible for the interception of communications.'

He paused and Bella nodded, wondering what on earth all this had to do with a typist at Ruislip.

'There's been an important breakthrough in the last weeks. They've found that voice transmissions, as opposed to Morse, from the Luftwaffe could be picked up on VHF, but the only trouble is that no one at Y Section can speak German. Fly in the ointment, what?'

She nodded again, a stir of excitement making itself felt.

'Now we've had a message here asking us to locate German-speaking WAAFs and you, I understand, are fluent in several languages, German included.'

'Yes, sir.'

'Excellent, excellent.' A glimmer of a smile twisted his lips briefly. It was common knowledge at Ruislip that he was furious that the powers that be considered him too old to engage the enemy in the air and had consigned him to a desk job, making him taciturn and short-tempered in the extreme. 'You'll be having an interview this afternoon to test your linguistic ability, a mere formality in your case I should imagine, and then there'll be some red tape and security clearance. All this is strictly confidential and not to be discussed with anyone, do you understand?'

'Yes, sir.'

'Good, good, that's all.'

She stood up and saluted, her head whirling, and as she reached the door he added, 'It'll be a darn sight more interesting work than what you've been doing here, so make the most of the chance, all right?'

'Yes, sir. Of course.'

Once outside the office she stood for a moment, breathing deeply as excitement took hold. Suddenly everything was different; she was going to be able to do something that would really make a difference, she told herself, her heart racing. And she would make sure she was the best operator Y Section had, come what may.

Later that evening at the house the girls sat in the sunshine in the garden eating their evening meals on their laps. It was the last day of May and blossom filled the air with fragrance, birds singing in the trees. Aware of her promise, Bella hadn't said a word to anyone about what had happened that day, but now, looking at the smiling faces of the other girls and listening to their banter, she realized another chapter of her life was ending. She had imagined she would be here until the end of the war but she would soon be gone. Another WAAF would work at her typewriter and sleep in her bed here at the house. Life was such a transient, ephemeral thing even though it seemed perpetual as you were living it.

She shivered in spite of the warm air and Rachel, sitting at the side of her, said, 'What's the matter? Someone walked over your grave?'

She smiled and nodded. This time last year she had been the happy young daughter of parents she adored, living in her beloved childhood home and knowing she had found the love of her life in James. Even with the growing rumblings of war, everything had seemed wonderful. How trusting and innocent she'd been, she thought wistfully, her heart aching for the girl who had vanished like the morning mist. She missed her.

And then she shook herself mentally, spearing a piece of meat with her fork and putting it in her mouth. She was alive, she was healthy and in her right mind, and she had a lot to be thankful for, not least the promise of this new line of work that sounded as though it could be amazing. *One day at a time*. It had become her mantra in the last months and she nodded to it now. One day at a time and another new beginning.

Chapter Fourteen

Belinda sat in the morning room finishing another of the letters that she knew she wouldn't post. There was a pile of them in the drawer of her writing bureau already, all addressed to Bella. It was ridiculous, she admitted to herself, but somehow writing them made her feel closer to her daughter even though Bella would never read what she had written.

She finished by signing '*your loving mother*', and then slipped the letter into an envelope before putting it with the others, sighing heavily as she did so. People would fear she was losing her mind if they knew about the letters, and maybe she was. Certainly she could hardly bear to look at her reflection in the mirror, she hated herself so much.

In the terrible weeks after Archibald had died and Bella had gone to London, she had paced the house each and every night, having cat naps now and again but barely sleeping at all. In the day she had taken long walks whatever the weather, unable to sit and rest. In the end she had collapsed one day and Wright had sent for the doctor. Dr Hogarth had told her in no uncertain terms that she had to take the medication which he'd prescribed the day of Archibald's death or that she wouldn't see the year out.

'You're skin and bone,' he had said grimly, 'and this state of affairs cannot go on. Wright tells me you don't eat or sleep, which is not what Archibald would have wanted. Surely you see that?'

He hadn't mentioned Bella but he must have wondered why her daughter had disappeared so suddenly after Archibald's death, even before the funeral. No doubt the gossipers had had a field day discussing that.

She had listened to Dr Hogarth that day and begun eating again, taking the elixir each night before bed that guaranteed at least a few hours of oblivion. She didn't deserve the easy way out after what she had done, she'd told herself. She deserved to suffer each day.

She stood up and walked to the window. It was a beautiful soft June day and as she looked out her thoughts turned from herself to the evacuation of the British soldiers from Dunkirk the week before. Following an appeal over the BBC, the Admiralty had contacted the owners of small vessels, such as yachts, river launches and cabin cruisers, almost all of which had been crewed by weekend sailors, to augment the force of over two hundred Royal Navy vessels. Some six hundred boats of one description or another had risen to the occasion in Operation Dynamo, rescuing the British Expeditionary Force from certain annihilation.

Harrowing tales had been reported of the evacuation: the horrors as men on the beaches were bombarded by the Luftwaffe; the nightmare of their escape on the armada of small ships and little boats. She knew the eldest of the Wynford boys had been killed; Wright had told her the news which he'd heard from Skelton, the Wynfords' butler, who was a friend of his. It was common knowledge that many men, when eventually treated, were found to have maggots in their wounds under field dressings or were suffering from gangrene. Belinda shut her eyes for a moment, picturing Philip's son, ruddy-faced and laughing in his white flannels as he'd played cricket on the lawns of Evendale with his brothers and friends. She shuddered, pity sweeping over her for a moment.

Now that the possibility of invasion was real she knew folk were living in fear; reports of German parachutists dressed as nuns was a common rumour, along with other fanciful ideas. For herself, strangely, in view of how she had been in the past, the thought of Hitler and his Nazis arriving on these shores didn't send her into a panic. But then, perhaps it wasn't so strange, she told herself in the next moment. The worst that could befall her had already happened when she had lost Archibald and Bella, the one to death and the other to a silence so profound it was unbearable. She knew her daughter had joined the WAAFs because Mrs Graham at the London house had told her so, and after the cook had imparted the news, it had seemed inevitable. Bella would never have sat twiddling her thumbs, she had realized.

She turned, surveying the room bathed in sunshine. She had gone to the rose garden that morning and cut some blooms to bring into the house. It was run on a skeleton staff now; only Wright and Mrs Banks and the cook remained in the house, all of whom were well over sixty years of age, and the gardens and grounds had been left to run wild when all the outside staff had joined up. Palmer would turn in his grave if he could see his precious ornamental gardens, she thought ruefully; it was probably just as well he had died before the war had started. But the rose garden had still presented some magnificent flowers he would have been proud of. None of the bedrooms apart from her own were used now, and she rarely went into the drawing room or dining room, eating her meals in the breakfast room and living mostly in the smaller morning room where she was now.

The one good thing when most of the staff had departed was that Johnson had gone with them, disappearing not to work in a munitions factory or to do other war work but to join her sister, who had a small B&B establishment somewhere or other. It had been some days after the maid had gone that Belinda had realized some of the family silver was missing, or to be more accurate, that Wright had brought it to her attention. He had accused Johnson outright of taking it and had been for calling in the police, but she had been in the throes of grief at the time and hadn't been able to cope with what that would have meant. It had validated everything she'd always thought about the woman, however. A week or so later, after

Wright's day off, he returned to the house in a taxicab with the missing items. He'd apparently gone to the B&B himself and faced Johnson and her sister. She didn't know what had occurred, he wouldn't say, except to assure her that Edith Johnson would be looking over her shoulder in fear of the police for some time to come, and he hoped she wouldn't be able to sleep at night.

She had been touched at Wright's loyalty and indignation on the family's behalf; it had been one bright spot in a dark, dark time. Mrs Banks had been supportive too; old age had mellowed her somewhat. What the two of them had gleaned about the circumstances surrounding Archibald's death she didn't know, but they treated her with both respect and kindness, and she was grateful.

She knew she looked different these days; there was no colour in her cheeks and her eyes showed pain in their depths which had aged her beyond her years. The black of her mourning clothes added to an image that was austere and unembellished, and the only pieces of jewellery she wore were her wedding and engagement rings. She rarely had visitors and when she did she was polite but never took up any invitations to return the visit.

There was a cursory knock at the door of the morning room and then Mrs Banks bustled in with a tray of tea and little cakes and pastries. Encouraging her to eat was a constant theme of the housekeeper and cook and although she knew they meant well, it was wearisome. Nevertheless, she always forced some food down; she knew she was too thin.

'Your afternoon tea, ma'am.' Mrs Banks eyed her sternly, giving Belinda no option but to sit down and take the cup of tea the housekeeper poured and then select a cake and pastry from the small array in front of her. Only when she had bitten into the little sponge cream cake did Mrs Banks leave the room.

As she ate, Belinda thought about how fortunate they were that the farm still provided them with so much. In February when rationing had begun housewives all over the country had been less than impressed: butter, sugar, bacon and ham could only be bought on the production of ration books, and even then four ounces of butter and bacon or ham uncooked didn't go far, nor did the twelve ounces of sugar allotted. Meat rationing had followed in line with the government's livestock control scheme and had been rationed on the basis of value. Fellburn's farm had meant things had continued pretty much as normal with supplies of cream and butter and cheese to the house, although Belinda was sure it would be frowned on if the authorities knew and fines levied. Frankly though, she didn't have the mental energy to concern herself with it. Most of her waking thoughts were about Bella: where she was, what she was doing in the WAAFs, whether she was safe, and most of all what her state of mind was.

She had just finished her first cup of tea when Wright tapped on the door and put his head round it. His voice low, he said, 'Colonel Wynford has called, ma'am.'

'What?' She was glad the cup was empty as it teetered and then tipped into the saucer. She hadn't seen Philip or

Felicity since Archibald's funeral when they'd obviously decided they had to attend for appearance's sake. She hadn't spoken to them and they hadn't come back to the house with family and friends. Making a tremendous effort she pulled herself together, saying, 'Would you show the colonel in here, please, and ask Mrs Banks to bring another cup.'

'Yes, ma'am.' Wright hesitated, and then said even more quietly, 'The colonel doesn't look too good, ma'am, just so you know.'

'Thank you,' she said softly. 'He's lost a son, he must be grieving.'

'Aye, yes, ma'am.'

Once the door had closed behind the butler Belinda took a long, deep breath and by the time it opened again she was outwardly composed, but then the formal greeting she'd been about to make froze on her lips. When Wright had said that Philip didn't look too good it had been an understatement. He looked ghastly, shrivelled even. Rising, she held out her hands, saying, 'Come and sit down. Wright is bringing another cup and you'll have some tea, won't you?' as though he was always calling at the house.

For a moment she thought he was going to burst into tears and watched as he made a valiant effort to control himself. It was some moments before he managed to say, 'I'm sorry to turn up unannounced, but—' He stopped abruptly, shaking his head.

Somewhat at a loss, Belinda took his arm and pushed

him down in the chair facing the small sofa where she'd been seated. He was ill, she thought. That was the only explanation for such a change in him. He sat with his head bowed and she saw that the once thick mop of hair was thinning and his hands were trembling. Clearing her throat, she murmured, 'What is it?' before adding quickly, 'I heard about Anthony. I'm so very sorry.'

Wright came with the extra cup and saucer at that moment and it wasn't until they were alone again that Philip raised his head and looked at her. 'We – we heard today that Randolph and Gerald were among the one hundred thousand British troops south of the Somme, which were cut off at Saint-Valery with the French Forty-First Division. The Germans had considerable superiority in numbers and air supremacy and they attacked without mercy.'

Belinda put her hand to her mouth, her voice a whisper. 'Not Randolph and Gerald too?'

He nodded. 'It was nothing short of a massacre, apparently. The Germans were bombing roads packed with civilians trying to escape—' Again he paused before groaning, 'All three, Belinda.'

'Oh, Philip.'

'And James estranged from us. Did you know he joined up as a doctor in the army when war broke out? The last we heard he was in Boulogne.'

Again she murmured, 'I'm so sorry. How is Felicity bearing up?'

A change came over his face for a moment. 'Felicity?

Well enough, I think. She was always a distant mother. Anthony's wife has taken it hard, but she has the twins to console her. Twin boys.' A glimmer of a smile touched his mouth. 'They're the image of Anthony. And Randolph's children will be a comfort to his wife, a boy and a girl. Gerald's daughter is a baby but his wife's family will rally round. This damn war.' He swallowed hard. 'They wouldn't let me fight – the legs, you know, and my age I suppose.'

He was silent for a moment and then he said, very softly, 'I don't really know why I came here today. We had the telegram and I confess I went to pieces –' he shook his head – 'and Felicity told me to pull myself together in front of the servants. *The servants!*' His voice had risen and now he took a shuddering breath before he mumbled, 'Sorry, sorry.'

She didn't think about her next action, leaning forward and taking one of his hands in her own as she said, very quietly, 'You needed to talk to someone, that's natural.'

Whether it was her words or the genuine compassion in her voice she didn't know, but it released a flood of emotion in him. She had never seen a man cry before; her father had always been tight-lipped and although Archibald had been emotional when she had told him she was pregnant with Bella, his tears had been ones of joy and soon over. This was different, this storm of grief that racked Philip's frame. She found herself on her knees in front of him; the sounds coming from him were barely human, and when Wright appeared in the doorway she raised her head and said, 'Brandy, quickly.'

'Brandy,' Wright repeated; then turning, he hurried out of the room, returning a few moments later with a large glass of brandy as he stood staring at his mistress holding Colonel Wynford, wrinkling his eyes at the agonized cries coming from the other man. 'Ma'am?' he said after a minute or so.

'The colonel heard today that Randolph and Gerald have been killed too,' Belinda said, having to raise her voice to be heard over the terrible noise Philip was making.

It was a full five minutes before the sounds lessened but eventually Philip lay slumped in the chair, his hands over his face, and it was only then that Belinda said, 'Drink this brandy, it will help.'

She thought for a moment he hadn't heard her and was considering telling Wright to fetch her smelling salts, but then with one hand still covering his eyes he reached out with the other and she placed the glass of brandy in it, nodding to Wright that he could leave. Once she had seated herself again, she waited until he had finished the brandy before she said, 'Is there anything I can do, Philip?'

He raised his head and looked at her through swollen pink lids. 'Belinda, I'm so sorry. Not just for coming here like this but – but for everything.' His voice shaking, he added, 'Have you heard from Bella?'

She shook her head. 'I know she joined the WAAF when war broke out. That's all.'

'I wrote to her. When she was at the London address I wrote a letter explaining how it had happened and that you were not to blame in any way. I heard nothing back, but then I didn't expect to. There've been many times I've wanted to come and see you in the past months, to see how you were, but –' he stared at her for a long moment – 'I didn't think you would want to see me.'

Would she have wanted to see him? Probably not, she answered herself. Not the old Philip, anyway. Not when her whole being and spirit had been so devastated; but now, now he was feeling the same, albeit for a different reason. Or perhaps it wasn't so different. He had lost three of his sons and James would have nothing to do with him; she had lost Bella and moreover her daughter – their daughter – hated them both. She sighed deeply. 'When you say I wasn't to blame, that's not true and we both know it. You didn't force me, Philip. And afterwards, when I knew there were consequences, it was my decision not to tell you and to let Archibald believe Bella was his.'

'You were so young and you must have been terrified. You did what you thought was best.'

'That's all true but it's no excuse, not really. My actions have ruined two young people's lives and caused the death of the man I loved. A good man. I have to live with that. Sometimes I don't know how I can but I have to, because if there is the slightest chance in the future that Bella might come and see me, I have to be here. I don't expect forgiveness – what I did was unforgivable.'

'You are very hard on yourself,' he said softly. 'You were such a child in those days in many ways and as I said, you must have been so frightened. And, Belinda, don't forget all the joy that Bella brought into Archibald's life. He was so proud of her and so happy to be a father, and but for Bella he would never have experienced that.'

'But at the end, knowing she wasn't his killed him.'

'You don't know that for sure. His heart had been failing for some time but even if that was the case, it was a few moments of shock compared to all the years of love and happiness being a father brought him.'

'I – I wish I could see it like that.'

'Try,' he said, very gently. 'And Bella and James will get on with their lives, it's what young people do. They're hurt now and angry but they'll find love again.'

'Bella will always hate me.'

'Always is part of the future and none of us know how that will be.' He paused, and then said painfully, 'The only certain thing in life is that it will end in death.'

They sat in silence for a few moments before she said, 'What will you do now?'

'Go on as before, I suppose.' He rubbed his hand across his mouth. 'What else?'

She nodded. It was what she was doing, after all.

'When we got the telegram today I realized something. I have acquaintances by the dozen, I have companions, some of whom I've known since boyhood who I get drunk with, a – a mistress to provide what Felicity doesn't like to give, and people we socialize with every damn week, but there is no one I can talk to or –' embarrassment coloured the next words – 'cry with. To be truthful I don't know what brought me to your doorstep because I'm fully aware I've no right to ask for your help.' She watched the muscles in his cheekbones tighten as he added, 'But I'll be for ever grateful.'

She didn't know what to say and so she remained silent but as her eyes met his, her face was soft with compassion. She had always imagined that Philip led a charmed life, that he was shallow, taking what he wanted when he wanted it and to hell with everyone else, and that had caused a hard knot of resentment deep inside, but now she felt it melt away. It was a relief, a release. It didn't change the pain and guilt she felt about Bella but nevertheless, some of the tenseness she lived with daily evaporated.

He cleared his throat before he said, 'May I come again? I won't make it a regular occurrence – I know you would not want that – but if just now and again I could call it would mean so much.'

His voice had been low and hesitant, quite unlike the confident individual she'd always known, and it was this that made her say, 'Of course, if it would help.'

'Thank you.' He stood up, turning away and rubbing vigorously at his eyes, and she pretended not to notice that his face was damp when he said, 'If you hear anything from Bella, would you let me know? It would put my mind at rest to know that she is safe and well.'

She too was on her feet and she nodded.

'I care about her, you know. I always have. Of course, I didn't suspect the truth for a moment but I always felt an affinity with her somehow.'

'She's like you,' Belinda said with painful honesty,

feeling she was betraying Archibald's memory. But it was true. She and Archibald had been two of a kind – passive for the most part and content with the mundane. Bella wasn't like that. She was fire to their water, like her natural father. Like James too, her half-brother. No wonder they had fallen so quickly in love; they were similar in many ways – animated and ardent and spirited. She had always liked James the best out of the Wynford boys; he'd had a social conscience the others didn't possess, besides his natural charm and humour. This thought caused her to say softly, 'I'll be praying for James.'

She walked with him to the front door and watched as he mounted his horse before riding off down the drive. Wright joined her, his voice concerned as he said, 'Three of his four sons taken. It doesn't seem fair, does it, ma'am.'

It was some seconds before she turned back into the hall. 'No, it doesn't seem fair, but then war never is, is it. It's like a great heartless machine just mowing down the good and the bad indiscriminately.'

'A machine built by men, ma'am.'

'Yes, you're right.' She suddenly felt exhausted, her limbs leaden. If James didn't return from France alive what would Philip do? And Bella, where was she? She could be in all sorts of danger and she would never know.

'But Hitler must be stopped, ma'am,' Wright said impassively. 'The alternative is unthinkable.'

She stared at the old man. 'Even if Britain's youth is sacrificed? Boys like the colonel's sons?'

The rheumy, faded eyes didn't waver. 'Mr Churchill

said that all he had to offer was blood, toil, tears and sweat. It's all any of us can offer, ma'am, young and old alike.'

She nodded slowly, and then said from the heart, 'What would I do without you, Wright?'

The wrinkled face stretched in an uncharacteristic smile. 'As the master used to say, ma'am, no one is indispensable but some are more dispensable than others.'

She found herself laughing. 'Yes, he did, I'd forgotten.'

She was still smiling as she walked back to the morning room but once she had shut the door her face straightened. It suddenly seemed as if the war had come a whole lot closer. Three of the Wynford boys would never be coming home and Bella and James were still in the thick of it; James in France and Bella who knew where? Clasping her hands together, she cried out to God, 'Protect her, please protect her. It doesn't matter if we're never reconciled, I can live with that, but don't let her die. Please, God, don't let her die.'

PART FOUR

Oh, I Do Like to Be Beside the Seaside

1940

Chapter Fifteen

Bella sat with the other girls in the kitchen of the house in Ruislip, where they'd gathered to hear Churchill's broadcast to the nation. It was 18 June and her last day in London. Tomorrow she was leaving for her new post and she'd been presented with a sealed envelope containing a railway warrant to Hastings before she'd left the office that evening. Her bags were packed and she had written to Kitty and Lucy to tell them she was being moved and that she would be contacting them at some point. Tomorrow would be the beginning of a new adventure, but tonight she was waiting for 'the old beast', as Rachel called Churchill, to speak.

She glanced at the pamphlet from the Ministry of Information that one of the girls had pinned to the wall. It was so ridiculous that they'd all fallen about laughing when it had come through the letterbox, and it never failed to amuse if one was down in the dumps. And she felt a little odd tonight, nervous and excited. But sad too.

'Do not believe rumours,' it declared. 'Be calm, quick, exact . . . Do not give any Germans anything . . . Hide your food, your bicycles, your maps. See that the enemy gets no petrol.'

The recommendations, along with the publicity picture showing a smiling housewife in a housecoat secreting a biscuit tin at the back of her coal cellar, were almost insulting.

If Britain was invaded, did the Ministry really believe that a sweetly smiling little lady politely informing a tough Nazi paratrooper that she wasn't allowed to give him a biscuit would hold water? Bella thought for the umpteenth time. Nevertheless, it was amusing and they had all agreed that it must have been conjured up by a man. So many of the male sex seemed to have a mental image of a woman as the cosy little housewife. The time-honoured sex divide that allocated homemaking to women and world affairs to men was still alive and well, even in the midst of war when women were taking on roles hitherto denied them and doing them well. Every one of the girls, including herself, had experienced men both inside the services and outside showing their disapproval.

And then her mind was switched to the radio as the BBC announcer introduced the Prime Minister and his familiar voice came across the airwaves:

'*What General Weygand called the Battle of France is over. I expect that the Battle of Britain is about to begin . . . The whole fury and might of the enemy must very soon be turned on us. Hitler knows that he will have to break us in this island or lose the war. If we can stand up to him, all Europe may be free and the life of the world may move forward into broad, sunlit uplands . . . Let us therefore brace ourselves to our duties, and so bear ourselves that, if the British Empire and its Commonwealth last for a thousand years, men will still say, "This was their finest hour."'*

When the broadcast was finished Bella looked round at the other faces and then smiled as Rachel said, 'Well, he can pack a punch, I'll say that for him.'

'Oh, he's the man for the hour all right,' said Betsy, whose father was a staunch Trade Union man, 'but he's no friend of the working class, not in peacetime. Still, it's not peacetime, is it, and Chamberlain was about as much good as a chocolate teapot.'

'Talking of chocolate . . .' Another of the girls, a spirited redhead whose parents owned a sweetshop, went into the cupboard and brought out a package. 'Mum and Dad sent me this and I thought it'd be nice if we shared this lot today, with it being Bella's last night.' The package proved to contain umpteen bars of chocolate and other confectionery, and when several bottles of wine were added to the mix it guaranteed an evening of fun and laughter.

Later that night as Bella lay in bed feeling somewhat tipsy, she reflected that but for the war she wouldn't have known the sort of easy comradeship that existed in the WAAFs. It was a silver lining in her particular cloud. Here she was off to Hastings tomorrow, and if things had been different – if she and James hadn't been torn apart and her life taken such an unexpected turn – by now she would have likely been a doctor's wife in the north-east. Her chest tightened as the familiar pain of loss took hold.

Despite herself, the contents of Colonel Wynford's letter – she refused to think of him as her father – came into her mind. He had gone to great lengths to make it clear that her mother was blameless in what had occurred all those years ago on Armistice Day, but whether that was true or not there was still the matter of the lies her mother had told once she had realized a baby was on the way.

She twisted restlessly under the covers, thoughts swamping her head. It was the years her mother had lived a lie that she couldn't come to terms with and couldn't forgive, she told herself bitterly. And had she and James not fallen in love her mother would still be doing that.

Turning over, she resolutely cleared her mind. She needed to sleep so that she was fresh for tomorrow and when all was said and done it was only the future that mattered. She was finished with the past.

The journey to the Fairlight station above Hastings was uneventful. She had been told that the special operators in the Y Listening Service worked in exposed positions on the south coast, logging and passing to Bletchley Park, Station X, all the German transmissions they could pick up, and that she would receive the appropriate training as soon as she arrived.

It had been a fine summer's day when she had set off on the train from London but there was a damp drizzle in the air when she eventually reached her destination. Although it was mid-afternoon she was immediately introduced to the woman who would train her to operate radio receivers and told that there was a pressing need for her linguistic talents and every hour counted. Somewhat overwhelmed as well as being hungry and tired, she tried to concentrate on what she was being told and appear at least a little intelligent.

Later that evening she and another girl who had arrived just after her were taken to the mess for a meal – stew on one side of the plate and prunes and custard on the other – which they gobbled down within moments, and then on to their living quarters by the hut corporal. 'Your things have already been put on your beds,' she informed them crisply, 'and the girls you share with are all in the same line of work. You can discuss what you like with them but to anyone else your jobs are confidential. Once you're fully trained you'll work in a caravan close to the Fairlight cliff-edge because it gets good cross-Channel reception, and you'll be doing six-hour shifts. Any questions?'

Winnie, Bella's new companion, said a little tentatively, 'Where's the bath hut for the WAAFs?'

The corporal pointed to a large shed-like structure in the distance. 'That's the one for the WAAFs. The airmen's ablution block is twenty yards beyond it but they've been known to wander into ours by mistake when they've had a drink or two, so be warned.'

She opened the door of the Nissen hut she'd brought them to. 'As I said, you'll be working shifts and there's normally at least three or four girls sleeping at any one time, so keep the noise down. Get a good night's sleep and report for training after breakfast. Time is of the essence.' So saying she turned on her heel and marched off, leaving them staring at each other.

The Nissen huts, with their corrugated-metal covering, were not popular for sleeping accommodation in the winter. They were poorly insulated with just a central pot-bellied, floor-fixed black stove for heating. On this damp but warm summer's evening the hut seemed almost welcoming, though, as they stepped inside and looked around.

Four of the ten beds the hut held were occupied by sleeping WAAFs, and Bella and Winnie saw that their belongings had been placed on the two beds furthest from the stove. Once they had unpacked they trudged off to the ablution hut before returning and getting into their pyjamas, holding a whispered conversation so as not to wake the sleeping girls while they shared a packet of biscuits Bella had brought with her.

It transpired that Winnie, an attractive blonde girl with a smattering of freckles across her snub nose, had lived in Germany for a while with her family some years ago. Her father was in the army and had been stationed there. Like Bella, she had seen the evils of Hitler's regime and when war had been declared had left her home in Coventry and joined up.

She was delighted about being involved in the Y Service, excited and thrilled that the work was so hush-hush. 'It's like we're spies or something, isn't it,' she whispered happily. 'I couldn't even tell my dad what I was going to do except that it's important. He's ever so proud, though. I bet your family are the same?'

'Not really,' Bella said quietly, the familiar pain constricting her throat for a moment. 'My father died just before war was declared and I don't have anything to do with my mother.'

'Oh, I'm sorry. Have you got any brothers or sisters?'

She thought of James and the other Wynford boys, her half-brothers. 'No. I'm an only child.'

'That's probably a good thing in a way,' Winnie said softly. 'Less people to worry about. I've got two brothers and my dad in the army. Hubert and Peter were both in France and my mum didn't sleep for a week when Dunkirk was going on, but they both got out OK.' She sighed. 'Physically anyway. They lost a lot of friends and Mum says they're not the same boys they were.'

Once they'd settled down to sleep on the creaky beds that protested if you so much as moved a muscle, Bella lay awake for a long time, tired though she was. Winnie had prompted her conscience, she admitted to herself painfully. She knew her mother would be worried about her and she supposed she got a certain amount of satisfaction in punishing her by continuing to remain incommunicado. She didn't want to correspond with her but perhaps she could send a short note, just a line or so, and with no address so her mother couldn't write back, and tell her that she was all right? She didn't deserve it, not after what she had done, but it would be the humane thing to do and with all the terrible cruelty and barbarity going on in the world, it would be something positive? She had never thought of herself as a vengeful person until her father had died.

She twisted and turned on the narrow bed with its thin mattress for a long time; she heard some other girls come into the hut but pretended to be asleep. She didn't want to talk to anyone; Winnie had unintentionally stirred up a host of memories and try as she might she knew she couldn't escape one undeniable fact – she still loved her mother. It seemed like the worst betrayal of her father but she couldn't help it.

Eventually, the decision made that she would pen a note the next day, she drifted off into a troubled sleep, her dreams populated with dark, disturbing shadows and a feeling of dread that only evaporated in the light of day.

Over the next days and weeks, Bella and Winnie were soon on terms of easy familiarity with the knobs and dials of the radio receivers and could twiddle them with the best. They listened in to the messages transmitted between the Luftwaffe pilots and control stations, their headphones clamped on tightly as their ears strained to catch every single word. Everything they heard had to be meticulously logged and then carefully translated into English. It was painstaking work and stressful at times but also rewarding.

Bella became familiar with a range of German regional accents like the other girls, and found that after a while she could even distinguish the voices of individuals, any of whom, she realized disconcertingly, could have been one of the men she'd met from the Air Wireless School at Halle-an-der-Saale. She tried to put this out of her mind; it made it more personal than she liked. They were the enemy of course, but she couldn't help recalling their fresh, eager faces and how young they were. So many servicemen who were little more than boys were dying on both sides and it was heartbreaking. This war wasn't their fault and yet they were being asked to make the ultimate sacrifice.

Cracking the simpler aspects of the enemy pilots' code was a matter of time and patience. For example, they knew that *Indianer* meant Indians – Allied aircraft – and *Kirchturm* referred to church tower or height. The logged interceptions were all sent to the code-breaking headquarters at Bletchley in Buckinghamshire via the Air Ministry, where the raw material was meticulously analysed and compared with other intelligence data.

Bella and the other girls were vitally aware of the

responsibility of their work and that it was crucial to winning the war. Although this made each one of them more focused on doing the best they could, it also caused a taxing and fraught job to be even more pressured. They couldn't afford to make mistakes: human error wasn't an option when lives depended on their accuracy. Consequently, on the evenings when they were off duty and could visit the pub or a dance hall in the village, some of their number let their hair down with abandon. There were plenty of WAAFs who had a liking for gin, and plenty of airmen or locals who bought it for them. Nevertheless, it was an unspoken rule among the girls that they always made sure that each of their number made it back safely to barracks.

Throughout a baking hot July the war hotted up too. German forces had landed on the Channel Islands; the Luftwaffe were attacking ships in the Channel and began their first daylight raids. The news was mostly bad. Bella found immersing herself in her work meant she was usually asleep as soon as her head touched the pillow, and when a volunteer was required for an extra shift she was always the first in line. She needed to fill every minute of the day and night and work helped to keep personal thoughts at bay. On the rare occasions when she had some spare time she wrote to Kitty and Lucy, both of whom seemed to have settled into their new postings although Kitty grumbled that her hands would never be clean again.

She had been at Hastings for two months when, at the

beginning of August as Alsace-Lorraine and Luxembourg became part of Germany, she was called into the office of Group Captain William Crawford of Special Signals Intelligence. He was an imposing figure of about forty or so, over six feet tall with wide shoulders and a lean frame and steel-grey eyes. It was common knowledge in the camp that his wife had died in childbirth and the baby shortly afterwards. Whether it was this tragedy that made him so reserved and aloof no one knew, but he had a well-deserved reputation for suffering fools badly and WAAFs in particular. Rumour had it that he considered the services no place for women, and this was at the forefront of Bella's mind when she knocked on the door of his office.

A terse 'Come in' followed. She walked in and stood in front of his desk. It was a moment or two before he looked up from the document he had been studying. As the full force of a pair of piercingly grey eyes with all the softness of granite met hers, Bella fought the inclination to blink. She stared back at him, keeping her face impassive although her stomach muscles had tensed.

He raked back a lock of dark hair which had fallen across his forehead before he said shortly, 'I understand that you're damn good at your job.'

'Thank you, sir.'

'Privately educated.'

'Yes, sir.' He had made it sound like a crime, and now Bella's voice was as clipped as his had been. He clearly had a chip on his shoulder; the rumours had been spot on.

'You speak several languages and your supervisor thinks your talent is exceptional – you picked up the regional accents immediately, for example.'

Bella continued to stare at him. She wasn't sure if he expected her to comment and so she remained silent.

'Furthermore, you're prepared to –' he consulted the papers in front of him – 'go the extra mile whenever necessary.' He sat back in his chair. 'Your supervisor is needed in another unit in Hornchurch and she has recommended you to take her place. It will mean that as well as doing your own work you will oversee others and be in charge of monitoring newcomers. She feels you have a natural authority.'

Again Bella got the impression that he was sceptical but now her voice was cool and firm when she said, 'Yes, sir.'

'You will be promoted to corporal herewith, of course.'

She almost said 'Corporal?' but just managed to stop herself in time. 'Thank you, sir.'

The telephone on his desk rang and before he reached to pick up the receiver he said shortly, 'That's all for now.'

She saluted and turned away, leaving the office and shutting the door quietly behind her. Then she stood for a moment. Had what she thought had just happened *really* happened? She'd been promoted? But he'd offered no word of congratulation or praise, in fact he'd seemed to resent it. His whole manner had verged on arrogant, but then she'd encountered this thinking before in the air force from the day she had joined up. Some men just seemed to think that a woman's place was – if not in the home – then certainly not doing a man's job.

She became aware that she was clenching her teeth and forced herself to relax. Group Captain William Crawford might be a thoroughly irritating man, but it was up to her not to dwell on the things he said – no, not so much what he had said but the manner in which he had said it, she corrected herself. Whatever, hopefully she would have very little to do with him in the future and that would suit her just fine.

She nodded at the thought, and then set off to find Winnie and tell her and the others the news. Corporal McFadyen! Who would have thought it.

William Crawford finished his call and then sat staring into space in spite of the hundred and one things he had to do. He'd made a hash of that interview, he told himself. The very least he should have done was to offer his congratulations to Mirabelle McFadyen; certainly she had received a glowing recommendation from her superior, who wasn't one to give praise lightly. But she'd caught him on the raw from the moment she had walked into the office so cool and self-contained, a product of her class if ever he saw one. Born with a silver spoon in her mouth and every inch a lady.

And then he shook his head at himself. She had joined

up, hadn't she? Volunteered to do her bit rather than sit in luxury being served with afternoon tea by the servants and decrying what the war had done to limit the supply of stockings. It was his own prejudices he was projecting here; he'd always considered the upper classes – especially those who had never done a day's work in their life – to be a waste of space. Since being in the RAF he'd come across plenty of officers' wives who had nothing in their heads beyond their bridge clubs and cocktails before dinner. There had been more than one occasion in the past when Hilda had accompanied him to some do or other and the other women had looked down their aristocratic noses at her in an oh-so-genteel way. He ground his teeth. And his wife had been worth a dozen of them. A hundred. Like him, she'd been working class and proud of it.

A picture of Hilda flashed across the screen of his mind and he sighed. They had known each other from their schooldays in the poorer part of the East End of London and had married in their teens. Hilda had wanted a large family, at least half a dozen – three boys and three girls, she'd told him, laughing, several times in the first couple of years. The laughter had grown less as a decade had passed with no signs of a baby and then, out of the blue, she'd become pregnant. They'd been in Cairo at the time and he'd just been promoted to Group Captain in the RAF. Everything had seemed perfect.

Suddenly the memories were too much and he stood up abruptly, walking out of his office and telling his secretary he was going for an early lunch. It didn't do to think, he told himself bitterly as he walked to the mess, or reflect on what might have been. What *should* have been. Somewhere up there in the heavens the gods smiled at mere mortals thinking that they had their lives mapped out and were just waiting to show them how wrong they were. Well, he'd been shown all right.

He bit tightly on his lip, forcing away another memory of a tiny white coffin being lowered into the ground to rest beside that of Hilda. He rarely visited the cemetery on the outskirts of London where his wife and daughter were buried; it was too painful and the dark desire to join them, to take what he considered the easy way out, frightened him at such times with its intensity. But the war might provide the answer; he took more risks up in the air than he knew he should but he didn't care. All he asked was that when his time was up he was able to take a good few of the enemy with him so that it was worth something. Rumours were running rife that Goering intended to throw everything Germany had got at them in the air, but that didn't frighten him. Fear was born when life was precious, when it contained something you cared about, and that had ended for him two years ago.

He walked into the mess, his face stony, and chose a table away from everyone else to eat his food, not looking to left or right.

Bella, seated on the other side of the room with Winnie, stared at the hard flinty face and stiff body. He really was the most uncaring, cold-hearted man she'd come across, she thought irritably, still annoyed by his attitude when he had talked to her. And a misogynist into the bargain. He might be good-looking in a severe, frosty kind of way but what woman in her right mind would be attracted to such an individual?

Winnie, noticing the direction of her gaze, nudged her. 'Gorgeous, isn't he?' she whispered softly. 'All detached and remote, a man's man.'

Bella's eyes fixed on her friend's face. 'Winnie, he's not remote, he's just plain rude,' she whispered back hotly.

'Well, all the girls swoon after him.'

'This one doesn't.'

'I wouldn't say no.'

'*Winnie.*'

'Well, I wouldn't,' said Winnie, undeterred by the shock in Bella's voice. 'I love the strong, silent type.'

Bella grinned. 'You love *any* type.'

Her friend grinned back. 'That's true. Life's too short to be picky. I want to have fun and live a little before I pop my clogs. Did I tell you that I'm meeting one of the pilots in the pub tonight? That tall, blonde-haired one called Stephen. He's got a friend if you're interested.'

'I bet he has,' Bella said wryly. 'Anyway, I'm doing an extra shift this evening.'

'All work and no play . . .' Winnie shook her head. 'You know, you and the group captain ought to get together, you're just the same. He's got a reputation for being the original ice-man and you're the ice-queen.'

Bella made a face, determined not to take offence. 'I'm perfectly happy as I am, thank you very much.'

Winnie's gaze drifted back across the room. 'He *is* a dish, though,' she said dreamily, 'and you know what they say about the quiet ones . . .'

Chapter Sixteen

In a very short time it became apparent that Hitler planned to annihilate the RAF and to increase attacks on Allied shipping. Bella and the other WAAF operators could overhear German pilots communicating with their bases about shipping movements in the Channel. On 10 August 'Eagle Day' was announced in Germany, the date by which the Luftwaffe planned to win air superiority from the RAF, and the raids by German planes increased in ferocity. Five days later the RAF reported that they'd shot down nearly a hundred and fifty out of a thousand raiding aircraft, losing only twenty-seven of their own planes.

Now the work of the Y Service became even more vital. From Fairlight, overheard messages would go through warning the navy and No. 11 Fighter Command at Uxbridge what the Luftwaffe were planning, and air cover would immediately be dispatched to protect convoys. Bella and her fellow operators knew that these convoys, containing food and fuel for the nation, had to get through safely and that every message they intercepted was vital. The Y Service were building up a fuller picture from their stations of the workings of the Luftwaffe, and it was clear that Hitler and his Nazis believed themselves to be invincible and that Britain had no chance against them. There was a supreme arrogance underlying what Bella and the others overheard, an absolute confidence in the Führer and his assertion that they were the master race.

In the middle of August the Luftwaffe suddenly switched its attacks to targets in southern England, and the Battle of Britain began in earnest. The PM delivered another pep talk to the nation, paying tribute to the RAF pilots in their Hurricanes and Spitfires who were giving their all with no thought for self.

'*Never in the field of human conflict was so much owed by so many to so few*,' Churchill had declared, MPs cheering and clapping before he'd gone on to say that Britain bristled with two million soldiers, rifles and bayonets in their hands, who were standing ready to resist invasion. The enemy coming ashore on Britain's soil was what everyone was expecting and dreading.

His speech was stirring stuff as usual and what the nation needed, Bella thought, especially when one was tired and feeling the strain of the horror of what was happening. She was now working double shifts as a matter of course but she enjoyed the work, gruelling and distressing as it could be at times.

She had written a short and unemotional letter to her mother to say that she was safe and well. It had relieved her conscience in one way, but in another she couldn't rid herself of the guilt that she was betraying her father in easing her mother's mind a little. She couldn't win whatever she did, she told herself ruefully. That was something she would just have to accept, she supposed.

In the third week of August she suffered another huge blow. She received a tear-stained letter from Maud and Delia to say that Kitty had been killed in an air raid. Kitty had put their mother down as her next of kin. It was clear the twins were devastated and Bella felt the same; it was hard to take in that the gutsy, vigorous Kitty was no more.

A few days later, as the RAF bombed German gun installations on the French coast that had been shelling Dover, she was called into Group Captain Crawford's office again. Since their last meeting Bella had become aware of the group captain in a way she hadn't been before. Her personal antennae sensed if he was around, which was as annoying as it was uncomfortable. He had nodded at her briefly once or twice when he'd passed her in the mess, and a couple of days after her promotion had stopped to ask if everything was all right in the new role, but on those occasions he hadn't smiled and the grey eyes had been like polished stone.

They were beautiful eyes though, she thought, as she stood in front of his desk again. The colour of a stormy sea and the black lashes surrounding them were thick and long, almost feminine. He glanced up and she caught at the thought, telling herself not to be so pathetic. In spite of herself she felt her cheeks growing hot and prayed he wouldn't notice.

'Sit down, Corporal McFadyen,' he said quietly, and once she was seated he leaned back in his chair, surveying her for a moment. 'You and the other girls are doing an excellent job but with German attacks increasing in intensity we're moving the unit to Hawkinge near Folkestone. It's been decided that we'll be more useful there. We're leaving tonight.'

'Everyone, sir?'

He nodded. 'I'd better warn you that this corner of Kent is in the firing line, so to speak. Have a word with your staff and warn them that things will get hot in the next weeks.'

'Yes, sir.'

'Is there anyone who in your opinion won't be able to cope if things get bad, as they are likely to do?'

Her chin lifted. 'Among the WAAFs you mean? No, no one. I can't speak for the airmen, of course.' There it was again, the covert implication that the RAF was no place for women.

He had detected the sarcasm, she saw it in the narrowing of his eyes. And then to her surprise she saw a quirk to his mouth. Not a smile as such, but a definite movement of his lips. It made him more human, and Bella didn't like what it did to her.

'You have faith in your girls,' he said softly.

'Yes, I do, sir. Every one of them wants to serve her

country and is prepared to do whatever it takes to stop Hitler and his Nazis. That's why we joined up.'

'I appreciate that,' he said smoothly.

'But you think that there are some jobs that only men can do,' she responded before she had time to think about her words. Then she quickly added, 'sir'.

He stared at her for some moments, the handsome face thoughtful. 'Not exactly. More that there are things that I believe are more suitable for a man.'

He was splitting hairs. 'Sir, women are getting stuck in as MT drivers, balloon operators, parachute packers, flight mechanics, radar and wireless operators – to name just a few jobs. And it's the same in civvy street. Women are doing everything that the men did and sometimes—' she stopped abruptly, realizing that her tongue was running away from her.

'Sometimes?'

She breathed out. 'Sometimes a lot better, sir.'

The quirk turned into a grin. 'You're a very single-minded young lady, Corporal.' His voice was impassive but not disapproving. 'One could almost say uncompromising.'

'I've found that women have to be that way in the RAF, sir, and I'd say it's a fair summing-up overall.'

'Would you indeed.'

Bella got the impression that he was finding the conversation amusing and it grated on her. She didn't want to be patronized. Her voice cold, she said, 'The thing is, women always have to do something just that little bit better than a man to be taken seriously.'

'Do you really believe that?'

'Absolutely. Look how long it took for women to get the vote. And it's only twenty-one years since Nancy Astor became Britain's first woman MP, and she was treated pretty badly by the male element in the House of Commons.'

His head was tilted slightly to the side as he surveyed her searchingly. 'Actually,' he said quietly, 'she was the second woman to be elected. A year before the viscountess won her seat, a woman was elected for a Dublin constituency for Sinn Féin, Countess Something-or-other. She made herself ineligible by refusing to take the oath of allegiance to the monarch though.'

Bella stared at him, irritated. And of course he would have to know that, she thought, aware that she was being unfair but annoyed nonetheless. She shrugged. 'That may be so, sir, but it doesn't really change the point I was trying to make. Women are paid less for doing exactly the same job as a man and I can't see that is right, and they are still considered the weaker sex who need to be protected and looked after.'

'And you wouldn't like to be protected or looked after?' he asked mildly.

'No. Yes.' He was confusing her. She'd noticed the gravelly note in his deep voice before and it was both attractive and disconcerting. 'What I mean is, in certain circumstances possibly, but when I am doing my job – and I think I speak for the majority of other women here – I would like to be treated as a man by my male colleagues.'

William's gaze ran over the thick golden hair and lovely face with its dark-blue eyes and full lips. He could have replied in a number of ways but he didn't want to antagonize her further and he was aware that she was annoyed with him although he wasn't quite sure why. He nodded. 'I see.' If she seriously thought that any red-blooded male would see her as anything but a woman she must be mad.

That thought coming out of the blue disturbed him and he sat up straight, returning to the matter in hand when he said briskly, 'I'll leave you to take charge of the move, Corporal, and instruct your girls accordingly. I'm sure I don't need to tell you that this is all highly confidential.'

'No, sir.' Or should that have been yes? Bella asked herself, aware of being flustered in spite of her efforts to be calm and professional.

'Good. That's all for now.'

'Thank you, sir.' Once outside the office she went straight to inform the other girls that they were on the move to Kent and that they would be in the thick of things, although that bothered her a lot less than the conversation with the group captain. She didn't want to think of him as a man, and an attractive man at that, but she couldn't help it. Winnie had called him the strong, silent type and maybe he was, she thought ruefully; perhaps that was why when he unbent just a little it was so beguiling?

And then she mentally shook her head at herself. Less of the silly schoolgirl notions and more of the calm, strong woman she purported to be, she told herself sternly. She was done with men, and even if she wasn't, he would be the last person in the world she would get involved with and she was sure that would be fully reciprocated by him too. It was clear they rubbed each other up the wrong way and were chalk and cheese; he had no time for determined, independent women and she certainly had no time for men like him whose views of women were in the Dark Ages. However attractive they were.

The move to Hawkinge went like clockwork but this was a very different kettle of fish to the station they had left. In their quarters Bella and the other girls had no peace, with fighter planes ceaselessly landing and taking off and the nearby harbours constantly under attack. Aircraft zooming overhead and the terrible rhythm of machine-gun and anti-aircraft fire made up their days and nights, and the screaming whines of planes crashing to earth out of control made her feel sick every time she heard it. Furthermore, and she fought against this at first, the knowledge that the group captain was often up there in the skies made it even more personal. She found herself wishing he could have stayed in Hastings where it had been quieter, but he hadn't and that was that.

As the Battle of Britain reached new heights, Folkestone and Hawkinge were repeatedly shelled from across the Channel. If Bella and her companions weren't at their posts, tracking the choreography and reporting their findings, they were dashing in and out of air-raid shelters and praying against direct hits on their position. Despite the ceaseless bombing and shelling they never left their sets while they were on watch, though. Her conversation with the group captain before they had left Hastings came back to Bella time and time again, and she felt so proud of the WAAFs in her unit. The pressure was enormous, and she often fell into bed at night with her mind screaming for the oblivion of a few hours of sleep as did the other girls, but not one of them broke down or lost control.

They had been at Hawkinge for some weeks when an incident happened that she feared might lead to her being court-martialled. On the whole the men and the WAAFs responsible for the interception of communications in the unit got on well; the men appreciated that the WAAFs were doing an excellent job and although some of them had been wary at first of having women amongst them, a comradeship had grown. They all worked long hours and extra shifts when necessary, which was much of the time, and because of this got to know each other well in a short period.

Bella was at her post when one of the men, a young man whom she knew was concerned about his wife in London who was expecting their first child in days, suddenly began shouting and screaming, ripping off his earphones and frightening everyone to death as he began to make the most unearthly noise. His hysteria, borne of exhaustion and the fact that he had lost three of his friends in as many days, was understandable but she knew how it would affect morale, and as the senior WAAF on duty she acted instinctively. Brushing aside two of his friends who were trying to reason with him, she slapped him hard across the face twice.

Stunned and shocked, he stared at her blindly for a moment, but the noise stopped. Then he began to weep.

'Take him to the mess for some coffee,' she said to one of the other men, as shocked as they were by her actions. He was senior in rank to her and she knew this could have repercussions.

Sure enough, that evening as she came off duty, she was summoned to Group Captain William Crawford's office. He was sitting behind his desk as she walked in after knocking, and she was struck immediately by how tired and grey he looked. They were losing pilots every day in the *danse macabre* overhead.

She had prepared herself for the worst, so when he smiled and said, 'Sit down, Corporal,' it took the wind out of her sails.

'Thank you, sir,' she said politely, sitting down and folding her hands in her lap as though her heart wasn't racing nineteen to the dozen.

'I heard about what happened today,' he went on. 'Not from the man in question initially, but it prompted me to call him in and have a word. He was embarrassed and ashamed but understood you did what was necessary in the circumstances and was actually full of praise for you and the other WAAFs, who do an excellent job under dire conditions. He will be back at his post tomorrow. I trust that won't be a problem?'

'Of course not, sir,' she said quickly, relief washing over her.

'He's a good man, Corporal.'

'Yes, sir, I know that and he's anxious about his wife on top of everything else.'

'Quite.' William nodded. In reprisal for RAF bombings Hitler had threatened to raze British cities to the ground and Londoners had been put on the front line since the beginning of September. He sighed heavily. Every evening wave after wave of Luftwaffe bombers droned over the capital, the bombs falling impartially on rich and poor alike. The King and Queen had been in Buckingham Palace when the building was hit, and the British Museum and Downing Street hadn't escaped either. Thousands of people were being killed and injured and every day the city's red buses had to pick their way past new bomb craters to get Londoners to work.

Overstretched rescue services were performing prodigious feats daily, and heroism by the police and firemen was the norm. He thought about the tale one of his friends had told him the other night. Mark had been on leave with his family in the capital the week before and a police station at the end of their street had been hit. The windows had been shattered and there were heaps of rubble everywhere, but it had borne a sign saying, 'Be good, we're still open.'

It was typical of the Londoners' cockney humour, but for the poor devils like the airman who had broken down today the fact that his nearest and dearest were in the thick of it must be damn awful.

Looking at Bella, he said softly, 'It's one hell of a time to be separated from those you care about, Corporal.'

'Yes, sir, it is.'

'Have you got people in London?'

The softness of his voice and the personal nature the conversation had taken had thrown her. It made him more human and she didn't like that. It was difficult enough as it was to deal with him, she thought ruefully, as she made a valiant effort to pull herself together.

He was waiting for her to answer and she cleared her throat before saying quietly, 'Not relations, but we have got a London house and I've known the staff since I was a little girl.'

William nodded. 'Where's your family's main residence?'

'The north-east. I haven't been back there since before the war broke out though, it's all a bit difficult. What – what I mean is, my mother and I have been estranged for a while. A – a family problem.' Now why had she told him that? she asked herself, immediately regretting it.

'I'm sorry to hear that,' he said quietly. He wanted to ask more but he knew it would be intruding on her privacy. There was certainly more to this woman than met the eye, though; in spite of her forthright manner and confidence he recognized a sadness about her, perhaps even sorrow connected with grief? Not that it was any of his business, he told himself in the next instant. She did her job and she did it well, that was the only thing that mattered.

His voice becoming brisk, he said, 'Well, I just wanted to let you know that there will be no consequences from what happened today, in case you were wondering. In fact, I think you did what was necessary in the circumstances, Corporal.'

'Thank you, sir.' She hesitated. 'Actually, I suppose I acted automatically. It didn't occur to me until afterwards that I had struck a senior officer.'

He suppressed a smile. 'Perhaps not something to make a habit of?' he said drily.

'No, sir.'

There was a twinkle in his eye despite his tone.

'Is that all, sir?' she asked primly.

He nodded. Once she had left the room, closing the door quietly behind her, he didn't get on with the paperwork on his desk, however, his thoughts wandering. He was flying again tonight and now more than ever no one knew who would be coming home, if you could call Hawkinge home. And that hadn't bothered him a jot until recently. The only request he'd made of the Almighty was could He make it quick – he'd listened to too many of his men screaming when their planes were shot down in flames by the enemy and they couldn't get out. It had seemed ironic that men who wanted to survive, who had everything to live for – wives, sweethearts, families – were dying and he was still here. He knew he had taken risks, he had a couple of medals for bravery to prove it, and he'd felt a fraud accepting them. It wasn't bravery that had made him put himself in the firing line time and time again, more that he didn't care.

Somewhere in the far distance he heard the unmistakable whine of an aircraft in its death throes and winced, hoping it wasn't one of theirs.

In the moments of silence when it was quiet again, he asked himself a question: Did he still not care? Was he still the same man he'd been before a certain lovely, blue-eyed Corporal had come into his life?

He got up abruptly, turning and looking out of the window onto the square beyond. He didn't like the way his mind had gone. It was a betrayal of Hilda, of the love they'd had for each other. His marriage hadn't been easy, he admitted to himself, not in the latter years when Hilda had been so desperate for a child that it had consumed her, changed her into someone he barely knew, but he had still loved her. He wasn't sure if she had still loved him by the time she had died although she had returned to being the Hilda of their early days when she had found out she was pregnant, the bitter acrimony and harsh words melting away as her stomach had swelled.

He rarely allowed himself to dwell on those last painful years when nothing he had done or said was right. She had blamed him absolutely for their failure to have a child, but at the same time had refused to see a doctor or even discuss it with anyone. She was the youngest of three girls and her two sisters both had big families, which proved there was nothing wrong with her; she had flung this at him over and over again. He, on the other hand, was an only child and so the fault clearly came from his side. He'd made the mistake once of pointing out that his parents had only married in their forties and his mother had fallen pregnant with him straight away, but she'd become so angry and abusive on that occasion that he'd never repeated the mistake.

Stop thinking. He nodded to the voice in his head. It didn't do any good to think. He'd nearly driven himself mad after Hilda had died, dissecting the past and wondering what he could have done differently, but gradually he'd come to realize that once other people were part of your life matters, to some extent, were taken out of your hands. Autonomy was the answer. No one to answer to or for. It didn't provide happiness, but then what happiness was there in this world that was tearing itself apart?

He turned and sat down again, clearing his head of everything but the report he needed to write. Facts, in black and white. No emotion clouding the issue. That he could cope with.

Chapter Seventeen

September was a difficult month for Bella and the other Y Service WAAFs, and October was no better. By now they had become familiar with the German reconnaissance pilots' voices, and would have recognized them as individuals even without their call signs. Some of them were characters and knew perfectly well that the WAAFs were listening in to them, flirting with them in English and reminding Bella of the young Luftwaffe officers she'd met in Germany before war had been declared. Much as she loathed Hitler and the Nazis, she felt some of the pilots had been brainwashed by the Hitler Youth from when they were small and weren't fully responsible for the position they now found themselves in. It made the job harder. They were certainly as brave as English pilots and more than once, when one of them was shot down by a flight of Spitfires or Hurricanes, she found herself hoping that they would get out alive.

She thought of all the sad letters she'd written when she was working in the casualties section and the tears she had cried for the families of the men who'd been killed, their wives, mothers, sweethearts, and knew that German women's hearts would be breaking in just the same way. It was easy to hate Hitler and Goering and the monsters in charge of the concentration camps, but these boys? That was different, and Winnie and the others felt the same. Nevertheless, they had a job to do, and one which demanded cool heads and a degree of detachment whatever the circumstances.

As the weather got colder and November arrived in a flurry of snow showers and heavy frosts, it became clear that the Luftwaffe had lost the Battle of Britain and Hitler had decided to try and defeat his only fighting foe by starving her out. The German threat to Britain's Atlantic lifeline was very real and the front line manned by sailors of the Royal Navy and seamen of the Merchant Navy was of vital importance. This wasn't to say that the Luftwaffe stopped their raids; in the middle of November the mediaeval city of Coventry was devastated by the worst air raid of the war when over a thousand civilians were killed.

It was the day after this when Bella and her watch were on duty that she was called into William's office again. They hadn't spoken more than one or two words since the incident concerning the airman, but as soon as she looked at him she knew it was serious. 'One of your girls, Winifred Kirby,' he said without preamble. 'It's bad news, I'm afraid, and I thought it best if you break it gently to her.'

'Winnie?' she said, her heart sinking.

'Her mother. She was killed in the attack on Coventry last night.'

Bella stared at him. Winnie was always saying how her mother worried about the menfolk who were all away fighting but so far they'd survived without a scratch.

'I'm afraid she's required to go tomorrow for identification purposes. Apparently her father and brothers are overseas and she's next of kin. I'm very sorry. Was she close to her mother?'

Shocked to the core of her, Bella nodded. 'Yes, sir. Very.'

Again he said, 'I'm sorry. There's a pass for her here and her travel warrant. It's an early train in the morning – perhaps you could see that she is all right to catch it?' And then his voice gentled. 'Sit down, Corporal. This has clearly been a blow. Is Winifred a particular friend of yours?'

'We started at Fairlight station on the same day.' She sat down, feeling a little nauseous. Winnie was going to be devastated. 'She – she only got a letter from her mother this morning but we were leaving for a shift and she said she'd read it this evening when she'd got more time to enjoy it.' Bella's voice caught in her throat. This was Kitty all over again. Loss and heartache.

'It's an uncertain world we live in.' He was finding it hard to see her so distressed and not be able to do something. 'My secretary has put instructions on where Miss Kirby needs to go in the envelope, it should all be clear.'

'Thank you, sir.' She stood up and took the envelope he held out to her, their fingers touching briefly in the barest of contacts. Nevertheless, she felt the impact in the quickening of her heartbeat and after saluting hurried out of the office as though the Devil was at her heels.

Their shift had just finished as she rejoined the others and Winnie was waiting for her so they could go to the mess together. There had been a couple of mad dashes to the air-raid shelters during the afternoon, but for the moment at least it was relatively quiet. As she approached Winnie outside the building where they worked and saw her friend's bright face, she knew what she was about to say would change Winnie's life for ever.

'What did he want you for this time?' Winnie called when she was still a little bit away from her. 'You haven't been slapping any more senior officers you haven't told me about, have you?' The man in question was completely back to normal now and also the proud father of a bouncing baby boy, hence the liberty to joke about it.

As Bella reached Winnie, she stared at her friend and Winnie's expression changed. 'What is it?' she said, her face straightening. 'Are you all right? What's happened?'

There was a bench nearby and rather than go into the mess or anywhere else where there were lots of people, Bella pulled her over to it. In the distance a flight of Spitfires was coming in to land and there was the faintest sound of anti-aircraft fire, probably from one of the nearby harbours which were constantly under attack.

It was almost dark and a bitter wind was blowing.

Winnie shivered as she said again, 'What's happened? I thought we were going to the mess?'

'In a minute.' They were both going to need a cup of coffee. 'I've got some bad news. The group captain thought it'd be better if I had a word with you.'

Winnie's face froze. 'My dad? Or is it one of the lads?'

'Oh, Winnie, I'm so, so sorry. It's your mother.'

'Mum? No, it can't be.'

'It was the attack on Coventry last night.'

'Is she injured?'

Bella was holding Winnie's hands tightly and she shook her head. 'She's gone, Winnie.'

'Not my mum. Please, God, not my lovely mum.' As Winnie began to cry Bella pulled her close and the two of them clung together. Bella knew she would remember this moment all her life; her friend's heartbreaking sobs, the cold dark night, the fighter planes landing and more taking off and the other sounds of the station. She hated Hitler and the Nazis, she told herself fiercely, every one of them. She hoped they would all burn in hell for eternity.

The air-raid warning started but neither of them moved. Men were running and shouting and more planes were taking off as the Luftwaffe zoomed in, a dogfight erupting in the skies above with bombs falling on the perimeter of the camp. They'd seen it all before since they had been stationed at Hawkinge – the ceaseless bombing and shelling and pandemonium, and just a few days ago two airmen and a WAAF had been killed by enemy fire as they'd run for cover, but this night, in these moments, grief took priority over the German planes. It wasn't that either of them thought they were invincible, far from it, but there were some things that were more important than being shot and this was one of them.

It was some time before Winnie sat up and pulled away, wiping her face with the handkerchief Bella silently gave her. 'I never imagined Mum would be hurt,' she whispered brokenly. 'Dad and the lads, yes, I've gone through them being killed or taken prisoner a hundred times, but never my mum. I don't know what I'll do without her, Bella. She was the one who held us all together.'

Somewhere close there was the terrible screaming whine of an aircraft crashing to earth out of control and they both winced as they heard the ground-moving thump as it hit land and then exploded. They could see flames in the far distance and umpteen running figures, and Bella drew Winnie gently to her feet. 'Come and have a hot drink,' she said softly. 'We shouldn't be out here.'

She was going to have to tell Winnie that she was expected to go and identify her mother tomorrow, but for now that could wait.

The next morning she travelled to the station with Winnie and saw her friend onto the train. Neither of them had slept for more than an hour or so, and Winnie was white-faced and silent. They hugged before she climbed aboard, and Bella gave Winnie the bag containing sandwiches and cake for the journey, along with a few bars of chocolate that some of the other girls had contributed from their precious supplies from home. Everyone had been shocked and sympathetic about the tragedy; several of their company had lost loved ones since the war had begun and it was always at the backs of their minds, whatever they were doing.

Bella's last glimpse of Winnie was of her sitting by the window as the train began to trundle off, raising her hand and mouthing *Thank you*. Her friend's bravery brought tears to her eyes, and once back at the station and with two hours to spare before she went on duty, she decided to take a walk to clear her head. She left the base, walking for a mile or so to where a narrow river made its way to the nearby sea. It was a cold morning but in the trees on the bank birds were singing, oblivious to the horrors human beings had wrought as they went about their business of finding food.

She sat down on a fallen tree stump, thinking about Winnie and praying for strength for her friend as a weak winter sun touched her face with its rays. In the distance she could hear the engines of their planes and she wondered if the group captain was flying that day. She had heard Winnie weeping quietly for most of the night beneath her blankets, and she knew that if William died – it was the first time she had allowed herself to think of the group captain as William – she'd cry for him. It was crazy, because they'd only spoken a few times and she didn't know him at all, but nevertheless, should something happen to him she would be beside herself.

Was this what they called being on the rebound? she asked herself in the next moment. Was she imagining that she felt something for him because of what had happened with James? Was it a crush of some kind because he was an older, experienced man with something of a tragic past? Certainly there was no question of a relationship between them; he didn't know she existed in *that* way.

Suddenly impatient with herself, she jumped to her feet. She was being ridiculous, that was the long and short of it, and she would die on the spot if he ever guessed that she liked him. Turning, she began to walk back to the base, realizing that she was freezing cold and more than a little hungry, which she felt slightly guilty about in the face of Winnie's misery. In the mess the night before Winnie had drunk a mug of cocoa but had been unable to eat a thing, and she'd been so upset for her friend that she hadn't wanted anything either. Now, though, she was starving, so did that make her shallow? Probably. Or just human, perhaps?

It was a long day and she thought about Winnie constantly once she'd finished her shift, which had been a particularly harrowing one. One of the Luftwaffe pilots whom all the girls looked forward to hearing because of his sense of humour and banter had been shot down in flames and he had been unable to bail out. She'd listened to him as he had screamed and screamed for his mother and cursed the Führer, and once he'd fallen out of reception range she had gone outside and vomited. And then she had wiped her mouth and smoothed her hair and gone back inside to continue working. She and the other girls knew that their work was no tennis party or seaside picnic; it demanded everything from them and there was no place for womanly sensitivity or sympathy and pity, but sometimes such qualities rose to the surface despite their professionalism.

The war and particularly the rigours of the Y Service required them to deny the very qualities that hitherto, as women, it had been natural to embrace. Even expected of them. Now, in the work they were involved in, it led to the deaths of young men like the Luftwaffe officer and they were expected to hate the enemy and feel no pity despite the carnage they played a part in. But that was the job, Bella told herself that evening as she waited for Winnie, and she wouldn't want to be anywhere but here doing her bit.

Winnie arrived back at the base when it was dark, pale-faced and shattered. Mercifully, in the circumstances, her mother had barely got a scratch on her and it was thought that she had suffocated in the dust and rubble. She had looked as though she was just asleep, Winnie told Bella brokenly, and the doctor at the morgue had had to restrain her when she had shaken her mother to wake her up, unable to believe that she was dead.

'Everyone was very kind,' Winnie said wearily, 'and there were lots of us waiting to identify loved ones. I was sitting with a mother who'd lost her little girl and they promised her the child would be buried with her teddy bear.' She gulped and shook her head. 'Her daughter had been crying for it in the air-raid shelter so the mother ran back into the house to get it and the shelter had a direct hit.' She stared at Bella. 'Why do such things happen?'

'I don't know, Winnie.' Again she thought of Kitty.

'Her husband was killed at Dunkirk, the little girl was all she had.'

'Try and not think about it,' Bella said softly, 'not tonight. You're all done in.'

'Our mum brought us up never to swear but I've had awful words in my mind all the time. Against Hitler, against the Nazis and SS, even God.'

'That's perfectly natural.' They were sitting in the mess, where Bella had tried to persuade Winnie to eat something. Her friend's chalk-white face and dazed eyes worried her.

'Did you feel like that when your dad died?'

'I was angry, yes, but –' she hesitated and then decided that telling her story would take Winnie's mind off things and it might help her – 'at my mother rather than God. And the man I was engaged to.'

'You were *engaged*?'

Bella told her the whole story, leaving nothing out, painful though it was. She had kept it all inside for so many long months it was a relief to talk about it. She didn't know how Winnie would react, whether she would be disgusted and think the less of her, but when she'd finished, her friend's face showed nothing but compassion.

'And you haven't seen your mum since the day you left home?' Winnie said softly after some moments.

'No.'

'Nor James?'

Bella shook her head. 'I'm over him now and I'm just grateful that we never, you know, jumped the gun. I mean we could have done, people do, don't they, but he was very respectful.' She sighed. 'He's a nice person; he'll be a wonderful doctor.'

'Do you believe what the colonel wrote in his letter? That it was all his fault?'

'I don't know, Winnie. Sometimes I do and sometimes I don't. But that doesn't excuse my mother for what she did afterwards and everything that happened because of her lies.'

'No, it doesn't, and I see that, I really do, but I suppose she was young and frightened and confused. She thought you'd have a lovely life being brought up in a beautiful home with a dad who loved you, whereas if she had told the truth about everything it would have been catastrophic. She could never have foreseen what would happen.'

'That doesn't make it right.'

'No, it doesn't.' Winnie paused. 'But oh, Bella—'

'What?'

'Go and see her when you can. Talk to her face to face and listen to what she has to say. She's your mum and nothing changes that, and you know she loves you. I'd give anything to have just one more day with my mum, anything.'

Bella put her hand over Winnie's.

'Do you love her?' Winnie asked after a long moment.

'I tried to tell myself I didn't, I told her I hated her, but—'

'You do,' Winnie finished for her. 'So go and see her before it's too late. It can't make things any worse than they are now.'

'But it's a betrayal of my father.'

'That's not true. You told me yourself he adored your mum and you were precious to him. Do you honestly think that he would want you both to be at odds? He sounds a lovely man and if he'd lived I think he'd have forgiven your mum, knowing that he was still your dad in everything that mattered. You said you'd come to terms with losing James and that's good, but if you don't see your mum you'll never really be able to move on with your life, Bella.'

'I'll think about it.'

'Do it, for me if nothing else. You haven't taken any leave since you joined up because you said you'd nowhere to go and would rather keep working. That's not healthy in mind or body.' The WAAFs in Y Service were given four days and nights more leave than was allowed to other airwomen because of the intensive work and mental and physical strain, and Bella was the only one who hadn't availed herself of this in spite of Winnie nagging her about it in the past. 'The section isn't going to fall apart because you're not here for a few days, now is it?'

'I know.'

'So you'll do it?'

'I promise I'll think about it.'

Winnie sighed, recognizing that was all she was going to get. Leaning forward, her face drawn and tired and her eyes pink-rimmed, she said softly, 'I loved my mum all the world and the only thing that's of any comfort at the moment is that she knew that and I've no regrets. It's terrible seeing that still outer shell with what made her *her* gone. Don't leave it too late. That's all I'm saying.'

Bella nodded. Winnie meant well, she knew that, but she had to be sure that she was doing the right thing before she made such a momentous decision. Nevertheless, her friend's words had both challenged and unsettled her. To err was human and to forgive divine, but there wasn't much divine about her, she acknowledged ruefully. But she had promised to think about it and she would.

Chapter Eighteen

As the month of November wore on it was generally agreed that a bleak Christmas lay ahead for a besieged Britain. With vital shipping space needed for war supplies, the country was becoming used to food shortages. Housewives were told that carrots would have to take the place of dried fruit in their Christmas puddings and Lord Woolton, the Minister of Food, asked the population to make sacrifices during the festive period.

For Bella, Winnie and the others who had become conditioned to what passed for meals dished up by the RAF cooks, the lack of things like bananas and other fruit was incidental. As Winnie remarked, everything tasted the same anyway and the taste was pretty dreadful.

The attacks by the Luftwaffe on British cities continued; in the Midlands Birmingham and other towns were hammered night after night, and at the end of the month Liverpool and Southampton were subjected to intensive raids lasting over seven hours.

Then, at the beginning of December, it became apparent

that Goering had changed his tactics yet again. The Germans were now making a major effort to knock out British industry with special squadrons trained to attack specific targets. Bella and the other girls discovered that the German planes were equipped with new navigational devices, and Coventry, Birmingham, Sheffield, Manchester and Glasgow suffered tons of high explosives and thousands of incendiaries raining down from the skies. After this, ports came under attack from the four hundred bombers sent over Britain each night.

The girls in Y Section were now often working sixteen-hour days as a matter of course and it was exhausting. Because they were on the front line and often came under bombardment, sometimes Bella felt as though the Luftwaffe were everywhere, but in spite of the intense nature of their work and the manifold disadvantages of daily life on the camp, there were good times too. Inevitably, an undercurrent of tragedy clouded their days and nights – several of the WAAFs had lost family members, as Winnie had, or sweethearts and even husbands – but perhaps because of that and the fact that they lived with danger every moment, the happy times were even more precious.

It was Winnie's birthday in the middle of December, and knowing how much her friend was grieving, Bella decided that she and the other girls in their hut would put on a surprise midnight feast for her. Some of the girls were able to donate goodies which had come from home, and Bella and the others bought extras, all of which were stored in a cardboard box under Bella's bed. A couple of the WAAFs were dating pilots at the base and they managed to get them a bottle of brandy and some wine to go with the feast of fruit cake, chocolate biscuits, toast with cheese and pickles, peppermint creams and treacle toffee from a WAAF whose mother made it her mission in life to keep her daughter supplied with sweets she made herself, and a long baked jam roll Bella had cadged from one of the RAF cooks who'd lost both parents in the Luftwaffe raid on Liverpool at the end of November and was sympathetic to what Winnie was going through.

So it was, after the midnight visit of the duty WAAF officer was over and the coast was clear, that they woke Winnie up and had a couple of hours of sitting on their beds wrapped up like Eskimos with their feet encased in aircrew long socks, drinking cocktails of brandy and wine from beakers and demolishing the food. It was gone two o'clock before they settled down to sleep, and it was only in the morning that Winnie – who, being the party girl, had been plied with cocktail after cocktail – discovered that she had spread shoe-polish blacking on her face instead of cold cream after lights-out. Both products were sold in the same size tins.

Winnie had finished the night with a toast to her mother before they'd retired, and as Bella lay in the darkness listening to the cacophony of snores in the hut she thought about what her friend had said: 'Mum, from when I was small you were always my best friend. Thank you for giving me life and I love you more than words can say.'

It had been short but it had affected Bella profoundly. Her own mother had given *her* life, and she had never doubted that her mother loved her. Her childhood had been a happy one and she'd always known that she came first with both her parents. Maybe, just maybe, her mother had been more concerned for the baby she was carrying than for herself when she'd made the decision that had ended so badly two decades later?

She tossed and turned for a long while, sleep a hundred miles away, but as dawn broke she knew that she had come to a decision which she had been putting off for too long. She would ask for leave and go and see her mother, perhaps at Christmas if that was possible. She needed to see her face to face and really understand her mother's state of mind all those years ago and how she had lived with herself once she'd made the decision she had – whether she'd had regrets, felt ashamed and guilty, and whether she had really loved her husband.

As she lay watching it grow lighter, she knew she was a different person to the innocent girl who'd left home all those months ago. Her time in the WAAF had made her more broad-minded and opened her eyes to many things. The social mix of girls from every conceivable walk of life had meant that she had soon dropped her conventional outlook – she'd had to. Biddy, one of the girls in their hut, had been working the streets of London's East End as a prostitute before she had joined up, having been put on the game by her father at the tender age of twelve. Another girl had been living in sin with her boyfriend before she had volunteered and it had been her choice, not his, having witnessed the unhappy life her mother had had with her father and been determined never to tie herself to one man legally. Another WAAF, Camilla, an upper-crust socialite, had admitted she'd only married her ridiculously rich husband on the understanding that theirs would be an open marriage: 'He's thirty years older than me, darling,' she'd drawled in her la-di-da voice after a few drinks one night in the hut, 'but still good-looking enough, although he hasn't got the stamina in the bed department, know what I mean? But he wanted me and Daddy was all for it – it was a step up the social ladder – so . . .' She had shrugged.

Her mother wasn't cut from the same cloth as Camilla and as Winnie had said, she would have been frightened and confused when she'd found out she was expecting a baby, expecting *her*. Maybe she'd really believed she was doing the right thing, and not just for herself and her unborn child but for her husband too? Certainly there'd been no more children so perhaps it had been his only chance of experiencing fatherhood?

Once the others began to stir, the process of helping poor Winnie scrub the shoe-blacking off her face took priority and it took all Bella's time to calm her friend down and convince her that no one would notice that her skin was a shade or two darker than usual. By the time that they went to the mess for breakfast she'd determined to ask for some leave that very day. She'd go and see William – the group captain, she corrected herself, she really mustn't keep thinking of him in personal terms – as soon as possible before she changed her mind.

William smiled as Bella walked into the room and asked her to sit down. He was exhausted, having flown on several sorties that had been harrowing in the extreme over the last week. They were losing less aircraft than the Luftwaffe but still the beggars kept coming, he thought with a touch of respect for the German pilots' dedication. 'How can I help you, Corporal?' he asked pleasantly, aware of a slight flush creeping over his face at the sight of her.

'I'd like to ask for some leave, sir.'

He nodded. 'Absolutely.' He wondered why she had come to ask him personally rather than just requesting it through the normal channels. Had she wanted to see him? And then that hope – ridiculous and inappropriate though it was – was dashed when she continued, 'The thing is, sir, I'd like at least ten days if that is possible? At Christmas? I – I wanted to go and see my mother.'

He remembered she had told him she was estranged from her mother. In fact, he remembered every single thing she had told him about herself. Quietly, he said, 'It's rather a long time, and at Christmas too. Is it important?'

She hesitated, and then said slowly, 'To me, yes. You probably won't remember but I told you some time ago that my mother and I haven't been in contact for a while. We have things to sort out and I don't want to leave it any longer, with the war and everything. The last time we parted it was on bad terms –' she stopped abruptly before continuing – 'or perhaps I should say that on my side it was on bad terms. I said some things I shouldn't have.'

'We all say things we shouldn't.'

'No, these were really bad things.' He was the last person in the world who she wanted to know about her past, so when she found herself continuing she didn't know why. She told him all of it, even about James, and he sat quietly the whole time without interrupting or saying anything.

When she'd finished she was staring down at her hands in her lap and he had to restrain himself from jumping up and taking her into his arms to comfort her. The inclination shocked him as much as if he had followed through on the impulse, revealing, as it did, that this woman meant a great deal more to him than she should. His voice soft, he said, 'You do realize that everything you have done and said is perfectly natural, don't you, and that no fault whatsoever with regard to James lies with you. You and he were the innocent parties in what was a tangled web of human relationships.'

He watched the colour spread over her face; then, her voice a whisper, she said, 'My head knows that, it's trying to convince my heart that's the problem. I feel –' she gulped in her throat – 'ashamed, I suppose, and guilty. If James and I hadn't fallen in love my father would still be alive.'

That was true, he acknowledged, desperately searching for something to say to help her. 'I can understand you thinking that way – it's inevitable, I suppose – but it's completely wrong because the events of what – twenty years before? – were the cause. Nothing you or James did was anything other than what people do when they fall in love. They want to be together, to announce it to the world.'

She stared straight into his face now as she asked, 'Have I shocked you?'

Neither of them was aware that she hadn't added the customary 'sir', but both knew that in the last moments something had changed. 'No, you haven't shocked me,' he said, his voice still soft. 'You haven't shocked me at all.'

'Lots of people would be.'

'Some, perhaps, but there will always be people who are simplistic and judgemental without knowing the true facts of a matter.'

'Yes, I suppose so.' She hesitated. 'We didn't – I mean James and I, we didn't . . . So that was a blessing,' she finished awkwardly, her face flaming again.

He knew he had absolutely no right to ask but he had to anyway. 'How do you feel about him now? Do you still love him?'

She looked away from him for a moment and then met his gaze again. 'Not in that way, no. I care about him, I don't want anything to happen to him of course, but it's different now – another thing I feel guilty about, to be truthful. I was so sure that he was the one for me at the time so how could I fall out of love so quickly? I never thought I was a shallow person—'

'You're not,' he said quickly, too quickly. His eyes dropped from hers and he cleared his throat. 'Getting back to the matter in hand, I'll clear your leave. Would going on the Friday before Christmas suit? It would mean you're back here on Monday the thirtieth?'

'Thank you, sir.' Protocol had been resumed.

'Good, good.' He nodded briskly and as she stood up he rose to his feet too. 'I hope all goes well when you see your mother,' he said, returning the salute Bella gave and watching her until she had left the room without looking back. Then he slumped in his seat, staring blankly ahead, lost in the depths of the revelation of what she'd confided.

One fact stood out from all she had said. She wasn't involved with anyone. How many times had he lain awake lately wondering if there was someone of her own class, some aristocrat or landowner that she had an understanding with? Nights when he'd thrown his greatcoat over his pyjamas and walked to the ablution block for a cold shower to alleviate the torment of his body when he'd imagined her in his bed. And she hadn't slept with this man who had turned out to be her half-brother. He knew he ought to be more glad for her than for himself but he'd be lying if he said he was.

And then he shook his head at himself. For crying out loud, what was he thinking? None of this made any difference. He didn't even know if she had feelings for him, and even if she did it was a non-starter. She was recovering from what must have been one hell of a body blow; he was still mourning a wife and child, and in civvy street they came from opposite sides of the social spectrum. And, not least, there was a damn war raging.

As though to emphasize the last point, the air-raid sirens began to wail their eerie cry, but instead of standing up and hurrying to one of the shelters he remained sitting at his desk. It would solve all his problems if a blast took him out, he thought grimly. No more fighting within himself about his attraction to a female officer under his command, and feeling like the most contemptible person on the planet when he pictured a small white coffin lying beside a larger one under the earth. He was a mess, he knew he was a mess and he wouldn't inflict that on any woman, much less one who had been through her own hell on earth. And besides all that, he'd had his time of crying, waves of sorrow crashing over his body with such force that he knew he would never be the same again. He didn't have anything to offer a woman and he didn't want to love again; to trust his fragile self-esteem to another human being. He had loved Hilda but she'd broken him long before she had died in the years before she'd become pregnant; humiliating him and grinding his pride into the dust because he couldn't give her a child.

He made a sound deep in his throat, angry at the self-pity which he despised.

Squaring his shoulders he stood up, pulling on his cap. He had a job to do.

Chapter Nineteen

On the long journey to the north-east by train and taxicab, Bella said not a word to her fellow passengers, her thoughts consuming her. Intermittent snow showers over the last days had made the countryside outside the train windows white, painting a pretty Christmas-card appeal to even the most industrial towns, but she was in such turmoil that nothing really registered. She was oblivious to the appreciative glances of more than one male, eating the sandwiches she had brought with her without tasting them and staring blankly out of the windows, her mind flitting between the forthcoming meeting with her mother and the last conversation she'd had with William. The former filled her with nervous trepidation and the latter with horror, and both made her feel physically sick.

How could she have told him about James and the rest of it? she asked herself for the hundredth time. She must have lost her reason. It had to be some sort of mental suicide, she decided. That was the only thing that made the remotest sense. He would look at her differently now – at the back of his mind he'd always be remembering what she'd revealed.

In the days leading up to her conversation with him she had decided to take some responsibility for her feelings about her mother and the whole scenario. To stop repressing and avoiding them. But that was a different kettle of fish to blurting out the whole sorry tale the way she had. She *must* be mad. It was the only answer.

By the time she arrived at Fellburn House she felt like a wrung-out rag. She hadn't let her mother know she was coming and she couldn't have said why. Perhaps it was because she needed to see her in her normal state of mind, whatever that was, without giving her mother the time to prepare some new fabrication or sob story.

One thing she knew for sure, Bella thought, as she stood at the bottom of the steps leading up to the front door of Fellburn with the snow settling on her head and shoulders, and that was that forgiveness wasn't easy. It suggested that she had to condone or forget what had happened to her father, neither of which she could do. The past wasn't gone. It lived on in every memory and recollection, good and bad. It couldn't be transcended or excised, it had to be faced and dealt with but could she do that? She still didn't know.

She walked slowly up the steps to the front door, wondering suddenly if she had done the right thing in coming home. She turned and looked for the taxicab that had brought her from the station, but it had already disappeared. The hushed silence of the snowy night settled around her, so different to the mayhem and constant noise of the base. In these surroundings you could almost believe that there wasn't a war.

She looked at the bell pull and still she hesitated. Was she going to make things a whole lot worse in coming home? For her mother as well as herself? Had it been sentimentality on her part after what Winnie had said about her mother that had driven her here? Winnie's mother wasn't her mother and her friend's experience of family had been different.

She was shivering but it wasn't with cold, and as she stood there with her bag at her feet she had never felt so small or alone. And then she straightened. She could either do this or walk away. It was as simple as that. She rang the bell.

It seemed aeons later, thousands upon thousands of years, that the door opened and Wright stood staring at her as though he couldn't believe his eyes. And then Bella found herself ushered into the hall, the old man taking her bag in spite of her protests that she could carry it herself. 'Oh, Miss Bella,' he kept repeating, his rheumy eyes full of tears, 'Miss Bella.'

She tried really hard not to cry herself but the butler's patent delight touched something deep inside and it went some way to melting the twisted knot inside her. Her voice soft, she said, 'Is my mother at home, Wright?'

'Indeed she is, miss. Come this way.'

As though she was a visitor, which she supposed she

was, she thought painfully, he led her towards the morning room, saying as he did so, 'Your mother doesn't use the drawing room any more, miss, not since the rest of the staff joined up. There's me and the cook and Mrs Banks left and we do our best but it's a big house as you know.'

She didn't reply; the fact that she was home was causing a whole host of emotions to surge through her. She wanted her father to be here, to hear his voice and see his eyes light up at the sight of her but that would never happen again.

And then Wright was opening the morning-room door after a perfunctory tap, still holding her bag as he said in ringing tones, 'It's Miss Bella, ma'am.'

Belinda had turned her head towards them but she didn't rise from the sofa on which she was sitting for a moment, staring at her daughter in disbelief. And when she did try to get up she almost fell backwards, causing Bella to spring forward and reach out to her before stopping some two feet away and standing still.

Behind them, Wright said, 'Can I get you anything, Miss Bella? Coffee? A snack?'

Without turning, she said, 'Coffee would be lovely, thank you, Wright. It – it's been a long journey.'

'Right you are, miss. And shall I take your bag up to your room?'

The question asked more than the mere words and she nodded, still without turning. 'Yes, please.'

In the few seconds before the morning-room door closed behind the old retainer, Bella saw that her mother had changed since she had last seen her. It wasn't just that she seemed to have aged ten years or more; her face was a dull, pasty white and she was thin, terribly thin. But her eyes were the same and they were looking at her with such love in the depths of them that Bella's throat closed. They continued to stare at one another for a split second more before Bella crossed the divide and knelt down beside the sofa. Her mother looked ill, very ill, and it frightened her. Taking one of her hands, she said softly, 'Hello, Mother.'

'You've come home.' It was a whisper.

'Yes, I thought we could spend Christmas together,' she managed to say past the huge lump in her throat.

Her mother became still. Her eyes were closed and now from under the compressed lids there appeared tears.

'Don't cry, please don't cry.' And then she too was crying, sobs that tore through both of them as she held her mother close without saying a word.

Some time later Wright came in with a tray of coffee and by then they were sitting side by side on the sofa, utterly spent. There was lots that had to be said, Bella knew that, but for now it was enough that she was home.

Christmas was a quiet affair. On Christmas Eve they drank mulled wine and ate mince pies that didn't have a trace of carrot in them. Where Cook had obtained the dried fruit for them and the pudding on Christmas Day, no one asked. She'd told her mother about Kitty and they remembered her in prayer before they went to their separate bedrooms.

On Christmas Day Bella awoke early, her heart heavy. She'd pulled the curtains back before she'd gone to sleep and now she lay and watched the snowflakes falling from a laden sky.

She had told her mother that she'd forgiven her and she had, but it was all still so painful, especially here at home. Her father's presence was everywhere. It seemed as though at any moment he would walk in. Perhaps everyone felt the same when a loved one was taken, and poor Winnie would be mourning her mother more than ever on this special day.

Throwing back the covers, Bella pulled on her thick dressing gown and walked across to the small armchair which stood in the bay of the window. Tucking her feet under her, she sat looking out at the snowy scene as she reflected on the last months. This was her home and yet now it felt strangely alien; she wasn't a part of it any more. The base was her life, with all its danger and hard work and constant noise and mayhem. It was too peaceful, too tranquil here. She missed Winnie and her other friends and – her heart thudded – and William.

She'd fallen in love with him; she couldn't fight the truth any more, she admitted to herself. Useless to try and explain it away by putting it down to a strong physical attraction; it was so much more than that. It was probably emotional suicide but she loved a man who had a reputation for being cold and arrogant and there was nothing she could do about it, even though he kept everyone firmly at arm's length.

But he hadn't with her, not always anyway, she thought in the next moment. Admittedly he hadn't told her anything about himself, but why would he? The disclosures had all come from her side, but as her commanding officer he would hardly pour out his heart to one of his WAAFs. Nevertheless, she'd seen a side to him she was sure none of the other girls had, or was she just fooling herself here? Probably, she told herself wearily.

The small fire that Mrs Banks had lit in the bedroom's ornate little fireplace the night before was just ashes now, but it had been enough to take the worst of the bitter chill off the room although when Bella breathed out it was a white cloud. The cold didn't prompt her to move, however. She let thoughts of William flood her mind; imagining what it would be like to be in his arms, to be loved by him, really loved.

Belinda knocked gently on the door of her daughter's bedroom before opening it. Bending, she picked up the tray holding two cups, a fine bone china teapot and milk jug and a plate of Cook's shortbread, and entered the room. Bella was sitting in a chair in the bay of the window.

'Happy Christmas, darling,' Belinda said softly, her heart full to bursting as Bella turned and smiled at her. Their heart-to-hearts over the last days had been crushing now and then but for the first time since Archibald's death she'd begun to hope that she might find a way forward through the guilt of the past. She didn't entertain even the possibility of freeing herself from it; it would always be with her, but if Bella could be part of her life again that would be enough.

Bella had told her more than once that she forgave her, and she believed her daughter had, but forgiving herself was something else entirely. She prayed every night to Archibald that he would forgive her for what she had done to him, telling him that if she had her time over again she would make a different choice, that she'd throw herself on his mercy and tell him about the few mad moments in Philip's study that had resulted in a small life growing inside her. She should have trusted in his innate kindness, his gentleness, his love, she knew that now. She had made the wrong choice and they'd all suffered because of it.

'Come and sit down,' Bella said, interrupting her train of thought as she indicated the other armchair in the bay.

She did as she was told after pouring them both a cup of tea and handing Bella hers with a shortbread biscuit in the saucer. Looking out into the snowy morning, she said, 'All the terrible things that are happening in the world and yet it looks so peaceful out there.' She took a deep breath. 'I need to tell you something – the eldest three Wynford boys have all been killed.' They hadn't mentioned Philip in the present sense, only referring to him when she had told Bella how things had played out on that Armistice Night, and she was aware of this when she added, 'And Felicity has left Philip.'

Bella was silent for a moment. Then she said, 'And James?'

'The last I heard he was with the army as a doctor somewhere abroad.'

Bella nodded. Trying to make his life make sense the way she had when she had joined up.

'He doesn't communicate with his father and only occasionally with Felicity.'

Again Bella nodded. So the colonel had lost all his family in one way or another? She didn't know if her mother expected her to feel sorry for him but she didn't, she wouldn't, she told herself fiercely. By his own admission in the letter he had written to her when she had still been in London before joining up, the colonel had seduced her mother that night. She didn't doubt for a moment that all he had been interested in was a brief gratification of the flesh, but with his friend's young wife? It was despicable. She hated him. She would always hate him. 'I'm sorry about Anthony and the others,' she said shortly.

Belinda took a sip of her tea. She recognized that she needed to change the subject by the tone of her daughter's voice. 'I thought we might go to church this morning if you'd like to?'

Bella hesitated. Like her parents, the Wynfords had always attended the parish church in the village when they weren't in London. It was expected. 'You go, but I'd prefer to stay home.'

'Then I'll stay with you. We can listen to some carols and have a sherry before lunch.'

'That'd be nice.' Bella glanced at her mother and then

reached out and took one of her hands. 'I do love you,' she said softly.

Belinda smiled a teary smile. 'I don't deserve it.'

'Yes, you do.' She squeezed her mother's thin fingers. 'It's time to stop punishing yourself now.'

She knew she would never be able to do that but it wouldn't help Bella to say so. She needed to mend and nurture her relationship with her child and part of that meant bearing her own pain and guilt and letting Bella get on with her life without worrying about her. She'd always been a weak person; all through their married life Archibald had wrapped her up in cotton wool and she had let him, enjoyed it, but that had to end once and for all. She had to take responsibility for herself, she realized, with sudden crystal-clear clarity, and that needed to start now, today.

Forcing a brightness into her voice, she said, 'You're right, of course. My wise little owl. I'm so proud of you, my darling, you know that, don't you? I know you can't tell me what it is that you do in the WAAF, but just that means it's something important and worthwhile. I was going to ask if you enjoy it but perhaps that's the wrong word in the circumstances?'

Bella nodded. She thought about the young Luftwaffe pilot who'd been shot down on the day that Winnie had gone to identify her mother, and all the other deaths she'd listened in on. 'It makes a difference,' she said quietly, 'but that has consequences.' She and the other girls never talked about the fact that they played a part in enemy planes being shot down by the RAF but they knew it was so. Nevertheless, they owed it to their country to behave with consummate professionalism and do the work to the best of their ability.

'Let's make a snowman this morning,' Belinda said suddenly, wanting to dispel the sad look that had come across Bella's face. 'Remember we used to do that every Christmas Day when we came home from church if there was any snow?'

Bella grinned. 'I do.' The three of them, she and her parents, had always topped the snowman off with one of her father's hats and scarves they kept for the occasion and an old pipe of his.

'I miss him,' Belinda said softly.

'Me too.'

They looked at each other, and in that moment Bella felt closer to her mother than she had ever done.

Bella travelled back to the base on the Monday after Christmas as had been arranged, and until she reached Hawkinge – which had become known as 'Hellfire Corner' in recent weeks – she was unaware that the Germans had chosen the previous night to try and set fire to the city of London. The raid had been planned with typical German thoroughness and timed to coincide with the tidal low point in the Thames; the water mains being severed at the outset by high-explosive parachute mines before ten thousand firebombs were unloaded.

Everyone was talking about it at the base and Winnie

told her that for a time the situation had raged out of control and the city had become an inferno as firemen were unable to use the mains supply or obtain water from the Thames. When the water came on again, supplied from more distant mains, the exhaust pipes of fire engines became red hot through the continued high-pressure pumping by twenty thousand firemen.

'Ernie Foster, the pilot who's going out with Biddy, was in London last night on a forty-eight-hour compassionate leave 'cause his parents were killed in a direct hit on their house on Boxing Day and he needed to sort out where his brothers and sisters were going to be housed,' Winnie said as Bella unpacked her bag in the hut. 'Apparently soldiers and civilians all mucked in to help. We've been told on base by the Air Ministry that the raid was broken off because the weather deteriorated unexpectedly over low-lying German airfields. Otherwise there'd be nothing left of London. It shows God's on our side, doesn't it,' she added. Winnie's mother had been a fervent churchgoer and Winnie had imbibed her impassioned belief in the Almighty with her mother's milk, although her faith had faltered for a while after her mother had been killed.

Bella said nothing. There were even more horrific, unbelievable reports emerging about the concentration camps that the Nazis had set up, and so many men, women and children were dying in this war. She just didn't know what she believed about God any more. Why didn't He smite Hitler and put an end to the devastation rather than let it continue month after month? It was something she'd brooded about on and off lately but was no nearer to finding an answer and so most of the time she put it on the back burner along with all the other things she didn't understand about the war, like why Kitty had been taken so young.

She and Winnie talked a little more before Winnie had to go on the night shift, but as Bella settled down in her narrow little bed in the hut where some other WAAFs were sleeping, she found she couldn't turn her mind off.

It was New Year's Eve tomorrow. 1941 was almost upon them and no doubt it would hold more heartache. She would be back at her post in the morning doing a job that was harrowing but necessary, she thought sadly. But would they win the war? They were just a small island desperately holding out against invasion, and the Third Reich was huge. It had become a monster, sweeping across countries like a stormcloud, raining down death and destruction wherever it touched. She shivered, but the icy chill was from within rather than without. For the first time she considered the possibility that they might become an enslaved people and it was terrifying.

And then, unbidden, some verses of her father's favourite hymn came into her mind:

God moves in a mysterious way
His wonders to perform;
He plants his footsteps in the sea,
and rides upon the storm.

Deep in unfathomable mines
of never-failing skill
He treasures up His bright designs
and works His Sovereign will.

Ye fearful saints, fresh courage take;
the clouds ye so much dread
are big with mercy and shall break
in blessings on your head.

Bella lay in the darkness as a sense of peace from somewhere outside of herself stole over her; she felt her father's presence and could almost smell the cigars he liked to smoke. '*Fresh courage take*,' she murmured softly. Yes, God was in the storm and He knew they were on the side of right not might. She didn't know why she had been feeling so low but she wouldn't give in to fear. And everything else in her life – the plans for the future she'd once thought so important; the uncertainty every day held; even this love for William that could never be – was out of her hands anyway, and in a strange way there was comfort in that.

She had gone to bed as though prepared for an expedition to the Arctic, wearing more clothes than she had worn in the day, and now she snuggled down under the thin RAF blankets on top of which was her greatcoat, and shut her eyes. As she fell asleep, the words of Winston Churchill in a speech he'd made in the summer reverberated in her head, and they seemed to be a confirmation that all was well although nothing had really changed:

'We shall defend our island, whatever the cost may be, we shall fight on the beaches, we shall fight on the landing grounds, we shall fight in the fields and in the streets, we shall fight in the hills: we shall never surrender.'

PART FIVE

Sunshine, Sand and Snakes

1941

Chapter Twenty

As the plane door opened, air that could have come from an oven burst in and Bella felt sand gritting her teeth. They'd been warned about the heat but it was hotter than she had ever imagined. Even after a week in Egypt she hadn't got used to it.

She, Winnie and Camilla had sailed from England in September after being medicated, lectured and equipped, and so secure had been the blanket of secrecy surrounding their departure that they hadn't been allowed to tell even their nearest and dearest where they were bound for.

They had already endured a sandstorm at Heliopolis when they'd first arrived at the station there which had been the first point of call after arriving in Egypt. The temperature had risen to boiling point and because the camp was under canvas most of the tents had been whipped away, and pandemonium had reigned for a while. The sandstorm had made a noise like the shrieking of a thousand lost souls and it had been utterly unnerving. Their temporary living quarters – a square hole dug in sand, baked hard by continuous wetting and drying with some steps down in local bricks and a tent on top – had left a lot to be desired. Three narrow iron beds had been squeezed into the small space and although these had survived the sandstorm intact, they'd been half-buried in the process.

The WAAFs' value as fluent German-speaking members of the Y Service had been proven during the Battle of Britain when they had intercepted transmissions between German bombers and their bases, but from May, after a night that had nearly taken the heart out of London when over five hundred German planes had indiscriminately dropped hundreds of high-explosive bombs and incendiaries in a few hours on the capital, bomber activity had gradually begun to slacken.

Rommel was creating havoc in French North Africa, however, and when Bella was asked if she was prepared to accept a new posting to Egypt, she agreed with alacrity. William had also asked her, when he called her into his office, to recommend two other WAAFs in Y Service who would accompany her in monitoring aerial threats to the troops in the desert. She'd had no hesitation in choosing Winnie and Camilla. They were the two girls she was closest to but moreover both were excellent at their job.

William's presence had been required urgently in Cairo and he had gone on ahead to liaise with the commander-in-chief a few weeks before. Ridiculously – and she knew it *was* ridiculous because she meant nothing to him beyond being extremely good at her job and running the section for him – she felt as though a light had gone out with his leaving. It hadn't fully dawned on her until he had gone but just the fact that she might catch sight of him in the day sometimes, even in the distance, brought a buzz of expectation that carried her through the most difficult and arduous of days. He had come and sat with her in the mess once to discuss a particularly sensitive situation concerning a married RAF officer and a young WAAF who was pregnant and had named the officer as the father, which the man in question was vehemently denying. The WAAF was part of Bella's section and William had wanted her view on the matter. She'd been inordinately pleased he'd trusted her enough to talk in confidence about it, but sitting drinking coffee with him in a relaxed setting had upset her equilibrium for days.

Bella thought of this now as they left the plane for the jeep that was waiting for them. They'd been told they'd be the only airwomen on camp and that living conditions would be basic, but that paled into insignificance beside the fact that she'd be within sight and sound of William again. Thank goodness no one could read her mind, she told herself ruefully, especially William. She would die a thousand deaths if he ever suspected her true feelings.

When they arrived at the camp expecting a repetition of their sleeping quarters at Heliopolis, Bella was pleasantly surprised. Although the airmen were in tents, a small hut had been constructed within a little fenced compound for them and it included a very basic brick ablution facility. There was a cold-water shower and a lavatory whose 'flush' went into a tank sunk into the floor, which they were told one of the Egyptian workers would empty and disinfect weekly. The interior of the hut was spartan: iron beds with thin, biscuit-type mattresses and a shelf over them with hooks from which to hang things; bomb boxes at the foot of each to store possessions and windows of fine wire mesh for ventilation.

The sergeant who'd taken charge of them and shown them to the hut didn't seem over-pleased to see them, his weathered, sunburnt face surly as he said, 'Proper VIPs, you lot are. Your group captain had my men working flat out to get all this ready in time. Right tartar, he is.'

Bella eyed the man coldly. William had told her before he had left for Egypt that morale was low there and the working conditions terrible. They were to take over from some RAF personnel who had been injured and were awaiting repatriation to the UK, and she understood that the sergeant had probably been through hell, but this was William he was criticizing. 'I'll pass your opinion on when I speak to him, shall I?' she said, her voice sweetly poisonous.

He glared at her. 'I'm just saying, that's all.' He turned away, muttering something under his breath that finished with 'no place for damn women', but they ignored him. Once he'd gone, they stood looking around them. The air had been desiccated outside and wasn't much better in the hut. Bella wondered if she could ask William to have an electric ceiling fan installed at some point but they'd have to manage for now.

'Home, sweet home.' Winnie plumped down on one of

the beds, which didn't give an inch. 'I didn't expect the red carpet but that sergeant was a bit much, wasn't he.'

Bella nodded. In spite of the way that women in all the services and in civilian life too were proving themselves, there were still some men like the sergeant who were determined to view the female sex as a liability.

'Darling, the poor man's probably frustrated,' Camilla drawled in her languorous way. 'No little wifey to see to his carnal needs and all that.'

Winnie grinned. 'You've got a one-track mind, Cammy.'

'Maybe.' Camilla took off her cap and ran her fingers through her blonde curls, sitting down on the middle bed as she said, 'It was sweet of the group captain to get this organized for us, wasn't it.' She cast a sly glance at Bella. Camilla didn't miss much and she rather suspected there was some kind of attraction between the group captain and Bella. Subtle, almost undetectable, but there nonetheless. She knew better than to say anything to Bella, though, adding, 'Shows he cares about us and all that,' and watching Bella for her reaction.

Winnie snorted. 'He knows we'll work better if we get some sleep at night, that's all.'

'Oh, darling. You're so cynical.'

'Pot calling kettle, Cammy,' said Winnie easily.

'Me?' Camilla opened her eyes wide and pouted. 'I'm just a naive, trusting soul. An innocent little lamb in this big, bad world.'

Winnie gave another snort. 'And Adolf Hitler is really Father Christmas.'

Camilla put her hand theatrically on her heart. 'I'm wounded.'

Bella was only half-listening to the two rib each other. The sergeant had told her that as corporal in the hut and therefore in charge, she would be required to report to Group Captain Crawford in half an hour to receive instructions. It was taking all of her self-control not to dash over to the station commander's office, which William was apparently sharing, this very minute.

She began to put her things away, deep in thought. Over the last little while she had done nothing but tell herself that she was being ridiculous and acting like a schoolgirl to believe herself in love with him. She didn't even really know the man for a start, not properly, and what she did know wasn't exactly conducive to them getting along on a personal level. Besides which, and this was probably the crux of the matter, he'd given no indication that he was attracted to her.

'You all right, Bella?'

She became aware that Winnie was staring at her and quickly forced a smile. 'Fine, just fine.' And she was, as long as she didn't let her heart rule her head, she told herself firmly.

'So are your quarters comfortable enough for the time being? Not exactly the Ritz, I know.'

'They're fine, sir.'

'Good, good.' Considering he had been anticipating this meeting all morning, William knew he was making a hash of it. Just seeing her again had thrown him. He waved at the chair in front of the desk. 'Sit down, Corporal. Would you like some coffee? That's one thing they do well here as long as you like it strong and black.'

She didn't. 'I'm all right, thank you, sir.'

'Good journey?'

She nodded.

'Right.' He cleared his throat. 'Well, as you know, you and the other girls will be monitoring aerial threats to our troops. Rommel is a force to be reckoned with and this backlash against the Germans on the ground in Libya, Morocco and Egypt is strategically important. Of course, what we really need is for America to stop prevaricating and nail their colours to the mast, but as yet –' he shrugged – 'there are too many isolationist forces encouraging the president to stay out of the war. It's all very well for Roosevelt to say he'll do everything in his power to crush Hitler and the Nazis, but words without action are meaningless.'

'Yes, sir.' She wondered if he knew that her heart was only just beginning to stop pounding after her first sight of him.

'The Nazi noose is tightening around Leningrad and it won't be long until Hitler enters the gates of Moscow but we can fight them here and make a difference. It's vital work and therefore hellishly dangerous.' He hadn't wanted her here for that reason and yet he knew she had better experience in the work than any of her male colleagues. Special Signals Intelligence was saving lives and he couldn't argue with that; he just didn't want Bella put in jeopardy, but of course he had been unable to voice that to his superiors. They'd wanted the best the RAF had got out here and that was Bella and the other WAAFs.

'I understand, sir.' She hesitated. She knew their location was known to the enemy and in Heliopolis she and the others had seen things which had shocked them. The three of them had visited one of the medical wards before they'd left to try and offer comfort and a cheery face to some of the patients in the hope that hearing news from home might work as a tonic. Many of the invalids had had desert sores caused by the terrible swarms of flies that settled on and infected any exposed wound, and even in the hospital sand was all-pervading. It got into the sheets, the dressings, into all the interstices of the men's bodies, between broken limbs and the plasters that encased them. Bedbugs added their own form of torture to burnt and gangrenous flesh and diseases like sandfly fever, dysentery and even diphtheria were evident.

'We know the risks,' she said. When men were suffering so horribly, how could she and the others *not* do what they could? The nurses they'd seen had been amazing and it was clear that calls were made on them that far exceeded the confines of physical care. All too often anxious men, fearfully mutilated, would call upon them to boost their male self-respect by flirting with them and asking them for a kiss, and they always obliged.

'If a kiss can make a man face himself again in the

mirror, why not?' one of the nurses had said to her who worked on a ward for seriously burnt patients. 'I give them with all my heart and it's just part of the service.'

These women were the real female heroes of the war, Bella told herself now. Exhausted, often as not, but still keeping themselves bright and clean and kindness itself for their patients, joking and laughing even if their patients' courage so incapacitated them that they had to flee to a quiet place and let the tears flow.

'What is it?'

She came back to herself to see William staring at her, his grey eyes narrowed. Quickly, she said, 'Nothing, I was just thinking of the hospital in Heliopolis, that's all.'

'And?'

He wasn't going to let it go. 'The men are so brave despite everything they've gone through and the nurses are magnificent.'

He nodded, his eyes intent on her face.

'We went to visit and they were telling us of all the horrors they hear about in the course of their work – tank crews trapped in burning vehicles, awful maiming by mines, and – and oh, so much more.' She shook her head. 'I don't know how they do it. Every day watching patients they've grown fond of dying and all the time working flat out dressing wounds, taking temperatures, administering medicines and trying to instil hope where there is none.'

'There's all different kinds of bravery,' he said softly.

'Yes, I suppose so.' She was aware that the conversation

had developed an intimacy that wasn't in keeping with what would be expected between a group captain and a corporal, or perhaps it wasn't the conversation at all but more the way they were looking at each other? She forced a shaky laugh. 'It just makes what I do seem very tame.'

'You have willingly put yourself in the front line – that's far from tame.'

There was a knock on the door and one of the Egyptian workers entered, carrying a tray on which reposed a pot of coffee and two cups. He placed it on the desk, saying, 'Your coffee, sir,' and giving a funny little bow before leaving, but not before Bella noticed the sidelong glance at her. In spite of herself she found her cheeks were hot.

'Sure you won't have a cup?'

William seemed completely at ease and she found it acutely annoying even as she recognized she was being ridiculous. Nevertheless, it goaded her into saying, 'Actually, sir, I will.'

There followed a moment or two of silence while he poured them both a cup and passed Bella hers, the smell pervading the office. She took a sip and tried not to wince; it was so strong she was sure she could have stood a spoon up in it.

'I've arranged for some daily labour to keep your living quarters and washing facility clean. The Egyptian attitude to women leaves something to be desired so if you run into any trouble let me know. The labour gang mostly consists of young boys and if they can avoid work, they will.'

She smiled. 'I can be quite forceful when I want to be, sir.'

'Of that I have no doubt,' he said lazily, smiling back.

Her traitorous heart had only just calmed down and now raced again.

'You and the others will be working in the administration office next door to this building, and both myself and the station commander should be on hand if you need us.'

'Right, sir.' At least the office accommodation was solidly built and had electric fans, which might help a little with the intense heat.

'There are two guard dogs that patrol with their handlers at night around the security fence, and you girls will be eating in the warrant officers' and sergeants' mess with other officers. Some of the drivers here are German prisoners of war. I'd prefer you have no conversation with them for several reasons, the main one being that only myself and the station commander and the remaining personnel in the administrative office know that you speak fluent German and the purpose you're here for. As far as anyone else is concerned you've merely been drafted in to help with the administrative side of things.'

'Yes, sir.'

'I know there's no need to remind you and your WAAFs that your work is highly confidential but I'm doing it anyway,' William continued quietly. 'And just be aware that although the Egyptian workforce should be loyal, one can never assume anything. They live hand to mouth and the temptation to earn extra money for their families must be considerable.'

She nodded. She'd had to force down the last sip of coffee and her mouth felt coated inside. 'Is there anything else, sir?'

'Nothing except to say that I'm here and please bring any problems that you and the others might encounter to me personally. Incidentally, I've arranged for fans to be fitted in your sleeping quarters. Ideally it would have been done before you arrived but everything takes ten times longer here.' He smiled again. 'But then I've never been known for my patience.'

Bella stood up, hoping she didn't look as flustered as she felt. 'Thank you, sir.'

'Take some time to familiarize yourselves with your new surroundings before you begin work tomorrow. You and your girls will be working eight-hour shifts, by the way. I want an operative listening in at all times. I'll leave you to sort that, Corporal.'

'Yes, sir. Thank you, sir.' She saluted and left the office, and once outside in the sweltering heat stood for a moment to regain her equilibrium. Bring any problems to him? she thought with dark humour. If he did but know it, the biggest problem she was likely to have was William himself.

Chapter Twenty-One

Over the next weeks, Bella, Winnie and Camilla settled in to their new environment. On trips into town, Egyptian cigarettes, cheap petrol, unwashed humanity, exotic perfumes and frying chippattis and other street food all created a smell that Bella would associate for the rest of her life with hot foreign climes, along with the scent of the thick cream they plastered on their faces to keep their skin from drying out in the intense heat and the amazing saffron skies at night in the desert.

Bella had the battle with the Egyptian labour force that William had predicted, and which she won hands down with a mixture of firmness and bribery by the means of a weekly bar of chocolate if the work was done to her satisfaction. She knew a smattering of the language and with her prowess in that realm soon was able to understand it and speak it enough to control the little gang of Arab boys. They were quickly forced to recognize that they couldn't pull the wool over her eyes. One of them, Achmed, took it upon himself to be her right-hand man and make sure the others did their work properly, but she didn't fool herself that it was respect for her that instigated this, more the weekly bar of chocolate and his natural inclination to boss the others about.

It had clearly been a shock to the airmen to have three WAAFs disturb their bachelor existence but apart from the sergeant and a couple of other old diehards, most of the men made it clear that they were very happy about the situation. There was a great deal of flirting that went on with Winnie and Camilla and the airmen, but Bella kept herself to herself on the whole. When she knew that Camilla had become involved with one of the pilots she had a word with her friend about security and not giving any hint of why they'd been brought to Egypt.

'Darling girl,' Camilla had drawled, 'the last thing we talk about is work. In fact we don't do much talking at all, to be frank,' she'd added with a lascivious wink and a little giggle.

At the beginning of December the Japanese bombed Pearl Harbor a day after President Roosevelt appealed personally to Japan's Emperor Hirohito to avoid war with the US. Hundreds of Japanese war planes made a massive surprise attack on the US Pacific Fleet in its home base in Hawaii, as well as American bases in the Philippines and on Guam and Wake islands in the middle of the Pacific. A peaceful Sunday afternoon was shattered as the planes caught the US Navy completely unawares and in two hours sank or seriously damaged five battleships, fourteen smaller ships and two hundred aircraft, killing over two and a half thousand people and injuring hundreds.

The next day, on the eighth of December, William called Bella into his office to put her fully in the picture as to what was happening amid all the rumours flying around the camp. His face grim, he told her to be seated before he said, 'I wanted to let you know that Britain has declared war on Japan today along with declaring war on Finland, Romania and Hungary, who've failed to respond to ultimatums that they stop military operations in support of the German armies. America's now entered the war at last – of course they had no option to do otherwise after the bombing of Pearl Harbor. I understand from my superiors that the Japanese prime minister has undertaken to purge Anglo-American influence in the Far East once and for all.' He paused, and then said quietly, 'We live in unholy times, Bella.'

He had never used her Christian name before, and he must have gathered she was known as Bella rather than Mirabelle. This registered as much as what he had told her. She nodded, flushing, as she said, 'This is grave, isn't it, sir, for our people in South East Asia.'

'It would be worse if Japan hadn't made the mistake of attacking the US and bringing them into the war. They will find they've got a tiger by the tail. But yes, it's grave.' He sighed. 'After the First World War and the devastation and loss of life it caused, most people thought it would never happen again. This will be catastrophic on an unimaginable scale.'

She nodded. 'It makes you realize that things that have happened before in your life seem petty compared to such worldwide tragedy.' And then, suddenly realizing what she had said, she stammered, 'I didn't mean you – I wasn't referring to your – your wife and—'

'I understood what you meant,' he interrupted.

'I was talking about me,' she said, her face scarlet. 'I didn't mean to imply—'

'Relax, Bella,' he said softly. Damn it but she was beautiful. He should never have allowed her to be brought out here, she'd have been safer in England. 'And I agree with you in part. Of course personal loss or grief is just that, personal, which is why it affects the human soul so deeply. When – when my wife died it was hard but my daughter –' he shook his head – 'that was something else. That tiny coffin . . .'

'I'm so sorry, sir,' she whispered.

They looked at each other steadily for a moment, both knowing that a line had been crossed; then William merely nodded. He had to bring this back to a professional status – what the hell was he thinking, talking to her like this? He cleared his throat. 'I think that's all for now, Corporal. I'll leave you to tell your two WAAFs the situation. Of course it won't really affect us here short term, but I wanted to let you know what was happening.' What he'd really done was to seize on an excuse to see her alone again face to face, he told himself angrily, which was as stupid as it was improper.

She had stood up as he was speaking. 'Yes, sir, thank

you. I'll let the others know.' Considering how she was feeling she was amazed her voice was so calm and brisk, but once outside the office she bit down hard on her bottom lip, tears hovering. His face when he'd spoken of his daughter . . . And she'd been so insensitive. How could she have said what she'd said? She simply hadn't thought, but she should have.

She had just come off a shift when she'd gone into William's office and she knew Winnie was working and Camilla was sleeping in the hut, so she made her way to the mess, oblivious for once of the burning sun. This was what came of lowering your guard for even a minute and letting another human being infiltrate your defences, she told herself bitterly, as she got herself a coffee and a biscuit. It made you feel rubbish and just proved that the decision she'd made to be autonomous was the right one.

Nevertheless, as she sat sipping the coffee, the look in his grey eyes as he'd stared at her after talking about his child was burned into the screen of her mind. It confirmed what she had been trying to ignore since the first day she had met him. He liked her. And that made everything a hundred times more complicated.

In the run-up to Christmas several things of importance occurred on the world front: the Japanese invaded Malaya and the Philippines, and Hitler and Mussolini declared war on the US. Japan's lightning advance in South East Asia reached Hong Kong, and the garrison of British and

Commonwealth troops was hopelessly outnumbered but putting up a brave fight in the week before Christmas.

Their situation put a damper on any celebrations at the camp in Egypt, and Bella and the others had to fight daily against allowing themselves to become despondent and afraid by the way the war seemed to be going.

She had purposely avoided William since the conversation in his office but that didn't mean that she didn't live in a state of heightened awareness, which in itself was exhausting. Camilla, on the other hand, was as happy as the day was long with her new RAF beau, who apparently was also married.

'It's not infidelity,' Camilla drawled comfortably when Winnie challenged her one day. 'Nicholas knows I need rumpy-pumpy and he wouldn't expect me to go without. It keeps me happy, after all. I'm his wife and it's his rings I'm wearing but when I'm over here and he's in England . . .' She shrugged. 'Anyway, he turns a blind eye at home so actually this is even better for him, and if our getting together sends Martin off with a smile on his face when he's flying over enemy territory that's all to the good.'

'I doubt his wife would agree,' Winnie said flatly.

'Darling, she's probably doing the same.'

'Cammy, you don't know that.'

'Well, if she isn't, she's a fool. No one can expect a man to be faithful in a war. Martin loves her and she loves him and this is just sex between us, after all. It won't hurt anyone.'

Winnie had related the conversation she'd had with

Camilla to Bella one day when they were in the hut together, shaking her head as she'd said, 'Now I'm no angel as you know, but if I have some fun I always make sure that the man in question isn't married or engaged or anything and that he knows the score – no strings attached, precautions a necessity or no deal and that it's easy come, easy go on both sides.'

Bella had nodded, but when she'd thought about it she wasn't sure that Winnie's ideology was any better than Camilla's. It all seemed so unemotional and contrived somehow for what should surely be something special? But perhaps she was the one who was out of step in this world that had changed so radically in the last couple of years? Everyone seemed to be living for the moment, knowing each day could be their last, and she could understand that; it made sense. Nevertheless, when she gave herself to a man love would have to be involved, so where did that leave her if she wasn't prepared to commit emotionally? After she'd made her head ache thinking about it she decided enough was enough. The future would sort itself out and she wasn't going to worry about it.

A few days before Christmas she got a letter from her mother saying that James had been badly injured and had died shortly after being shipped back to England. His parents had been with him, she wrote, and there had been some kind of reconciliation between him and his father before he'd drawn his last breath. Philip was devastated, of course, with all four of his sons gone and his marriage to Felicity over.

She sat in the hut and cried for some time, feeling bereft. All the 'might-have-beens' and 'what-ifs' swirled through her mind as well as the pain and sorrow that a young life had ended so tragically. They'd loved each other once; in fact, she still did love James, but not in the same way she once had. Of necessity, when she'd found out the truth, her love had begun to change, but she'd harboured a secret hope that some time in the future they'd meet and lay old ghosts to rest. Be friends, love each other as sister and brother even. But now it was too late. He had gone.

Winnie found her after a little while. She silently passed her friend the letter, tears still streaming down her face, and after Winnie had read it she sat down and hugged her. They hadn't discussed James since the day she had told Winnie about her past months ago.

As Bella dried her tears with a handkerchief Winnie had passed her, she said quietly, 'This war, Winnie. What's going to be left at the end of it?'

'I don't know.'

'It's monstrous, isn't it.'

Winnie nodded. 'My mum used to say that for evil to abound all it took was for good men and women to say and do nothing. Well, we're not doing nothing, we're doing *some*thing, and that's what James and all the others have died for. I hope Hitler and Mussolini and the rest of them get what's coming to them soon, but until that happens we fight on. That's the way I see it.'

'You're right.' And they had to keep believing that they

would win the war, because anything else was unthinkable. James and his brothers and the rest of the men, women and children who were sacrificing their lives deserved it.

Winnie was reading the letter again and now she said slowly, 'Bella, do you get the impression that your mother feels sorry for Philip Wynford? Or is it me? Perhaps I'm reading it wrong? What do you think?'

'What?' Bella took the letter back. She had only been concerned with the news about James but now as she reread her mother's words, she said grimly, 'She can't be, not after what he did and what happened to my father because of him. It's awful about the boys but she can't feel anything for him personally, can she?'

Winnie was wishing she had thought before she'd spoken. 'No, I'm sure she doesn't. It's probably that she knew his boys and all of them being killed has affected her too. That's only natural, isn't it.'

Bella stared at her friend. 'Because of that man my father's dead and James and I were separated. If I thought my mother felt anything for him I'd never speak to her again.'

Her eyes returning to the page in her hand, she read it once more. The Colonel had wrecked all their lives and in a way he was responsible for what had happened to James. James would never have joined up if he had been married to her and working as a doctor in a poor district where he was desperately needed. She knew he wouldn't have.

'The colonel's one of those men who's dubbed a nice fellow by everyone,' she said slowly, 'the sort who gets on with other men and charms all the ladies. He's got a way with him, he always has had. I thought he was lovely when I was growing up. Surely, though, my mother can see through him now regardless of what's happened with his sons?'

'Of course she can.'

Bella nodded, still staring at the letter, her stomach beginning to churn as she wondered what was happening back at home. It was so far away, and the trouble was that much as she loved her mother, there was no denying that as a person she was weak and easily led. Her mother had once told her that her grandfather had governed her mother's actions and decisions before she was wed and after that, her husband. Even the brief interlude with the colonel had happened because essentially her mother had allowed a will stronger than hers to dictate to her. But surely, *surely*, her mother wouldn't be so stupid now?

Winnie was staring at her with concern, and Bella shrugged, saying with a calmness she didn't feel inside, 'It really is of no account one way or the other, is it, not when you think about what folk are going through in this war and what's happening in the world. Our little problems don't matter and besides, I can't do anything here, so it's no use worrying about it.'

'I suppose so,' Winnie said doubtfully, not convinced by Bella's manner in the slightest. 'You're not going to write to your mum and say anything, are you?'

Bella shook her head. 'I'll wait till I see her again and find out what's what then.'

Winnie nodded, relieved. 'Better face to face.'

Bella stood up. 'I'd better go and relieve Cammy. Don't mention this to her, about James. It's between the two of us, all right?'

'Of course.'

Once she was outside the hut, the blistering heat and dust made England seem even more distant. Nevertheless, Bella found thoughts of her mother intruding for the rest of the day. She told herself that her mother and the colonel weren't answerable to her, that they were grown adults after all, but that didn't help. When she finished her shift and Winnie replaced her, she left the office with the weight of the world on her shoulders.

She walked straight into William without even seeing him, deep in thought as she was, and as the impact nearly sent her flying backwards he caught her arm to steady her. 'I'm sorry,' they both said at the same time, and then as he smiled she tried to do the same but to her horror burst into tears.

His smile wiped away, he said, 'Hey, hey, what is it?'

She shook her head, attempting to move away, but he was holding her arm and wouldn't let her. Through her tears, she mumbled, 'It's nothing really.'

'Now that I doubt,' he said softly, his deep, faintly husky voice concerned. 'Come on, come and have a cup of coffee and talk to me.'

'No, not inside.' She didn't want to be where other people were because she knew she wouldn't be able to control the tears yet.

'All right, let's walk a bit.' He was still holding her arm and he led her across the sandy expanse of the camp square and towards the man-made garden at the side of the warrant officers' and sergeants' mess. This had been established before Bella and the other WAAFs had arrived when tons of soil had been brought in and dumped on the sand to a height of five feet. It was a blaze of colour in the day with flowers and shrubs, and at night several of the plants perfumed the air with a sweet scent. A couple of benches had been made in the little oasis and the Arab boys watered the vegetation several times a day. William had told her in the past that the RAF officer who had instigated the project had been a keen gardener before he'd joined up, and had wanted to bring a little sanctuary of England into the harsh desert surroundings. He'd been killed just as the garden was completed.

Once they were seated they sat for a few moments in silence, Bella wiping her eyes with the crisp white handkerchief William had passed her. The midnight marvel of the African sky hung above them, blazing stars set in indigo depths which mixed now and then with the homing lights of aeroplanes arriving at the base. It was very warm despite the late hour, and the perfume surrounding them was heady. After she'd composed herself somewhat, Bella said, 'You were working late?'

'I often do.' He didn't add that he always found it difficult to sleep, not so much because of the heat although that was a factor but more because of his thoughts. His voice soft, he added, 'I sometimes come and sit here for a while – it's soothing to the senses, isn't it.'

She nodded. One of the Arab boys had told her in his broken English that it was considered a prize when they were on what he called garden duty. She understood most of the local labourers were from a village close to the camp where mud houses roofed with date palm fronds plastered with mud was the order of the day. She'd asked him what he normally ate after she'd seen a small sack containing dates tied round his waist, and he'd told her that although some of the villagers grew barley and wheat along with onions, dates were the main staple of their diet. His mother made *bazin* from barley flour which she kneaded into dough and they ate it uncooked, but that was for the family evening meal, and always with dates. After that she'd often slipped the boys some biscuits or cake from the mess, which had added greatly to her popularity. It was a harsh existence for the boys and she could imagine that working in the green and scents of the garden after being surrounded by great stretches of desert would be appealing.

'I don't want to intrude, but if something is troubling you would it help to talk about it?' he said after a few seconds.

'I – I had a letter from home, from my mother.'

'Ah.'

'James has been killed,' she said flatly, 'and it made me realize that somehow I always felt he would survive the war and that we could perhaps meet in the future as friends.'

'You still love him.' It was a statement not a question.

'No. Yes. I mean –' she took a breath – 'not in the way I did, I'm sure about that, but as, well, as a brother I suppose. And now the way it finished can never be put right, if you know what I mean.'

'I think so.' He hesitated and then turned towards her. 'But perhaps if the nature of his love hadn't changed it would have been too painful for him anyway?'

She stared at him in the shadowed darkness. 'I hadn't thought of that,' she admitted after some moments.

She had no idea how captivating she was, William thought wryly. He doubted if this poor bloke would ever have been able to get her out of his system.

'But it wasn't altogether James dying.'

'No?'

'My mother said how devastating it was for the colonel, his last son being killed after the other three, and of course it would be, but—'

'But what?'

'The tone of what she'd written, it suggested . . . Oh, I don't know. The colonel's wife's left him and they're getting a divorce.'

He shifted slightly on the bench, looking out into the black night again as he said softly, 'You think there may be something between your mother and him? Is that what you're saying?'

'I – I suppose so. I mean, what happened in the past . . .' She took another deep breath before she could say, 'It's a link, isn't it. They liked each other then. And – and when it all came out and he said it was all his fault, my mother wouldn't have that. He didn't force her, that's what I mean.'

'I see.'

'My father died because of him,' she said bitterly. 'I'd never forgive my mother if she started a relationship with him.'

'Never is a long time.'

'*Not for me.*' She'd shouted at him but she didn't apologize, repeating in a quieter tone, 'Not for me. It would be as though my father's memory meant nothing to her. What they did has hurt so many people, it would be like saying that they don't care about any of that.'

'But you don't know if they do care for each other in that way. I remember you told me that growing up, the two families were quite friendly? Perhaps that's all it is? Friendship? And pity on your mother's part, now his sons are no more.' He didn't state the obvious, that this man's only surviving child was her, but it hung in the air between them. She'd talked about a link but that fact was a darn sight more than some tenuous connection. He could understand why she didn't want to acknowledge that the man who had loved her and brought her up as his daughter wasn't her real father, but the truth was he wasn't and this colonel fellow was. And it was ironic that this very thing was a bond between her mother and the man in question, considering Bella's hatred of him.

'It could be,' she said, quietly now.

'But you don't think so.'

'I don't know.' Her voice broke as a mist of tears blurred her vision. 'But I'm frightened.'

He wanted to gather her up in his arms, to kiss her and make love to her until nothing else mattered in the world, but in the next instant she had stood up, saying, 'Thank you for listening but I shouldn't have bothered you. You've enough on your plate as it is. I understand we lost three men today.'

He nodded, rising to his feet. 'I'm afraid so.' One of them, Squadron Leader Stewart, he'd known from before the war and counted as a friend. Lionel had been there for him when Hilda and then Joy had died in a way others hadn't. 'We need to facilitate our troops on the ground but everything comes at a cost,' he said levelly.

'I'm sorry.' In spite of his demeanour she felt the deaths had had more of an impact than he was letting on. Then, without considering her words, she spoke from the heart. 'Do you think we've got any chance of winning this war, sir?'

He looked at her in the pocket of England, the Egyptian night all around them. 'I don't let myself consider anything else,' he said simply. 'We will win, end of story.'

She nodded. It was the answer she had needed. 'Goodnight, sir.'

'Goodnight, Corporal.' She soon disappeared into the darkness but he continued to stare after her for some time before sitting down again, reaching in his pocket for his cigarettes.

Chapter Twenty-Two

Christmas came and went, and any celebrations were dampened by the way the war was going. President Roosevelt's words about the assault on Pearl Harbor – '*Our enemies have performed a brilliant feat of deception, perfectly timed and executed with great skill*' – had resonated with Bella and many others, and over Christmas Japan's lightning advance in South East Asia saw Hong Kong falling to the enemy. After a seven-day battle on the island, the hopelessly outnumbered defenders – six thousand in all – were compelled to surrender unconditionally. In the final stages of the battle, the infantry battalions were facing two entire Japanese divisions, a force estimated at forty thousand men, and with the colony's reservoirs in enemy hands and the garrison down to twenty-four hours' supply of water, the odds were overwhelming.

On New Year's Eve everyone got a little tiddly and sang 'Boogie-Woogie Bugle Boy' and the 'White Cliffs of Dover' in the mess, somewhat cheered by the reports of

Winston Churchill's fighting speech to both houses of the US Congress on Boxing Day. His Christmas visit to Washington appeared to be rousing American opinion to a new level of enthusiasm in supporting Britain's war effort, which everyone agreed couldn't be a bad thing. According to newspaper accounts the Prime Minister had made full use of his oratorical powers, striking all the right notes including copious quotations from Abraham Lincoln and mentioning his own American mother.

'He's a wily old bird,' was Winnie's summing-up of Churchill's trip to the US and Bella had to agree with her. The Churchill–Roosevelt personal relationship had apparently never been closer and it was yielding dividends for Britain. On the other hand, as the New Year unfurled, her own personal relationship with William – if it ever had merited such a description – couldn't have been worse. And it was her own fault, she reflected miserably. Partly at least. And all due to the island of Malta.

From early on in the war the island had been of key importance in controlling the sea route across the Mediterranean, vital to maintaining Axis supply lines. This Allied base was a thorn in the side of the German command and Rommel had realized its significance, meaning the Luftwaffe bombed Malta remorselessly. Air raids were constant, the island was in a state of siege and in danger of starvation, and as Bella saw it, she *had* to go to Malta. The monitoring staff on the island were insufficient and under-trained in dealing with the quantity of radio/telephone message traffic from the numerous

German bombers threatening it and things were getting worse. There were the Queen Alexandra nurses at the hospital, but no WAAFs or other servicewomen.

In the first week of the new year she had gone to see William, requesting that she be sent to the island as she had better experience in this vital work than any of the male RAF personnel there. He had listened to her without speaking and then flatly refused to consider such a notion. 'Out of the question,' he'd said firmly. 'All servicewomen, apart from the QAs, have been evacuated and for good reason.'

She'd stared at him, more than a little taken aback. 'I'm part of the RAF. My being a female shouldn't matter if I'm qualified to do a particular job better than anyone else who's available.'

'You've got no idea what it's like there. The island is being pulverized.'

'I know that, which is why I could be of help.'

'Absolutely not.'

'But that's ridiculous. I believe I could help to save lives—'

'And lose your own in the process?' he interrupted coldly, his grey eyes icy.

'So it's all right for a man, perhaps a married man with children, to die doing their job but not a single woman like me? That doesn't make sense and you know it. I'm needed out there. I'm far more experienced than any of the men, which is why I came over here in the first place.'

'Permission denied, Corporal.'

She glared at him, her temper boiling at his high-handed manner. 'I can't believe you're being so unreasonable,' she bit out furiously. 'You're seriously telling me that you're prepared to sacrifice lives I could help save because of some outdated misogynistic views you have about women?'

'That's enough.' He didn't raise his voice but his tone was deadly.

'I don't think so, *sir*,' she added venomously. 'I don't think it's nearly enough.'

'*Corporal*.'

And to think that she had imagined herself in love with this man, she thought through her blazing anger. He hadn't listened to her, not really. She had seen his face change with the first few words she'd spoken when she'd come into the office, disapproval and condemnation etched all over his features. So what if there were no other WAAFs on the island, or any other servicewomen, come to it – that was neither here nor there. How dare he dismiss her out of hand simply because of her sex? 'I need to be there,' she said stubbornly, holding on to her temper with a huge effort of will. 'Our people need all the help they can get.'

'I'm sorry, Corporal, but what is it about permission denied that you don't understand?'

She had the childish impulse to stamp her feet and scream at him in her frustration but somehow she mastered it, turning without saluting and storming out of the office, banging the door behind her. Later that day she talked to Winnie about it in the privacy of the hut but the conversation didn't go well.

'I can understand why he refused to let you go, Bella,' Winnie said flatly, knowing what her friend's reaction would be.

'*What?* Why?'

'Look at it from his point of view. They've evacuated all servicewomen off the island and other women are being got out now too, it's so dangerous. He's responsible for bringing us across here from England and where we are is bad enough – Malta is a hundred times worse.'

'I know that, for goodness' sake,' said Bella irritably. 'And like I said to him, that's exactly why they need me there. You know the monitoring staff they've got there can't cope with the amount of work and they're not experienced or trained as well as us. I could make a real difference.'

'You're making a real difference here.'

'Winnie, if I was a man and had gone to him with the same proposal, you know as well as I do that he wouldn't have stood in my way. He's like Sergeant Potts and some of the other RAF men who think women should be sitting at home baking cakes while the world falls apart.'

Winnie stared at her friend's indignant face. She loved Bella like a sister but sometimes she could be so thick, she thought testily. 'I don't think the group captain is at all like that, and have you considered that he might – he just might – be more concerned about you as a person than a woman, if you know what I mean?'

'I don't think I do,' said Bella, flushing in spite of herself.

'Well, think about it, because that's all I'm saying on the matter.' A blind man could see that they liked each other and she wasn't the only one who'd noticed it either, Winnie told herself. And what was the problem anyway? The group captain was a widower and Bella was unattached. All right, he was her superior officer and so on, but there were far more questionable liaisons going on in this war. Anyway, she wasn't going to say any more because she would only get it in the neck from Bella. 'I'm going to relieve Cammy,' she said expressionlessly, 'and I suggest you get some sleep before the night shift,' and without giving Bella a chance to comment she walked out of the hut.

Bella plumped down on her bed, which didn't give an inch, feeling hot and sticky and angry. William put himself in danger every time he flew a plane and at the camp they all lived daily with the fear of being bombed, she thought indignantly, so why was her transferring to Malta so different? It was just geography.

She flung herself face down onto the flat pillow, feeling wretched, even as she admitted to herself that knowing she would be a vital asset in Malta wasn't the sole reason she wanted to go there. They were in a mess there and it would mean that she would have to work even harder and longer hours than she did here, and she needed that, needed to be so exhausted that she fell into bed too tired to think and had her mind occupied every moment she was awake. The past haunted her and now there was this added possibility about her mother and Colonel Wynford, and try as she might she couldn't put it out of her mind.

She lay for some time thinking about things and particularly Winnie's comment about William. Was it because he cared about her that he'd been so dismissive to the point of rudeness? The thought created feelings she could do without and she brushed it aside, telling herself that even if there was a grain of truth in it, that didn't make it right. Everyone was agreed that the gallantry of the airmen, ground crews and gun crews on Malta was extraordinary, and all she wanted to do was to use her skills to support their heroism. It was vital to glean any information possible about enemy movements to stop some of the slaughter that was happening. William must see that, surely?

She turned over, the ever-present noise outside the hut a dull background throb to her thoughts as she replayed their conversation over and over in her mind. She'd been unforgivably rude to a senior officer; at the very least he must be absolutely furious with her. But she tried to excuse herself: he hadn't even made any attempt to *listen* to her, let alone talk things through. It had been like speaking to a block of stone.

It was another hour before she accepted the inevitable; she would have to seek him out tomorrow and apologize for her conduct and take any punishment he saw fit. She'd been completely unprofessional, which was galling in itself because it didn't exactly enhance the standing of the WAAFs in general in his mind.

Eventually she fell into a troubled sleep, still fully dressed and with her shoes on, to dream of long corridors stretching endlessly from which there was no escape and people calling her name over and over. Her father came towards her, his arms outstretched and his face smiling, but even as she flung herself into him he turned into the colonel, and then James appeared dressed in a doctor's white coat splashed with red, his hands covered in blood. He shouted at her to run, to run and not look back, but when she tried to move she found her feet were glued to the ground and she couldn't break free. Somewhere in it all William was there, but she couldn't see him. She knew she had to get to him and then she would be safe but soon even his voice began to fade and she was all alone in a darkness so consuming it was alive, sucking the very essence out of her mind and body.

She awoke some hours later and wearily got ready for her shift. Camilla had come in while she had been sleeping and was snoring in her bed. Bella found herself envying her; Cammy never thought about anything too deeply.

The night sky was black but shimmering with stars as she walked to the administration block and when she relieved Winnie and clamped the earphones to her head they were still warm. She and Winnie exchanged a few words but didn't mention William, and once she got to work only her job mattered. Dawn had broken when a hand was laid on her shoulder, her earphones removed and a soft voice said, 'Stay absolutely still. Don't move.'

She froze. It wasn't so much what William had said but the deadly tone he'd used. He moved very slowly to stand in front of her and she saw he was holding a revolver. It was only then that she noticed the cobra in a corner just a few feet away, its broad flattened head distinct from its long ribbed neck, which had expanded to form a hood. 'It feels threatened,' William whispered, 'so easy does it. Stand up and slowly back out of the room.'

She'd always been terrified of snakes and now she found she couldn't move, much as she wanted to. There had been grass snakes in the grounds at Fellburn and they'd made her feel faint, harmless though they were.

'Bella?' The soft whisper came again. 'It's fine, everything's fine, just do as I say, all right? I won't let it hurt you, I promise, and it's probably more frightened of us than we are of it.'

That she doubted. But she'd behaved like a hysterical female the day before and she was blowed if she was going to do the same today. Somehow she got her legs to move, and as she did so she realized she'd been swinging them to relieve the odd cramp or two she got from sitting still, which had probably caused the snake to believe it was in danger. Quelling the urge to run screaming like a madwoman, she slid slowly off the seat and then stood for a moment, willing her shaky legs to support her before backing away.

When she had reached the door William slowly followed her, his eyes never leaving the venomous snake which was swaying slightly in its corner, looking every inch as lethal as it was. She'd been warned about the Egyptian cobra, one of the most venomous snakes in North Africa, before she had left England, along with several others which were poisonous, but had been told she was unlikely to encounter one close up. Well, this was about as close up as it got, she thought feverishly, stepping into the area beyond the administration office and feeling as though she was going to faint.

The next moment he had joined her and shut the door behind him, saying, 'It must have got in during the night somehow, maybe when you changed over at midnight I'd imagine. Our Arab boys are supposed to check all the huts and offices twice a day for undesirables, so someone's slipped up. I'll send one of them to deal with it – they're used to catching them with a pole thing and popping them into a sack – amazing really.'

She was aware that he was trying to defuse the situation, but it wasn't working. That thing had been in there with her ready to strike and she hadn't known. Cammy wouldn't relieve her for another hour, when the rest of the administration team would start to come in too; how quickly would its venom have worked on her? Would she have had time to get help, and even if she had would it have made any difference?

She was trembling and he put his arm round her, giving her a brief hug as he said, 'Everything's all right, it's over.

Come through to my office. I wanted to talk to you before the day starts properly.'

As Bella followed him she wasn't sure what had shaken her more, the snake or the hug. Of the two, she came down on the side of the latter.

The office that William shared with the station commander was empty except for a young RAF officer who was looking through a file at the filing cabinet. William told her to sit down and turned to the young man: 'There's a cobra in administration. Get one of Mohammed's boys to deal with it, would you, and then bring us some coffee.'

'A cobra?' The officer looked as alarmed as she'd felt. 'Yes, sir.'

Once they were alone, William said quietly, 'That was an isolated incident and won't happen again. It's unusual for them to come into buildings like that but we're on the edge of the desert here.' He'd had the shock of his life when he'd come to talk to her and seen that thing in the corner of the room, with Bella blithely unaware of the danger she was in. This damn country, he thought savagely. All sand and snakes and a blazing heat that saps the life out of you. Thank God she hadn't panicked, that could have been disastrous for both of them. Why had she had to come into his life in the middle of a war? *He loved her*; seeing that thing about to attack had forced him to acknowledge that for the second time in his life he loved a woman to the very depths of his soul, but this love was different to the one he'd had for Hilda. Hilda had been his childhood sweetheart and he'd cared deeply for her but as in everything else, there were levels of love. And then he dismissed the thought; the past with all its issues concerning his wife and the lead-up to her becoming pregnant at last was too complicated to think about now. Too painful. On top of which he had to tell Bella he was party to sending her into even more acute danger than the one she'd just experienced.

'I came looking for you for a reason,' he said quietly, 'and one which I won't deny I'm not happy about. Nevertheless, after you'd gone yesterday I discussed your proposal about Malta with the station commander.'

Bella stared at him. 'I'm sorry for the way I behaved,' she said quickly before he could say any more. 'I shouldn't have spoken the way I did, sir.'

He smiled, shaking his head. He'd decided to admit part of the truth and now he said softly, 'You were right to some extent. I admit I'm old school and I was brought up to protect the fair sex –' his tone was wry – 'and it goes against the grain to send a woman into such a dangerous environment.' Her, most of all. 'But not because I think men are superior, I'd like you to believe that. I feel that men and women have different strengths, that's all, but I'm forced to concur that this war has changed things. When I thought things over yesterday I came to the conclusion that I was too –' he hesitated – 'close to the situation, and you're right. You being a female shouldn't interfere or influence a decision if you are the best person for a job, whatever the circumstances.'

There was a knock at the door and the young RAF officer came in with a tray of coffee. He set it down on the desk in front of William, saying, 'Mohammed has dealt with the problem, sir, and all's well.'

'Thank you, Tollett. Go and get some breakfast.'

'I've had—' The man stopped abruptly. 'Yes, sir. Of course, sir.' He left quickly, closing the door behind him.

William poured the coffee and handed her a cup and for once she didn't mind the strength of it. It was exactly what she needed to soothe her jangled nerves.

'So, the upshot of what I'm saying is that we feel you would be a great asset in Malta. But you do realize what you're letting yourself in for? Things are about as bad as they can get there.'

She nodded. 'I know, sir.'

'There's head knowledge and then there's experiencing such conditions.'

'I feel I can really make a difference, sir. It's what I joined up for.'

He settled back in his chair, his grey eyes surveying her over his coffee cup as he took a swig before saying drily, 'Of course it is.'

'Can I just say thank you, sir? For letting me go but for saving my life too?'

He chuckled. 'I'm not sure I did that, Corporal. In a stand-off between you and a cobra I don't think the snake would have a chance.'

His face had mellowed and she wondered how she could have been so angry with him just twenty-four hours ago. 'I hate snakes,' she admitted ruefully. 'I can cope with anything but them.'

'You coped just fine, Corporal.'

The warmth in his voice and the look in his eyes belied the formality and caused the colour to rise in her cheeks. As the silence stretched and held, Bella found she was holding her breath.

It was William who broke the moment, looking away as he said, 'We'll fly out to Malta within the week. You'll need to explain the situation to your WAAFs. One of the administration team who has an understanding of German will take your place in the shift rota – they'll need to get him up to scratch, of course.'

She'd only registered the 'we'.

'I'll be accompanying you,' he said expressionlessly. 'Unfortunately the officer in charge of Special Signals Intelligence in Malta was killed two days ago and I've offered to take his place until the new man arrives. Like you, I feel I can be more use out there than here at the moment.'

'Yes, sir.' She wondered if he would have offered to go if she wasn't going and then berated herself for the presumption. *Vanity, vanity, all is vanity*, she told herself wryly.

Nevertheless, the fact that he was going with her suddenly made the incident with the snake of no importance at all, and when a few minutes later she left the office she felt she was floating on air.

Chapter Twenty-Three

Belinda stared at Philip before nodding enthusiastically. He had just told her that he was giving Evendale over to the army for a convalescence home for badly injured soldiers and officers and that he was going to be involved in the running of it. 'There's plenty of room for the medical staff and patients alike,' he said with boyish eagerness, 'and the grounds are ideal for recuperation as well as the farm. Lads who were farm labourers or worked in the country might find solace in doing the same again, don't you think? It'll be therapy for the mind as well as the body.'

It was the first time she had seen a trace of the old Philip since James had died, and now she leaned forward and grasped one of his hands as she said, 'I think it's a marvellous idea, wonderful.'

'It'll mean I'm doing something useful.'

She nodded again. She knew how the injury to his legs had frustrated him and that he had wanted to be in the thick of the war, but some days he could barely walk.

'Have you talked it over with Felicity?' The divorce was going through but they were still legally married; Philip had agreed that Felicity could divorce him on the grounds of adultery and he wouldn't contest it. He'd told Belinda it was the least he could do in view of his past behaviour.

He snorted. 'She's getting her pound of flesh, that's all she's worried about. She was never happy in the country anyway, always hankering for the bright lights.' Then, his expression softening, he said quietly, 'I don't know what I would have done without you, Linnie, in the last months. Topped myself probably.'

Belinda wasn't quite sure how the pet name had come about but now when he visited, which was often, he called her Linnie all the time. He had never overstepped the boundaries of friendship though or said anything out of place, for which she was grateful.

She always kept a tight control on her feelings where Philip was concerned. She was well aware she had just been another notch on his proverbial bedpost all those years ago, but it hadn't been like that for her. Apart from the physical attraction she felt for him there was something more, something she didn't want to acknowledge. Betraying Archibald had been the most shameful experience of her life and she regretted it with all her heart, but those minutes in Philip's study had taken her to a place she hadn't known existed. She took hold of her thoughts as she often had to do in his presence, her voice betraying none of her inner turmoil. 'More tea?'

'Thank you.' He watched her as she poured the tea,

his eyes lingering on her sweet profile and causing the ache deep inside that he had given up trying to master.

He didn't quite know when he had fallen in love with her but from the moment he had made her his, she'd always been in his heart and mind so he supposed it was that night. He hadn't admitted it to himself then, nor in the following years when she was happily married to Archibald with the daughter whom they both adored. He'd been glad for the pair of them; Bella had made a huge difference in their marriage which was plain to see.

Belinda offered him the plate of cucumber sandwiches and he smiled his thanks, taking a couple of the tiny squares. It wouldn't be too extreme to say he lived for his visits to this house, which had become as necessary to him as living and breathing.

It had been that dependency in part which had prompted him to offer the Evendale estate to the authorities. He needed to have something to occupy him, mind and body, something worthwhile. He couldn't right the wrongs of the past but in doing something for the men who'd fought in the war, he was honouring the memory of James and his other sons.

The last meeting with James had been nigh on unbearable, his guilt at wrecking his son's life made worse by James's compassion towards him. Compassion he hadn't deserved. Felicity had left the ward at one point and it had been then that James had squeezed his hand, whispering, 'Tell Bella I wish her nothing but happiness if you see her and that she must love again.'

Tears streaming down his face, he'd nodded. 'I'm sorry, my boy. I'm so sorry.'

'I love you,' James had murmured. 'I always have and nothing has changed that.'

Within moments he had slipped into unconsciousness and an hour later had drawn his last breath. Philip had looked down at his son's face and seen the little boy he once had been, and he had thought he would go mad. But he'd gone on. One always had to go on.

Belinda's voice brought him out of the darkness as she said softly, 'Philip? Are you all right?'

'Yes, yes.' He swallowed hard, pulling himself together. 'Have you heard from Bella recently?'

She never showed him their daughter's letters but spoke to him about their content. He knew Bella was somewhere in North Africa and involved in work that was highly secret and no doubt dangerous, but he hadn't mentioned the risk factor to Belinda. Ignorance was bliss.

'Not in the last few weeks.'

He nodded. He knew she'd written to Bella about James's passing and that would have been hard for Bella.

After a little silence they talked about inconsequential matters until Philip took his leave. He kissed Belinda lightly on the cheek, drinking in the nearness of her and the faint perfume of apple blossom from the shampoo she used. Felicity had favoured expensive, heavy scents. He much preferred the naturalness of Belinda's.

He paused as he left the room, glancing at the portrait above the fireplace. Archibald gazed back at him, one arm round his wife's shoulders and Bella nestled in front of them. The perfect family.

He'd liked Archibald when the man was alive, Philip thought ruefully as he stepped into the hallway. He supposed he still did like him, even though he was the obstacle that prevented him from declaring his feelings for Belinda. Archibald had been the best of men but in death he had assumed virtual sainthood, certainly in Bella's eyes, whereas Philip was the pantomime villain and wicked seducer, a cad in every respect. The worst thing was that the cap fitted.

Belinda stood at the threshold of the house as Philip drove away in his horse and trap. Petrol was scarce and they had all taken to the old mode of transport wherever possible. She supposed life itself had been something of an anachronism since the outbreak of war.

It was bitterly cold but dry and bright, although heavy snow was forecast in the next twenty-four hours. She remained looking down the drive long after the horse and trap had disappeared. Philip always disturbed her when he called. She knew that he had no intention of doing so and that the fault was entirely hers but nevertheless, he unsettled her. Of course, she would never, *never* have admitted that to a living soul, or the fact that if his visits should cease she'd feel bereft.

They were only friends, she told herself as she stepped back into the relative warmth of the house. He obviously was interested in Bella's welfare now he knew she was his daughter – that was only natural, especially after losing the boys – but Philip had been involved with so many women in the past and she didn't fool herself that she meant anything to him beyond being Bella's mother. And he perhaps had a fondness for her because of that.

She would have liked to have grown old with Archibald. Theirs had been a relationship of gentle harmony and that's what was important in one's twilight years. And then she balked at the term – she had only just had her forty-fourth birthday; she wasn't old, was she? Worn out? Unattractive?

She walked across to the large gold-framed mirror in the hall and peered at her reflection. An unlined, wide-eyed face looked back at her, the skin still supple and youthful. There were a few silver strands in her blonde hair but not many and it was still as silky and thick as ever.

What on earth was she thinking? She jerked away from the mirror, guilt swamping her. It didn't matter what she looked like and she didn't want to be attractive to Philip, she told herself, as though someone had accused her of that very thing. In the last year since Bella's visit she had learned to live with herself on a day-to-day basis, never looking very far ahead and accepting the sudden storms of remorse about Archibald that would sweep in when she least expected it as just punishment for what she'd done. Bella had told her that she had to stop punishing herself, but how could she when it had been Archibald who had suffered the penalty for what she had done? And Bella too, and poor James. They had all been innocent of any wrongdoing.

She walked into the morning room and held out her hands to the crackling log fire burning in the large fireplace; they only ever used the wood on the estate now coal was harder to come by. She glanced up at the same picture that Philip had looked at moments before. *They say that time heals*, she thought sadly, but she supposed it was what you did with the time that matters. For healing to take place you need to let go of the guilt and grief and she couldn't; she didn't feel she had any right to.

The doctors had told her that Archibald's heart attack had been inevitable, that it could have happened at any point in the preceding years and he'd been living on borrowed time for a while, but that didn't make any difference to how she felt. It had been the brutal revelation that Bella wasn't his child that had caused the final attack, and that was something that could never be rectified.

When she heard the sound of a horse's hooves outside the window of the morning room she sighed heavily. Who on earth was it now? She'd actively discouraged callers since Archibald had died but there were still a few ladies, elderly on the whole, who kept up the genteel country ways of paying an afternoon visit now and again. They'd sit, mostly in black these days, smelling of lavender and mothballs and talking about inconsequential things as though the war that was raging didn't exist in their world. And perhaps it didn't at that.

She heard voices in the hall and then Wright tapped on the door and opened it, saying, 'The colonel's back, ma'am,' in his impassive tone.

'Philip.' She moved forward to greet him. 'What's wrong? Did you forget something?'

He waited until the door had closed behind Wright and they were alone before he said, 'Not exactly.'

There followed a silence which, when Belinda realized he wasn't going to break it, caused her to say awkwardly, 'Well, do sit down. I'll tell Wright to bring more coffee—'

'Not for me, thanks.'

'Well, sit down anyway.'

He still didn't move from his stance just inside the door but said, 'I'd better leave. I shouldn't have come.'

'Philip, what's the matter?' In all the time they had known each other she had never seen him like this. What on earth had happened between the time he had left and now when he had come back?

'I want – I need to tell you something. Will you just listen without saying anything?'

She stared at him. 'Philip, you're frightening me.'

'No, don't be frightened. Not of me. Never of me.' He swallowed hard. 'What I'm about to say I'll never refer to again and I say it without hope or expectation. I love you, Linnie. I've loved you for a long time and I've never felt for anyone what I feel for you. You know my reputation –' he waved his hand – 'and I'm not about to deny that most of it is true, but believe me when I say that none of them meant anything, but you –' again he swallowed, his Adam's apple jerking – 'you were different.'

Belinda stood quite still, frozen with amazement although her heart was pounding so hard it hurt.

'I am grateful for your friendship and it's the most precious thing in my life, which is why I've hesitated to speak before, but just now, as I drove away, I thought if something happened to me and you didn't know how I felt I couldn't bear it. Which is selfish, I know. But then I've realized I am a selfish man as Felicity told me every day of our married life.' He smiled painfully. 'Now I'm going to leave you, and the next time that we meet everything will be as it was before. I will never embarrass you again by mentioning this, you have my word on that. Can I still count you as my dearest friend, Linnie?'

She couldn't speak but she nodded.

'Thank you.' He reached out and took her hand. 'Life is a damn funny affair, all things considered, isn't it,' he said softly. 'Damn funny.'

They gazed at each other, sadness in their faces, and then Philip turned on his heel and left without saying anything further, shutting the door quietly behind him.

Chapter Twenty-Four

Bella and William left for Malta in the middle of January on a flying boat from Cairo escorted by British fighters. Winnie had been in tears when they'd said goodbye, hugging Bella as though she would never let her go, and even Camilla had been misty-eyed.

They arrived at the receiving station at Kaura Point which had been set up to monitor transmissions from German bomber traffic based in Sicily to the north in the middle of a heavy air raid, which they were told was par for the course. 'The beggars don't stop day or night,' the young officer who greeted them said cheerfully, monitoring his language in view of her presence. 'And make sure you know what's coming at you. One of our men confused a Messerschmitt 109 flying low over the sea with a British fighter in trouble a couple of days ago until the swine aimed a volley of machine-gun fire at him. Lucky to be alive to tell the tale, he is, silly bu— silly devil,' he corrected himself quickly. 'It missed him but careered on, shooting up the airfield. I'll say one thing for the Hun, they don't know what fear is.'

It wasn't the most reassuring of introductions to her new abode but it was not unexpected. William smiled at her. 'Make sure you wear your tin hat,' he said drily, making her smile.

Within days she had organized the Maltese unit to work at maximum efficiency; under her guidance the men were working unbelievably long hours to ensure round-the-clock monitoring but she never asked them to do anything she didn't do. She and her German-speaking eavesdroppers warned of impending attacks, advised on targets, alerted fighters when they'd been spotted by the enemy, listened in on weather reports, determined the strength of enemy formations and contacted threatened shipping convoys.

She initially encountered a little of the wary hostility she'd met in the past, but her cool-headedness and intellectual grasp of what was needed convinced even the most hardened woman-hater that what she contributed was valuable. She was even permitted to dine in the all-male mess, which William told her was a first for a WAAF. 'The general consensus of opinion is that you're a thoroughly decent type,' he grinned as she frowned at him. 'So why that face?'

'Because the RAF, like the other services, is behind the times,' Bella answered tartly. 'All-male indeed, as though women are the inferior sex and it's an honour to be included with the men.'

'Aren't you even the tiniest bit honoured?' he teased, laughing out loud as she glared at him and threatened to empty her bowl of fruit and custard over his head. They usually ate together, which for Bella was something of a mixed blessing simply because she enjoyed his company too much. She had never really understood the term 'bitter sweet' before, but she fully appreciated it now.

She had been accommodated in a hotel, being the only woman at the station, which meant dodging bombs and shrapnel and picking her way across the rubble every morning to the safety of a labyrinth of tunnels where she worked, and returning to her sleeping quarters at night. Women and children were being evacuated now from the towns and villages and it was difficult to determine when one air-raid ceased and the next began, which meant a number of casualties every day. After a direct hit one night on the house next to the hotel, William insisted that she be installed in safer lodgings in the tunnels. To her embarrassment a cave-like storehouse near the mess was cleared for her, and a bed, a couple of orange boxes for her belongings and a chair were put in there, and a wooden door made to fit the structure.

'One of the Arab boys will bring a bowl and pitcher of water every morning,' William told her as he handed her a piece of soap and a towel, 'but it'll be no more showers for the immediate future I'm afraid.'

She hadn't protested. The terrible screams of agony and wails from the house next to the hotel, where a whole family had perished, were too fresh in her mind. A young couple and three children had lost their lives, as well as elderly grandparents.

Knowing it was vital to glean any information possible about enemy movements consumed her days and nights, and to some extent she found she was developing a fatalistic attitude about her mortality. She didn't want to die or be horribly injured, but if it was profitable in defeating the enemy, it was worth it. She said this to William one evening and he looked at her with the expression she'd come to recognize, one of quizzical despair.

'Forgive me if I don't share your enthusiasm,' he said flatly.

'Oh, you know what I mean.'

'Unfortunately, yes. When God made you He forgot to press the self-preservation button.'

She tried not to smile. How could he be funny and annoying at the same time? 'I don't *want* to be hurt—'

'Well that's something, I suppose.'

She ignored the interruption and continued, 'But if it's for the greater good . . .'

'The greater good for whom?'

'Everyone. The war effort. The fight against the Nazis.'

'And you think that the Nazis will notice if you kick the bucket?'

'Of course not. That's not what I'm saying and you know it.' She glared at him over the mush on her plate that was masquerading as cottage pie although she dreaded to think what the animal was that had given its life for such a concoction.

He sighed. 'I can't deny you've made a difference here.'

'Thank you,' she said tartly, moderating her tone as she added, 'You have too.'

'Thank you, Corporal.' He grinned at her.

They rarely kept up the formality since they'd come to Malta and in spite of herself she gave a little giggle. He'd helped her set up the new working programme and dealt with the inevitable red tape, but he still flew on raids when he could, which she hated. Of course she couldn't say so on any level. She had no right – they weren't together and even if they had been she wouldn't have tried to prevent him doing what he felt he needed to do. Nevertheless, she suffered the torments of the damned till she knew he was safe each time.

As January gave way to February various reports reached them; the Allies had failed to halt Japan in Malaya; Germany was pushing back the Eighth Army in the Western Desert and Singapore was under siege. According to newspaper reports, Reinhard Heydrich, right-hand man to the Gestapo chief, Himmler, had admitted to something called the final solution for the Jewish problem – the total extermination of an estimated eleven million Jews in Europe. The Germans were setting up special camps with facilities for the mass annihilation of men, women and children, even babes in arms.

Bella caught a couple of the airmen in her unit talking about the believability of such claims and wondering if they were propaganda by the Allies. 'I was in Germany just before the war,' she told them grimly, 'and I have no doubt that they are true. Hitler won't stop until his Nazis have murdered every last Jew in the world. That's his aim. It always has been. World domination and the elimination of an entire race of people and everyone who disagrees with him. You might say he's mad and he is, but it's a sane madness which is worse than the lunatic kind. He's more than prepared to kill his own people – Germans – if they disagree with him, not just those from other countries.'

The two men stared at her. 'What was it like in Germany then?' one of them asked.

'Terrifying,' she said simply.

In the middle of February Singapore, the great naval base and fortress considered to be impregnable, surrendered to the Japanese. It was a far-reaching military defeat and the consequences for the Allies was grave, as everyone recognized. The fall of Singapore deprived the Allies of their only major dry dock between Durban and Pearl Harbor. Now the enemy had acquired the valuable naval asset for future operations in the Indian Ocean.

To some extent, the world beyond the stricken island of Malta made little impact on Bella. Working as she was meant she had no time to brood about whatever was happening at home between her mother and Philip Wynford or take too much notice of the disastrous war news. She and the rest of the team were regularly working fourteen-hour days, snatching some sleep and meals when they could, but they knew they were making a difference to the number of Allied casualties, which was everything.

And William was with her. She was aware that he had become essential to her well-being but had given up trying to fight it; no doubt one day he'd say goodbye even if it was at the end of the war – he hadn't said anything to suggest that she meant more to him than a colleague and, she liked to think, close friend – but she'd deal with that when it happened.

Anyway, she told herself on numerous occasions, they were so different in lots of ways and a relationship between them would never work. Whatever he said to the contrary, he wanted a woman like his wife had been, someone who wanted to settle down and have babies and devote herself to family life for the rest of her days. And there was nothing wrong with that – she had imagined something similar with James although she would have been working with him too in his practice – but she had changed in the aftermath of her father's death and there was no going back. She wasn't sure *what* she wanted, if she was being honest, but it wasn't being the little wife stuck at home. But neither did she want a life without William in it. So there was the dilemma; she wanted to have her cake and eat it, as her father would have said. Impossible situation. But with life so uncertain, it was no use worrying about the future anyway.

In the first week of March, over a late supper in the mess, William said he had something to tell her. She had just finished a gruelling day and was bone tired, but his first words brought her out of the dazed stupor she'd fallen into as she ate without tasting the food.

'You're wanted back in Cairo, and to be honest your work's done here. You've trained the staff and the new officers are now up to speed – we've got an efficient and well-organized team with round-the-clock monitoring. The thing is, Messerschmitts are attacking our North African airfields and harbours and the Eighth Army in the desert need all the support they can get. Things have changed in the last weeks since we came here.'

She stared at him. She would go where she was most needed, but— 'Are you returning too?'

'Not until the new Special Signals chappie gets here.' He didn't add that the first officer who'd been meant to arrive to relieve him had been killed as he'd stepped on the island in an air raid. It had thrown the powers that be into a tiz-woz and they had only just decided on yet another replacement. He didn't mind that so much as the fact that stuck here he wouldn't be able to protect Bella or know she was all right; not that his protection against machine-gun fire or a bomb would cut the mustard anyway, he thought wryly. But while she was close it was something. 'I'll drive you to Luqa airfield after supper tomorrow – there's a number of women and children who are being evacuated to Egypt and you'll join them.'

He didn't sound as though he minded her leaving at all, or that he was having to stay. Pride came to her rescue. 'That's fine,' she said expressionlessly. 'It will give me time to make sure that everything is in place here.'

'Back to being able to have a shower,' he said cheerfully, so cheerfully she wanted to kick him.

She forced a smile. 'Quite.'

'You've been an amazing asset here, you know that, don't you,' he said softly.

Again she forced a smile. 'Thank you, sir.'

He frowned at the formality but in the next moment they were joined by a couple of other officers who immediately engaged William in conversation about the way the war was going.

As soon as she could, Bella made her excuses and left them to it, and once in her little hidey-hole she shut the door firmly behind her. At least in Cairo she'd have Winnie and Cammy, she thought, waves of self-pity sweeping over her. And who needed men anyway? Relationships with the opposite sex caused nothing but trouble. The only thing worthwhile in life was the undemanding friendship of other women – as soon as love or sexual attraction or whatever you wanted to call it reared its head, it brought nothing but heartache and turmoil. So she would go back to Cairo tomorrow, and she wouldn't think about William at all. What he was doing; whether he was safe; if he was getting over-tired, which could mean as a pilot he wasn't on the ball; whether he was eating enough and sleeping . . .

She flung herself down onto the narrow camp bed, pulled the wafer-thin pillow over her head and quietly cried herself to sleep.

The next morning she quickly became aware that the monitoring team knew of her departure later that day. Whether William had told them or someone else she didn't know, but everyone said they would miss her and thanked her for what she had done. That evening she was touched when a few bottles of wine were produced along with some cake. The impromptu party brought a lump to her throat, but she carefully avoided William and stitched a bright smile on her face until it was time to leave.

William carried her kitbag to the jeep despite her protests that she could manage. Once they were on their way, he said quietly, 'Everyone's sorry to see you go. You'll be missed.'

By you? 'They're a nice bunch, sir,' she said flatly.

He nodded without taking his eyes off the road. The sky was black, pierced by stars, and as she'd thought many times since arriving abroad it was so fundamentally different to an English sky – larger, higher, more exotic – which was silly really because the sky was the sky after all, she told herself.

'Your WAAF friends will be pleased to see you back safe and sound. They must have been worried about you.'

'I suppose so, but there's danger everywhere.'

'Not quite like here.' As though to emphasize his point, some huge explosions in the distance rent the air along with the normal drone of aircraft and screaming whines of others in trouble. The Luftwaffe were continuing to bomb remorselessly. 'There'll be nothing left by the time the Nazis have finished.'

She made no reply to this and after some moments of silence, he said softly, 'You're very quiet.'

The road was dusty and bumpy and there was bomb

damage all along the route. Even though it was a little before midnight, normally there would have been a few people about. But they'd seen no one. She shrugged. 'I thought you'd want to concentrate on your driving, sir. The road's full of holes and craters.'

Another 'sir'. The easy camaraderie of recent weeks was definitely a thing of the past, William thought wryly. It had been her express wish to come to Malta – did she blame him for the fact that she was being recalled to Cairo? Keeping his voice non-committal, he said, 'Have I said or done something to offend you, Bella?'

She clenched her teeth and it took a moment to unclench them before she could say in the same tone he had used, 'Of course not, sir.'

The third 'sir' did it. Much as he didn't want to put the idea in her mind if she hadn't been thinking that way, he said, 'I had nothing to do with you being ordered back to Cairo. Unfortunately you're too good at what you do and it was decided on high that the Eighth Army could benefit from your expertise. We go where we're sent in this war.'

'I know that.'

'And you believe me?'

'Yes, I believe you.'

'Then what's the matter?'

'Nothing is the matter, sir.' She'd rather be hung, drawn and quartered than admit the truth. If he didn't care than neither did she, she told herself fiercely. 'Everything is absolutely fine.'

He muttered something under his breath that she thought could have been, 'To hell with it,' but said nothing more for the rest of the journey until they reached the Luqa airfield. She saw a group of women and children waiting together in the distance and presumed they were the ones who were going to accompany her to Egypt. As they came to a stop, she climbed out of the jeep clutching her briefcase which contained secret documents for the station commander at Cairo, and William threw her kitbag over his shoulder. Two Wellington aircraft were standing a way off, and as they neared the evacuees, William said quietly, 'Take care of yourself until I'm back in Cairo, won't you,' as he glanced down at her.

His deep, slightly husky voice had carried more than the actual words had conveyed and Bella looked at him, their eyes meeting and holding.

'Group Captain Crawford?' An airman met them in the next moment, smiling as he added, 'We're getting everyone on board now, sir.'

The group of women and children were already walking towards the first Wellington. The runway was blacked out to provide less of a target for the Luftwaffe and suddenly William said, 'What the hell's happening there?' as a third aircraft which had been about to take off hurtled into one of the stationary Wellingtons, bursting into flames.

The women and children were scattering, screaming, and guided by the firework display German raiders homed in on the airfield within moments, adding to the mayhem.

Deafening explosions vied with machine-gun fire from enemy planes as people ran for cover, and William grabbed her hand, shouting 'Move!' as bullets whizzed past them. They dived for cover, face down, only to realize that they were underneath a petrol bowser.

Seconds later, the mines which had been on the errant Wellington blew up with another mighty explosion. William seized the briefcase and covered the back of her head with it as he shielded her with his body, flying shrapnel raining down with savage force.

'Keep still, don't move,' he shouted in her ear above the mayhem as the carnage went on and the Luftwaffe made the most of the opportunity, but she couldn't have done anyway with her face pressed into the ground by the briefcase and his weight covering her.

The minutes until the din and chaos finally died down seemed like hours and she was conscious of thinking that if she was going to die in this war then let it be now, with him, rather than without him in the future. Then she was aware of a couple of airmen pulling him off her as they said, 'Are you all right, can you move?' as the battle in the sky above them went on and the flames lit up the scene on the ground.

The briefcase fell to the side of her and to her horror she saw deep scars in the leather made by the shrapnel; William had saved her life yet again. Now that his weight was off her she struggled into a sitting position and then was conscious that the two airmen were kneeling by his side and there was blood everywhere. One of the men tore open William's jacket and put his ear to his chest, saying to the other, 'He's breathing, just,' and then to her, 'Can you walk, Corporal?'

'Yes, yes, I'm all right,' she said frantically. 'See to him.'

Their aircraft had chased the enemy planes further afield for the moment, and as the two men lifted William between them she trotted after them, aware that one of her legs was hurting but not even bothering to look to see how bad it was. William had the appearance of a corpse.

They took him to the nearest building, which was the control room, laying him on the floor as one of the men said, 'Get the medics here, tell 'em it's bad.' She'd seen the bodies of some of the women and children outside and RAF men helping others; they'd been like sitting targets, she thought grimly, fighting back the tears.

The next few hours were horrendous. Her leg needed stitches and so she was transported to the hospital along with William and the other injured. Her only concern was for William and she was terrified he was going to die.

The QAs at the military hospital proved to be wonderful despite the pressure they were under. Once her leg had been dealt with, they got permission from one of the doctors dealing with the badly injured for her to see William. He had been placed in a small side room off the main ward and she'd been told he needed an urgent operation once he was stabilized – one of many if he came through this one. Drips and monitors surrounded the bed and as she walked quietly to his side she thought for a moment that he'd already passed away. His face was white, a dull pasty white, and he didn't look as though he was breathing, but then his eyes opened. They were slightly vacant for a moment and then his lips parted to whisper her name, 'Bella.'

'I'm here.' She bent over him and clasped one of his hands. It was cold despite the warmth of the room.

'Are – are you all right?'

He looked at death's door – he *was* at death's door – and he was asking her if she was all right? She had told herself that no matter what, she wouldn't cry, but now her eyes misted and her voice was choked as she murmured, 'Thanks to you, yes. You saved my life – again.'

He closed his eyes for a moment and then a flicker of a smile touched his colourless lips. 'Let's not go for a third time, my darling.'

She blinked, finding it impossible at that moment to utter a word. Did he realize what he'd said?

She wasn't sure but nevertheless it gave her the courage to put her lips on his before she sat down at the side of the bed, still holding his hand. 'You need an operation,' she said quietly. 'But you're going to be all right.'

His doctor had said much the same and William knew he had been lying too. 'I want you to know –' he couldn't take a deep breath, it was too painful and he had to pause some moments before he could continue – 'to know that I love you. I think I've –' again the pause – 'always loved you, even before I met you, if that makes sense.'

Who cared whether it made sense or not? Softly she said, 'And I love you, so much.'

He was silent, lost in the depths of the revelation in her eyes, but then he murmured, 'If you mean that, kiss me again.'

Gently she laid her mouth on his and following this they were silent for some moments, the sounds of the ward beyond the little room filtering through now and again. He'd closed his eyes and she thought he was sleeping until he whispered, 'I've been such a fool, wasting time, precious time.'

'Then that makes two of us.'

A nurse entered the room, checked the drips and took his pulse, her calm professional manner giving nothing away. She glanced at Bella, her voice low as she said, 'The doctor wants a word with you before you go, Corporal, and I'm sorry but he needs to rest now.'

'Can I come back later?'

The nurse hesitated. 'Ask the doctor when you speak to him.'

She kissed him again before she stood up but there was no response and it was clear this time that he was sleeping. She left the room with the nurse, who pointed out a small, sandy-haired man at the end of the main ward. 'That's Dr Easton,' she said briefly, before returning to William's room and shutting the door. Bella stared after her, her stomach churning. Something about the exchange made her think that the nurse didn't expect William to survive the operation.

Dr Easton confirmed her fears when she spoke to him after he had taken her into his office and sat her down in a chair. 'You understand he's very ill, Corporal? Shrapnel isn't compatible with the human body and frankly he's peppered with it.' His voice had been somewhat brusque but as her hand went to her mouth, his harassed expression mellowed and he said quickly, 'I'm sorry, it's been a long night and it isn't over yet.'

'He – he's going to have an operation today?'

'Hopefully, but that in itself . . .' He shrugged. 'I don't want to give you false expectations.'

She swallowed, determined not to break down in front of him.

'I understand from one of the men who brought him in that he saved your life?' he said after a moment.

She nodded.

'You know him well?'

Again she nodded.

'And would you say he's a strong character, a fighter?'

'Definitely.'

'Then that's in his favour. I never underestimate the power of the human spirit but I think you should prepare yourself, nevertheless.'

'I understand,' she said quietly. 'Can I come and see him again?'

'Normally I'd say no but in view of the circumstances I'll make an exception, though not today. Tomorrow or maybe the day after.'

'I've been called back to Cairo, that's why I was at the

airfield and Group Captain Crawford was seeing me off when it all happened.'

'Let's say tomorrow, then. You understand I'll do what I can, but he'll be taken back to England as soon as possible if he rallies a little? It will be a long road to recovery and he'll need further operations and by someone more qualified than me for the tricky ones, I'm afraid.'

'So – so there is a chance he could get better?'

The world-weary eyes softened. 'You're in love with him.'

It was a statement rather than a question but she answered anyway. 'Yes, I am.'

'And he with you?'

'Yes.'

'That's good. They fight all the harder if they've something to live for.' He'd been sitting at his desk and now he stood up, signifying that the conversation was over.

It wasn't until Bella was in the jeep being driven back to the base by one of the airmen that she realized Dr Easton hadn't really given her an answer.

The next day she was turned away from the ward by a sympathetic but firm nurse. 'It was a long operation yesterday, Corporal McFadyen, and the group captain still isn't really conscious.' She didn't add that they were all amazed that he was still in the land of the living, considering he was a human sieve. Even Dr Easton. 'Come back tomorrow.' Everyone knew that the handsome officer had got so badly injured saving the life of the pretty corporal and they thought it was terribly romantic, as her tone conveyed when she whispered, 'Once he's properly awake I'll tell him you came, I promise.'

Bella thanked her and left to endure another sleepless night of tossing and turning; partly because her leg was so painful but mainly because of William.

The following morning she arrived at the hospital prepared to do battle. She was going to see William come hell or high water. She had been told she was flying to Cairo the next day and the thought of leaving him alone here was bad enough, but she couldn't go without seeing him.

The same nurse was on duty and greeted her with non-committal professionalism when Bella asked how William was. 'He's as well as can be expected.'

'How did the operation go?'

'I understand Dr Easton was satisfied he'd done all he could for the present.'

How was it medical staff could say something and nothing at the same time? Bella asked herself frustratedly. She'd prepared herself for how he was going to look as she walked into the small clinical room but it was still shocking to see him so white and still. And then he opened his eyes and it was the same William as he smiled at her. 'Bella.'

She bent and kissed him on the lips; she was done with pretence now and frightened, so, so frightened for him. Pulling a chair close to the bed she took one of the hands lying limply on the smooth coverlet as she whispered, 'Oh, William.'

'I'm glad we're done with sir,' he said, grinning.

It should have reassured her but it made her want to cry. One of the nurses had obviously shaved him and there was a small nick on his chin which somehow made him look even more vulnerable. 'You're looking a bit better,' she said softly. It wasn't true, and they both knew it.

'I'm glad you're a bad liar if we're going to spend the rest of our lives together. We *are* going to spend the rest of our lives together?'

Forcing herself to match his bravery, she said lightly, 'Are you proposing, Group Captain Crawford?'

'Hell, yes.' He'd spoken too vehemently and now she watched him flinch slightly and take a breath. 'And before you answer, I want to tell you something. I meant every word I said the last time I saw you, in case you've been wondering. I was a fool, I should have spoken before, but I wasn't sure how you felt, not that that should have stopped me.'

He was struggling for breath and now she said, 'Don't talk any more, they'll throw me out if I upset you.'

He was quiet for some moments, getting his breathing under control and fighting the pain that felt as though his chest was clamped in an iron band, and she stroked his forehead, her eyes full of love and concern.

'I need to make you understand,' he said softly when he was able to. 'I love *you*, just as you are, all right? I don't expect you to change, I don't *want* you to change.'

'Are you saying you think I'll be difficult to live with?'

she murmured teasingly in an effort to hide the amazement that he'd known how she felt.

He smiled faintly, fighting the exhaustion that had him wanting to close his eyes and sink into oblivion, because he needed to make the most of every minute he had with her. 'Hilda was a good woman and I loved her, but –' he hesitated, not sure how to put it because the last thing he wanted was to denigrate Hilda in any way – 'she was a product of her upbringing, her heritage if you like.' He tried to take in air without breathing too deeply. 'Her own self-worth was wrapped up in being a mother first and foremost—'

She bent and placed her lips on his, stopping his words. Raising her head, she whispered, 'Ask me to marry you properly.'

He moved his fingers so that he was now holding her hand rather than she his, his eyes tight on her face. 'Will you be my wife, my darling?'

She gazed into his face, her love plain for him to read. 'With all my heart,' she said softly. For a fleeting moment she remembered that other proposal under a blue English sky and her ecstatic response; it seemed a hundred years ago and she had changed so much that she felt as though it had happened to another person – or perhaps grown up was the right definition, she thought. She had been so young then, not so much in years but in her mind, in the essence of her. 'I love you, William Crawford.'

'And I you, Bella McFadyen.'

His eyes were closing in spite of himself when she whispered, 'I have to leave for Cairo first thing tomorrow.'

His grip on her hand tightened and he forced his eyelids open. 'Oh, Bella.'

'I know.' There were tears in her eyes and she bent and laid her head next to his on the pillow, and it was like that that he gave in to the overwhelming exhaustion and slept.

PART SIX

The Full Circle

1943

Chapter Twenty-Five

'Some of you may hear me in your aircraft, on board your ships, or as you wait for battle in the jungles of the Pacific islands or on the Italian peaks. Some of you may listen to me as you rest from your work, or as you lie sick or wounded in hospital. To many of you, my words will come as you sit in the quiet of your homes. But, wherever you may be, today of all days in the year, your thoughts will be in distant places and your hearts with those you love. I hope that my words, spoken to them and to you, may be the bond that joins us all in company for a few moments on this Christmas Day.'

As the notes of the National Anthem crackled across the airwaves, Bella bit her lip as she looked at Winnie. The King had said exactly how she was feeling – her thoughts were in a distant place and her heart was with William.

'Aw, Bella, I know you're disappointed you didn't get leave,' Winnie said softly in total understanding.

The two of them along with Camilla were now based at Allied Supreme Headquarters in Algiers and all three had hoped to go home for Christmas after two years abroad, but especially Bella. William was in England and she hadn't seen him since she'd left him in Malta, but the Italian invasion had meant that her vital interception skills could not be spared. She was eternally grateful that he had slowly recovered from his devastating injuries, and only recently he had come through a serious operation to remove a piece of shrapnel which had settled close to his heart. It had been the last surgery of many and it would have been wonderful to have celebrated together, especially at Christmas. But he was in England and she was here, and never the twain shall meet, she thought ruefully, smiling at dear Winnie, who'd been a constant rock throughout.

Not that Algiers was the worst posting in the world. The piercingly white sunlight and bright colours and gardens loaded with citrus fruits would have been wonderful if William were there to share it with her, and they had been lodged at a hotel where the food was good and there were even dances and socials at service units which Camilla took full advantage of. Camilla had only been at the new posting for a week or so before she had found herself a new beau, married of course. The stoical Winnie despaired of her. But now, on Christmas Day, there was work to do and they were busy with preparations for Operation Shingle, the amphibious landings at Anzio, planned for less than a month away.

Bella knew it was vital work she was involved in and most of the time she found comfort in that, but sometimes the homesickness was overwhelming – not for a place but for a person, William. They hadn't even had time to exchange rings, she reflected sadly, and it was all their own fault. Why hadn't they spoken of their true feelings before? Why had it taken a catastrophic event like the one at the airfield for their love to come into the open?

She had written to her mother to tell her about William and had received an enthusiastic reply. Her mother hadn't mentioned the colonel then, nor in the letters that had followed. It had put Bella's mind at rest to some extent, but not completely; but as her anxiety about William had been foremost, the situation in England – whatever it was – had gone on the back burner. Her mother tended to write about the shortages in the shops; the embargo on bellringing that had been lifted this Christmas; the festive party planned for the village children by the WI – ordinary, mundane things that were still happening somewhere in the world and which were reassuring and comforting, like slippers warming in front of the fire on a cold winter's day.

It wouldn't be too extreme to say that in spite of the highly secret and important work she was doing, Bella lived for William's letters. She floated on air for days after one had arrived and suffered the torments of the damned if they were delayed, especially after one of his operations. Initially, once he'd arrived back in England he'd been confined to bed for some six months, which had driven him mad; then slowly, as each surgery was successful, he was allowed to do more. Now he had returned to Special Signals Intelligence in England, but to a desk job, much to his disgust. His doctors had insisted that his flying days were over, and although she would never admit it to him because she knew how much it rankled, Bella was relieved. The strain on his body from his extensive injuries along with the operations to remove pieces of shrapnel would have taken a toll, although she knew William dismissed that.

She had written to him saying that he was still playing a huge part in the war even if he wasn't up in the air leading sorties against the Luftwaffe, and had received a typically William reply – sardonic, rueful and full of irritation with the poor medical team in charge of him.

'Come on.' Winnie took her arm, pulling her out of the hotel and into the bright sunlight where a gharry with open sides was waiting for them, Camilla already inside, bright-eyed and bushy-tailed. 'You're coming to the Christmas get-together at the base and no argument, *and* you're going to dance and enjoy yourself. William wouldn't want you to mope on Christmas Day. We've been working since seven this morning apart from coming back here for a late lunch. All work and no play . . .'

In spite of not wanting to go, Bella found she enjoyed the festivities, aided by a few glasses of wine and hope for the future. General Eisenhower was convinced that the coming year would see an Allied victory and his optimism was infectious. The enemy was being rolled back by a series of military successes and the successive assaults by the RAF on Germany throughout the year had caused firestorms which had consumed cities.

Boxing Day brought a return to continuous hard work but with a huge boost to morale when the German warship *Scharnhorst* was sunk, and as the New Year dawned an atmosphere of expectation took over. It was needed; many like Bella were impatient for the onslaught that would mean the start of the endgame. Servicewomen and -men were battle-weary and homesick; some had been away from loved ones for years, something they had never imagined at the beginning of the war. Things like ENSA, the Entertainments National Service Association, otherwise known affectionately as Every Night Something Awful, helped with their concerts, which were enormously valuable in boosting morale.

Winnie continued to look on the bright side every day and Bella was unfailingly grateful for her friend's positiveness, particularly when William's letters were held up for weeks on end. They were beautiful letters and she kept every one, reading them again and again: '*I'm just living for the day that we're together again and I can hold you in my arms day and night, in fact I'll never let you go*,' he'd written in the last one. '*I miss you beyond words and pray constantly for your safety. It should be me in the thick of it, not you, my darling.*'

Bella had felt slightly guilty when she'd read that. Since the Allied Forces led by Eisenhower had retaken Morocco and Algeria from the Nazis the year before, it wasn't so dangerous as it had been, and there were compensations to being in North Africa. Open-fronted fruit shops displayed piles of glossy melons, purple eggplants, baskets of tomatoes, strings of red peppers, fresh dates on their yellow stalks, lemons and oranges and candelabra bunches of bananas, and compared to the greyness of England the Middle East was bursting with colour.

She glanced at Winnie now, who was tucking into pancakes filled with pineapple jam after their evening meal of chicken in some exotic sauce. The hotel certainly didn't stint in the size of their servings. As though she'd read her mind, Winnie grinned at her: 'I'm going to be a barrel at the end of this war. I can hardly fit into my uniform. Even Cammy's getting fat. She was highly indignant last night when apparently lover boy said her love handles had doubled in size.'

Bella raised her eyebrows. 'Bit rude.'

Winnie giggled. 'I don't think she chooses them for their sweet-talking,' she said with customary naughtiness, winking lewdly. 'Her benchmark is set on something else entirely.'

Although they had been working at the base since early morning and it was now eight o'clock in the evening, they were returning there as soon as they'd finished their meal. Operation Shingle was due to take place the following day, on the twenty-second of January, and they were needed at their posts practically round the clock.

As it turned out they didn't leave their radio receivers once they were back at base until well into the next day, but it was worth it. The surprise landing by thousands of British and American troops had been a complete success; they'd stormed ashore at Anzio thirty miles south of Rome and gone swiftly eastwards, cutting the supply lines of the hundred thousand German troops on the Garigliano front. The invading force had met hardly any opposition, having achieved total surprise, and reinforcements of both men and materiel were continuing to pour ashore as an armada of landing craft, with powerful naval and air cover, shuttled to and from the beachhead.

Bella and the others normally still worked shifts but it had been all hands to the pump for the last forty-eight hours. Once the main thrust of the day was over she told Winnie and Camilla to go back to the hotel and get some sleep while she remained on duty. The next main objective of the forces was to strike inland to Littoria, the site of the pre-war international airport for Rome. Its capture would provide an excellent base for the Allied air forces and after that the plan was full steam ahead to Rome.

She knew the coming weeks would be tough and the need to listen in to the Germans as important as ever. The Allies needed to take Monte Cassino, the rock fortress which blocked the road to Rome and which had already cost the lives of hundreds of soldiers, and it wouldn't be easy. Every little snippet of information they could glean about the enemy's intentions and also their morale was vital.

Sure enough, the next weeks were harrowing. Bella and the other radio operators heard distressing reports on both sides and it couldn't help but affect them deeply, but they immersed themselves in their work with no thought of self. Then finally, in the middle of May, British and Polish troops captured Cassino, and the three WAAFs were told they were being sent back to Cairo. They were all exhausted, but Bella had become increasingly uneasy about Winnie over the last weeks. The fatigue which dogged Winnie in recent days seemed extreme and different to a normal tiredness. Her friend was usually so chirpy and positive, however dire the situation, but she'd been suffering with a gippy tummy and a lack of appetite for a while and Bella didn't like the change in her.

They arrived back in Cairo to the welcome news that they had been granted a week's leave at a house in Alexandria that had been taken over as a leave centre, before they would return to more top-secret work. Bella was hoping that the rest and change of scenery would be the tonic Winnie needed, and when the warrant officer who'd been charged with driving them to the house pulled into a large garden courtyard off a broad, palm-tree lined boulevard, she thought it was just the thing. The large white stone house bordered on both sides by stately eucalyptus trees was beautiful.

It was sunset, the sky above them like a saffron sea with the sun dropping like a ripe red African orange in a golden haze.

They were welcomed at the door by a plump, smiling housekeeper and a little maid who was apparently her daughter, and after a glass of sweet tea three-quarters full of peeled fresh almonds they were shown upstairs to three of the six bedrooms the house held. The double beds were covered by snow-white sheets, the walls were whitewashed and there was a small basin in each room along with a tall, thin wardrobe.

Fatima, the housekeeper, showed them the shared bathroom with its small tub and toilet as proudly as if it was her own home, and then ushered them downstairs for the evening meal she had prepared.

They ate in the dining room with the doors open onto the courtyard garden at the front of the property. It was laid out with running fountains, jasmine and bougainvillea in abundance and divided into small separate areas by paths and flowering bushes. The scent stealing into the room was heavenly. At the back of the house was an orchard of ancient, gnarled olive trees.

It was an oasis in the desert, the three of them agreed, as they sat at the dining table listening to the twitterings of hundreds of sparrows. Fatima told them that the little birds nested in the huge bougainvillea vines which filled the courtyard with a cerise-flowered canopy in places. After the relentless months of work without a break, it was almost too much to take in.

Bella slept deeply that night on the bed that consisted of one massive central bedspring with a sawhorse to either side and a mattress. The shutters at the window opened onto the orchard but Fatima had told them to keep their shutters closed at night because of insects.

Lutfiyah, Fatima's daughter, whom Bella thought couldn't be more than eleven or twelve years old, brought a breakfast tray of coffee and a platter of freshly prepared fruit and pastries to the room at eight o'clock. Enjoying the luxury of breakfast in bed, Bella took her time over the meal before she wandered along to Winnie's bedroom next door, only to find her friend still fast asleep with her own breakfast tray untouched. Camilla, on the other hand, was downstairs in the courtyard when Bella ventured forth, holding an animated conversation with the young boy who tended the garden. He was another of Fatima's children, she'd discovered.

'He's going to accompany me into town later,' Camilla told Bella. 'Fatima doesn't want us wandering about on our own – I think she's worried we might be whisked off to a harem or something.' She giggled. 'Fat chance. Do you and Winnie want to come to the bazaar? There doesn't seem a lot to do here.' Bella suspected 'not a lot to do' equated to no airmen dancing attendance.

'Perhaps,' Bella prevaricated. Winnie had seemed so tired and out of sorts over the last weeks, she suspected her friend might like to just sit in the garden in the shade and enjoy the unfamiliar indulgence of doing nothing, rather than traipsing around the hot, dusty shops and bazaars.

Just before lunch, when Winnie still hadn't made an appearance, Bella went upstairs to her friend's room. Winnie was preparing to come down for lunch but looked pale and wan, and admitted she felt nauseous. 'I think it's one of these foreign bugs I can't shake off,' she said wearily. Then she forced a smile as she added, 'At least it's helped me lose a bit of weight so I fit into my uniform better.'

Bella gave no answering smile in return; for the first time she noticed that Winnie was considerably thinner than she had been a while ago. 'Winnie, you need to go to the doctor and ask for something, explain how you've been.'

'You know me, I'm not keen on quacks.'

'Nevertheless.'

'I'm fine, Bella. A few days here will sort me out. It's a lovely place, isn't it.'

'Don't change the subject,' Bella said, softening the admonition with a smile. 'You're going to see the doc when we're back at base no matter what you say, all right?'

'We'll see.' And then as Bella frowned, Winnie added, 'If I don't feel better I'll go, OK?'

Six days later they were back at base and the following morning Winnie saw the medical officer, who took some bloods and said he was sure there was nothing for her to worry about. He gave her a box of what looked like horse pills, which Winnie had to cut into quarters before she could get them down, along with a bottle of foul-tasting medicine which Winnie promptly tipped down the sink, much to Bella's chagrin. 'I promise you, if I didn't feel sick before I took that then I certainly would after,'

Winnie said firmly. Bella had to admit that the mere smell knocked one backwards, and conceded that she had lost that particular battle.

They had been told in strictest confidence that the reason they'd been recalled was because their skills were needed with regard to the long-awaited invasion of Europe. It was going to be the biggest combined land, sea and air operation of all time and needed meticulous planning, total secrecy and a complete understanding of what the Germans were thinking and doing.

'These last days are crucial to success or failure,' the station commander told Bella when he took her aside the morning after they'd returned from leave. 'We need to know what the Germans are thinking before they do. It's like a game of poker, bluff and counter-bluff.'

She nodded. 'Yes, sir.' She knew nothing about poker.

He hesitated, and then said gently, 'How's Group Captain Crawford?' The general consensus was that the man was a walking miracle, but then William did have a damn good reason to fight to get well, he thought, looking at Bella. He hoped it worked out between them; he'd liked William very much.

Bella went slightly pink. 'The last operation was another success as far as I know, sir.' She didn't add that she was worried because she hadn't had a letter in over two months. Moving about from one place to another always caused problems, she told herself, but she missed him so much and his letters brought a semblance of sanity into an otherwise mad world.

'Capital, capital.' He felt embarrassed; he always steered away from making things personal, even with his long-suffering wife. Having been reared in a strict military family, he had been taught from infancy all about discipline and the necessity of the stiff British upper lip. One had to set an example at all times and remember one's privileged position. The lower ranks might show their feelings, but an officer? Never. Even when one witnessed one's best friend impaled on barbed wire and the enemy taking potshots at him all night so that he screamed for death, one maintained self-control and restraint in front of the men. The nightmares were more difficult to master. 'Keep up the good work, Corporal,' he said heartily. 'We're on the winning side. Always remember that – we are on the winning side.'

'Yes, sir.' She hoped so. She so hoped so, but the reports of the 'secret weapon' that Hitler had up his sleeve were becoming more alarming. There was no doubt that something existed, from the conversations they'd eavesdropped on: a pilotless, jet-propelled aircraft carrying high explosives – the *Vergeltungswaffe* or reprisal weapon, the Germans called it – and aimed at England. Where William was. The 'V-1'.

Chapter Twenty-Six

'I'm sorry, Corporal.'

The medical officer was a nice man and he truly seemed sorry, Bella thought dazedly, as she stared into the lined face. Somehow, she found the words to say, 'But she was all right a few weeks ago. It can't be that serious.'

'These things often don't become apparent until it's too—' He stopped abruptly. 'Until it's serious.'

Too late. He had been going to say until it was too late. Bella sat frozen in her seat. Winnie had been due to hear the results of her blood test the day before but had suffered a fainting fit combined with a nosebleed in the morning and had been shipped off to sickbay. Bella had visited her there in the evening and been somewhat reassured to find her with a little more colour in her face and looking less washed out. With this in mind, she said, 'She looked more herself last night. Much better.'

'The result of a blood transfusion and other medical interventions.'

'But it can't be this thing you're talking about, this blood problem.'

'A blood cancer, Corporal. And of course we're transferring her to the military hospital for further tests later today, and then depending on what they find, back to England, but –' again he paused – 'I thought you should know. I know the two of you are great friends.'

'No, this isn't right. She's come through the war and we've been bombed at times and . . .' Her voice trailed away. 'It isn't right.'

'I'm sorry. Perhaps they'll be able to do more once she's home. Medical science is making great strides in this area, I understand.'

But he didn't believe that; she could read it in the sympathy on his face that he couldn't hide. 'Does she know? Have you told her?'

'Not in so many words, but I suspect she has some idea by now that something is badly wrong.'

'But she's so young to have something serious. Could you have made a mistake?' She was clutching at straws and she knew it.

'I only wish that was so, but as I said, other tests will be carried out both here and in England. I would be very happy to be proved wrong.'

Her father, James, Kitty and now Winnie? It couldn't be. She wouldn't let it be. 'Can I see her?' She had come along to the sickbay between shifts, but the medical officer had intercepted her before she'd visited Winnie and sat her down in a quiet corner.

'Of course, m'dear.' The doctor nodded at an orderly who was hovering close by. 'Sami will take you to her. She'll be leaving for the military hospital later – perhaps you'd see to it that her belongings are brought here.'

'Yes, sir,' she said mechanically, feeling as though she had been knocked for six. Two or three days ago she and Winnie had sat in the courtyard garden drinking gin cocktails and talking about what they would do when the war was over. Her plans had been tied up with William but she'd said she'd like to travel with him and see more of the world before settling down; perhaps live and work here and there for a time. Winnie, on the other hand, had confided that her dream was to meet someone and live in the country, away from the city where she'd been born and grown up. 'Somewhere with fields for children and dogs to run in and where I can keep hens. Nothing big or grand, but the front garden would have a little picket fence and be full of hollyhocks and Michaelmas daisies, and the back garden would have a small stream running at the bottom of it. I'd love a garden,' Winnie had said wistfully, so wistfully that Bella had hugged her and promised that she'd come to visit her in her little cottage and collect eggs from the hen house, and they'd sit talking about old times in the garden.

Winnie hadn't wanted a millionaire's mansion or fame and fortune, she told herself bitterly as she followed the orderly into the sickbay, just to fall in love with a good man and live a peaceful life raising a family in the countryside. Was that so much to ask, God? Was it?

Composing her face as the orderly drew back the curtain from around the bed, she thought at first that Winnie was asleep. Then, as her friend opened her eyes and smiled, Bella said softly, 'How are you feeling now?' Stupid question, she thought, but what else could she say? And Winnie looked worse today, much worse.

'Lazy,' Winnie said, grimacing.

'You? Lazy? That'll be the day.' She realized now that Winnie had been pushing herself over the last weeks, refusing to give in to how she was feeling until it became too much. The work had been the important thing, she thought, with a surge of resentment against the war and what it asked of people.

Winnie stared at her. 'You know, don't you.'

'Know? Know what?' She thought she'd done a good job of hiding her feelings.

Winnie held out her hand and Bella took it as she sat down by the side of the bed. 'It's all right,' Winnie said softly. 'I'm not scared of dying.'

'*You're not going to die.*' She'd spoken too loudly and now she lowered her voice as she repeated, 'You're not going to die.'

'But if I do, I'm not scared.' Winnie squeezed Bella's fingers. 'I want you to know that. I saw the look on Dr Wood's face this morning and he's spoken to you, hasn't he? He went on about more tests and this, that and the other, but I could read what was in his eyes.'

'Winnie—'

'No, listen. Listen to me, Bella. I made my peace with

God after Mum died and something happened then. I can't explain it but I've felt Him very close since. Before she went I'd just gone along with what she believed and the whole Catholic thing because it was all I'd ever known – God, Jesus dying on the cross for us, the virgin birth, but after she died and I was so angry –' she shook her head – 'I don't know how to explain it except to say one night it all became real for me, me personally. So I'm not scared. I know I'll see Mum again.' Her voice softened still more and she murmured, 'Don't cry, Bella. Everything's all right.'

Gulping against the tears, Bella's voice came out like a wail when she cried, 'But what about me? What am I going to do without you?' And then she clapped her hand over her mouth, horrified at the selfishness. 'Oh, I'm sorry, I'm sorry, that was awful.' For a moment she thought Winnie was crying and then she saw her friend was trying not to laugh.

'Oh, Bella, your face!'

And as Winnie gave way to laughter, Bella reluctantly drummed up a smile, even as she thought, *How can I let her go?* Only Winnie could laugh at a moment like this.

They talked for a while but Bella could see that Winnie was so tired she could barely keep her eyes open, and after some minutes she kissed her on the forehead, saying, 'Have a nap. I'll come and visit in the hospital when I can.'

'Bella?' Winnie's hand held on to hers for a moment longer. 'Don't fight this. You're amazing and I love you but you can't control everything. Sometimes you have to let go and accept that what will be, will be, or you'll end up tearing yourself apart. Do you understand what I'm saying?'

Bella nodded. 'I understand, but I don't think I know how to do that,' she said with painful honesty, looking down into Winnie's white face. She wished she had noticed Winnie wasn't well earlier; she wished she'd made her go and see a doctor weeks ago; she wished – oh, she wished a hundred things, but it was all too late.

'Try, for me?'

Bella nodded again.

'We had some good times, didn't we? Even in the midst of all the heartache?'

'We did, Winnie, we did.' She had been about to say that they would have some more, but in view of Winnie's earlier words she bit it back, saying instead, 'You're more than a friend, you're the sister I never had, you know that, don't you? So – so try and get better, for me?'

Winnie didn't reply to this. Instead she said, smiling gently, 'You're a force of nature, Bella McFadyen, do *you* know *that*?'

'I'll see you soon.'

'Take care and tell Cammy to behave herself.'

'Fat chance.'

Bella forced a smile as she said goodbye, but once outside she bit her lip hard and told herself she couldn't cry, not here. The air was scorching and even in the sickbay it had been humid and sticky, but Winnie's flesh had been cold. The pain as this thought hit home caused a whimper deep in her throat which she stifled quickly. She felt very small and very alone as she stood there under the blazing Egyptian sky, and very far from home and William.

Three days later it became apparent that Winnie was too ill to risk being moved from the military hospital in Cairo, and a short time after this she slipped away in her sleep. Bella had been given permission to be at her friend's side for the last forty-eight hours while Camilla held the fort in the radio operators' room back at base, and everyone had been kindness itself, bringing her cups of tea she didn't want and sandwiches she couldn't eat.

Just once in the last twelve hours Winnie had surfaced from a drugged sleep and as Bella had felt the hand in hers move, she saw Winnie's eyes looking at her with recognition. 'Bella,' she whispered.

'I'm here, Winnie. I'm here. I'm staying with you.'

'Bella, I saw it. The cottage and the garden and Mum's there, waiting.' Winnie had drawn in a rasping breath. 'It's beautiful, Bella. So – so beautiful.'

Bella was overcome, and tears blurred Winnie's face as she found the strength to murmur, 'I'm glad, Winnie.'

'B– Bella?'

'Yes, what is it?'

'Don't be sad, n– not for me. It's so beautiful . . .'

'I know, darling. I know.'

Her voice taking on a strange strength, Winnie said, 'The

roses, they smell so sweet, and there's bluebirds. Bluebirds singing in the trees. I never expected bluebirds . . .' She had closed her eyes then, her fingers relaxing in Bella's hand and a smile touching her colourless lips.

Minutes later, Winnie had gone to her cottage and her mother's arms.

Bereft, Bella put her head in her arms on the bed and wept uncontrollably.

Chapter Twenty-Seven

'Part of me never expected this day to come, and now it has I wish it hadn't,' Camilla said mournfully as she and Bella stood on the deck of HMT *Corfu* in the pouring rain of a British autumn. 'I shall have to divorce Nicholas, of course. I simply couldn't go back to the stuffy life we had before the war.'

'Absolutely not,' Bella said with heavy sarcasm. They had still been in Cairo when the war had ended in May after the Germans had surrendered. The price of victory and defeat had been fifty-five million dead and many more injured and crippled for life. Their station commander had asked them to stay on for some more weeks as Japan had yet to surrender and their expertise and experience were needed in what he called the 'tidying-up' operation, but the work had been much more low key and Camilla had taken full advantage of this, conducting an enjoyable but risky balancing act between three married lovers, none of whom knew about each other. While Bella had been desperate to get back to England to William, Camilla had engaged in evenings in the Nile Club, the Gezira, the Auberge des Pyramides and other establishments, drinking cocktails, eating dinner, sporting in hotel rooms and generally having a high old time.

Camilla grinned at Bella now, flicking back her silky hair and adjusting her umbrella. 'I know,' she said complacently, 'I'm a romance whore, aren't I.'

'Well, I wouldn't have put it quite like that.'

'Winnie would have done.'

They became silent for a moment, each thinking it should have been three of them standing there.

'I do miss her too.' Camilla slipped her free arm through Bella's. 'Not like you, I know, but –' she sighed – 'it seems so unfair, doesn't it.'

'That's because it is.'

Camilla nodded, and then waved at a naval officer she'd been flirting with since they embarked, nearly taking Bella's eye out with the umbrella as she did so. They had left Port Said in the middle of October and when they'd passed Gibraltar a couple of days ago Camilla had become melancholy and had confessed she was dreading seeing her husband again. Now the ship was in the process of docking at Southampton and Bella knew that Camilla hadn't told anyone in England she was coming home. 'I need time to adjust,' she'd said firmly when Bella had tried to persuade her to let someone know. 'I shall find a little hotel somewhere and just prepare myself for a couple of days.'

Now, glancing at the naval officer who was still looking

at them and the glint in Camilla's eye, Bella had a pretty good idea of how the preparation would play out. 'You're incorrigible,' she whispered.

'Darling, all the nice girls love a sailor,' Camilla whispered back, arching her finely drawn eyebrows. 'And this one is fancy-free with no ties whatsoever, so who knows?'

Bella was only half-listening; the dock was getting nearer and she was searching it for a familiar face. She had only let William know she was coming home; she wanted to see him first, and then they could go and see her mother together if everything turned out all right. She didn't know why the 'if' was there or even when it had come. Perhaps it had been when they knew the war was over and one day soon they'd be going home, or maybe even before that, when Winnie had died, or yet still before, after the deaths of James and Kitty. Then there was her father . . . It seemed that everyone she loved, she lost. William's letters had still been as passionate as ever but it had been a long time since they had seen each other and he had endured so much. People change. He was an honourable man; if his feelings had changed he wouldn't tell her by a letter or even hint at it. He would wait until he saw her face to face.

Her heart was beating so hard it constricted her throat as they gathered their bags together. She and Camilla hugged and promised to write and then Camilla joined her naval officer, who was waiting for her, a big grin on his face. Slowly the ship edged into its berth as she stood at the railings again, peering at the folk on the dock.

And then she saw him. A tall, dark-haired figure, bareheaded in spite of the pouring rain and standing slightly apart from everyone else milling about. As he would be, she thought with such a surge of love she felt faint. He had always been a loner. If he didn't want her she would die. Her heart would still go on beating but that part of her that made her *her* would be no more.

He met her at the bottom of the gangplank after the formalities of disembarkation, his arms open wide and such love on his face that she flew into them like a homing pigeon, dropping her bags and oblivious to everyone around them. Lifting her right off her feet he held her to him, his endearments incoherent as he smothered her face with kisses.

People moved around them; some smiling, some disapproving and some frankly envious, but they were in their own world. It was some minutes later before they drew apart, breathless, dishevelled, but still unwilling to let go of each other.

'I couldn't see you,' he murmured, kissing her again. 'There were all these people and I couldn't see you. I thought something had happened, you'd changed your mind . . .'

'About us? Never.'

'Oh, my love.'

He looked older, she thought, but of course he would after everything he had been through; all the operations, the fighting to get well. His hair was greying at the temples but it made him look even more handsome, distinguished.

He bent and picked up her bags and she saw to her surprise that they were practically the last ones on the dock. 'Come on, I reserved a taxicab. It'll be waiting, I hope,' he added with the smile that was so infrequent but so magical.

The cab was still there and the cheerful little man who greeted them took her bags and stowed them in the boot of the car while they climbed inside. He kissed her again, and they only drew apart when the cab driver said, 'Where to, guv?'

'Back to the Angel Hotel where you picked me up,' William said, before turning to her and adding, 'I thought you'd need to rest after your journey and have a quiet night and something to eat, so I booked a couple of rooms.'

'Two rooms?' she queried softly. She wanted to sleep in his arms.

He looked at her, long and steadily. 'I've got a special licence in my pocket. If you'll still have me, we can be married tomorrow. I confess to being old-fashioned . . .'

'I love old-fashioned.'

She was married in a vibrant silk dress she had bought on a shopping expedition with Camilla just before they left Egypt, her hair, which had been bleached even fairer by the foreign sun, held in place by jewelled combs. Her attire would have been perfectly suitable in Cairo, but on a cold October day in England she had the appearance of an exotic bird of paradise. William thought she was the most beautiful thing he had ever seen. He had asked the friendly taxicab driver of the day before if he would pick them up the next day and also be a witness at the register office. The man had been tickled pink, offering to bring along his wife as the other witness.

William and Bella held hands as they made their vows, exchanging the wedding rings that William had bought when he had made the arrangements a few days ago. Much to his relief, Bella's fitted perfectly and as the registrar pronounced them man and wife he took her into his arms and kissed her as though he would never let her go, causing the taxi driver's wife to shed a few tears. Once back at the hotel they treated the middle-aged couple to a champagne lunch before waving them off, whereupon William promptly took her in his arms again, kissing her long and hard.

'I suffered the torments of the damned last night,' he whispered huskily, his arm round her as he drew her into the lift to the bedrooms. 'Knowing you were so near.'

Bella had been feeling a little nervous. He'd been married before and was an experienced lover, and she didn't want to disappoint him, but the look on his face dispelled any misgivings and she put her arms round his neck, drawing his mouth to hers. 'I want you so much,' she murmured against his lips.

She'd expected that they'd probably go to his room so when the lift continued upwards to the next floor, she said, 'William?' as the lift doors opened.

He smiled but didn't answer the unspoken question,

leading her along the carpeted corridor to the end door and opening it before whisking her up into his arms and making her squeal. 'The bridal suite,' he said, before kissing her again and then setting her down in a room that was all frothy cream lace and pink satin and fresh flowers. 'I know it's a bit much but like I said, I'm old-fashioned.'

'It's perfect.' She giggled at the flamboyant painted cherubs on the ceiling.

Smiling ruefully, he walked across to a small table where an ice-bucket, champagne and strawberries were waiting. Popping the cork, he filled the two flutes on the table with the icy-cold sparkling liquid and handed Bella hers. 'To us,' he said softly and simply.

'To us.' The champagne tasted of strawberries and honey and it was delicious, much nicer than any she'd had before; or perhaps it was being here with William that made it so delectable? she thought, taking another sip.

He took her glass and placed it and his own on the table and as he took her in his arms, he murmured, 'You're so beautiful, so very beautiful.'

They undressed each other slowly, and as she peeled off his shirt and his chest was exposed her fingers traced the scars amongst his body hair. 'Oh, William,' she breathed softly. He had gone through so much and she hadn't been there.

'It's fine, I'm fine,' he said, kissing her until she couldn't think of anything but her need of him.

He was gentle with her, mindful of her innocence, but when her passion equalled his and he entered her she moved with him in perfect harmony towards a climax that splintered the world into fragments and left them both shaken and satiated. Afterwards she lay cradled in his arms under the blankets and it was like that she drifted off to sleep, feeling at rest within herself as she had never done in her life before.

They made love again before going down to dinner in the evening. The restaurant was crowded but William had reserved an intimate table for two in a small alcove, and they drank wine and laughed and talked over an excellent meal although Bella was barely conscious of what she was eating. They were married, she was his wife, she kept thinking in wonder. In between the main meal and dessert, he lifted her left hand and kissed her wedding ring before pressing a small box into her fingers. 'I know this is the wrong way round, the engagement ring should come first. But then again we don't seem to have done anything in the traditional way, do we?'

She opened the small velvet lid and gasped. The three glittering diamonds on a loop of gold were exquisite. 'It's utterly beautiful,' she murmured softly, her eyes sparkling as he took the ring out of the box and slipped it beside her wedding band. Again it fitted perfectly. 'But I didn't get you a wedding present.'

'Yes, you did, twice,' he said with a wicked grin and then chuckled as she blushed.

She had never seen him smile so much, she thought as

the wonder flooded in even more strongly, but then their courtship – if you could call it that – hadn't been a traditional one, as he'd said a minute ago. They had lots to discover about each other, but time was on their side now at last. William had reserved the bridal suite for five nights – a mini honeymoon, he'd called it – and she didn't intend to let anything of the outside world intrude. Soon enough she would have to think about her mother and pay a visit up north with all the memories that would involve, but not for the next little while. That belonged to her and William alone.

Chapter Twenty-Eight

It was only shortly after two in the afternoon but already the light was fading, Belinda thought, staring out of the window of the morning room as she was inclined to do for long periods these days. It had tried to snow earlier before an icy rain had taken hold. Wright was sure it would be a bad winter and the old butler was usually right about such things.

She turned from the window and walked across to the fire that was burning and crackling brightly in the hearth. Two brass lamps with fluted pink glass shades had been lit by Mrs Banks a few minutes ago and were filling the room with a warm glow. The atmosphere was one of warmth and peace but Belinda didn't feel peaceful. In fact, she didn't think she'd known a moment's real peace since the day that Philip had declared his love for her three years ago. He'd been true to his word since then. In all his visits here and hers to Evendale, he hadn't referred to it again and she doubted that he ever would.

She sighed, sitting down in one of the armchairs set

each side of the fireplace. Clasping her hands in her lap, she stared into the flickering flames from the big log burning in the grate.

There were times when the emptiness of her life seemed overwhelming. And then she refuted the thought, telling herself she had so much to be grateful for. Since Philip had turned Evendale into the convalescence home for military personnel she visited it almost every day, reading and talking to the patients and playing cards with them or walking in the grounds with those men who could manage to go outside. It had given her purpose, something worthwhile that she could do.

She'd wrestled with herself for some time after Philip had revealed his feelings. And then she'd had to accept that she loved him. It had been a relief to acknowledge it, if only to herself. The seeds of her love had been sown long ago on Armistice Day and an act that should have made her hate him had had the opposite effect. She didn't understand that or herself.

They'd caused each other immense grief, she told herself sadly, and not just themselves but worse, those they loved, and yet this feeling between them had grown, which was surely against all logic and reason? But whatever they felt for each other, there was Bella. She might be Philip's natural child, flesh of his flesh, but she hated him with a passion.

Belinda sighed again. If she told Philip that she loved him and wanted to be with him she knew she would lose her daughter for ever. One day soon Bella would come home, God willing, and much as she cared for Philip, their daughter came first. Although they had never discussed it and she had never told Philip how she felt, he must know that any intimate relationship between them was impossible. Ironic, really, that Bella should be so like him in her nature – spirited, determined, intelligent, intense – when it was those very qualities that would prevent Bella from ever forgiving him for his part in the tangle of the past.

Where Bella loved, she loved with all her heart and soul, and it was the same with the opposite side of the coin. There had been a definite coolness in a couple of Bella's letters after she had first written to her about Philip's grief when James died, and she had been very careful not to mention him again.

Mrs Banks came bustling into the room in the next moment with a tray of coffee which she placed on the small table next to Belinda's armchair. 'It's bitter out there today, ma'am. You're in the right place and no mistake.'

Over the last few years since most of the staff had gone, she and Mrs Banks had settled into more of an easy informality and Wright had become increasingly protective of her, bless him, Belinda thought fondly, as she said, 'I was going to go to Evendale today. I'm reading *Great Expectations* to that young officer I told you about, the one who was blinded and is suffering from shell shock, but I think I might leave it till tomorrow and see if the weather is more clement.'

'Definitely, ma'am,' Mrs Banks said firmly. She and

Wright didn't altogether approve of the mistress going to what had become a convalescence home-cum-hospital; it was kind of her to want to comfort the poor souls there, but some weren't quite right in the head and you never knew what they were going to do next. The mistress had said there were plenty of male nurses to handle the difficult ones, but still . . . 'Now eat a couple of them teacakes, ma'am, they're still warm,' she said in her motherly fashion before she left the room. The mistress was too thin in her opinion, and the sadness that had settled on her since the master's death and Miss Bella's leaving rarely lifted, except sometimes when the colonel called. Through an unspoken mutual agreement she and Wright never discussed the mistress's friendship with Colonel Wynford, nor what they had gleaned on the day of the master's death and Miss Bella subsequently leaving the estate. As Wright had said in the kitchen on the day it had happened, the mistress had been just a young girl when she had come into this house and she had made the master happy. His statement had said more than just the actual words and had been a declaration of how they would deal with things.

Belinda looked ruefully at the plate of teacakes. She wasn't in the least bit hungry but she knew she would have to force down at least two or three to keep Mrs Banks happy.

It was nearly four o'clock when Philip came to the house and dark outside; an icy sleet was falling and as Mrs Banks showed him into the morning room where

Belinda was sitting reading, he said by way of greeting, 'What a wretched day. I hate sleet, it's neither one thing nor the other.'

'I'll bring some tea and cake, ma'am,' Mrs Banks said before she shut the door, leaving them alone. She'd warn Cook the colonel was here too, she thought as she bustled off to the kitchen. He often stayed for dinner when he called late afternoon like today.

'I just wanted to make sure nothing was wrong after you didn't come today.' He smiled at her and Belinda smiled back. There was rarely a day that she didn't go to Evendale or he to Fellburn.

'I'm perfectly all right, Philip,' she said quietly, her sedate manner at odds with the warm glow inside that his concern about her always produced. 'The weather has been so dreadful I thought I'd leave it until tomorrow.'

'Sensible girl.' He dropped down into the other armchair opposite hers and stretched out his hands to the warmth of the fire, his easy manner evidence of the close relationship that they shared these days.

He had brought the fresh smell of wind and rain with him and Belinda wondered how a room could change so much with the entrance of one person. But that was Philip.

'What?' He'd raised his eyebrows, his head to one side as he smiled at her, and she realized she'd been staring.

Flushing, she said, 'Nothing, nothing. I was just wondering if you can stay for dinner?'

'Absolutely.' He grinned. 'Why do you think I left it so late to call?'

'You're dreadful,' she said, laughing softly.

His expression changed and his voice was slightly husky when he said, 'I love to make you laugh.' Then in the next moment he changed the subject as he always did if the atmosphere became charged, his tone light. 'You'll never guess what Oliver did today, not in a month of Sundays.'

'Oh, yes?' Oliver was a favourite patient of hers. The young lad had been no more than sixteen when he had joined up at the beginning of the war because he had wanted to go off and fight with his three older brothers. He had seen each of them die; two at El Alamein and the third during the liberation of Rome, but it had been in the last weeks of the Battle of the Bulge that Oliver had lost both his legs in an explosion and suffered burns to his hands and face. He had sunk into a deep depression which had been made worse by the fact that his parents and two sisters had been killed in the Blitz. Belinda had spent a lot of time sitting with him in the gardens at Evendale, wheeling him down to the lake where it was peaceful and quiet and the kingfishers flitted over the water or up into the bluebell wood in the spring. As the weather had got colder, knowing he was better when he was outdoors, she'd pushed the wheelchair to Philip's farm, where the farmhands and some of the inmates always made a fuss of him. She'd often come home and cried at how gentle the big tough men were with the lad.

'He wheeled himself down to the lake and went skinny dipping, in this weather! Caused a hell of a panic when one of the other fellows saw him and thought he had finally become unhinged. Half a dozen of 'em went rushing down thinking he'd tried to drown himself and he pulled himself out, bright as a button, and said he'd wanted to feel alive again. They got him back inside and warmed him up but the doc said it's a good sign. Good sign! I don't know who's dafter, the doc or Oliver.'

She could tell he was secretly delighted; he had a soft spot for Oliver too. 'I'm glad and I can understand what the doctor means, and what Oliver meant too. He's so young still but he's missed all his youth because of the war, times of doing crazy things just for the fun of it.'

Philip nodded, sadness sweeping across his face. 'Sometimes I look at them, Linnie, and think my lads were the lucky ones, being taken out of this damn world rather than being brought back maimed and crippled and blind and out of their minds.' His voice broke as he muttered, 'And they're so brave, all of 'em in their different ways. It humbles me, especially when I think of the mess I've made of my life.'

'Philip—'

'I know, I know.' She had taken his hand and he looked down at their entwined fingers. 'But it's true, Linnie. I was selfish, selfish and shallow for too many years and it hurt people I loved, people I still love. I cared about Bella before I knew she was my daughter – you know that, don't you. There was always something about her but I put it down to the fact that she was your child. And Archibald. He was a good friend and I did a terrible thing to him.'

'*We* did.'

'M'dear, you were little more than a child—'

A tap on the door before it was opened brought their hands apart, but they were still leaning towards each other when Mrs Banks said, her voice unusually high, 'It's Miss Bella, ma'am,' and the next moment Bella walked into the room followed by a tall, dark-haired man.

Such was her surprise that for a moment Belinda couldn't move. Philip's reactions were quicker. He stood up but any remark he was about to make died at the blazing anger in Bella's face. For some seconds they remained in a frozen tableau: Bella glaring, Belinda seated and Philip at a loss to know what to say, and then the man behind his daughter took her arm, his voice cool and calm as he looked at Belinda and said, 'We haven't been introduced but you must be Bella's mother. I'm William, William Crawford.'

When in the next instant Bella made a kind of strangled cry and tore herself out of his grasp, rushing out of the room and almost knocking Mrs Banks over who was still standing on the threshold, he said quickly, 'Excuse me,' and followed her, to find her fumbling with the handle of the front door. 'Stop,' he said quietly. 'Just stop, Bella,' turning her to face him.

'Do you know who that is in there?'

'I presume it's your mother and Colonel Wynford, from your reaction.' She was trembling, he could feel the tremors under his hands which were gripping her shoulders.

'They – they were—'

'They were sitting in front of the fire talking, that's all.'

'That's not all and you know it. You saw them.'

'I saw nothing more than two people talking, Bella, and neither did you.'

'It was the way they were with each other, you *must* have sensed it?'

He was silent for a moment, wondering how he could put what he felt bound to say. He knew she had been apprehensive about coming to see her mother because deep down she was frightened that the suspicions that had been aroused years ago, when her mother had written to her about James's death, would be confirmed. And he understood that. She had loved the man she'd known as her father and had been devastated when he'd died the way he had; not only that, but she'd lost the man she was going to marry and her whole world had been turned upside down. Her mother wasn't the person she'd thought she was and had fallen from the pedestal, and to Bella the man sitting back there was to blame for it all. Quietly, he enfolded her into his arms and after a moment her stiff body went limp. 'My darling, I love you more than life itself so listen to what I'm going to say.'

She went to pull away, and he held her close as he said, 'No, listen to me. You asked me if I sensed something back there and I need to answer that truthfully for your sake. What I saw was two people who care deeply for each other, how deeply I don't know and neither do you, but there was a wealth of sadness there too.'

Her voice was muffled when she said, 'They *should* be sad.'

'Possibly, but are you going to waste the rest of your life wishing that on them? Are you? Hate's a deadly thing, my darling. It eats its way through everything. It will darken your life, *our* life, and cause you untold damage. You have to let go of it.'

She raised her head, her eyes swimming with tears. 'I *want* to hate him.'

'Oh, Bella.' Her innate honesty caused him to pull her in to him again, cradling her against his chest for a moment before moving her to look down into her face once more. 'If you leave here now like this you will live to regret it.'

'My father deserves better than me flinging my arms round them and wishing them well.'

'No one is asking you to do that, least of all me.'

'It feels like that,' she said, her bottom lip trembling like a child's.

'Sweetheart, bring reason to bear for a moment. If your mother and this man care for each other, really care for each other, you can't do anything about that. You can't control how they feel or tell them what to do and in trying to fight against it you'll tear yourself apart.'

She stared at him. 'That's what Winnie said.' She shook her head as she murmured, 'Not about the colonel, but me wanting to make her better somehow. She – she said sometimes you need to accept that what will be, will be.'

'She's right.'

'But this is different.'

'Yes, it is.' He took a deep breath; it was going to be hard to say what he knew he should. 'This is about forgiveness.'

She pulled herself from his arms, taking a step backwards. 'You're telling me I should forgive him?' she said incredulously.

'For your sake, not his.'

'I can't do that, William.'

'Can't or won't?'

'Both.'

He nodded. That devastating honesty again, but it was one of the things he loved about her. 'Will you come back into the room and talk to your mother?' Their bags were in the hall; they had been going to stay for a few days but he didn't know if she would balk at that now.

She made no answer but just inclined her head as she bit hard on her bottom lip.

They entered the morning room together. William suspected that the colonel had advised Belinda to stay where she was and to let them talk in private after Bella had rushed out of the room. Now Belinda stood up and came to them, taking Bella's hands as she said, 'My darling,' while Philip made to leave. As he walked away, Belinda surprised him as she said, 'Wait, Philip.'

He paused, standing beside William as Belinda drew Bella over to the sofa and pressed her down on it, sitting beside her. Something had clarified in Belinda's thinking when she'd seen the look on Philip's face as their daughter had glared at him with such hatred. 'You've come home,' she said quietly, stating the obvious.

Bella nodded, unable to speak.

'I'm glad, so glad, and I don't want to upset you, my darling, but there's something I need to say.'

Bella was rigid.

'You're right in what you supposed when you walked into this room and saw Philip and me together, but quite wrong if you think that we have acted on it. You think we care for each other, yes?'

Still Bella didn't speak or move.

'As I said, you are right.' Belinda was still holding her daughter's hands. 'But you have to understand that the past and its effect on you means that we will only ever be friends, nothing more.'

As Bella tried to remove her hands, Belinda's grip tightened. 'There were many factors that contributed to what happened all those years ago, Bella, and you're old enough to understand that. Philip's not the only one to blame. I came into this house as a young bride and Archibald was a different man in those days to the one you knew. It wasn't his fault, things had happened to him, things which I don't feel I can go into, but he was locked inside himself and I didn't have the experience or understanding to realize he needed help. I was desperately unhappy and I believe he was too. Then, that night at the Armistice Ball . . .'

She paused, glancing at Philip before continuing, 'When I realized there were consequences the decision was mine, and mine alone, to tell Archibald the child was his, and Philip never knew he had a daughter. The pregnancy, the knowledge that we were going to have a child, changed Archibald – and our marriage – more than words can express and he became the man you knew, happy and fulfilled. A loving father and husband.'

'But it was a lie.' The words were low, pain-filled.

'Yes, it was, but it saved him, saved our marriage, I believe that now. The McFadyen men struggled to produce children –' Belinda shook her head – 'but that's by the bye. I sound as though I'm trying to make excuses for what I know was inexcusable, and maybe I am, but I'm telling you the truth, Bella. It wasn't planned, it was never repeated, it was moments of madness and it was wrong, but it gave me you. I should have had the courage to tell Archibald the truth when I knew I was expecting a baby, which would have avoided the tragedies of the future. I'm totally to blame for them—'

'*No.*' Philip took a step forward before stopping. 'No, you're not. You were a slip of a girl – the fault was mine, totally mine.'

Their gaze caught and held, and Bella dropped her eyes from the well of sadness, her thoughts in turmoil, assailed by so many emotions she couldn't have put a name to any of them. She stood up and walked to William, standing by his side, needing his strength. As he put his arm round her she looked at her mother. Philip was standing to one side of the couch, and it was to the two of them that she said flatly, 'William and I got married a few days ago when I returned to England. I wanted to come and tell you myself rather than writing.'

Belinda's eyes were glittering with unshed tears and her lips were trembling but she managed to whisper, 'That's wonderful. I'm so pleased for you both.'

William smiled at his mother-in-law and then held out his hand to the tall, distinguished fellow who was Bella's natural father. 'How do you do, sir?' he said politely, for all the world as though things were quite normal and he hadn't just had the most extraordinary introduction into a family anyone was likely to experience. 'It's good to meet you.'

As Philip took his hand, he murmured, 'Please, call me Philip,' and as his eyes met William's they expressed his gratitude.

In the kitchen, Mrs Banks had pounced on Wright, who'd just walked in after returning from doing some errands in the town. Taking him aside while the cook prepared a tea trolley with sandwiches, cake and coffee, she explained what had occurred while he had been 'gallivanting' as she put it, much to the old man's indignation who'd never gallivanted in his life.

'You could have knocked me over with a feather when Miss Bella stood there on the doorstep, and I couldn't do any other than to show her and this man, who turns out to be her husband, in to the mistress, could I? But oh my, then the sparks flew when Miss Bella saw the colonel sitting there. She was up for flying out of the house till he, her husband, caught her. Nearly knocked me on my backside, so she did. Anyway . . .' She went on to explain what she knew although she didn't admit to eavesdropping at the morning-room door – Wright could be a bit strait-laced about things like that – finishing by saying, 'And then it all went quiet so I thought I'd better see about getting them some refreshments. Eeh, the things that happen in this house.'

'And the colonel's still in there?'

'Oh aye.'

Wright was hastily pulling off his coat and changing into his indoor shoes. 'I'll come along with you and help you with the tea things.'

'Aye, I thought you might.'

They looked at each other for a long moment.

'It'd be grand if things worked out for the mistress, wouldn't it,' Mrs Banks said softly.

'Don't you go counting your chickens afore they're hatched.'

'I'm not, I'm just saying it'd be nice.'

Wright's stern face cracked into something that resembled a smile. 'Aye, lass, it'd be nice.'

Chapter Twenty-Nine

'I'm glad you decided to stay for a while. Your mother needs you, you know.' William and Bella were standing in what had been her childhood bedroom. It wasn't as she remembered in some ways. It was damp and cold, rather than warm and cosy, and the fire in the small grate didn't make much impact on the overall chilliness. Her mother had explained that they didn't use any rooms they didn't need to these days since the beginning of the war. 'She's lonely, Bella.'

'I know.' It was the only reason she was still here when everything in her wanted to leave. 'But – but this with the colonel.' She shook her head. 'I can't bear it.'

He put his hands on her face, raising it upwards and bending down and kissing her. 'They can't help how they feel any more than we can, my darling.'

'No, it's not the same.' She jerked herself free. 'It's not.'

'Because you don't want it to be?' he said gently.

The truth of that caused a lump in her throat and a

smarting in her eyes. To combat the weakness, she said fiercely, 'You're on his side.'

'My sweet, there's no "sides".' He took her in his arms again. 'But if there were then I'm on yours, for ever and a day.'

She tried to smile and then shook her head. 'I knew this would happen. He's manipulated her like he did all those years ago. You must be able to see that?'

There was a long pause.

Bella looked at him. 'You don't think so, is that it?'

'I don't know what happened all those years ago and neither do you but it wasn't rape, Bella. And if he was the person you think he is, he'd have his feet under the table here or have persuaded your mother to marry him and live at the Evendale estate. Neither of which has happened.'

'You like him.' The words were flat, dull-sounding.

'I neither like nor dislike him. I don't know him. But you heard it from your mother's own lips that they haven't been intimate apart from that one time many years ago. Now do you believe her?'

Bella nodded.

'Then I don't think you can accuse him of manipulation. I think—' He stopped.

'What? What do you think?'

'I think you ought to talk to him, just the two of you without your mother present, and hear what he has to say about, well, everything.'

'*Talk to him*?' Then, each word coated in bitterness, she said, 'Why would I want to talk to *him*?'

William took a deep breath. 'Because he is your father, Bella. Biologically, just biologically, I know, and Archibald will always be your father in every way that counts, but nevertheless, it's his blood that runs in your veins.'

'Don't say that.' She didn't raise her voice but it was so pain-filled that William winced.

She plumped down on the bed, staring blindly ahead, and he sat down beside her, taking one of her hands but she didn't respond in any way. After a moment, he murmured, 'I love you.'

Dully, she said, 'I love you too.'

'Think about what I've said, that's all. I can't tell you what to do – you're your own woman and it's your decision – but just think about it, all right? For me?'

Bella nodded. They had sat in the morning room, the four of them, after the tea trolley had been wheeled in, and she had forced down one dainty little sandwich, feeling as though it would choke her as she had listened to William making conversation with her mother and Philip Wynford. She had wanted to scream at him that this wasn't fooling anyone, that it was a travesty, a sham, but she hadn't because she'd been aware of her mother's drawn, white face and the way her hands had been shaking as she'd held her teacup and plate. She had only looked at the colonel once as he had made his goodbyes after refusing to stay for dinner even though her mother had weakly protested, and then only because she'd had to. He had stopped in front of her, his voice expressionless as he'd said, 'Goodbye, Bella.' She'd looked into the face that was still handsome and she didn't trust herself to speak, merely inclining her head. And now she had dinner with her mother to get through before she could return here and pretend to fall asleep so that she could be alone with her thoughts.

William didn't release his hold on her hand and they sat in silence for some moments before he said, very softly, 'I do understand, my love.'

No. No, he didn't. In spite of their consuming love for each other, how could he? She didn't expect him to. He had been through his own trauma; he'd told her about the years during his first marriage when Hilda had got more and more depressed and bitter, blaming him for their lack of a child and becoming almost deranged, and then the tragedy of her death and little Joy's. She understood that he knew pain and sorrow and rejection and could empathize in that regard, but that was different to understanding the core of how she felt. Only God could do that because He saw the human heart in all its frailty.

Turning, she laid her head on his shoulder, and they sat like that for a long time until it was time to go down to dinner.

Bella had known that the Evendale estate had been given over to be used by the military as a hospital and convalescence home, but nothing had prepared her for the change in the house and grounds she had been used to visiting since she could toddle.

She had gone to sleep eventually the night before,

determined not to seek Philip Wynford out, and then awoken in the morning knowing she would go and visit him that day. What had transpired in the hours of sleep she didn't know; she was just sure she had to go.

In contrast to the day before, the morning was bright and sunny although bitterly cold, and as William drove her through the grounds of Evendale in the horse and trap she was glad he'd come with her. They'd decided the best plan was not to inform Belinda of the proposed meeting but to say they needed the horse and trap to go shopping in town for some bits and pieces. Petrol was still in short supply and Archibald's car was covered over and tucked away in the barn where it had been stored since the outbreak of war.

As they pulled up outside the house there seemed to be men everywhere; some in uniform and some not; some on crutches and others in wheelchairs, and some looking able-bodied but being escorted by both male and female nurses or orderlies. Others sat in the late autumn sunshine at long benches and tables on the verandah that covered the width of the house, playing cards, talking, reading or sitting with their eyes closed.

'It's so different,' she murmured as William helped her down from the trap. 'Busy.' But that didn't really describe the atmosphere that was all at odds with the Evendale she'd known; it was purposeful now, functional.

William tied the horse to a post at the foot of the steps leading up to the verandah as a young man came towards them, his arm being held by a female nurse. The boy couldn't have been more than nineteen or twenty and on his left side where his other arm was missing his face was horribly scarred, his ear and eye gone. He was well wrapped up, and as he reached them he said excitedly, 'Look, my horse and trap. Are we going for a ride today?'

The nurse smiled at them as she said, 'Not today, Sidney. Perhaps tomorrow.'

'Yes, tomorrow.' He nodded like an obedient child. Looking straight at William, he said, 'My name is Sidney. What's yours?'

'William.'

'How do you do, William?' Again the tone was that of a child minding its manners.

'How do you do,' said William gently.

'Why don't we go and find your milk and biscuits?' The nurse's voice was bright. 'I think there are chocolate ones today.'

'Ooh, chocolate. I love chocolate ones. May I have three?' He had forgotten them immediately, turning away and shuffling off with her, still chattering away.

'Oh, William.' She found she was gripping his arm, her voice tear-filled.

'I know,' he said quietly. 'Poor devil.'

'He's one of the lucky ones.' A white-coated doctor had come up behind them. 'He's reverted to childhood and he's happy.' He held out his hand. 'I'm Dr Hedley. How may I help you?'

'I'm – I'm here to see Colonel Wynford,' Bella said.

'Philip? Does he know you're coming?'

'Not exactly. I'm Bella McFadyen. My mother—'

'Belinda's girl?' the doctor said warmly. 'Nice to meet you, Miss McFadyen. Your mother is highly thought of here. She has a gift with the patients – even the most severely damaged seem to respond to her.'

'Actually, it's Mrs Crawford,' William put in, chuckling as a horrified Bella turned to him with her hand over her mouth. 'We got married a few days ago,' he explained to Dr Hedley, who was smiling broadly, 'but I can see I'm going to have to work on the name.'

'My wife signed a cheque in her maiden name only last week,' the doctor said as the three of them began to walk up the steps to the house, 'and we've been married five years.'

He led them through the front door, which was propped open, and into the hall, which again had changed out of recognition. Trolleys and wheelchairs stood in a row against one wall with varying bits and pieces against another, replacing the small velvet seats and occasional tables which used to adorn the space. Likewise the delicate scent of bowls of flowers had been replaced by the smell of antiseptic. Magnificent paintings still graced the walls in places, but this wasn't the Evendale of her childhood.

'I would imagine Philip's in his office,' Dr Hedley said, leading them along the hall and then into a corridor beyond where he knocked on one of the doors, opening it after a moment and popping his head round. 'No. Well, we'll try the day room.'

They followed him further and into what had been the ballroom. The great expanse of polished floor was the same, but now everywhere Bella looked there were men sitting in armchairs or at tables or in wheelchairs. Some, she saw, had no legs but arms; others no arms but legs; still others had all their limbs but appeared motionless. There were faces so scarred and distorted she looked away quickly, afraid to be caught staring. The buzz of conversation was loud and suddenly from one table maniacal laughter burst forth and she saw two male nurses hurry over to a man and lift him out of his chair, whisking him out of the room.

As the terrible laughter died away she saw Philip in a corner of the room near the windows that stretched down one wall. He was kneeling by a wheelchair in which a man was sitting, or what was left of him – a stump of a body and one arm.

Dr Hedley followed her gaze. 'There's Philip with Corporal McCabe. Sad case. Only twenty-five. His wife couldn't cope with his injuries and won't visit. He gets depressed at times and it takes him so he won't eat or talk and has to be watched round the clock in case . . . well, you know. Philip's got a way with him and tries to catch him before the black dog takes hold – he can recognize the signs better than we can. He makes the lad laugh, spends hours with him and sits up all night when it's necessary, but that's Philip all over, isn't it.'

Was it? Bella stood between William and the doctor in the middle of the room and as she watched, the young corporal threw back his head and a peal of laughter, real laughter this time, echoed round the room. The two patients nearest him, also in wheelchairs, were laughing too at something Philip had said and one of them clapped him on the back, causing him to nearly pitch forwards from his kneeling position. Righting himself, Philip stood to his feet, grinning, and it was then that he noticed Bella. The smile slid from his face; he said something to the three men and then began to walk towards them.

William turned to Dr Hedley. 'I wondered if I might have a look round while Bella talks to the colonel,' he said quietly.

The doctor's eyes narrowed; he clearly sensed something wasn't quite right but rose to the occasion, saying cheerfully, 'Of course, of course. I've a few minutes spare, I'll come with you.'

They moved off as Philip reached them, his eyes on Bella. 'What's wrong? Is your mother all right?'

She drew in a long breath. 'Mother's fine. I – I wanted to talk to you privately. She thinks we've gone into town.'

'I see.' His face, like his voice, was grim. 'Then we'd better go to my office, we won't be disturbed there. I take it your husband won't be joining us?'

It was strange to hear William referred to as her husband. 'No, no, he's having a look round with Dr Hedley.'

Once in the office which had been Philip's study he gestured to the chair in front of his desk for Bella to be seated. The room was very much an office now; little remained of how it had looked all those years ago on Armistice Day – which was intentional on his part. Filing cabinets stood all along one side; there were no pictures on the walls and his desk and chair were utilitarian. Boxed files were stored on the bookcase, and next door to this room was one where three secretaries worked. A communicating door had been put in and now he walked across and turned the key in the lock. He didn't doubt that Bella had come to warn him to stay away from Belinda and as he sat down at his desk he prepared himself for the onslaught.

Her first words took the wind out of his sails because she said very quietly, 'Do you love my mother as much as she loves you?'

He blinked, then said simply, 'More. Much more.' And as she nodded, he added, 'She has never said she loves me, let me make that perfectly clear—'

'But she does,' Bella interrupted, her voice small. 'Was – was it always that way, when my father was alive, I mean?'

There was a long pause before he answered. She could hear the occasional shout outside the office and once someone calling a doctor's name. Then he said slowly, 'I don't know what you want me to say, Bella, or what would make things better or worse for you.'

She moved her head impatiently and they were both unaware that it was a mannerism of his. 'I want the truth, that's all. Just the truth. I hate being lied to.'

There seemed another long pause before he answered

her. 'Then the truth it is. But I shall need to go right back in time to explain. Are you comfortable with that?'

She nodded.

'When I first made your mother's acquaintance she was a young bride, Archibald's new wife, and they were one of many couples who visited here. We had a great many parties and dinners in those days – my ex-wife liked to entertain and the house was always full. Before – before Armistice Night I had noticed that she always seemed a little sad and on the periphery of things. Archibald was set in his ways, he didn't like to dance or join in the fun—'

'There's nothing wrong with not wanting to dance,' Bella cut in sharply.

'You wanted the truth,' he reminded her after a moment of silence. 'Do you wish me to continue?'

Again the impatient movement of her head.

'That night, Armistice Night, was different to any other. The war was over at last, everyone was elated, euphoric, the atmosphere . . . well, you probably experienced something similar yourself in Cairo. I danced with your mother because Archibald, as ever, was talking politics with other like-minded individuals, and it was then that I – I really saw her, I suppose. *Her*, not Archibald's wife. We laughed and we danced and there was magic in the air and we were all a little intoxicated with life as well as wine. I knew your mother was an innocent, Bella. I've got no excuse for what followed. Although she was married she was as unworldly as they come and I took advantage of that. In my defence I didn't plan it, it wasn't premeditated. It just happened.'

'I don't believe something like that ever just happens.'

'No, you're right.' He nodded. 'I could have stopped and I didn't. She was different to any other woman I'd known and looking back I fell in love with her that night, but until the day I found out you were mine we never spoke of it again. She devoted herself to your father and she made him as happy as a man could be, and we had nothing to do with each other beyond friendship. I know you will find this difficult to believe but I liked your father very much, liked and respected him. Again I have no excuse for what I did to him.'

'It was cruel.'

He looked down at the desk. 'It isn't enough to say that I am sorry, I know that. You and James, all of it. I ruined my boy's life.' He hesitated, lifting his head. 'He spoke of you when he was dying – he wanted me to tell you that he wished you happiness and that you must love again. He still loved you but he'd found peace at last, which is something. Oh, don't cry, Bella.' He had the desire to go to her and take her in his arms but he knew she wouldn't want that. His voice cracking, he whispered, 'I can't ask you to forgive the unforgivable but if you could just understand your mother's part in it all and why she did what she did when she found out she was expecting you, that would help her. If she had told Archibald the truth and he'd thrown her out, her parents wouldn't have helped her, and if she had told me the scandal would have been devastating because these things always get out. Your life would have been tainted. It was like that in those days.'

She wiped her eyes. 'It would have been better in the long run.' Straightening, she took a long breath. 'The hospital, this home, Evendale, is it for James?'

Her intuition surprised him even as he realized it shouldn't have; she was a remarkable young woman. Quietly, he said, 'Yes, in part, and for the other three too and all the lads who went to fight and never came back, but James especially, yes.'

She nodded. 'He would have liked that.' James's dream had always been to care for people, to watch them heal and recover and have the best life that they could. His dreams were dead and buried now, like him, but perhaps not completely, she thought, as a glimmer of hope rose in her. Maybe, wherever he was, he knew what his father had done in memory of him? Winnie would have said that, in fact she would have been sure of it. 'That lad you were talking to in the wheelchair, Dr Hedley said you've got a way with him. James – James would have been pleased.'

It was a huge concession and Philip knew it. Softly, he said, 'Thank you.'

'He also said that Mother's the same and that she's highly thought of.'

'Yes, yes, she is.'

It was said with such tenderness that Bella felt a physical pain in her chest, as though someone had suddenly jabbed her with something sharp.

She dropped her gaze from his and bit on her lip. *Why did they have to love each other?* It wasn't fair. They were asking too much of her. But then they hadn't asked anything, she told herself in the next moment, and that was the trouble. Her mother hadn't even told Philip that she loved him but had continued to live her solitary life at Fellburn, and he hadn't made any attempt to persuade her to do otherwise. And she knew why.

She drew in a deep, silent breath. It was because of her. Her mother knew how she felt about the colonel and was prepared to sacrifice any happiness she might have had with him, and he had accepted it, loving her mother as he did.

She looked down at her hands clasped in her lap. The colonel wasn't a bad man. He had done a bad thing but he wasn't a bad person. Terrible, inhuman things had happened in the war; the cold-blooded and systematic attempt by the Nazis to destroy an entire section of the human race, for one thing: proven stories of unbelievable horror were emerging. POWs were telling of the living hell they'd endured in Japanese camps. Hate had been the driving force and it had turned human beings into monsters. What had happened on Armistice Night had been a mistake with tragic, wide-reaching consequences and a sickening betrayal of her father, but it hadn't been evil.

After a moment she raised her head, and with a break in her voice, murmured, 'The wonderful man who raised me will always be my father.'

'Of course he will.'

'But – but you said a little while ago that you couldn't ask me to forgive the unforgivable. What you and my mother did wasn't unforgivable – it was stupid and selfish and became a huge tangle when James and I fell for each other. There are so many "ifs" connected with it, aren't there. If I hadn't been conceived that night. If my mother had told my father the truth and confessed when she found out she was expecting me. If she'd told you, even when James and I first fell in love, so somehow you might have separated us. If my father's heart hadn't been so fragile. If the war hadn't come so that James could have been a doctor somewhere and lived out his life . . .' She gulped hard against the tears and shook her head sadly. 'I hated you when I found out.'

'Yes.'

'But I don't hate you any more.' She smiled wanly at him. 'And – and I think you and my mother should be together if that's what you both want. I've got my own life to live with William and we're already thinking it won't be in England.'

'Because of the past?'

'No, not really.'

'Your – your mother and I, then?'

'No. At least –' she looked straight into his deep-blue eyes – 'not mainly because of that. I'm not ready to settle down and have a family and William accepts that. I'd like to carry on working for a time and travel too. We both would.'

'I don't know if your mother will believe that. That she and I are not the reason you want to live abroad, I mean.'

'She will after I've spoken to her.'

It was said with such authority that Philip had to restrain a smile.

'And I can see that you and Evendale would be good for her,' Bella said with painful honesty. 'She needs you.'

Philip swallowed deeply; tears came into his eyes and he said gruffly, 'Bella, I'm sorry—'

'If we're going to move on in the future I think we've had enough sorrys for a lifetime.' It was said without rancour, and quietly. 'We've got to look to new beginnings like the rest of the world or what's left of it.'

He wanted to say that he was proud of her but it was the sort of thing a father would say and he didn't feel he had the right. He cleared his throat. 'Thank you.'

She stood up as she said, 'I need to go and find William now.'

As she made to go out of the room Philip rose to his feet but didn't move from behind the desk. 'I'm glad you've found someone to spend the rest of your life with and he's a good man, I can see that.'

'Yes, he is. A very good man.' She paused before opening the door. 'I'll go and speak to Mother now and then we'll go into town for some lunch and do some shopping this afternoon, just William and I.'

He knew that she was telling him the coast would be clear for him to state his intentions after she had paved the way and he inclined his head, again saying, 'Thank you.'

Bella looked at the man who was her natural father for a moment longer. When she was a little girl and she had come with her parents to Evendale for numerous picnics in the grounds in the summer – elaborate occasions with lots of other families and children to play with – she'd liked the colonel and she'd known he liked her. He had always made a fuss of her more than the other children and she'd always made a beeline for him, sitting on his knee and demanding his attention with childish precociousness. As she'd got older there had been high teas and Christmas and birthday celebrations when she had played with James, but Evendale had been synonymous with the colonel. When her school days were over and before she went to Paris she'd accompanied her parents to dinner here and a dance or two; it had almost been like a second home in a way, and the affection she'd had for its owner had been as strong as ever. Every shred of that had been burned away in the heat of her hate on the day her father had died and she had carried on hating Philip, nurturing and feeding the emotion. And now?

She opened the door and stepped outside before shutting it behind her. She leaned against the wall for a moment, needing its support. Now she didn't hate him, she thought wearily, but neither did she want anything to do with him and that would be necessary, if only a little, if he married her mother. But she had meant what she said; her mother needed Philip Wynford and the purposeful life she would lead with him here, and, selfishly perhaps, she wouldn't have to worry about her when she and William went abroad. They would be free to make the new beginnings she had spoken about in there.

In spite of the sadness she was feeling, along with the guilt that she had stood aside so that her mother and the colonel could come together, she felt a moment's excitement about the future. And then the guilt swamped her again: would her father have understood what she had just done, that it was purely for the sake of her mother's well-being? She hoped so – oh, she did so hope so – but she'd never know and she had to live with that. He had been a gentle man, a man of peace and not war, and he had always gone out of his way to give someone the benefit of the doubt and extend the olive branch of forgiveness, but even so.

Her thoughts in turmoil, she levered herself off the wall and as she did so William turned the corner of the corridor and came hurrying towards her. Her distress must have been mirrored in her face because as he reached her he took her in his arms, saying, 'It's all right, it's all right. Whatever's happened, I'm here.' His kiss was gentle but the tenderness was too much and as her face crumpled, he said, 'Hang on, dearest, till we're out of here. Come on, we're leaving,' and with his arm round her he led her into the baronial hall and then to the waiting horse and trap. It was only when they were halfway along the winding drive and the house was out of sight that he stopped the horse, saying, 'Oh, my love,' as he took her in his arms again.

She gave way to a bout of body-shaking emotion and

he let her cry it out. After a minute or two, she raised her head, taking the crisp white handkerchief he gave her and wiping her eyes. 'It's – it's my father,' she whispered shakily.

He was wise enough not to ask which one but waited for her to continue.

'I told the colonel that he and Mother should be together and that I'd talk to her, but then I thought of my father that last morning and wondered what he'd think of me.'

'He would have thought, like me, that it was sacrificial on your part and intended only for your mother's good. He loved her, Bella. You know that. And he loved you perhaps even more. I never met him, unfortunately, but from what you've told me he was deeply compassionate as well as being wise. If he had lived I'm sure he would have forgiven your mother because he knew that whatever she had done no one would replace him in your affections and that he was one hundred per cent your father in every way that mattered.'

'But you don't *know* that.'

'Bella, my love, there is no perfect ending in all of this and you will always be assailed by doubts now and again, but answer me this. Could you have lived with yourself if you hadn't done what you did today? And if, maybe, you could have, what do you think it would have done to your soul to continue hating the colonel and keeping two people who are both heart sorry for what they did apart? What would be accomplished by that except further pain and sorrow? Your mother has punished herself for what she did far more than any court of law could have done. She's broken, Bella, you've seen that. You know it. Her life is a litany of guilt and regret and even though you have forgiven her she will never forgive herself, not really.'

She nodded, knowing it was true.

'And the colonel knows that he destroyed any affection you might have had for him in the past and that in the future he'll be tolerated under sufferance by his only living child.'

Again she nodded.

'The wounds of the past are still raw for you, my darling, I know that, especially here with so many reminders of your father, but what you did today is the first real step to finding peace. Time will help and I hope I'll play a part too,' he added with the quirk to his mouth she loved.

Softly, she murmured, 'I love you, Group Captain Crawford.'

'And I love you, my darling wife. Now, shall I take you to see your mother?'

She kissed the mouth that she'd once thought was so stern. 'Yes, please, and afterwards we'll go into town for lunch, just you and I, and I'll let you buy me lots of expensive clothes this afternoon.'

'Thank you,' he said gravely with a twinkle in his eye, glad to see her smiling, and as he clicked to the horse to start moving again, she nestled her head on his shoulder.

* * *

When they reached Fellburn William went upstairs to their room so that Bella could talk to her mother in private. Belinda looked up in surprise as her daughter walked into the morning room, where she was sitting reading a book she had no interest in. 'Back so soon, darling? I thought you were going into town to do some shopping?'

'We will in a little while. I wanted to talk to you first.' A log fire was blazing in the hearth and as Bella walked over and held out her cold hands to it, she glanced up at the portrait above the fireplace. Softly, she said, 'We were happy then, weren't we.'

Belinda's voice had a little catch in it as she said, 'Yes, we were.'

'What I mean is, you made him happy, we both did. He had twenty years of happiness he wouldn't have had if you had confessed about me when you found out you were pregnant.' She sat down in the armchair facing her mother and leaned across, taking her hands. 'I need to tell you that William and I won't be staying in England in the immediate future. We both want to live and work abroad, see the world, travel, be free.'

Belinda didn't reply for a moment, her eyes widening, and then Bella could see she had to make an effort to say, 'I – I understand.'

'I hope so, because I know I'm not like you in some ways. I'm twenty-six years old and you'd had me by that age and were content to be a mother and a wife, but I want more. That's the only way I can describe it. I'm not ready to have a family, not yet. In the future, but not for some years.'

'Does William agree?'

'Yes, he agrees.' Bella smiled. 'But there's one thing stopping me from travelling. Stopping us.'

'What is that?'

'You.' She had decided on the ride home how she would broach things and now her voice didn't falter as she said, 'I wouldn't be able to be so far away if I didn't know you were being looked after and that you were happy. It was different in the war, I had no choice, but now I do. And I want you to be happy, Mother.'

'Bella—'

'No, listen to me. I can see how you feel about Philip Wynford but I needed to make sure how he felt about you so I went to see him this morning.'

Belinda pulled her hands away, her voice uncharacteristically sharp as she said, 'You did *what*?'

'I went to see him.' Bella leaned forward and took her mother's hands again. 'And I saw Evendale, what it's like now. When I got there he was with a young man, Corporal McCabe? He was as gentle with him as James would have been, as understanding. And we spoke with a Dr Hedley, William and I. He said you had the same kind of gift with the men there as the colonel does. That they all love you.'

Belinda made a little sound in her throat, a painful sound, and now Bella slipped from her chair and knelt by her mother's side as she said, 'Philip loves you very much and he needs you. Now if I've got this wrong, if you don't care for him as he does for you, then William and I will put our plans on hold and stay in England.'

'But you hate Philip, Bella.'

'Not any more, I promise you that.'

'Those first moments when you got home—'

'Took me by surprise,' Bella finished for her. 'And I'll be honest, I was angry.'

'Then what's changed?'

'Me, I suppose,' she said ruefully, shaking her head. 'Winnie always used to say that I liked to control everything and that's true. It's not an attribute, it's a failing. And you know, since I've recognized that, I've realized that James and I would have been unequally yoked if we had married. I need someone as strong or stronger than me, like William. So, do you want to be with Philip and the life that will bring with it? Because if so then you have my blessing, and you know I never say anything I don't mean, for good or ill.'

'Will – will it mean losing you? Will I see you again?'

'Oh, Mother.' She reached up and took Belinda in her arms. 'You will never, ever lose me. We'll come back to England and visit and we can write often. I love you, I'll always love you. You must know that?'

And when Belinda didn't answer but began to cry softly, her face buried in Bella's bosom, Bella cradled her closer, murmuring endearments as one would to a distressed child, and she knew in those moments that the last remnants of childhood had gone from her for good.

* * *

It was an hour later when Philip arrived at the house and Bella and William had already left for town thirty minutes before. It was Belinda, and not Wright, who opened the front door to him. She had been standing waiting at the window knowing he would come at some point and on seeing him had flown into the hall, all sense of decorum leaving her. Wright, who had come from the direction of the kitchen as the bell had sounded, quickly retraced his steps, returning to the cup of tea and piece of cake he had been enjoying. As he walked into the kitchen, Mrs Banks was pouring herself a second cup of tea and she and the cook looked at him. 'Well? Who was it?'

'The colonel.'

'You were quick.'

'Aye, well, the mistress had already opened the door to him.'

'Had she?' The tone said more than the words conveyed. 'Well, don't go in yet asking if he's stopping for lunch.'

Wright glared at the housekeeper. They had worked together for well over forty years and had been firm friends for almost as long, but that didn't mean she didn't irritate him on occasion, like now. 'Why do you think I came back here then, if not to give 'em a few minutes?'

'I was just saying, that's all.'

'Aye, well, there's no need to say, is there.'

In the hall, Philip stood looking at Belinda. In spite of what Bella had said, he hadn't been sure of his reception but the way she was looking at him, and the fact that she had opened the door herself, emboldened him to say,

'I have something to ask you. May we go into the morning room?'

She was incapable of answering him, merely nodding and leading the way as her heart pounded so hard she was sure he must be able to hear it.

Once in the privacy of the morning room, Philip shut the door and walked across to the couch where she had seated herself, but instead of joining her he dropped to one knee and took her hand. Looking into her face, he murmured, 'Linnie, oh, Linnie. You know how I feel. I love you as I have never loved anyone before, neither a woman nor my own flesh and blood. I once said I'd never mention it again but after Bella came to see me today . . .' he paused. 'You know she came?'

'Yes, I know.'

'It – it gave me hope because I never thought in my wildest dreams I would be able to ask you to marry me. But I'm asking now, Linnie. Will you marry me? I don't expect you to love me as I love you but if you'll have me I'll do everything in my power to make you happy, I promise you that. I've loved you for a long time, since that first night, and I will love you to the day I die.'

She gazed at him, the need to pretend gone. 'And I love you, so much.'

'And you'll marry me? You'll be my wife?'

'Yes, I'll marry you,' she said almost shyly.

He stood up and drew her into his arms. Then he kissed her, not gently but with a fierceness that found an immediate response in herself, and they clung together for long seconds. When at last they moved apart he lifted his hand and traced the outline of her mouth with one finger. 'You're so beautiful,' he whispered, 'and so young. How can you love an old man like me?'

She smiled shakily, and such was the look on his face that she did indeed feel like a young girl again, just starting out on the road of life with the man she loved.

Chapter Thirty

The next few weeks were ones of mixed blessings for Bella. The day after Philip had proposed to her mother it had started to snow and it hadn't stopped for a full two weeks. Heavy falls blocked roads all over the north of England and in places ten-foot drifts were capable of swallowing men and animals alike.

Mr Irvin had continued to run Fellburn's farm all through the war and it was still thriving and making a profit, and he made sure the big house was supplied with everything they needed so that they were never short of food. The barn next to the stables was packed with chopped logs and kindling, so they had plenty of wood for the fires too, which was fortunate as the wind was bitter, blowing its way through any crevices and chilling rooms quickly.

Philip had fought his way to Fellburn a few times during the blizzards. He had never stayed long because Belinda worried about him getting home safely in the light. After a brief word Bella and William would leave him and her mother alone; the atmosphere was always a little awkward, and Bella was grateful for William's support. In spite of the weather Philip had made it his business to see the vicar of the local parish church and ask for the banns to be read; he and Belinda would be married a few days before Christmas and then honeymoon in Paris. On their return, Belinda would join her husband at Evendale. She had told Bella that she intended to sign Fellburn over to her and William lock, stock and barrel, and sure enough, as soon as the weather permitted, Belinda went to see the family solicitor to make sure that all the legal formalities were taken care of.

It all happened quite quickly, and along with the Fellburn estate, which included the working farm and so on, there was a large amount of money in the bank. Archibald had been a shrewd businessman; he had sold the rope-making works and the pottery in his latter years but continued to invest wisely, and when he had died Belinda had inherited a substantial legacy. She now declared that this was Bella's by right. 'It's what your father would have wanted,' she said to Bella and William over dinner the evening before matters were finalized. 'And I'm not going to Philip empty-handed,' she added with a smile. 'When my parents died and the house at Brandon was sold, my brother and sisters and I split the proceeds and I've never had occasion to dip into my portion.'

'But, Mother—'

'No, please don't fight me on this, Bella. I know you

both want to live and work abroad but should you decide, at any time, to come home then Fellburn will be waiting for you. The farm takes care of itself under Mr Irvin's management and Mrs Banks and Wright run the house. Everything will tick along quite nicely.'

Part of Bella's reluctance was because she knew William had been taken aback and somewhat horrified at the turn of events; he was now married to a very wealthy woman. That night she'd decided to take the bull by the horns and bring everything out into the open. They had just made love, and as she lay quietly in his arms, the room lit only by the light of the flickering flames in the fireplace, she murmured, 'Are you annoyed with me?'

'*Annoyed* with you? Good grief, darling, why should I be annoyed with you?'

'Because I didn't say no to Fellburn and the money. It's ours, you know. Not mine. "For richer, for poorer"?'

'I know, I know. I just didn't expect it would be for richer quite like this,' he said ruefully after a moment or two. 'Or so soon. It's very generous of your mother but it takes a bit of coming to terms with, my love. I'm sorry if I gave you the impression that I'm annoyed – of course you had to accept – but you need to understand that my beginnings were different to yours. I'm working class at root level and I'm not ashamed of that—'

'Nor should you be,' she interrupted vehemently.

'But some of that thinking, the way men thought when I was being brought up, has gone deep, I suppose. "Give me a child until it is seven," as the Jesuits used to say. If a girl made what would be termed as a good marriage meaning that she'd be taken out of her situation into a far better one, everyone would congratulate her and say how well she had done for herself. A man –' he shook his head – 'now that was a different kettle of fish. He'd have all kinds of labels stuck on him and none of them complimentary.'

'But that's so wrong.'

'I didn't say it wasn't.'

'Then if you know it's wrong you mustn't let it affect you, affect us.'

'I won't.'

She sat up slightly so that she was looking into his face, her voice earnest as she said, 'I'd get rid of it, all of it, if I thought it would come between us. I don't even want it in the first place. It's – it's like grave clothes in a way, the shrouds they wrap corpses in.'

'Oh, Bella.' His throat was full of emotion at her love for him, the passion that was such an integral part of her, but he found himself wanting to laugh too. 'My sweet, it's nothing like that.'

She pursed her lips. 'You know what I mean.'

'I do and I love you for it.'

'Everything was so simple during the war, William. We were fighting the Nazis and nothing else mattered but winning and stopping the evil they'd unleashed. Now things are so complicated. I wish we were back in Cairo.'

'I don't think you do, darling, not the way it is there at the moment.'

Rioting had broken out in Egypt at the beginning of the month. Two hundred people had been injured in Cairo while others had died in Alexandria.

'Well no, perhaps not, but I don't want to be here either and I have to be, don't I.'

'For the moment. I know the wedding day is going to be hard for you but it means so much to your mother for you to be there. Once that's over we will decide what we're doing, but for now let's make what we can of this time, darling. All right?'

'All right.' She snuggled down again, one arm over his chest. 'As long as we aren't at odds.'

'We aren't.'

Belinda and Philip tied the knot at the little parish church in Burnhope on a cold December day six days before Christmas. The bride looked beautiful and ethereal in a cream silk costume, the jacket edged with silver braid, and a matching hat, and Philip was in uniform. The wives and children of Philip's older sons attended the ceremony, along with Belinda's sisters and their families and a few friends. Wright, Mrs Banks and Mrs Brown – Fellburn's cook – had been invited too, but overall it was a quiet affair with a small reception at a hotel in Chester-le-Street where the couple were staying overnight before leaving to start their honeymoon.

It was a long day, and if Bella had spoken the truth she would have admitted that she hated every minute, but with William's help she performed the role she'd committed herself to when she had played Cupid. She made sure she was always smiling for her mother, laughing and joking with the assembled company as though she hadn't a care in the world.

Belinda had asked William to give her away, and as he had placed her hand in Philip's at the altar Bella had bit down hard on her bottom lip to stop the pain she was feeling. All over the church handkerchiefs were fluttering as the women guests dabbed their eyes, and even Wright was visibly moved. Everyone was thrilled for the happy couple and Bella felt as though she was a spectator at a play she didn't want to see.

The day had been bright and sunny first thing, but as they reached the hotel the sky had clouded over and the first snowflakes had begun to fall from a laden sky. By the time the five-course meal was drawing to an end it was coming down thickly, which prompted the guests to start taking their leave of the bridal couple sooner than perhaps they might otherwise have done.

It suited Bella perfectly. Her face muscles were aching with the perpetual smile she'd doggedly maintained throughout the day and she felt emotionally exhausted.

Belinda had sparkled all day and when she said goodbye to them both, she put her arms round Bella and held her close, whispering, 'Thank you, my darling, for making this happen,' as she kissed her. It was nearly too much. Somehow Bella found the strength to hug her back and whisper, 'Be happy, Mother,' as she kept smiling, and then one of Belinda's sisters was there at their side and after she had kissed her mother she and William left the over-warm room and walked into the foyer.

'Bella?'

She almost groaned as she heard Philip call her name but turned to see him hurrying after them, and such was the look on his face that she thought, *No, I can't do this, I can't pretend any more.* She had felt Archibald close all day; not in a disapproving way but just . . . close, and she had never missed him so much.

'I'll get the coats.' William squeezed her arm.

She wanted to tell him to stay but she didn't, and when Philip reached her he said softly, 'I just wanted to say I'll take care of her till my dying day, Bella.'

'I know you will.' She dragged up another smile.

'No, that's not all I wanted to say. Why do we say things like that?' he said almost irritably. 'I couldn't let you go without telling you that I know what this has cost you, not just today, all of it. Your father was so proud of you, Bella. When you were in Germany before the war he told me once that he knew you were going to do great things. We were sitting, just the two of us, in the orangery having a quiet drink to escape the assembled company, and he said, "She's not like other girls her age, you know, my Bella. She is going to do great things, you wait and see." Well, you did do amazing work during the war I'm sure, but what you've done over the last weeks and today for your mother is greater. He was right, you see. That – that's what I wanted to say. He understood his Bella and you will always be his. He knew it and I know it.'

She wanted to speak, but she knew if she tried then the last of her control would give way and the avalanche of tears that she'd been holding at bay all day would burst forth.

Somehow, Philip's words had revealed what the feeling of her father's presence had been trying to convey all day: he understood. He would have expected his daughter to behave in the way that she had because that was what he would have done.

'Archibald was the best of men,' Philip said gruffly, reading something of her inner turmoil in her face.

Bella still remained silent, but when she reached out her hand he took it, holding it against his chest for a moment, his face working. And when her body leaned in to him and she let herself be enfolded into his arms, the tears poured down his face.

William had hired a taxicab to take them all back to Fellburn and Mrs Banks and Cook chattered animatedly the whole way, Wright – who was sitting between the two women – suffering in silence, although Bella could see from the old man's face that he was wishing for the journey to end as much as she was. She knew the three faithful retainers had been thrilled to be invited to the church and the reception and that the two women were still bubbling over with it all, but she hadn't slept well for the last few nights and she was so tired she could barely function.

There had been a thaw over the last week and the

previous snow had melted away, but now the weather was bitterly cold and this latest fall was already a couple of inches thick and still coming down in great swirls.

Once they had pulled up on the drive at Fellburn and William was paying the taxi-driver, the man informed them mournfully that blizzards were expected over the next days and he didn't doubt they'd be snowed in for Christmas. 'All we need what with the rationing and all,' he grumbled, accepting the generous tip William gave him with an appreciative, 'Thanks, guv,' before wishing them all a merry Christmas and driving off.

Once in the house, Mrs Banks and Cook bustled away to take off their finery, the former then busying herself stoking up fires in all the rooms that were in present use, and the latter preparing a tray of tea and biscuits that Wright brought along to the morning room where Bella and William were sitting on the couch which he had moved close to the fire.

'Thank you, Wright,' Bella said, rousing herself to smile at the old man. 'Did you enjoy the day?'

'It was grand, Miss Bella.'

He had started calling her 'ma'am' when she and William had returned to Fellburn after their marriage but she had asked him not to, saying she preferred the old form of address. Wright was almost like a grandfather, she felt, albeit a somewhat stiff and formal one most of the time. 'I thought my mother looked beautiful.'

'She did that, miss. Aye, she did that.' His face cracked into what passed for a smile for Wright. 'And may I take the liberty of saying that you did too, Miss Bella,' he said gallantly.

'Thank you,' she said softly.

'Cook was enquiring whether you and Mr William would be wanting an evening meal later?' When they had arrived home mid-afternoon the light had already been all but gone and now it was quite dark outside, although the falling snow provided its own luminescence.

Bella glanced at William, who shook his head. 'Not for me – that meal at the hotel was enormous. Perhaps sandwiches?'

She nodded, saying to Wright, 'We'll have something about six o'clock and then I think an early night. It's been a tiring day.'

'Just as you wish, Miss Bella.'

They drank the tea and then must have dozed in front of the fire because when Wright brought the sandwiches at six o'clock he woke them up.

As soon as they had eaten they went upstairs and later, as she lay quietly wrapped in William's arms, she said softly, 'I don't want to do anything over the next days but eat and drink and make love.'

She could tell he was smiling when he said, 'Well, that's music to *my* ears.'

'And when Christmas is over we'll talk about what we're going to do and where we want to go.'

'All right, my love.'

'Because I don't want to stay here too long.'

'I know and we never planned to do that, did we. We

both want to carry on working for a while and travel, and nothing that has happened in the last weeks has changed that so don't worry.'

'It won't be for ever, but a few years at least.'

'Darling, we've got all the time in the world.'

She liked the sound of that, turning to him as she whispered, 'But we'll make sure we are together?'

'Absolutely.'

'I love you so much.'

'There's no words to describe how I feel about you.' He pulled her closer. 'Now, we've eaten and we've drunk. What was that other thing that you said you wanted to do for the next few days?'

She giggled, and then as his mouth found hers and he held her against the hard length of his body she gave herself up to the ecstasy of making love with the man she adored.

Chapter Thirty-One

The world in which 1946 dawned was deeply scarred and traumatized by years of war and conflict, and it was clear to many folk that life was going to be hard for both victors and vanquished alike.

A global food shortage meant that rationing increased in Britain, and in France riots broke out over the lack of bread in Paris and Rouen. Civil war was looming in India and there was trouble in the Middle East, but one of the worst-hit countries of the war was Germany. Famine was inevitable due to their agricultural industry being all but destroyed.

It didn't take long before everyone realized that the brave new world they'd dreamed of was just that – a dream.

In the second week of January William received a call from Intelligence. It appeared that Britain was keen to have operatives with experience of the German language and its dialects working with the German Control Commission, initially at Herford in north-west Germany but with a view to a swift posting to Berlin.

'They need people they can trust with some initiative,' William said as he sat with Bella in the morning room after the call. 'There's a hell of a lot going on out there. Nazis who still need bringing to justice, finding and restoring dispersed art treasures to their proper places, liaising with the locals as well as the Americans and Russians, which is proving awkward – and more besides. They're wondering if we'd be prepared to go out there for a while?'

Bella looked at him. It wasn't altogether what she'd had in mind. 'How long for?'

'That'd be up to us. It wouldn't be easy.'

She smiled. 'Since when have we liked an easy life?'

'There is that,' he agreed, grinning.

'And we'd be together?'

'Of course.'

She nodded. 'Let's give it a go.'

'Are you sure? It means we'll have to delay the honeymoon in hot climes for a while.'

'Would you think it terribly soppy if I said every day with you is a honeymoon?'

His answer was to take her into his arms and kiss her until she was breathless.

Their applications to work with the German Control Commission proved to be a mere formality. By the beginning of February all necessary papers were in place and they flew to north-west Germany. Belinda was a little tearful on parting but Bella knew her mother was happy with Philip at Evendale. They'd been across to see them several times since the wedding and her mother had blossomed in just that short time. The couple were already making plans to extend the facilities that Evendale offered by building workshops in the grounds to enable some of the patients to learn new skills like carpentry and welding.

That her mother had found her niche in life was obvious. Both the patients and medical staff clearly respected and liked her, and Philip worshipped the ground his new wife walked on. Bella was happy for her, for them both in fact, but she also welcomed the chance to put a bit of distance between them for a while. She was still coming to terms with their marriage to some extent and there were days when it was painful.

Once they had been transferred to the posting in Berlin, they both felt that they were in the thick of things again but in a different way to the last few years. The stark surroundings outside the military enclave where she and William mostly worked and where they had married quarters was horrific. As she described in a letter to Lucy, with whom she corresponded when time permitted, '*The stench of decay in the city is overpowering. There are vast wastelands of rubble stretching for miles and women and children are starving to death for lack of food and shelter. I want to help, Lucy, but the red tape is crippling.*'

'This is what war really means,' she said one day to William. They were returning to the base after interviewing a German woman believed to have knowledge about a ring of conspirators planning to undermine an aid programme in Bünde, not far from Herford. 'The devastation for children it leaves in its wake. What future can they have with no social infrastructure, no schooling?'

William nodded. They were passing what had once been a housing estate, but nothing had been left standing by the Allied bombing. As they stared out of the window of the armoured jeep, a figure like a skeletal ghost crept out of a hole in the ground and stood for a moment looking at them, cavernous eyes deep in a white face.

He tightened his arm round her. Nothing had prepared them for the level of suffering in Berlin. At times he berated himself for even mentioning the German Control Commission's request for their help, but at the same time he knew that they were doing an invaluable job in assisting the authorities which few operatives, men or women, would handle as well as Bella was doing. Furthermore, ordinary German women seemed to open up to her like the woman Bella had just interviewed, and she had a way with the children too.

The British, American and Russian occupiers were talking about corporate welfare programmes and rebuilding and so on, but it was going to be a long job and would need intricate planning. They knew many of the starving populace would die before such things were accomplished. Corpses were commonplace. It was going to be a grim road ahead.

They stayed in Berlin for three years simply because the need was so great. Through the bitter winter of 1947, when many folk said that the Russians had brought their

Siberian winter with them, the thermometer dropped to minus thirty-six degrees Celsius and it was the children who suffered the most, many of them orphans. Small frozen bodies were discovered every day, and it was then that Bella trod on some official toes when she and William got together with two middle-aged German sisters Bella had spoken with in the course of her work. Against the non-fraternization rules laid down by the military, they funded a soup kitchen in one of the few buildings in the area that was largely intact where the sisters and four other families lived, packed in together like sardines in a can.

Bella made it her business to ensure that there was always bread and a cup of hot soup for anyone who came to the sisters' door, along with blankets and a supply of warm clothes, particularly for babies and little ones. She arranged for the *Kinderklinik* – the German-run medical clinic in the district – to receive a supply of medicines like penicillin, painkillers and baby milk and bottles twice a week, and she and William funded all this themselves. Perhaps the most controversial thing they did, as far as the Allied authorities were concerned, was to set up a little school in one of the rooms of the house where the sisters, who had both been schoolteachers before the war, provided some sort of education for the children who came in. Bella's fervent belief that education could only be a good thing met with hostility from more than one of their colleagues at the base.

'What are them brats being taught, eh?' one irate man snarled at her. 'How to be the next generation of Nazis?

My brother came out of one of the concentration camps weighing less than six stone and he'll never be any good again. You want to feed and educate that lot out there when he and his pals – none of whom made it apart from him – ate rats and mouldy bread to stay alive? You think if the boot was on the other foot they'd be helping us, *eh*?'

Bella hadn't flinched when he'd shouted in her face but she had been thankful that William hadn't been present. He wouldn't have been able to keep his hands off the man. But she could understand in part why he was angry and it had moderated her tone when she'd said, 'There are babies who don't have the strength to swallow the milk that would save them, and dead children are brought to the clinic every day. I couldn't do anything to help your brother and the millions of other folk who were starved and tortured but I can do something for the babies and children right in front of me. I'm sorry you don't understand but that won't stop me doing all I can, and if the boot was on the other foot as you said and it was your children dying of cold and starvation, I hope a German woman would try and do what she could for them. And education is a fundamental right for any child. Hitler preached indoctrination of the worst kind and the only way to combat that so it never happens again is through education.'

He had continued to glare at her, eyes blazing, before giving a 'Huh!' and stalking off, leaving her pale and shaken. He'd come up to her when she'd been sitting in the canteen and as she glanced about her and met some of her other colleagues' eyes, they had looked away, their faces stony. A condemnatory silence had ensued.

The combined hostility had the effect of stiffening her back both physically and mentally. The triumphalism of the victor in these heartbreaking circumstances was as inhuman as anything the Nazis had done, she told herself, and if they couldn't see that, then she felt sorry for them.

It was in the summer of 1949, a couple of months after the end of the Berlin blockade by Russia, that Bella and William finally left Germany for good. Two weeks after the stranglehold on the city had ended and a new democratic Germany had been born – which didn't include the Soviet-occupied East Zone – they'd had a long talk about their immediate future. Only the British, American and French zones had come together to form the Federal Republic of Germany and the situation regarding Russia had worsened by the day. International anxieties about the sinister intentions of the Soviet Union had grown, although the forming of a new alliance by eight Western countries – the North Atlantic Treaty Organization, or NATO – was intended to act as a deterrent against aggression as any attack on a member state would be construed as an attack on all.

Nevertheless, Bella and William felt that the remit of their jobs had changed considerably. Furthermore, welfare programmes were in place along with rebuilding work, and they decided it was time to leave. The last three years had proved every bit as traumatic as the work they'd carried out during the war and although they had flown home on leave several times, spending time with Belinda and Philip and seeing the growth at Evendale, which was amazing, the weight of their jobs had always been with them.

'I don't want to be a spy in peacetime,' Bella had said during their discussion in their married quarters. 'It was different in the war.'

'It was.' William smiled at her. 'Quite different. They're beginning to call the situation with Russia the Cold War, but I don't see us as part of that. We'll leave the spying to the men in mackintoshes and bowler hats, shall we? Those that like the cat-and-mouse games.'

She nodded. 'I want to see more of the world, a warmer world for a start. It's always raining here.'

It was still raining on the day they flew out of Berlin. In spite of being the middle of July it was as cold as November and an icy wind was blowing as they got out of the taxi at the airport. Bella's hat went flying off her head and after William had chased and retrieved it, she said wistfully, 'I want to see the hot saffron skies we saw in Egypt night after night, William, and have a sunburnt nose.'

He laughed. He often laughed these days. 'Saffron skies and new beginnings, my love,' he said, pressing the hat firmly on her head.

'Lots of new beginnings in lots of places,' she agreed

as they walked into the buzzing airport, excitement making her eyes sparkle. This was the start of their great adventure and she intended to enjoy every minute. She and William, together, as she knew it would always be. What more could she ask from life?

Epilogue

1953

Bella gazed out of the open window of the taxicab as it made its way along the familiar country road to Fellburn. Pale shimmering fields of freshly mown hay made a mosaic against grain fields which had mellowed to the bronze of harvest, and the air was rich with the perfume of eglantine, the wild briar, and the mass of flowers growing in the grassy green verges.

This was England as she'd pictured it in the last years of travelling, she thought, and of all the places that they'd visited there was nowhere else she would rather they raised a family. Her hand stroked her rounded stomach. They were expecting their first child in a couple of months in September, and she smiled as she felt a strong kick against her fingers.

William's hand covered hers. 'Happy?' he asked softly.

She nodded. 'It was time to come home and put down roots.'

'Yes, it was time, sweetheart.'

Their extended honeymoon had taken them all over

the Mediterranean for a year, then on to the United States and Canada before they'd finally settled in Ahmedabad, the largest city in Gujarat, India, for twelve months. Gujarat had proved to be different to anything that they had experienced before with the deafening bustle of streets thronged with children and beggars, tongas, bicycles, camels and cars. Temple bells had clanged and radios had blared from seemingly every house they passed and the noise had taken some getting used to at first, but they had grown to love the vibrancy of India, although the poverty of some of the people had bothered Bella, along with the fact that girls seemed to be treated as inferior to boys in even the wealthiest families.

The city was situated on the edge of the desert and there was the scorching heat to acclimatize to, as well as snakes and scorpions and locusts, but bright-eyed monkeys lived in the mango trees in the garden of the white stone house they rented and brought their babies when they came to beg for food each day, stealing what they could when the opportunity presented itself.

Bella and William had become adept at bargaining in the local markets and shops too, and when the powerful and sand-laden wind was whipped into a frenzy it obscured the sky and turned the air a fevered tawny colour. But the desert skies were that amazing unique saffron colour at sunset, their whole life was multicoloured, they made some good friends and even became able to distinguish the rank smell of a jackal far off when they drew their water from a well in the garden of their little house.

Now, as the taxi passed between the wide-open gates leading onto the winding drive of Fellburn, that other life was already becoming a memory. But Bella had no regrets. The year in India had clarified something in Bella which had begun in Berlin. Sitting on their verandah with its flowering pots in the evenings and drinking tea as they listened to the chattering of the monkeys in the mango trees, she had told William about her longing to open a school, a boarding school for girls specializing in languages. Wealthy families would pay for their daughters' education, but for those girls who came from poor backgrounds there would be no charge.

'Languages can open up the world,' she'd told him earnestly, 'but so many girls from less privileged homes will never get the chance to know what they're capable of or have the opportunity to spread their wings.'

He had agreed with her without reservation and if possible she had loved him even more as he had entered into her plans to build an annexe onto the main house for themselves while the rest of the building would be converted into the school.

In all their travels in foreign climes there was one thing that didn't seem to change whatever the country – it was still very much a man's world. As the car rounded a corner and Fellburn came into view, she sighed in spite of herself.

William had caught the sigh, glancing at her as he said, 'What is it? I thought you were glad to be home.'

'I am. I was just thinking about the school and what

we're going to do and wishing it could be more,' she said quietly. 'In spite of the war and all the achievements and sacrifices that women made, girls, women, are still second-class citizens.'

'Change is coming, Bella. A generation of women have discovered that they are every bit as good as men and the genie is out of the bottle. Our children, whatever their sex, will be brought up knowing that and it will happen in other homes too. Have faith, my love.'

She nodded. 'I wish all men were like you.'

'You're very fortunate,' he agreed, deadpan.

And as she giggled, he grinned, taking her into his arms and kissing her in such a way that they were oblivious to the taxi drawing to a halt and the ancient, bent figure of Wright descending the steps.

Two months later to the day, in the bedroom of Fellburn House where she herself had been born, Bella gave birth to a bouncing baby girl. She was a big baby with wispy blonde hair, plump cheeks and a distinctly disgruntled expression at being expelled from the nice comfortable place she'd inhabited for the last nine months. William had been present throughout, and when the smiling midwife handed him his daughter wrapped in a snug cocoon of blankets, tears rolled down his face.

'She's beautiful,' he whispered huskily. 'Perfect. Like her mother.'

Bella smiled through her exhaustion. It had been a long labour. She knew William had been anxious throughout the whole of her pregnancy from the moment she'd told him she was expecting their child, even though he hadn't voiced his fears. It was natural, she supposed, after what had happened with his first wife, but although she had tried to reassure him in a hundred and one ways that all would be well, she'd also realized that until the baby was born nothing would put his mind at rest. Now he looked as though a weight had been lifted from his shoulders.

He came and sat down on the bed beside her once the midwife had finished her work, his arm going round her as the other cradled their sleeping daughter. Together they gazed down with rapt wonder at the little person they'd made. As one small arm struggled free of the cocoon and a tiny hand with minute fingernails grasped the edge of the blanket, William murmured, 'Determined too, again like her mother. She'll make her mark in the world and grow into a wonderful young woman.'

'As wonderful as her namesake,' Bella said softly, a catch in her voice.

They were naming her Winifred. Winnie for short.

A Woman of Courage

by Rita Bradshaw

It's 1890, and Josie Gray is an innocent and beautiful fifteen-year-old when Adam McGuigan, the youngest son of a dangerous and influential crime family, spots her singing in a public house in Sunderland. Adam is handsome and charismatic, sweeping Josie off her feet with his beguiling lies and promises. He charms her into marrying him on her sixteenth birthday, but on her wedding night the fairy tale ends.

Josie finds herself trapped in a living nightmare and there's no one to help her. Events spiral out of control, and when her life is put in danger she escapes with her baby son. Fleeing to a different country, Josie fights to make a good life for her child, and then love beckons again.

Believing in Tomorrow

by Rita Bradshaw

Molly McKenzie is only eleven years old when her abusive father beats her to within an inch of her life. Escaping from the hovel she calls home, Molly is found by kind fisherfolk, sick and near death. With them she experiences the love of a family for the first time and, even though life is hard, she is content.

Time passes and Molly's looking ahead to a future with the boy she loves, but then a terrible tragedy rips her life apart. Once again she's cast adrift in an uncaring world, but Molly is made of stern stuff and is determined to survive.

In the male-dominated society of the early 1900s, Molly has to fight prejudice and hatred, and rejection comes from all sides. Can she hold fast and become the woman she is destined to be?

The Winter Rose

By Rita Bradshaw

It's December 1902 and Rose O'Leary is looking forward to her baby girl's first Christmas. But then tragedy strikes: her husband dies at the shipyard where he works and within days his friend, Nathaniel, makes it plain he's determined to have her.

Rose flees with her child, but soon finds the world is a cruel place for a beautiful woman with no protection. More tragedy ensues and yet, although she's bruised and broken, Rose is a fighter.

Then, when she least expects it, love enters her life again, but she cannot escape her past and now it threatens not only her happiness but her very life. Will she ever find a safe haven?

'Raw passion and power on every page'

Northern Echo

The Storm Child

By Rita Bradshaw

It's mid-winter, and in the throes of a fierce blizzard Elsie Redfern and her husband discover an unknown girl in their hay barn about to give birth. After the young mother dies, Elsie takes the infant in and raises her as her own daughter, her precious storm child.

Gina grows into a beautiful little girl, but her safe haven turns out to be anything but. Torn away from her home and family, the child finds herself in a nightmare from which there's no waking. But despite her misery and bewilderment, Gina's determined to survive.

Years pass. With womanhood comes the Second World War, along with more heartbreak, grief and betrayal. Then, a new but dangerous love beckons; can Gina ever escape the dark legacy of the storm child?

'Expect the unexpected in this enthralling story with a wealth of colourful characters'

Coventry Evening Telegraph

One Snowy Night

By Rita Bradshaw

It's 1922 and the Depression is just beginning to rear its head in Britain, but Ruby Morgan is about to marry her childhood sweetheart and nothing can mar her happiness. Or so she thinks. An unimaginable betrayal by those she loves causes her to flee her home and family one snowy night.

Crushed and heartbroken, Ruby vows that, despite the odds stacked against her, she will not only survive but one day will show the ones she left behind that she's succeeded in making something of herself. Brave words, but the reality is far from easy.

Dangers Ruby could never have foreseen and more tragedy threaten her new life, and love always seems just out of reach. Can a happy ending ever be hers?

'Catherine Cookson would have been proud to put her name to this heartfelt and moving saga'

Peterborough Evening Telegraph

Beneath a Frosty Moon

By Rita Bradshaw

It's 1940 and Britain is at war with Germany. For Cora Stubbs and her younger siblings this means being evacuated to the safety of the English countryside. But little does Cora know that Hitler's bombs are nothing compared to the danger she will face in her new home, and she is forced to grow up fast.

However, Cora is a fighter and she strives to carve out a new life for herself and her siblings. Time passes, and in the midst of grief and loss she falls in love, but what other tragedies lie around the corner?

As womanhood beckons, can Cora ever escape her troubled past and the lost love who continues to haunt her dreams and cast shadows over her days?

A Winter Love Song

By Rita Bradshaw

Bonnie Lindsay is born into a travelling fair community in the north-east of England in 1918, and when her mother dies just months later Bonnie's beloved father becomes everything to her. Then, at the tender age of ten years old, disaster strikes. Heartbroken, Bonnie's left at the mercy of her embittered grandmother and her lecherous step-grandfather.

Five years later, the events of one terrible night cause Bonnie to flee to London, where she starts to earn her living as a singer. She changes her name and cuts all links with the past.

Time passes. Bonnie falls in love, but just when she dares to hope for a rosy future, the Second World War is declared. She does her bit for the war effort, singing for the troops and travelling to Burma to boost morale, but heartache and pain are just around the corner, and she begins to ask herself if she will ever find happiness again.

Snowflakes in the Wind

By Rita Bradshaw

It's Christmas Eve 1920 when nine-year-old Abby Kirby's family is ripped apart by a terrible tragedy. Leaving everything she's ever known, Abby takes her younger brother and runs away to the tough existence of the Border farming community.

Years pass. Abby becomes a beautiful young woman and falls in love, but her past haunts her, casting dark shadows. Furthermore, in the very place she's taken refuge is someone who wishes her harm.

With her heart broken, Abby decides to make a new life as a nurse. When the Second World War breaks out, she volunteers as a QA nurse and is sent overseas. However, life takes another unexpected and dangerous turn when she becomes a prisoner of the Japanese. It is then that Abby realizes that whatever has gone before is nothing compared to what lies ahead . . .

The Colours of Love

By Rita Bradshaw

England is at war, but nothing can dim land girl Esther Wynford's happiness at marrying the love of her life – fighter pilot Monty Grant. But months later, on the birth of her daughter Joy, Esther's world falls apart.

Esther's dying mother confesses to a dark secret that she has kept to herself for twenty years: Esther is not her natural daughter. Esther's real mother was forced to give up her baby to an orphanage – and now Joy's birth makes the reason for this clear, as Esther's true parentage is revealed.

Harshly rejected by Monty, and with the man Esther believed was her father breathing fire and damnation, she takes her precious baby and leaves everything and everyone she's ever known, determined to fend for herself and her child. But her fight is just beginning . . .

Beyond the Veil of Tears

By Rita Bradshaw

Fifteen-year-old Angeline Stewart is heartbroken when her beloved parents are killed in a coaching accident, leaving her an only child in the care of her uncle.

Naive and innocent, Angeline is easy prey for the handsome and ruthless Oswald Golding. He is looking for a rich heiress to solve the money troubles his gambling and womanizing have caused.

On her wedding night, Angeline enters a nightmare from which there is no awakening. Oswald proves to be more sadistic and violent than she could ever have imagined. When she finds out she is expecting a child, Angeline makes plans to run away and decides to take her chances fending for herself and her baby. But then tragedy strikes again . . .

Dancing in the Moonlight

By Rita Bradshaw

As her mother lies dying, twelve-year-old Lucy Fallow promises to look after her younger siblings and keep house for her father and two older brothers.

Over the following years the Depression tightens its grip. Times are hard and Lucy's situation is made more difficult by the ominous presence of Tom Crawford, the eldest son of her mother's lifelong friend, who lives next door.

Lucy's growing friendship with Tom's younger brother, Jacob, only fuels Tom's obsession with her. He persuades Lucy's father and brothers to work for him on the wrong side of the law as part of his plan to force Lucy to marry him.

Tom sees Lucy and Jacob dancing together one night and a chain of heartbreaking events is set in motion. Torn apart from the boy she loves, Lucy wonders if she and Jacob will ever dance in the moonlight again . . .